SLEWFOOT

NIGHTFIRE BOOKS
BY BROM

Slewfoot

ALSO BY BROM

Lost Gods
Krampus
The Child Thief
The Devil's Rose
The Plucker

NIGHTFIRE

A TOM DOHERTY ASSOCIATES BOOK

NEW YORK

SLEWFOOT

a tale of bewitchery

B R O M

SLEWFOOT

Copyright © 2021 by Gerald Brom

All artwork © 2021 by Brom

All rights reserved.

A Nightfire Book
Published by Tom Doherty Associates
120 Broadway
New York, NY 10271

tornightfire.com

Nightfire™ is a trademark of Macmillan Publishing Group, LLC.

The Library of Congress Cataloging-in-Publication Data is available upon request.

ISBN 978-1-250-62200-6 (hardcover)
ISBN 978-1-250-62198-6 (ebook)

Our books may be purchased in bulk for promotional, educational, or business use.
Please contact your local bookseller or the Macmillan Corporate and Premium
Sales Department at 1-800-221-7945, extension 5442, or by email at
MacmillanSpecialMarkets@macmillan.com.

First Edition: September 2021

Printed in the United States of America

0 9 8 7 6 5 4 3 2 1

This one is dedicated to my mother,

Catherine Shirley Brom,

who always said I could, when others said I could not

SLEWFOOT

Tread wary foot amongst these sacred stones,
for here, on October 5th, 1666, the devil Slewfoot
did take the lives of 112 good folk of Sutton Village.
May God save their immortal souls.

Marker mounted upon the ruined stonework of the old Sutton meetinghouse.

CHAPTER 1

The New World
Sutton, Connecticut, March 1666

A shadow deep in darkness.
    A whisper . . .
    Another.

"No."

More whispers—urgent.

"I do not hear you . . . I cannot hear you. For the dead do not hear."

A chorus of whispers.

"Leave me be."

You must wake.

"No. I am dead. And dead I shall remain."

You can hide no longer.

"There is nothing left for me out there."

There is blood.

"No . . . no more. I am done."

They come.

"For the sake of all, leave me be."

They are here, at your very door.

"I care not."

We have brought you a gift.

"I want nothing."

Blood. . . . Smell it.

"No, I smell nothing. I am dead."

But the shadow *did* smell the blood drifting around it, into it, becoming part of it, and with it came the hunger—but an itch at first, then, as the smell permeated the air, a painful clawing.

"Oh," the shadow moaned. "Sweet blood."

The shadow opened its eyes, shut them, then opened them again.

There, in the dirt, lay a four-legged beast, not a deer, not any animal it recognized, but a shaggy thing with split hooves and thick curling horns. It lay broken with its guts spilling from its belly, its eyes flickering and its breath fast and shallow.

The shadow drifted toward the animal. The beast fixed wild eyes on the shadow and began to quake, then bleat. The shadow fed on the fear, sliding closer, closer, pushing its smoky tendrils into the warm gore, drinking in both the terror and the blood.

The shadow began to find its shape, the blood forming arteries and veins, cartilage, bone, sinew and muscle. It began lapping the blood, then—realizing it now had teeth—tore into the animal, shoving its muzzle into the warm guts, devouring flesh and bone alike. The shadow felt a thump in its chest, another, convulsed, then a heartbeat, drumming faster, then faster. The shadow, which was no longer a shadow, lifted its head and let out a long howl.

Good, said the other.

"Good," said the shadow, now a beast. And for the first time in ages heard its own voice echoing off the cave walls.

Are you still hungry?

"Yes."

Would you like more blood?

"Yes."

There is more above.

The beast looked up, spotted a sliver of light at the top of a long craggy shaft.

4

What is your name? asked the other.

"I do not remember," replied the beast.

You will. Oh, but you will . . . and so will they.

"SAMSON!" Abitha called, trying to quell the rising panic in her voice.

She moved quickly, following the split-toe tracks as they wove through the shocks of dried cornstalks. She knew the goat couldn't have gone far, as she'd just seen the beast not an hour before. She reached the edge of the field and stopped, scanning the dense Connecticut woods. The trees, even at the dead end of winter and with all their leaves shed upon the cold earth, swallowed the light, making it difficult to see more than a hundred paces forward.

"Samson," she called again. *"Sam!"* The chill air made mist of her words.

She noted the heavy clouds above, could see dusk would be upon her soon. If she didn't find Samson by dark, then the wolves, or one of the wild men, surely would. Yet she hesitated, knowing how easy it was for a soul to enter that wood and never come out. She looked back to the cabin, debated fetching the musket. Deciding there was no time, she sucked in a deep breath, hefted the hem of her gray woolen skirt, and forced herself into that murky maze of trees.

She followed the tracks around a knot of blackberry vines and down an embankment, doing her best not to slip in the half-thawed mud and leaves. The branches and brambles tugged at her coat and long skirt. A limb caught her bonnet, pulling it from her head, unbinding her long auburn hair. She reached for the bonnet and her foot slipped out from beneath her, sending her sliding down the slope and into a boggy ravine.

"Hell and hell!" Abitha cried, then glanced furtively about. There was no one out here, but being careful had become habit, as she well knew the price should one of the sect hear her curse so.

She grabbed a branch and made to stand, but the branch snapped, sending her over onto her hands and knees, the muck sucking the boots from her feet. "Son of a whore!" she cried, this time not caring who heard.

Abitha spat out a speck of mud and began digging for her boots, found them, and tugged them from the bog. She tried shaking out the mud. When that didn't work, she began raking out the muck, the hard leather biting into her half-frozen fingers. When the pain became too much, she stopped, clutching her numb hands to her chest, trying to regain some warmth.

"Samson," she called, searching the soggy bog, scanning the endless wilderness, wondering how a girl from London ever ended up in such a brutal, unforgiving land. She felt the sting of tears and wiped at the corners of her eyes with the backs of her wrists, smearing mud across her cheeks. "Stop with the tears. You're not a child anymore."

She let that sink in for a moment.

Nay, be twenty come spring. A woman now . . . and a married one at that. Her brow tightened as she tried to count the months, realizing she'd been married nearly two years, found it all so hard to accept—a husband, a farm, the Puritans, especially the Puritans and their austere way of life. And all her days she'd been led to believe she'd be a maid to some lord or lady. Not much of a life to be sure, but at least she'd not fear starving come each winter. *Did not turn out so, did it, Abi? Nay, Father certainly saw to that.*

Her father had heard about the king's bounty for brides to the colonies, selling her off to the government for a handful of coins. She'd been promised to her husband, Edward Williams, before she'd even left the shores of England, a girl of only seventeen.

Being a teacher, Abitha's father had insisted she learn her letters right along with her two younger brothers. Thus, Abitha had no problem reading her promissory note, pulling it out during the long voyage over whenever she needed a good laugh, or a good cry.

> Virtuous, obedient young woman, fair of face and
> complexion, shapely figure, good upbringing from
> pious, well-mannered house.

Pious indeed, she'd thought, *if having a father who put more money to drink than bread and a mother who'd used cursing as a form of poetry counted.* And calling her virtuous? Well, if you ignored the outbursts of profanity, occasional thievery, and a propensity for brawling, then perhaps she was just the candidate to marry into a Puritan village. As to "fair of face," well, no one had ever told her that one before, not with her impish nose, not with a complexion that bloomed red with her temper and ruddy with the cold. And she guessed "shapely" meant something else to the man who'd penned this ditty, because her scrappy figure had rarely turned the head of any man she'd noticed. But it all lost its humor as the ship entered New Haven harbor. As it became real, she found herself sure her new husband would turn her away on sight. But if Edward had been surprised, so had she, as Edward wasn't all

6

she'd hoped. He was a fair-looking man, maybe even handsome, about ten years her senior, with a full head of dark wavy hair, but he had a swayback, a hunch, that caused him to walk with a stoop.

And what he might think of her, she couldn't tell, at least not then, because if Edward *had* been disappointed, he never let on—greeting her upon arrival with a timid smile. Then, after an awkward handshake and a brief, businesslike introduction, he plucked up her only bag and led her to his mule-drawn wagon, taking her away to her new life.

And here I be, she thought, *digging frozen mud out from my boots and chasing a stupid goat into the deep, dark wilderness.*

A distant howl snapped Abitha from her thoughts. She gave up trying to empty the muck from her boots and just shoved them back on, struggling up. Her long skirt was now covered in mud and soaked through, weighing her down, making the going even more difficult. She plucked a stout stick from the muck for balance and searched for the tracks, quickly picking them up again. They led her to the far side of the ravine, to a clump of boulders jutting out from the hillside.

Abitha studied the dark stones, was struck by how similar they looked to a giant crumbling stump, wondered if it might be the petrified remains of some ancient tree, tried to imagine just how huge such a tree would need to be to leave behind such an immense relic. She noticed something else, smaller boulders, upright and evenly spaced in a broad circle around the stump; she counted twelve of them. There was something peculiar to the way they were set, as though placed there by some bygone giant.

The hoofprints disappeared into a hollow at the base of the petrified stump. Abitha could see it was the entrance to a den or small cave and approached cautiously, scanning for signs of bears or wolves. But the only disturbance to the wet leaves was that of the goat.

She stepped closer and, setting a hand on the overhang and peering into the cave, found only darkness and shadow within. Yet, still she felt uneasy, as though eyes were on her, and regretted not bringing the musket.

"Samson?"

No response, nothing but that unsettling darkness.

"Damnable beast, why would you wander into such a hole?" And it struck her as odd how the tracks had been so direct, almost a beeline from the barn, as though the goat knew about the cave.

"Samson," she called again.

Nothing.

"Samson! Get out here . . . *now!* Do not make me come in after you." And in a soft whisper, "Please do not make me go in there." She contemplated going back to the cabin and returning with Edward, but she didn't know when he'd be home—could be hours. *We cannot lose the goat,* she fretted, knowing the beast had cost them dearly, another debt atop all their mounting debts. But it was more than that, it was knowing this was her fault, as she'd been the only one in the goat pen today, discovering the errant goat only when she'd come out to milk the two nannies for supper. But what she most dreaded was seeing Edward's face when she told him what she'd done, of having to bear his defeat at the loss. No, that she couldn't take.

"Samson," she pleaded. *"Please."*

She set her teeth, stooped, and stuck her head into the opening, waiting as her eyes slowly adjusted. The cave was larger than she'd expected, about the size of a wagon, with a low-hanging roof. She probed ahead with her stick, finding the floor, and slid in.

"Samson," she called, her words echoing off the back of the cave. Her eyes continued to adjust and she could see another chamber. *Nay,* she thought. *I'll not go in there. Naught can make me go back there.*

8

A slight rustle came from farther within, followed by a snort, like that of a goat. Abitha tensed, readied to flee. "Who's there?" she called, wielding the stick like a spear. "Samson? Pray tell, is that you?" She waited, clutching the stick so hard her hands hurt. When a full minute crawled by without another sound, she slowly let out her breath. *Stop being such a frightened goose.* She bit her lip and took a cautious step forward, another, and suddenly she was falling.

She landed on her side, flailing for purchase as she slid downward, clawing at the loose dirt seeking something, anything, to stop her descent. She caught hold of a protruding rock with one hand, then the other, and held tight as she tried to find purchase with her feet, gasping when she realized there was no ground beneath her, just a dark hole.

Abitha hung there breathing hard and fast, listening as the loose rocks tumbled down the shaft, seeming to fall forever, and that was when she heard it again, the rustling. This time she had no trouble locating its source—it was coming from the pit below her. Then she understood what had happened, that the goat had fallen in the pit.

"Oh, you stupid beast," she said. "You stupid, stupid blunderhead." She felt sure the goat's neck must be broken, or its back, and if so, the beast would no longer be any good for breeding, and you couldn't milk a billy goat the last she'd checked. "Oh, you're stew now, you fool of a beast. When I get—"

She fell quiet.

Another sound came from below.

She stared down the dark shaft.

Again, the sound, and she knew with absolute certainty it wasn't the goat, but whispering. It sounded like children. She couldn't understand the words—it seemed some other language. *The natives,* she thought, but no, this was something else, because she didn't just hear the words, she felt them, as though they were crawling beneath her skin. A chill raked her body and suddenly she *did* understand.

Let go. We will catch you.

Abitha redoubled her efforts to escape, struggling against the weight of her muddy skirt.

Again, the voice—closer now. She spared a glance downward, could see nothing, her feet disappearing into that terrible darkness. She got an elbow over, then managed to swing up a leg, hooking it on the lip of the pit. She rolled away from the hole, made it to her knees, scrambling as fast as she could for the entrance, toward daylight, lost her footing, stumbled—and that's when *something* touched her! She screamed, but nothing was there.

"Leave me be!" she cried, scuttling on all fours out the mouth of the cave, tumbling down the hill. She rolled up onto her knees, staring back up at the cave, waiting for it, whatever *it* was, to come out.

"You're not real," she whispered, shaking her head. "Not real!"

She wiped her hair from her eyes and saw it, there in the tricky shadows of twilight, a giant tree towering above her, impossibly immense, its leaves crimson, the color of blood. She couldn't move, couldn't so much as blink. She heard her name, far away, then closer, louder.

"Abitha!"

Abitha spun to see Edward holding a lantern on the far side of the bog, his stooped form silhouetted in the fading light.

She glanced back to the tree—it was gone, but in its place a sapling sprouted from atop the giant stump. "That was not there before," she whispered. *Nay, I could not have missed it, not with those leaves so red.*

"Abitha!"

She climbed to her feet, ran to Edward, skirting the bog, never so happy to see the man.

"Abitha. What—" He raised the lantern, looking her up and down, his eyes wide with dismay. And what a sight she made, covered in dirt and leaves, her

9

bonnet lost, her wet muddy hair stringing down her face, and—she only just realized—missing a boot.

"You poor girl, what—"

"I lost him, Edward," she said, talking fast, her voice breaking. "I lost him!"

"Who? Lost who?"

"Our new goat, Samson. I've lost him. I am sorry."

He scanned the dark. "We shall find him."

"Nay, you're not hearing me. Samson is dead. He fell in a hole. Gone . . . just gone, Edward." And she saw the understanding of what that meant for them dawn on his face. Without the billy to breed with their nannies, there'd be no kids come spring.

"Are you sure?"

"Aye. Edward. There's a pit." Her voice broke as she pointed back behind her. "He's at the bottom. I am so bitterly sorry. I . . . I—"

Edward reached for her and did a rare thing—embraced her. The hug was awkward and fatherly, as all his attempts at intimacy tended to be, but she knew he was doing his best to comfort her.

She pushed away. "Edward, did you not hear me? I lost Samson. *Me.* You *should* be cross. You have the right to be angry."

"Let us worry on this tomorrow," he said. "In the light of the day. If this be the Lord's will, then . . . then we shall make do."

She felt hot angry tears—anger *at* Edward, anger *for* Edward, because he wouldn't lose his temper, not at her; he never did. But she wished he would, wished he would curse her. Then maybe she wouldn't have to be so angry with herself.

"It were not God that left the gate unlatched," she snapped. "It were me. This is my doing. We cannot spend our lives blaming the Lord. That is no way to—"

"Enough!" he said, his voice suddenly terse. But she caught the fragility just below the surface and had to remind herself to not push too hard, to give him plenty of space to work things out his own way.

"Enough," Edward whispered, and turned, heading back up the slope, looking beaten and tired.

Abitha glanced back at the dark cave, then followed along.

As they approached the cabin, Abitha spied a white stallion hitched to the porch. *Oh no, not this night.*

Edward stopped, and for a minute Abitha thought he might turn and leave. Instead he inhaled deeply and headed in. Abitha followed.

Wallace, Edward's older brother, sat with his boots propped atop the table. Both men shared the same wavy hair, dark eyes, and brooding brows, but that was where the similarities ended, as Wallace seemed everything his brother wasn't—a huge breadth of a man, brash in voice and manner, square of jaw, a gallant-looking fellow by anyone's account.

"Edward!" Wallace called through a mouthful of ham.

Abitha had been preparing the table before heading into the woods, and Wallace had seen fit to help himself to one of the two small slices of ham. Abitha struggled not to shout at the man, that being the very last of their salted meat and there being no telling when they could afford more.

Wallace looked at the mud on Abitha's clothes and in her hair. "Dare I ask."

"We've lost a goat," Edward said, and added no more.

"Oh . . . I see," Wallace replied, taking another bite of ham. "I am sorry to hear of this." He held up the chunk of meat. "Hope you do not mind, brother. It is a long ride out here and I've not eaten dinner as yet."

You know full well we mind, Abitha thought, and looked to her husband, willing him to call the man out. *Do not make this easy, Edward. At least tell him it would've been courteous to have asked first. For once in your life, do not let him walk all over you.*

"Oh," Edward said. "Well . . . yes, it is good to be able to share the Lord's bounty."

"Abitha," Wallace said. "Fetch me a spot of Edward's sweet honey mead. Need to clear my throat. I have a bit of news to share."

Abitha hesitated, being in no mood to be ordered about by this man, not tonight, not in her own house. But there was more to it; they were almost out of mead. This being the end of winter, they were out of most commodities, and the man before them was a big part of the reason why.

Wallace waited expectantly. He wiped the grease from his lips onto his sleeve, then looked to Edward. "Something wrong with her?"

"Abitha," Edward said. "Some mead."

"But, Edward. There's just the last—"

"Abitha," he repeated sternly.

"Edward. I—"

"Abitha!" Edward snapped. *"Now!"*

Wallace watched the exchange with a bemused grin. "The patience you show this one, brother. You are a lenient man, to be sure. But some say too lenient. Do not mean to tend your house, but a stern hand in the home might save that one a thrashing in the village. That is all."

Abitha flushed, turned away, and marched to the cupboard. She knew all too well that Puritan women were to be seen and not heard, to be subservient and respectful to *all* men at *all* times. It had been drilled into her since the day she'd arrived, and she sure as hell didn't need Wallace to tell her once more. She sucked in a deep breath, trying to quell her temper, opened the cupboard, and lifted out a jug of mead. It was their last, and by the weight of it, all but gone. She grabbed a mug, filled it halfway, and sat it down with a thump on the table in front of Wallace.

"You can certainly tell when this one has her dander up," Wallace said, and smirked. "Face turns the color of a raspberry."

"You say you have news?" Edward asked.

Wallace's smirk fell away and he downed the mead in a go. "Edward, here, sit down. Abitha, a cup for Edward."

Edward took a seat at the table and Abitha brought him a cup and filled it.

Wallace tapped his cup. "A bit more."

Abitha glanced at Edward. Edward nodded and she poured out the last of the mead, barely enough to fill the bottom of Wallace's cup.

Wallace didn't hide his disappointment.

"There is no more," Abitha said tersely. "That is the last of it."

Wallace sighed. "Aye, hard times all around." He paused, searching for the right words. "Edward, it seems we are in a bit of a bind."

"Oh?"

Wallace cleared his throat. "I did my best with the tobacco . . . everyone knows that. Yes?"

"Only God can control the weather," Edward said.

"Yes," Wallace continued. "Exactly. I spared naught, as you well know . . . went to such trouble and expense to bring in the proper plant, the new sweet leaf that showed such promise. I did all things right. But yes, you speak true, I cannot bring the rain. That . . . only the Lord can do."

Oh, is it the weather that is to blame now? Abitha thought, fighting not to scoff. *The weather that made you take on tobacco even after you were warned by so many that the plant did not fare well in Sutton soil. But did you heed them? Nay, because you always know better, Wallace. Better than anyone.*

Wallace was quiet a moment, his face pained as though reliving a nightmare. "Anyway, I am not here to go over all that again. The crops failed and the venture did not work out. That is that. What matters now is our family's circumstance. I took on tobacco for *all* of us. You and Abitha too. As you know I had hopes to bring you in on it . . . to expand the operation to your spot out here. To honor Father's legacy and all he did for us by building a family enterprise."

He stared at Edward, his eyes all but demanding agreement.

Edward nodded.

"Well, it seems this venture has left us in a pinch." Wallace paused. "Seems . . . it seems we have a loan to repay."

"A loan? But . . . I thought you had gone in with Lord Mansfield as partner?"

"Yes . . . in a way. But . . . well . . . when the cost kept spiraling, he demanded some collateral."

"Your *farm?* Wallace . . . say you did not!"

Wallace peered into his empty cup. "No . . . no, I did not do that. I would never risk our father's farm."

Edward appeared relieved.

"I put up this place."

Edward sat straight up. "This place? You mean *my* farm? *Here?*"

Wallace nodded slowly.

Abitha steadied herself against the cupboard. "What . . . what do you mean?"

Wallace gave her a cutting look. "Mind you to stay out of this, woman."

Abitha bit her tongue, knowing too well that women were strictly prohibited from engaging in business affairs, that it was the very law.

"Wallace," Edward said. "Please explain this to me. I do not understand."

Wallace scowled, his face red. "How much plainer can I make it. I put this homestead up for collateral. I am sorry. I never thought it would come to this."

"But . . . you *cannot* do that. This is *my* land."

"Brother, it is not that simple, as you well know."

"It is. We . . . we have an agreement. I've made all payments on time. There is but the one season left."

"I am not saying this is fair. What happened with the tobacco was not fair to any of us. You think I do not feel bad about all of this? What I am saying is I am trying to be as fair as I *can*. Not just to you, but to all of us."

And when did you become so fair-minded, Wallace? Abitha wanted to ask. *Was it fair that you should inherit both farms simply for the being the eldest son, then push Edward to buy this one from you . . . these scraggly acres way out here in the wilds? And for a deal that made us all but paupers. Fifty bushels of corn per season. Fifty! At least twice, mayhap three times their worth. Was that fair?*

"But listen," Wallace continued. "Hear me out; it is not so bleak as you would think. I have worked out an agreement with Lord Mansfield."

"What sort of an agreement?"

"You can stay on here. You need not leave. Only you will be making your payments to Mansfield instead of me."

"So, I make my final payment to him?"

Wallace shook his head sadly. "There is no final payment, little brother. The property belongs to Lord Mansfield now. You work the land, giving him half the yield each year."

"Like some tenant farmer," Abitha said beneath her breath.

Wallace gave her a scathing glare. "Edward, I pleaded your case . . . explained the situation. Lord Mansfield is a fair man. He said he is willing to discuss terms for you to eventually own the land."

"How long?"

Wallace shrugged. "Twenty years, mayhap."

Twenty years? Abitha thought. *Twenty years! Edward, do not let him do this to us.*

Edward said nothing, just stared at the table as though lost.

"We are lucky to get that. I did my best. I am telling you."

Abitha began to shake, found both her hands balled into fists. *Edward, can you not see that this man is playing you, that he is always playing you?* But she knew no matter how many times she pointed it out, he could not. Edward could rarely read people's true intentions, leaving him vulnerable, and she had to watch as his brother took full advantage of this, over and over.

"There must be another way," Edward said. "Mayhap, if we, the both of us, put up a bit more each season to help you pay this off."

"No. I've been round this. This is the *only* way."

You must stand up to him, Edward, Abitha thought, taking a step forward. Edward glanced up at her, saw her outrage. Abitha shook her head vehemently at him.

"Wallace," Edward said. "I am sorry. But this is your debt. It is not fair to ask this of me. I have put everything into this place. You cannot just give *my* land away."

"Edward, who does this land belong to?"

"What do you mean?"

"Little brother," Wallace said in a gentle tone, the way you would talk to a child. "I've been doing my best to say this in such a way as to not make you feel small, as we both know you do not always understand the bigger picture. But you are forcing me to be blunt." Wallace leaned forward. "Who does the land belong to?"

"Well, it's not that simple. The land—"

"It *is* that simple," Wallace said sternly. "You are just not able to see it. Now, whose name is on the deed to this property?"

"Why . . . that be yours, of course."

"Of course. And as such it is my asset and therefore can be, and is, available to pay off my debts. It is *that* simple."

Nay, Abitha thought. *None of this is that simple, Wallace Williams. You made a deal for these parcels. And here we are with but the one season to go, and you . . . you what? You think you can just take it all away?* "No!" Abitha blurted out. "Why does it need be Edward's land? What . . . what about *your* land, Wallace?"

Wallace stood up, appeared ready to slap her. "Why is this woman speaking?"

"Abitha!" Edward snapped. "Enough. Please. Wallace, I am sorry."

"I have had about all I will take from that one."

"I will see to her. But this matter. It is upsetting for all of us. And you have to agree it is a fair question."

"What is?"

"Why do you not put up your own acres?"

"What part of this are you not understanding? These *are* my own acres."

"No, I mean your homestead."

"How can you ask that?" Wallace retorted, sounding wounded. "Would you have me give up the very home we were born and raised in? The farm that Papa built with his sweat and blood? And that would make no sense; my acres are worth ten times this place."

"Edward built *this* farm with *his* sweat and blood," Abitha said. "It was worth almost naught until he cleared it, brought in topsoil. It is *his* labors, not this land, that you are paying your debt with. Have you no shame!"

Edward looked at Abitha, horrified. *"Abitha!"*

"I have had enough of this!" Wallace growled. "I have signed this land over to Mansfield. It is done and that is all!"

"No!" Abitha cried. "It will never stand. You've signed a deal with Edward and you will be held to it!" Abitha knew she should stop. "What you have done is sold your own brother into servitude to pay off *your* debts."

"Abi!" Edward cried. *"Enough!"*

"Edward, do not let him cow you. Not after all our hard work. He—"

"Abitha! Not another word!"

Abitha saw Edward was shaking, that he appeared ready to bolt from the room. She closed her mouth.

"You have gone too far this time, brat," Wallace spat, his eyes furious. "Your tongue has earned you a hearing with the ministers. We will see what they think of your outburst."

Abitha flinched; she knew this to be no groundless threat. She'd seen several women set out in stocks for speaking their minds, one even lashed for far less than what she'd just done. And Wallace's threat might hold less weight if this were her first offense, but Abitha was already on probation for not keeping her tongue in check.

"Wallace," Edward pleaded. "Please . . . no. I am appalled by her behavior. Please forgive her. She is high-spirited . . . is still learning our ways. I—"

"No. . . . Enough excuses. She has been warned many times. I will be placing her on charges tomorrow. It is high time she learns her place." He picked up his hat and started for the door.

Edward stepped in front of the larger man, held up his hands. "Please, Wallace, do not do this. For me, please."

Abitha stood shaking, watching Edward begging to be heard. *This is my fault. When will I learn to keep my mouth shut?*

Wallace pushed past.

"All right . . . I am willing to work with you on this," Edward conceded. "The farm. I am."

Wallace stopped, gave Edward the look one would give a contrite child. "I am listening."

"I just need a little time to get my thoughts in order. That is all. It is a lot all at once. Surely you can understand that?"

Wallace waited.

"I . . ." Edward started, glancing fretfully at Abitha. "I am sure we can come to an agreement. I mean, I know we can. There has to be a way."

Wallace smiled. "Now, there is the little brother that I know and cherish. You sometimes forget that Papa left all this to me for a reason. He knew well of your weakness of mind and trusted me to look after you. You must trust me as well. We must not let Papa down."

Edward dropped his eyes.

Wallace let out a sigh. "And, Edward, to be fair, I guess I could have handled this better." He jabbed a finger at Abitha. "It is just hard to keep one's temper with that harpy nagging at us."

"I will see to her. But let me handle her in my way. Please say naught to the ministers."

"But *can* you handle her, brother? I am beginning to believe otherwise. Do you not see how she takes advantage of your gentle nature, plays you, bends you to her will with that poisonous, nagging tongue of hers? Look at her even now, glaring with such venom. I feel a few days in the stocks and a sound beating would be the best thing for that one."

"Nay, I can manage her. Abitha," Edward said sternly. "You will apologize. . . . You will beg Wallace's forgiveness. Now!"

Abitha gasped. Even knowing Edward was but trying to spare her punishment, it still felt as though he'd slapped her. She didn't trust herself to speak, so just stood there trembling.

"Abitha!" Edward all but growled.

Wallace smirked, and she knew he was hoping she would scream and curse, would throw something at him, anything to give him more leverage over Edward. She dug her nails into her palms as the tears welled up in her eyes. *You have to, Abi. You must.*

"It is no good, brother," Wallace said. "She will never—"

"I beg your forgiveness, Wallace," Abitha said, all but spitting the words out. She was shaking now, knew her face must be scarlet. "I should not have spoken so. Please forgive my disrespect."

Edward looked to the larger man. "There, see. She *is* trying."

"Her eyes are like knives," Wallace said. "I do not appreciate the way she is glaring at me."

"Abitha," Edward said. "Cast down your eyes."

Abitha continued to glare at Wallace.

"Abitha!"

She shifted her glare to Edward, wanting to slap him for treating her so in front of this beast. But when she saw the fear on his face, fear for her, it was then that the tears came, spilling hotly down her cheeks. She lowered her eyes, stared at her feet.

"Wallace, what more do you want? She is contrite. Please. This night would be a trial for anyone. I have promised to work with you. So, now let us put this behind us."

Abitha glanced up, caught the sly grin on Wallace's face.

"Perhaps you are right, little brother; there are bigger matters to settle here. We should not allow this one's ill-bred behavior to come between us. But I promise you this, the next time she butts into our business, she will receive the lash. Am I clear on that?"

"Yes," Edward said. "Of course."

"Are we clear on that, Abitha?" Wallace asked. It was obvious he was enjoying every second of this. "Do you understand your place? Do you? I need hear it from you so that next time there will be no argument. Do . . . you . . . *understand* . . . your . . . place?"

"I understand," Abitha said, keeping her head down, forcing the words out between her teeth.

Wallace smirked; he was positively gloating. Abitha had no doubt he'd gotten everything he wanted from this visit and more.

"Tomorrow then, little brother," Wallace said, his tone suddenly light. "After church. We can work out the details and let the ministers know where things stand." He put on his hat and left the cabin.

"Slow down, Abi," Edward called.

Abitha turned to see Edward trailing several yards behind her, all but lost in the morning mist, the sway of his back slowing his gait. She stopped and waited.

"We cannot be late, Edward. Not *this* day."

"We've plenty of time," he said over his labored breath. "We're almost there and I've not yet heard first bell."

Abitha nodded. "Indeed. I am just so nervous, that is all. I did but barely sleep last night." But worry was only half of it—she made no mention of her dreams of the giant tree, how it whispered her name, how its mighty roots slithered about like snakes, chasing her through the dark woods.

"We are in the right in this, Abitha. You know this, and with God's help, the ministers will see the truth as well."

God's help, she thought. *If only I could count on that. But where was God when I was watching my mother die and my father going mad with grief and drink? I wish I shared your faith, Edward. What a comfort that would be.*

And as though reading this on her face, Edward reached out and took her hand.

Abi pulled away.

"What is it?"

She didn't answer.

"You are still angry about last night?"

"It is hard not to be."

"Abi, I have said I am sorry, but if you need hear it again, then so be it. I am sorry. I had to address you so. You know it true. Wallace would've reported you otherwise."

She did know it. She also knew he was right, that she'd gone too far, but it still hurt. She saw him struggling for the right words and halted.

"I am lost without you, Abitha. I shouldn't need say it. . . . You know this."

She took his hand and he squeezed it tightly, that simple gesture saying so much more than all his words. But it was then that the bell clanged once, bringing awareness to just how close they were to the village. Edward dropped Abitha's hand and stood away. They both glanced fretfully about, knowing too well that public affection was yet one more offense on the long list of offenses and that zealous eyes were everywhere.

They continued along, the wagon ruts deepening as they neared the village, often forcing them into the brush to avoid the icy puddles. The bell tolled twice, and Abitha finally slowed down. "We do not want to be early, but right before the doors close."

"Wallace will be none too happy about that. I am sure he wishes to discuss this matter before church."

Abitha smiled. "Aye, I know." What she didn't say was that she didn't want to give Wallace any chance to confuse Edward before they met with the ministers.

Abitha smelled the river, then saw the gate loom out of the fog as though summoned. Tall timber fortifications disappeared into the mist on either side, their jagged tops like deadly teeth. These fortifications surrounded the entire village and were built to protect, to keep evil at bay. But Abitha shuddered as they entered; passing through the gate always felt more as entering a trap than a sanctuary.

There was no guard to challenge them—all were at church—so they picked their way down the lane, carefully skirting puddles and clumps of manure, passing through the orderly rows of modest thatched-roof houses.

Each home conformed to the one before it, all covered in unpainted clapboard and partitioned off by gray wattle fences made from saplings. Abitha searched for decorations—a wreath, a string of dried flowers—anything to break up the suffocating sea of gray. She found only drab waxed windowpanes staring back at her as though judging, weighing her soul, just waiting for her to say or do something wrong so they could condemn her before all.

No smoke rose from chimneys, the fires, stoves, and candles all snuffed out, as the occupants were either at church or silently on their way by now. The only sound Abitha heard was that of their feet crunching on the light frost, and in that moment, it felt as though Edward and she were lost in some gloomy ghost town.

Finally, they spied the commons ahead and could just make out the silhouette of the meetinghouse beyond.

"Now, remember what we went over," Abi said in a hushed voice. "Do not let that man—"

"I know, I know," Edward replied in a whisper. "We have been round this a dozen times. I'll do my best. That I promise you."

"I am sorry, Edward. I do not mean to nag. Just . . . just so much is at stake."

He smiled and gave her hand a quick, furtive squeeze. "You are no nag, Abi. You're a blessing. You give me strength. Worry not, I know what must be said. Let us just hope the ministers see the fairness of it all. Now you must make *me* a promise."

She gave him a wary look.

"No matter how things may go, you will mind your tongue and stay in your place. You're out of chances. One slip and Wallace will see you in the stocks with a good lashing. Now promise me."

"I promise," Abitha said, and thought, *Please, Lord God, help me keep my temper.*

The stocks materialized out of the gloom, stark warnings to all of the consequences for any who did not conform. Abitha felt a chill; she did every time she saw them.

There was a whipping post and five sets of stocks in the commons. Two of the stocks were standing, with a yoke that fit around one's neck and wrists, then three that clamped around one's ankles so that the person was forced to sit in the dirt. When she'd first arrived Abitha was shocked to see so many, couldn't fathom such a small community needing them all, but on more than one occasion since she'd come to town to find them full.

Abitha noticed a figure hunched on the ground. As they drew closer she saw it was a man, his legs in stocks.

"Joseph?" Edward inquired in a low voice.

It was indeed Joseph, but he didn't look up, turning his face away as though ashamed. He was clutching himself, shivering uncontrollably, and it took Abitha only a moment to see why. His blankets were on the ground beside him, just out of reach. She wondered why he would've tossed them away. It wasn't until she saw the mud on his back and in his hair that she realized of course he hadn't, that someone had done this *to* him.

"Oh, you poor soul," Abitha said, and quickly scooped up the blankets, bringing them over, then hesitated when she noticed the dried blood on his back, realized he'd been thrashed severely. "Joseph . . . I am so sorry." She gently wrapped the blankets around him, and that was when she saw it was more than mud in his hair, but manure too. And that, she knew, was not part of the sanctioned punishment, but someone's idea of sport. "Who did this to you, Joseph? Who took your blankets?"

Joseph didn't answer, just tugged the covers up over his head as though trying to hide.

"You should not do that," someone called.

Abitha looked round to see Wallace's daughter, Charity, and her friend Mary Dibble, walking past on their way to church.

"Uncle Edward, you would do her a kindness to tell her not to interfere."

"And you would do well to mind your own, Charity Williams," Edward said, in what was for Edward a severe tone. "You're not of age to be speaking so."

The girls stopped. "I meant no disrespect, Uncle. Just do not wish to see my aunt sharing the stocks with this man. Not in this cold." And though her words spoke of concern, her eyes showed nothing but contempt for Abitha.

A thickset woman, Mary's mother, Goody Dibble, walked up and joined the girls. "What is it now?"

"Abitha were aiding this sinner. I thought it good to warn her of the consequences."

"Abitha," Goody chastised. "Do you not know what this man has done? Why, he is guilty of skipping midweek church."

Thursday church, Abitha thought. She often forgot that those in the village proper had two services they were required to attend.

"Not only is he a truant," Goody continued, her voice rising, full of righteousness, "but also a liar. For he told Reverend Carter that he had been on his hands and knees with the stomach cramps during service. But he was found out when his neighbors came forth and reported that they'd witnessed him napping in his barn, both before and after service." She jabbed a condemning finger at the man. "This man did lie directly to the reverend."

And you, Goody, Abitha thought, *should be in the stocks for being a tireless gossip and sticking your nose in everyone's business.*

Two young men showed up, the brothers Luke and Robert Parker.

"He's still out here?" Luke asked.

"Aye," Charity said. "After what he has done, I am not surprised."

21

"Four nights was the sentence," Goody said. "I bet he'll not sleep through church again."

Luke casually bent down and plucked up a clod of manure, lobbed it at Joseph. The clod struck the man on the shoulder. Joseph let out a grunt.

"What are you doing?" Abitha asked, stunned.

Luke looked at her as though he didn't understand the question, then reached down and picked up another clod.

"He is doing his duty before God," Goody Dibble said. "Reverend Carter says that we must all help cast out the Devil . . . wherever he might lurk."

The others nodded and followed Luke's lead, the girls too, even Goody Dibble, all plucking up dirt clods and manure.

Abitha gasped as they began pelting the cowering man, Joseph letting out wounded bleats with every strike.

Abitha was startled by their intensity; there were no grins, or the laughter of those up to hijinks, nothing but set, grim faces. She felt she could've understood them better if it had been simple cruelty, but it was as though they were at war with Satan himself and Satan was somehow inside this poor man.

A large clod hit Joseph against the side of his head, knocking him over.

"Stop it!" Abitha cried, starting forward, but Edward grabbed her arm.

"Abitha, no."

"Let go," Abitha snapped, trying to twist free.

A stern voice came from behind them. "Why are you not in church?"

The group froze.

A man wearing a tall hat and a long flowing overcoat walked out from the fog. It was Reverend Thomas Carter, the head minister, a lean man, edging toward his fifties. His wide hat brim kept his long face in shadow but couldn't hide his ponderous brows and severe eyes, eyes that appeared to be judging each and every one of them. "Look at your hands. They're filthy."

The group appeared stricken, incapable of speaking.

"Clean up and get to church, *now*."

They dropped the clods and dashed away, leaving Abitha and Edward alone with the minister. Abitha hoped he'd not witnessed her with Joseph, as she was sure it wouldn't help their case if he had.

"Walk with me," the reverend said, and they did, heading toward the meetinghouse.

"Abitha, do you feel you were helping Joseph?"

Abitha's blood chilled. "I . . . I didn't mean to overstep, sir. I just . . . just—"

"You never mean to overstep, yet you keep doing it. Why is that?"

"I am trying. I truly am."

"Do you feel you are being merciful to Joseph?"

"I just thought . . . thought they were being so very cruel."

"Can you not see how your intentions undermine Joseph finding grace? Undermine this very community?"

"I am not sure, sir."

"Joseph must understand that his sins are condemned by all. It is not always easy, and yes, it can be cruel, but it is the only way. If one parent punishes the child for his poor behavior, only to have the other give him comfort for his tears, then the lesson is undermined and the family unity put in jeopardy. Can you see that?"

"Yes, I think so," she said, trying to make sense of what any of this had to do with pelting a man with manure.

"We must all fight the Devil together. If we allow the Devil to divide us, we shall perish. Yes?"

"Yes," she agreed.

They crossed the commons and approached the meetinghouse—a large grim structure that, like all the buildings in Sutton, was covered in unpainted clapboard and lacked any embellishments. When Abitha first arrived from London, she'd been surprised to find there was no church proper in Sutton—no building with a steeple and cross atop it—stunned to find that Puritans actually considered churches, no matter how austere, to be an offense against God. Thus, they held their services in the meetinghouse instead, in the same space as they held all their civil and social meetings.

But there was one bit of adornment added to the façade this day, a row of wolves' heads nailed above the door, their dark crimson blood staining the planks. Sutton paid a bounty for wolves and these trophies were meant to serve as a reminder to all that this land was wild and untamed, and that death and God's judgment could be upon them at any time. Abitha looked up into their dead eyes and shuddered.

They walked up the steps just as the adjunct minister, Reverend Collins, was preparing to shut the doors, bid him a good morning, and entered.

They were all here, the entire village of Sutton, over a hundred of them, packed into one room. Seating was arranged by land ownership and status, with the men on the left and the women on the right. Abitha gave Edward's arm a quick squeeze and he took his place. Abitha, even after two years, was still considered an outsider by most, so slid into her spot at the very rear on the women's side. She had yet to be confirmed into the community, partially due to her behavior, so was seated amongst the servants. In truth Abitha was glad not to feel the judgmental eyes of the congregation on the back of her neck.

"Abitha," came a hushed call.

It was Helen, waving her over. Helen was immediately shushed, as all women were required to remain silent through the entire service.

Wallace spotted Edward and pushed his way over, seating himself next his younger brother, leaning in on the smaller man, bending his ear.

The fool is probably going on and on about what their father, their dear Papa, would expect, Abitha thought. *I swear the man believes himself a conduit to their father's soul.* She bit her lip. *Careful what you say, Edward. Careful now. He's a snake, that one.* She'd spent a good part of last night talking Edward through and round this whole thing, but even though they both felt Wallace's claims were outside of anything either of them had heard of, that he had no real legal footing, they both knew the law in Sutton was often open to interpretation based on sentiment and bias, and far *too* often by how much wealth and land one possessed. She felt Reverend Carter a fair man, but the other two ministers were not so consistent in their rulings. She glanced over at Reverend Smith. Reverend Smith was Wallace's nearest neighbor and the two had been good friends since early childhood.

Abitha closed her eyes, crossed her fingers, and prayed for God's help this day. When she opened them, she caught Cadwell's son, Cecil, giving her furtive looks and realized a lock of her hair had fallen loose from her cap. Then she noticed Wallace's daughter, Charity, glaring at the both of them, making no attempt to hide her jealousy and disapproval. Charity fervently tapped her own bonnet and pointed at Abitha, drawing the attention of several of the women, most of them shaking their heads and giving Abitha condemning looks.

Lord, you would think I'd shown up with both my diddies a-hanging out. Abitha sighed, shoving the lock back under her cap. *Such nonsense,* she thought. *What possible harm can a loose bit of hair do?*

The doors closed with a resounding thud, signaling service was about to begin, and everyone faced forward, sitting stiff and straight on the hard, backless benches.

Reverend Thomas Carter walked up the aisle and they all stood as he removed his overcoat and took the pulpit. Reverend Carter didn't don the billowing robes that other ministers preferred, dressing instead in the same simple black coat and white collar that he wore most every day. He set down his substantial bible with a thud that reverberated through the entire room, setting it next to a large hourglass. He flipped the book open to the first mark, started to speak, when a timid tapping came from the doors.

Reverend Carter nodded to Samuel Harlow, one of the town deputies, standing in the back holding a long pole with a wooden knob on the end. It was his duty to prod or thump any who were not fully attentive. Samuel walked over and opened the door.

Ansel Fitch stood on the stoop clutching his hat to his chest, his eyes cast down.

"Come in, Ansel," Reverend Carter called over the congregation.

Ansel made a small bow and quickly scurried to a seat in the very back.

"Ansel," the reverend called.

"Aye."

"Stand up."

The man stood. Ansel was older than most; Abitha judged him to be in his late fifties. He was whip thin and a bit beaten down, with a craggy, bitter face and shifty eyes that tended to bulge at the slightest provocation, and they were bulging now.

Reverend Carter sighed. "You are late. You well know what that means."

"Please beg pardon . . . all of you. But I had other Godly duties that would not wait. I did spy two cats acting in a most unnatural manner. Walking side by side murmuring in each other's ears as only servants of the Devil might. I was but trying to find out what it was they were about. So, I ask you, good reverend, please grant me pardon this once."

"How many times have I granted you pardon now? Is it three, or four? Seems you are often following cats, or chasing some other hand of Satan come the start of church. It makes one wonder if it is your vigilance that is making you late, or if mayhap you just do not wish to crawl out of bed as early as the rest of us."

Ansel's face turned red. He glared at the reverend with his bulbous eyes. "I would have you know—"

"Enough! Your responsibilities to God start here in church. Now, come forward."

Ansel's face creased like a man forced to eat stinging ants. He shuffled forward and the reverend pointed to a spot on the floor, just to the side of the pulpit.

"There. Take your knees."

Ansel groaned and slowly knelt onto the hard planks, his knees cracking as he bent. As was the law, he would have to stay there, before everyone, through the entire sermon.

Reverend Carter returned to his bible and led them in opening prayer. After prayer, he flipped the hourglass and began his sermon. There were usually three sermons, one from each minister, over three hours of preaching.

On and on and on, Abitha thought, as she listened, finding it hard to understand how they could go over and over the same sentiments every Sunday. *It's not that complicated*, she thought. *Just do your best to treat others as you wish to be treated. What more needs to be said?* But in Abitha's experience the Puritans tended to make most moral matters as complicated as possible. Which surprised her, as edicts and rituals and canon, especially those smacking of Catholicism, were the very heart of all they wished to escape, their philosophy being one of eliminating all things between them and the Lord above. This not being more apparent anywhere than here in the meetinghouse, where all was stripped bare, there not being any adornment—no altar, no cross, not a sole decoration other than a large eye, that of God, painted on the pulpit, staring at them all, judging them all.

26

Abitha glanced at the eye, then quickly away as an intense feeling of uneasiness stole over her. It wasn't God she thought of when she met that unforgiving gaze, but her own father, of his rantings and ravings, especially there at the end, after her mother had passed.

The reverend was building up steam now, standing stiff and unyielding, leaning into the congregation as though against the very winds of Hell. He clutched the pulpit with one knotty hand while thumping the bible with the other, punctuating every condemnation as he lectured them on how they all could be more virtuous in the eyes of God.

Someone let out a cry, and Abitha glanced over to see Cecil rubbing the back of his head. Deputy Harlow had just thumbed him soundly with the long pole. She guessed he must have nodded off, or maybe was caught whispering to one of his friends.

Abitha straightened up, as did most, none wanting to appear to be unengaged. She tugged her shawl tight around her, trying to keep warm, swearing it was colder inside the meetinghouse than out. There was a large stove, but it was forbidden to light it during service, as someone, somewhere deemed it best to freeze during sermons, that it somehow brought them closer to God. *And who came up with that?* Abitha wondered. *What sadistic fool thought that a good idea?* She pictured a group of bitter old men in really tall hats huddled together in some smelly cellar, each trying to outdo the other in ways to make parishioners suffer.

Reverend Collins took his turn at the pulpit, then finally Reverend Smith. It was halfway through Reverend Smith's sermon that Ansel began to groan. Abitha could see him trying to relieve his agony by shifting from knee to knee. Most already thought him a loon, the way he crept about, spying on folks, always on the lookout for deviltry and witchcraft, but there on his knees, his shoulders sagging, he looked like nothing more than a broken old man to Abitha, and she couldn't help feel bad for him. But she found no sympathy in the eyes of the parishioners, only condemnation. It seemed at times as though they took great joy in others' failings, as it made them appear the better, the more pious, more likely to be included when the great rapture finally came and God gathered his flock to him.

The sun broke free of the heavy morning clouds. There were glass panes in the meetinghouse windows, a rarity in Sutton, most homes still having wax paper. The sun's rays fell on Abitha's face, warm and soothing, and as the minister's words began to fade into a distant hum, her eyes drifting over the congregation, coming to rest on Sheriff Noah Pitkin's graceful neck and strong jaw, his full mouth and easy smile. She thought, and not for the first time, how nice it would be to feel the press of his mouth on her lips, his strong hands on her breasts. She felt a mild stirring in her loins, blinked, thought, *Oh no, Abi. Do not do that to yourself. Not here.*

Her eyes cut to Edward and she felt a dash of guilt. Edward was good to her, and she wanted to do right by him. But it wasn't always easy as he tended to be more the kindly uncle than a husband to her. She knew part of it was his piety, but thought it was also his condition, the odd way his mind worked. She often had to remind herself that he was awkward with everyone, not just her. She glanced at the sheriff again and sighed. *I just need to feel desired, Edward. That is all.*

"Rise," Reverend Carter said, pulling Abitha from her thoughts. She stood and waited, as did all the women, as the rows of men silently exited from front to back. Edward glanced at her as he passed, and Abi tried to send him as much encouragement as she could. Wallace walked closely behind him, his meaty hand on Edward's shoulder, a broad confident smile on his face.

Oh, to be a man just this one day, Abi thought. *How I'd put that lout in his place.*

After all the men had exited, it was the women's turn; Abi, being on the last bench, felt her turn would never come. *Can you but move any slower,* she thought as old Widow Pratt toddled by. Finally, Abi got her chance, pushing past several of the younger women. She made it outside and spotted Edward, Wallace, and the ministers walking toward the town commons. She started after them when Helen pushed in front of her.

"Do you have it?" Helen asked, glancing furtively about.

"Huh?"

"The charm," Helen said in a hushed voice.

Lord, of course, Abitha thought. She patted her apron pocket, certain she'd forgotten in all the turmoil, but no, it was there. She'd put it there the previous day. She pulled out an item hidden in a small fold of sackcloth.

Helen's eyes grew wide. "That's it?"

Abitha nodded, pressing the item into Helen's hand.

The girl clutched it to her breast. "And it will work?" she asked in a whisper. "For Isaac. Like you said?"

"Indeed," Abitha replied, glancing past Helen. She could no longer see Edward. She needed to go.

"And I just put it under my pillow with a—"

"Yes, yes." Abitha spoke quickly. "Just do everything as I told you. But I make no promises. Sometimes the muses grace you with their gifts, sometimes they do not." But Abitha was pretty sure this charm would work, as it was plain to anyone with eyes that Isaac felt as strong for Helen as she for him.

"And what about—" Helen's eyes shifted to something behind Abitha and she darted away. Before Abitha could turn, she felt a hand on her shoulder.

It was Sarah Carter, the minister's wife. Abitha felt the couple had been spun off the same loom, as the woman shared her husband's preference for only the most austere of dress. Where most women preferred to dye their skirts and coats brown or indigo, Goodwife Carter covered her lean, spindly frame in only the simplest of black dress and plain white cap.

"Abitha," she said. "Your hair." Nodding toward Abitha's bonnet with a disapproving look.

"My hair?" Abitha asked, then understood: the long lock had fallen loose again. She quickly tucked it back beneath her cap.

"You need watch yourself better. It does not take much to lead these young men's thoughts astray."

"Yes, beg pardon, Goodwife Carter."

"It is not my pardon you need beg, it is God's."

Abitha bowed. "Of course, ma'am."

Goodwife Carter looked her up and down with her intense blue eyes. Abitha knew she was inspecting the length of her sleeves for too much wrist, the hem of her skirt lest an ankle might be showing, checking for any sign of adornment such as a bit of lace or colored ribbon or any other item that might go against the many sumptuary laws.

Do we not have enough to worry about? Abitha thought as she struggled to hide her annoyance.

"Long hair is a tool of the Devil," Goodwife Carter said. "Why have you not considered cutting it short, like the other women?"

"I have thought on it," Abitha lied. "But Edward . . . he likes my hair so." That not being a lie. Indeed, Edward often encouraged her to remove her cap in their cabin, and she would catch him admiring her curls. And she liked that—feeling attractive. There was much about her own appearance she would've loved to change, but not her hair; it was long, lush, and when washed, rolled into natural curls. Reverend Carter would've called that pride, and perhaps it was, but Abitha didn't see the harm in having pride in oneself.

"And, girl," Goodwife Carter added. "You are not as sly as you may think. Do not let me catch you plying your charms and potions. Not here . . . not anywhere in the village. I will turn my eye this once, but next time it will be in the reverend's hands."

Abitha flinched. She knew better, knew the risks, but she rarely came to town except for church, and word had gotten around that she was a cunning woman, a fact that was only partially true. She did indeed dabble—bartering minor potions and charms for small items when the opportunity arose—but she considered herself only a novice. Her mother though, she'd been a true cunning woman, and it was through her teachings—teachings cut short upon her untimely death when Abitha was just twelve years old—that Abitha had gained the handful of remedies, charms, and divinations she now possessed.

"You do me a kindness, ma'am. Thank you." Abitha made another quick bow, darting away before the woman could say more.

She found Edward engaged with Wallace, Reverend Carter, and the two adjunct ministers, Reverend Collins and Wallace's neighbor and good friend, Reverend Smith. Wallace appeared calm and well composed, and Abitha took that as a bad sign.

She drifted over, sidling up next to a large maple, getting as close as she dared, knowing if they caught her eavesdropping on business affairs, she'd receive a severe tongue lashing, or perhaps even the stocks.

"This is a simple matter," Wallace stated loudly and with ardor, as though his mere volume made it so. "The land is mine. There is naught else to be said."

Edward held his hat, wringing the brim. "But . . . I feel . . . well, you see . . ."

Oh no, Abitha thought. *He's floundering.* She caught Edward's eye, clutched her hands together in front of her chest, and gave him a tight smile, willing him to be strong. He straightened, closed his eyes, nodded, then opened them, setting them directly on Reverend Carter. Edward began talking clearly and directly, just as she'd coached him. They'd both agreed that Reverend Carter was their best chance. That if he could convince him, there was a strong likelihood that at least Reverend Collins would follow. "The land was promised to me first. That is the heart of the matter. To take it from me and give it to another amounts to going back on one's word."

Abi held her breath, trying to read the ministers' faces.

"Little brother," Wallace said, shaking his head as though in pity. "It is my land. We did establish this last night. You have no say on the land until you have paid it off, which has yet to occur. Until then, you are little more than a tenant."

Reverend Smith nodded. "I do see Wallace's point. Until the land is paid off it is legally his and he should be able to do with it as he wants, including using it to pay off his debts."

Oh, Abitha thought, *you are as stupid as a piece of wood.* She fought not to walk right over and set the man straight. And she felt it would almost be worth the lashing, if they would only listen. *Edward, you can do this. Remember what we discussed. Now, Edward, tell them or we lose everything we have worked so hard for.*

Edward cleared his throat. "As I have pointed out, I have cleared the fields of rock and tree, brought in soil. Have improved the land such that most of the value is from my labors. I have paid all but the last payment due. This alone should entitle me control of the land. But the real issue is more fundamental than that. This is about keeping one's word before the church and before God. I have kept my promises. All I am asking is that Wallace keeps his."

Abitha blinked. *Well said, Edward.*

Reverend Carter studied Edward for a moment, seemed to be appraising him afresh. He nodded. "Yes, Edward. What you say bears weight. If we do not stay true to our word, then who are we? That does makes sense to me."

"What does?" Wallace demanded.

"Wallace," Reverend Carter said. "Your agreement with Edward predates that with Lord Mansfield, does it not?"

"Yes, but—"

"Thus, I feel if you do not honor it, it amounts to taking back that which you have already granted and promised to another. Do you not see that?"

Wallace shook his head. "No, I do not. You are making no sense."

Reverend Collins nodded. "Yes, I see what you are saying. Wallace was not within his rights to promise away the land to Lord Mansfield, since he had already done so to Edward."

"Exactly," Reverend Carter said. "So it is my judgment . . . that so long as Edward makes his payments in a timely fashion, that the land, being thus developed by Edward's labors, shall be, for all but in deed, his to master. What say the two of you?"

Abitha let out a squeak, quickly covering her mouth.

Wallace's face clouded. "What? No! Absolutely not. I will—"

Reverend Carter raised his hand. "Enough, Wallace. You have had your say. Ministers . . . what say you?"

"Yes," Reverend Collins said. "I am in agreement."

Reverend Smith seemed on the fence, but reluctantly nodded. "I am sorry, Wallace. But I am inclined to agree."

"Then this matter is so settled," Reverend Carter said.

Abitha wanted to shout, wanted to run down and hug Edward. She'd not ever seen him so bold, so sure of himself. She felt ready to weep with joy.

Wallace appeared dumbfounded, as though not comprehending. "No, but what about Lord Mansfield? How will he be paid?"

"Your debt is a matter between you and him," Reverend Carter said. "You will have to find some other means."

"No!" Wallace growled, his face growing red. "That is not acceptable. I demand—"

"Wallace!" Reverend Carter snapped. "You will heel yourself now, or be put up on charges."

Wallace glowered at them, looked ready to punch the minister. "We will see what Lord Mansfield has to say on this."

Reverend Carter blinked, seemed taken aback. "This is Sutton, not Hartford," he said, sounding somewhat rattled. "We do not take orders from Lord Mansfield here."

Wallace glared at Edward. "What has become of you?" he spat. "You have allowed that woman to turn you against your very family. To betray your own father and his legacy. You should be grateful Papa is not here to witness such abhorrent behavior. The disappointment and shame of it would break his heart." Wallace gave Edward a final scornful sneer and stormed away.

CHAPTER 2

Edward brought in an armload of chopped wood, kicking the door shut behind him. He placed the logs and stoked the fire as Abitha finished preparing dinner—an egg scramble and yesterday's cornbread.

Abitha took a moment to unlace her fitted waistcoat, letting out a gasp of relief as she removed it, tossing it over onto the bed. She then undid her cap, tugging it from her head. *Could never do such a thing in Sutton,* she thought, knowing women were required to keep their caps on even while sleeping. *But I am not in Sutton, am I?* She shook loose her hair and ran her fingers through her long locks, taking a moment to enjoy how freeing that felt and giving thanks for the thousandth time that they lived out here in the wilds, away from all those prying eyes and wagging tongues.

She brought the pan over to the table and they both took their seats.

Edward clasped his hands together and Abitha followed suit as he gave thanks. "Amen," he said.

"Amen," Abitha said, and they began to eat.

"Why the long face, Edward? You should be smiling."

He looked up from his plate. "Huh . . . oh, yes. I know."

"Is it dinner? The cornbread is tough, I know. We've no more lard, but—"

"Oh no, Abitha. Not the food. You could make a pot of bark delectable. It is not that at all."

She waited; she'd learned to give him time.

He sighed. "Just Wallace. What he said about Papa . . ." He trailed off.

"You mean about being ashamed? That is nonsense and you know it well, Edward Williams. It is your brother who should be ashamed."

He nodded. "I agree. I know I do not always see such things clearly, but I do at least see that. It is more just that we are feuding. He is my brother. My family. The rift is so hard to bear."

"And Wallace knows that well, Edward. Wields it like a weapon, twisting your love to make you do as he wants."

Edward watched the fire for a minute. "You know well of my difficulties. How people are such a mystery to me. It is so hard to know what is expected . . . what to do, what to say. Growing up, other children picked up on that . . . and children can be cruel to those who do not fit in. Well, it was always Wallace who took up for me. He would not let anyone bully me . . . ever." Again, Edward drifted off.

Abitha wanted to point out that it was Wallace doing the bullying now. Instead she sighed. "Perhaps with time these wounds will heal."

Edward didn't respond, just continued watching the fire.

Abitha got up, walked over to the cupboard, slid out a tin, and brought it back to the table. She nudged it over to Edward.

He blinked. "What's this?"

"A little something I stirred up for you."

His brows furrowed.

"Well, open it, silly."

He tugged off the lid, revealing a handful of honey brittle wafers, and a small smile snuck across his face.

"We may be running low on all else," she said. "But thanks to your masterful beekeeping, we have honey aplenty."

He took one, bit into it, began to chew. "Thank you, Abi."

"You did well today, Edward," she said. "With Wallace. I felt so proud. I know how hard such things can be for you. But you handled yourself admirably."

"Why, yes, I did." He beamed and managed a chuckle. "And you over by that tree making faces. It did me such good. How can such a wee thing like you have such mettle?"

He started to put the lid back on.

"Nay, take another. You have earned it."

He did take another.

"One last payment to go, Edward, and we are free. Think about that. And once we are out from beneath this burden, we will have plenty. I will be able to buy sugar and lard and salt, enough to make you all the gingerbread you might want. Mayhap even some cloth to sew some new clothes. Would that not be nice? To not have to look like beggars for a change."

"God willing," he said, and then set his hand atop hers. "You are a blessing, Abitha Williams. I would truly be lost without you."

She laughed. "What a couple of odd ducks we are. Well, mayhap together we will find our place."

Abitha put the plates and utensils in a large pail to be washed come morning. When she was done, she found Edward tugging out the black leather satchel he kept hidden behind the cupboard.

He met her eye. "Would you read to me tonight, Abitha?"

She smiled. "I would. You know I would."

He brought the satchel over to the bed, removed his boots, and took a seat. He turned up the oil lantern, slid out a couple of books, and picked one. Edward could read, but it tended to be a slow process of sounding out each word.

"What will it be tonight, Edward?"

He handed her *The Faerie Queene,* by Edmund Spenser.

"Ah, I love that one."

"I know you do."

It was the one she'd brought from England. She recalled how nervous Edward had been the first time she'd showed it to him, insisting she burn it right away, as it was considered a sin to read any book other than the bible. She'd insisted he let her read him a few chapters, after which he agreed to keep it until they were finished. They were currently on the third read-through. She glanced at the six books he now possessed. It seemed every time he went to Hartford another novel appeared. She smiled. *Edward, there may be hope for you yet.*

Abitha undressed down to her shift and sat cross-legged on the bed next to him, opening the book to where they'd left off, and began to read.

Edward tugged over the satchel. He'd inherited it from his father. It contained a few charcoal pencils and several dozen sheets of old parchment. The parchment was filled with his father's long-winded interpretations of bible passages. Edward didn't keep them because of this, he kept them because he loved to draw on them—the fronts, the backs, blank or not, scribbling right across the words and letters, covering the pages with his bold, loose drawings. He pulled these out now, propping the satchel on his knee, using it as a backing board so that he could sketch while she read to him.

"It brings me such joy when you allow yourself time to draw," she said, plucking up one of the sketches. It was of her; most of them were. It was one of the first he'd drawn, and the face was crooked, the eyes lopsided, the lips little more than thick lines. She stifled a giggle—she looked like some sad scarecrow. Yet, despite the crudeness, she found she still recognized herself. She picked up another, a recent one, and was amazed by the contrast. Here her face and hair were etched out of soft flowing marks, the features brought to life with subtle shading. But what she liked best was that he'd made her look so lovely, and she hoped that this was how he really saw her.

"Edward, tell me, how is it each drawing gets better than the one before? Did you have lessons when you were a child?"

"Oh no, the only art lesson I ever had was the beating I received when my father caught me drawing. I believe I was around eight. I did not draw again until sometime after he died."

"How then do you do it? How does one teach themselves such a skill?"

He shrugged. "It is just a thing that is in me. I know not another way to put it."

"These new ones, they are wonderful. It is a crime that we cannot frame and hang them on the wall." She imagined the look of horror on Sarah Carter's face if she were to see one of these, and grinned. Abitha picked up another. She'd not seen this one before; it was of her sleeping, her hair swirling dreamlike around her moonlit flesh, the emphasis on her full lips and the swell of her half-exposed breast.

It's beautiful, she thought, *so beautiful.* She looked at Edward then, almost as though seeing him for the first time. She thought how handsome he appeared, sketching away with such passion, his full lips slightly parted, his eyes aglow with intensity. *Edward, I believe there is a romantic hidden somewhere beneath all your awkwardness.*

She held the sketch up. "Is this how you see me?"

He blushed, nodded.

Abitha smiled coyly at him and began tugging her shift slowly down, revealing first her shoulders, then her breasts.

Edward averted his eyes, keeping them glued to the parchment.

"I like the way you see me, Edward. Would you draw me . . . like this? Please."

He didn't say a word, just peeked up, all but hiding behind the parchment, and began to lightly sketch. His pencil gradually picked up speed until he was scribbling at an almost frantic pace. His eyes were alive, crawling all over her. His breathing grew heavy, and so did Abitha's as her pulse began to race.

"Edward, I seem to no longer be in the mood to read." She set down the book, reached over, and took the parchment and pencil from his hand, setting them aside.

She kissed him on the lips.

There was a moment when he seemed not to know what to do, then he kissed her back, pressing his lips passionately against hers, then their tongues met, and his hands were all over her.

They made love there in the dark to the sound of the crackling fire, neither one aware of the spiders, dozens and dozens of them, big and small, suddenly spooked from their hiding places and scurrying across the ceiling and floor. Neither one of them aware of the three small shadows hovering in the far corner of the room, watching them, waiting.

37

"I'll not lose your farm, Papa," Wallace whispered as he climbed the steps onto Lord Mansfield's stately porch. "That I swear to you." He clanged the large brass knocker three times and waited.

The butler opened the door, appeared confused. "Mr. Williams, sir. Ah, I was not expecting you today."

"Yes, well, I need to see Lord Mansfield. It is urgent."

"Hmm . . . let me check if he is available. Please come in. You may take a seat here in the foyer."

Wallace stepped in but didn't take a seat, pacing back and forth instead. He stole a peek into the adjoining parlor. It was the first time he'd been inside Lord Mansfield's home, and he was amazed by the brass fittings, beautiful oil paintings, and ornate rugs and furniture. Lord Mansfield was a Puritan, but even amongst the Puritans, wealth and class afforded many privileges. There were those who felt that wealth showed them to be in good standing with God and therefore should be flaunted. Wallace knew the man's ostentatiousness didn't fit well with Reverend Carter's teachings and was one of the reasons the minister held the man in such disdain.

"Wallace, sir," the butler called. "Lord Mansfield will see you in his study. Please follow me." The butler led him to the end of the hall and opened a door for him. "You may go in."

Wallace entered to find three men sitting upon elegant upholstered chairs. They were all smoking pipes and the room was thick with smoke, the smell of tobacco stinging Wallace's nose. The men were deep in conversation, so Wallace just stood waiting. Finally, Lord Mansfield looked up. "Ah, Wallace, do come over. Here, you know Magistrate Watson, do you not?"

A somewhat pudgy middle-aged man wearing a powdered wig and dressed in immaculately tailored clothing glanced over his shoulder and gave Wallace a nod.

Wallace nodded back. "Indeed, we've met."

"And his aid, Captain John Moore." The captain was a hard-looking man with dark, piercing eyes, dressed all in black. The butt of a flintlock pistol jutted out from his wide leather belt and his sword rested against the chair in which he was seated.

"I have not had the pleasure."

"Captain, this is Wallace Williams. We've been engaged in a spot of business together. He is Nathaniel Williams's son. The Nathaniel that helped settle Sutton."

"Why, I know well who Nathaniel Williams is." He stepped forward, extending his hand to Wallace. "It is an honor. I fought alongside your father when I was but just a lad." The two men shook.

"Yes," Lord Mansfield said. "Why, if it were not for Wallace's father, I am not sure I'd still have this lovely scalp of mine. When I took that arrow at Ferry Point, the one in my thigh here, it was Nathaniel who lent me his shoulder. Together we hobbled our way back to Fort Saybrook, and with those bloody savages harrying us the whole of it. Your father was a damn fine man, Wallace."

"Thank you, sir. Means a lot to me to hear you say that. You know how much he meant to me."

"He is sorely missed. Now, what is it? Bad news, I fear, by the look on your face."

Wallace sighed.

"I see," Lord Mansfield said. "Well, here, have a seat. Tell me where things stand."

"I am sad to report the problem lies with my brother's wife, Abitha. I conveyed your offer, your fair and generous offer. And I am sure Edward would've stepped up, would've done his part. As he has always done so before. But his wife continues to stick her nose in our affairs, taking every opportunity to place a wedge between my brother and me. It was she that pushed him to reject the terms."

"What, a woman?" Magistrate Watson asked, speaking up for the first time. "Why, man, did you not report her right away?"

"I should have. But my brother pleaded with me not to, and I promised him I would give her another chance." Wallace shook his head. "I regret that now. My brother, his mind is not sound, and she takes advantage of this, turning him against me."

"You are a good soul, Wallace," Lord Mansfield said. "To care for your brother so. I know he is family. But you need consider everyone's stakes in this matter, not just Edward's. You have a family to look after as well. He has forced you into a corner. Like it or not, you will have to go to Reverend Carter. The reverend will not stand for Abitha's behavior. And he will make Edward see reason, I am sure."

Wallace coughed. "I did, and, well . . . well, the harpy has filled Edward's head up with such nonsense that he convinced the ministers otherwise."

"What?" The three men appeared dumbfounded. "On what grounds? How is this?"

Wallace explained in detail, and still the three men appeared stunned.

"Reverend Carter has always been a thorn in my side," Lord Mansfield said. "The man can be so very literal. He does not always perceive the larger context of our tenets."

"Cannot see the forest for the trees," Magistrate Watson put in.

"Yes, precisely. That was the heart of the problem all those years ago. And why he broke away and settled there in Sutton." Lord Mansfield let out a long sigh. "Wallace, I owe it to your father to see to it neither you nor your brother lose your farms. There must be a way to make this work for everyone." He took a long draw from his pipe. "How about this? How about if we all shoulder a bit of the debt? I reduce payment and split the remaining debt between the two of you. Say . . . you both pay me a quarter of your farm's yield for ten years. Then everyone is free and clear. How does that sound?"

"That sounds more than fair," the magistrate stated.

Ten years! Wallace thought, and almost choked, then reminded himself it was better than losing the farm outright, and managed to nod. "I know Edward would do it. Do it for the sake of our father. But again, it is the woman that is the problem. I fear no matter how fair the offer, she will poison him to it."

"Then we need see to her," the magistrate said.

"Yes, we need to see to this Abitha," Lord Mansfield agreed. "Look here, Wallace, I know you wish to protect your brother, but I insist you report his wife's behavior to the reverend immediately. That is one bit of ground that he *will* most certainly side with you on. He does not tolerate disobedience in the home. A severe lashing and a few cold nights in the stocks and she will learn to keep her nose out from where it does not belong."

Wallace smiled thinly.

"Allow me to add something that might help," Magistrate Watson said, and walked over to the desk. He slid over a sheet of parchment, plucked a quill from the inkwell, and scribbled out a note. He folded it and handed it to Wallace. "It is just a nudge to let the reverend know that we hope he resolves things appropriately."

"And if that does not work, Wallace," Lord Mansfield said, "I strongly suggest you come up with a plan that will. What she is doing is an affront to the foundation of our society, an affront to you, to the good folks of Sutton, and to the good Lord himself. I know you are a Godly man, but if the Devil is working havoc through this woman, then sometimes one must step off the orthodox path to set things right. Do you get my meaning?"

"I believe I do, sir."

"Angels must often do dark deeds in the name of the Lord," Magistrate Watson added. "Do they not?"

Wallace considered this a moment, then nodded, more to himself than to the two men. "Why, yes . . . indeed they do."

Wallace shared a firm handshake with both men and headed away. As he rode home, it was the judge's words that he heard over and over again.

"Angels must often do dark deeds in the name of the Lord."

Wake.

"No."

They are here. You must kill them.

"Who?"

The people . . . smell them.

The beast did, smelled the blood beating in their veins. There were two of them. It opened its eyes.

You must kill them, Father.

"Father?"

Do you remember your name?

The beast considered. "I believe I have many names?"

Many indeed.

"Who are you?"

Your children. You must protect us, protect Pawpaw . . . from the people. Do not fail us. Not again.

"I am tired."

You need more blood.

The goat beast heard a thump from far up above, realized he could not only hear the people, but *feel* them, their souls. One was a man, the other a woman. The man was at the opening now.

We will call them, bring them to you. You can do the rest. It is time to feast.

"Yes, time to feast."

41

"That's close enough," Abitha said.

Edward ignored her, walking up to the mouth of the cave, his ax slung over his shoulder.

"Edward, you will fall in."

"Goodness, woman. Stop fretting so. I am not going to fall in."

"Stop!" Her voice suddenly severe. "It . . . *it's* in there, Edward."

He met her eyes.

"I know you will think me silly, but . . . well, I felt something in there. I truly did."

"What do you mean?"

"The Devil!" she blurted out. "I can feel it!"

"The Devil?" He smirked. "The very Devil? Here in our woods. I shall alert Reverend Carter right away."

"It is not a jest!" Her color was up, and it made him grin.

"Abitha, do you think old Slewfoot is going to grab me and carry me down into his pit?" By the look on her face, he could plainly see that she did.

"You think it funny?" She clapped her hands to her hips. "Well, you can just throw yourself in then, save me and Slewfoot the trouble. See how I care."

And he did see how she cared, and he could see she cared a lot. He stifled his grin. "Ah, Abitha, I am sorry. I do not mean to mock you. I will be careful. I promise." This seemed to placate her somewhat. But her eyes kept darting back to the cave, and he wondered just what it was she'd seen or thought she'd seen. Whatever it was, she wanted him to build a gate across the entrance. She'd said it was to keep any more livestock from wandering *in,* but he was now pretty sure it was to keep whatever she thought was in there from getting *out.*

Loud squawks came from overhead. Abitha started. They both looked up.

"Trumpeter swans," he said. "They're coming home."

Abitha pushed back her bonnet to watch the birds and several long locks of her hair fell loose, the rich auburn color lit up by the spots of sunlight dancing through the trees. *What a picture you make,* Edward thought. Wallace had quipped about her looks, about her freckles and scrawny figure. And perhaps she did lack the darling cheeks and dimples of Rebecca Chilton, or the shapeliness of Mary Dibble, yet to Edward, Abitha's striking green eyes seemed to radiate more life and loveliness than both of those young women together.

"Spring is almost upon us," he said. "We can start planting soon."

She flashed him an almost vicious smile, and he understood everything about that smile. "And, God willing, we will be done with *him* soon," she spat. "Wallace will have to find someone else to lord over. Glory, but what a wondrous day that will be. Will it not?"

"It will."

She stepped closer, reaching for his hand. He took hers, gave it a squeeze, but when he went to let go, she held on, pulling him close and slipping an arm around his waist, pressing her stomach against him. Edward tensed as thoughts of their lustful night returned. He blushed and drew back, suddenly unable to meet her eyes.

"What is it, Edward?"

"You know we should not act in such a way. The flesh makes us weak. About last night, I overstepped. I am ashamed."

She twisted loose from his hand, and the look on her face, it was as though he'd slapped her.

See, he thought, *such shameful lust only leads to pain. I will destroy that drawing, all the drawings. Lord, forgive me, I was so weak.*

She walked away from him, over to the cave. He could see by the set of her shoulders that she was upset. She pulled something from her apron, hung it in front of the cave. Edward stepped up for a closer look, saw that it was a cross made from twigs and feathers, bound in red yarn.

"What is that?"

"But a warding charm. Something my mother used to keep wicked spirits at bay."

He looked quickly around. "Abitha, you must not. What if someone sees?"

"None are out here but us."

"No more of these spells of yours. Do you hear me? It *must* stop." He realized the words had come out harsher than he meant.

"It is but rowan twigs and twine, Edward. How—"

"Twigs and twine that will see you tied to the whipping post!"

"Edward, you well know that several of the women make charms; they are considered nothing more than blessings." And this was indeed true, also true that home remedies, potions, and cunning crafts were used when folks could get their hands on them, surreptitiously of course, but it was common practice to be sure.

"That"—he pointed at the twigs—"is no simple blessing. Now you must promise to stop with your spells and charms."

"How is it that we had biscuits this morning, Edward? Your brother has saddled us with such a burden that it is only through my bartering these very spells and charms that we have flour and salt this day."

"Y-yes," he stammered. "Well, we will have to make do. It must stop as of today. It is just too risky."

"I am cautious."

"There is no hiding what we do from God. He will see us and he will punish us accordingly!"

"Why are you acting so, Edward? Is this about last night? You must quit this belief that God will punish you for seeking a bit of pleasure, for trying to find some joy in this harsh, cold world."

"For once just do as I bid. No more spells, Abitha. Swear to me!"

"You sound like my father. Must I swear off every pleasure in life? I am sick to death of this *want* to suffer needlessly. Suffering does not bring one closer to God." She plucked up the cross. "I was only trying to protect *you* from whatever wickedness lies within that cave. But if you prefer to have it come crawling out after you, then that is just fine with me!" She gave the cave one last fretful look, then stomped off.

Edward watched her march away, disappearing into the trees. *Why must everything I say come out wrong?* he thought. *Abitha, I could not bear it should anything happen to you, that is all I am trying to say. I cannot be alone . . . not again.*

Edward let out a long sigh and began sizing up the nearest trees to build the gate from. He noticed how rich the soil was in this area, thought what good farmland it would make once it was all cleared.

A low moan drifted from the cave.

Edward spun, ax raised. He waited—nothing, no bear, no devil. He lowered the ax. *You're hearing things.* But he'd more than heard that peculiar sound, he'd felt it, he was sure, like something had touched him. *She's done spooked you, that's all. All Abi's talk of devils has put devils in your head.*

He glanced back toward the cabin, hoping to see Abitha, but he was alone. He realized that the sun was gone, hidden behind thick clouds, and suddenly the forest seemed to be closing in, as though the very trees were edging toward him.

Another sound, this time more of a cry, a bleat maybe.

Samson? Of course. He almost laughed. *The goat. What else could it be?*

He stepped up to the cave, trying to see inside. The sound came again, faint, from somewhere deep within. He removed his hat and slid into the cavern, carefully prodding the floor with the ax, testing for drops. As his eyes slowly adjusted, he scanned the gloom, found only scattered leaves and a few sticks. There was a smell in the air, more than the damp leaves. He knew that smell—he'd slaughtered enough farm animals in his time—it was blood.

Another bleat; it seemed to come from the far shadows.

"Samson," he called, and slid deeper into the gloom, crouching as not to hit his head on the low ceiling, squinting into the darkness. *It's no good*, he thought. *I need a lantern.* He started back, then heard another sound, a whimper. *A child?* He shook his head. *Nay, just echoes playing tricks.* He continued out toward the entrance.

It came again, a sort of eerie sobbing. The hair on his arms prickled as the unnatural sound crawled into his head. *I should leave*, he thought. The sobbing turned into mumbling; someone was speaking to him. He didn't understand the words, then he did.

"Help me . . . please."

Edward froze. The words were those of a child, but they sounded hollow and he wasn't sure if he was actually hearing them or if they were in his mind. "Hello," Edward called. "Who's there?"

"Help me."

"Hold on, I will get rope and a lantern. Just wait."

"I'm scared."

"Just hold on, I shall be right back."

"I cannot, cannot hold on. I'm slipping!"

Edward hesitated—the voice, so strange, almost not human. But what else could it be?

"Help me!"

That had not been in his mind. He was certain.

"Help me!"

He saw a small face appear far back in the shadows, that of a child, a boy perhaps, almost glowing, some illusion of the light making him appear to float in the darkness like a disembodied head.

"Help me! Please!"

Edward swallowed loudly and began crawling toward the child as quickly as he dared, sliding on his knees, prodding the cave floor with the ax. He entered a smaller chamber, this one pitch. He grasped for the child, but the child flittered just out of reach. And it was then that Edward saw that the thing before him wasn't a child at all, but . . . *But what—a fish? A fish with the face of a child?*

Edward let out a cry, yanking his hand back.

The child giggled, smiled, exposing rows of tiny sharp teeth. Edward saw that the thing's flesh was smoky and all but translucent. He could see its bones!

"Oh, God! Oh, Jesus!"

Something touched the nape of Edward's neck. He jumped and spun around. Another face, there, right before his own. Another child, but not, its eyes but two sunken orbs of blackness. It opened its mouth and screamed. Edward screamed; they were all screaming.

Edward leapt up, ramming his head into the low ceiling with a blinding thud. And then he was falling—sliding and falling, clawing at the darkness. He slammed into rocks, then searing pain, again and again as he crashed off the walls of a shaft, and then finally, after forever, the falling stopped.

Edward opened his eyes. His face hurt, his head thundered, but he could feel nothing below his neck, knew this to be a blessing, knew his body must be a twisted and mangled mess. He let out a groan.

All should've been pitch, but the thick air held a slight luminescence and he made out rocks and boulders and *bones*. The ground was nothing but bones.

Where am I? But he knew. *I am in Hell.*

Then he saw it—the Devil, Lucifer himself. The beast sat upon its haunches, staring at him, its eyes two smoldering slits of silver light. Those simmering eyes pierced his soul, seeing all his shame, all the times he'd sinned, all the times he'd lied to his father, the times he'd profaned God's name, the books, those evil books he'd bought in Hartford, and most of all his lustful drawings, the ones he'd done of Abitha. "God, please forgive me," he whispered, but he knew God wouldn't, that God had forsaken him.

The ghostly beasts with the faces of children fluttered down, giggling as they circled him, but Edward barely noticed, his terrified, bulging eyes locked on the Devil.

The Devil clumped over to Edward.

Edward tried to rise, tried to crawl away, but couldn't do anything more than quiver and blink away the tears.

The beast shoved its muzzle against Edward's face. Edward could feel the heat of its breath as it sniffed his flesh, the wetness as it licked his cheek, his throat. Then a sharp jab of pain as the beast bit into his neck.

Edward stared upward, at the sliver of light far, far above, listening as the Devil lapped up his blood. The world began to dim. *I am damned*, he thought, and slowly, so slowly, faded away.

"Edward!" a woman called from above. *"Edward!"* she cried.

Edward didn't hear it. Edward was beyond such things. But the beast heard.

The other one, Father. Quick, now is our chance.

The beast shook his shaggy head. His belly full, he wanted only to close his eyes and enjoy the warmth spreading through his veins. "Tonight," he mumbled, barely able to form the words. The beast raised its front hoof and watched as the hoof sprouted a hand, one that sprouted long spindly fingers, which in turn sprouted long sharp claws. "I will kill her tonight." The blood took him and it was as though he were floating as he drifted slowly off into a deep slumber.

Tonight then, the children said.

Wallace trotted slowly along on his stallion toward Edward's farm. Going over and over what he must say, wondering how he'd been reduced to this, to pleading with Edward to accept Lord Mansfield's offer.

I did everything right, Papa. You know it true. Edward and I should be working to-gether, as you always wanted. Building our own tobacco empire . . . just like the plantations down in Virginia. Instead I am the fool of Sutton who knew naught about tobacco. Cannot go anywhere without seeing it on their faces. He spat. *No one but you, Papa, saw me working my hands to the very bone trying to save that crop, picking off worms day after day, even by torchlight. Is it right, I ask you, that I should now have to grovel before Edward and his harpy of a wife? Is it?*

Wallace reined up his horse at the top of the hill above Edward's farm, his stomach in a knot. *And you know the worst part of it, Papa? It will be seeing her gloat as I beg. I know not if I can bear it. Why does that woman despise me so? Why must she vex me at every turn? I have been generous, have done my best to welcome her into the fold.*

Wallace heard a shout. Turned to see Abitha, Charles Parker, his brother John and two of their boys, all heading toward him at a rapid clip. John was carrying a long loop of rope and a couple of lanterns.

"Wallace," John cried. "Come, quick. It is Edward. He has fallen into a pit!"

"A pit?" Wallace asked. "What do you mean?"

"Just come," John called as they raced by.

Wallace followed them down into the woods below the field.

"There," Abitha said, pointing to a cave opening tucked between some boulders.

Wallace took a lantern and peered into the cave. "Edward," he called. "Edward, are you there?"

"Anything?" Charles asked.

Wallace shook his head. "Naught but sticks and leaves."

"In the back," Abitha said, her voice rising. "The pit is in the back. I tell you he's fallen in. I know it. Please, you must hurry!"

Wallace glanced at the brothers, Charles and John. When Abitha couldn't find Edward, she'd gone over to the Parker farm seeking help, but neither of these men appeared in any hurry to enter the cave.

Abitha snatched a lantern from John and headed for the entrance, but John grabbed her, held her. "Hold there, Abitha. If there's one pit, there may be more. We must be cautious."

"We have no time to be cautious."

Wallace spied Edward's hat in the leaves. He picked it up and handed it to Abitha. It took the wind out of her and she stopped struggling.

"Here," Wallace said, passing his lantern to Charles. Charles had brought along their longest rope, and Wallace took it from him. He unfurled the rope, tying one end around a boulder. He tested the rope, nodded to John. "Keep her out here." He then slid into the cave, followed a moment later by Charles and his eldest boy, Luke.

Luke and Charles both held a lantern, allowing Wallace to lead while keeping his hands securely on the rope. He tested the ground with his forward foot as he went, ducking his head to avoid the low ceiling. With the light he could now clearly see that the dirt and leaves had been kicked up. The tracks led them to a smaller chamber at the rear of the cave. Wallace hesitated; he felt a chill, not that of cold, but a wave of foreboding that he couldn't explain.

The men brought the lanterns forward, revealing a pit of about six feet wide. Wallace spotted an ax by the pit. He tested the rope yet again, then moved into the chamber. After a moment, all three of them were peering down into the chasm. And again, that deeply unsettling chill ran through him; it were as though the very darkness was staring up at him.

There came a commotion behind them and Wallace turned to find Abitha looking over Charles's shoulder, her eyes full of dread.

"Do you see him?" Abitha asked in a hushed, desperate tone. "Anything?"

"You are to leave at once," Wallace said, but knew he was wasting his breath.

"There," Charles said, pointing. "Is that Edward's?"

A shoe sat against the wall of the cave. Abitha pushed closer. Charles grabbed her, trying to keep her from getting too close to the pit. *Edward!* she cried, her voice echoing down the dark chasm.

Luke crouched, held the lantern out, and squinted. "And that, there. What is that?"

Something white gleamed back at them from a rock jutting just below the lip of the pit. Wallace knelt for a closer look. *Oh, good Lord,* he thought. *A tooth, a human tooth.*

Abitha let out a groan. "Oh no, Edward. No." She slid to her knees.

They were all looking at the pit now the way one looks at a grave.

"Someone will have to go down," Abitha said.

Wallace tossed a small stone into the pit. They listened to the *ticktack* of the stone bouncing down the shaft. On and on and on it went, never really stopping, just fading away. They looked at one another, all knowing what that meant.

"We cannot leave him down there," she said. "What if he still lives?"

"It is too deep . . . too treacherous," Wallace put in, but what he didn't add was that no force on earth could compel him to go down into that pit. That every bit of him felt sure there was something foul and malevolent waiting below. "We cannot risk more lives."

"Well, if you will not then I will."

"Abitha," Charles said gently. "There will be no going down. No rope is so long."

"Mayhap he is not at the bottom, but upon some ledge."

"Abitha, please," Charles said, holding the lantern out over the pit. "Look down. Truly see." He held her arm tightly so she could peer over the lip, her eyes searching desperately.

"Edward!" she called, and they all stood there as the echo of her husband's name died out, straining their ears for a reply, a groan, a gasp, a cry, anything, but heard only their own breathing.

And Wallace saw it on her face then, as she stared at the tooth, that she knew the truth of it, that there'd be no surviving such a fall.

The villagers made their solemn way along the muddy path to the communal gravesite. The three ministers led the procession, followed by the casket and pallbearers, followed by the men of Sutton, the ministers' wives, the women of high standing, and then, only before the children, came Abitha. Even being the widow afforded her no privilege above her rank.

The site lay just out of town, and as they crested the rise, the north wind picked up, the sky appearing fit to burst. The villagers all clung to their hats and bonnets, picking up the pace, in a hurry to be done before the rain set in.

They came to the marker, a small common stone with no ornamentation other than the name *Edward Williams* chiseled onto its front, as the Puritans considered all equal before God and forbade any special adornment.

Reverend Carter took his place next to the stone, and the congregation circled around the freshly dug grave. The smell of the dank dirt hung in the air.

The pallbearers, Wallace, Charles, John, and Isaac, brought the casket forward, setting the plain pine box down beside the grave. The small casket landed with a hollow thud, as there was only a set of Edward's clothing within, along with his hat and the tooth wrapped in white linen—the tooth being included at Abitha's insistence.

Wordlessly they slid the box into the ground. There followed no eulogy, no songs or hymns, no personal words by family, no sermon, not even a prayer, no ceremony at all, as the Puritans wished to avoid any appearance of papistry. Abitha wondered what offense God could possibly find in a final prayer?

She found her thoughts turning then to her own mother's funeral. How her father had spared no expense, putting money they didn't have toward a grand gravestone. Even paying the choir to sing and the minister to read the eulogy he'd stayed up all night composing. How, when they'd lowered her coffin, her father had broken down, weeping openly. *But none of these things relieved your grief, did they, Father? Nor did drinking yourself out of employment, or dragging us to church three times a week.* Her last memory of the man came to her; it was just after he'd sold her off to the New World, him waving to her as the ship left port. A sad rag of a man with a bottle poking out from his coat pocket. She wondered if by now he too was in some pauper's grave with not even a small stone to mark a life lost.

Abitha searched the faces around her, searching for some sign that Edward's death mattered to them, but they were all like stone, not a tear to be found. Abitha wanted to scream, to cry out Edward's name, to heckle them and their cruel tenets and edicts, to laugh herself to tears, anything to break the oppressive silence.

The wind picked up and a few light drops of rain pecked at the mourners. The pallbearers took up the shovels and began rapidly filling in the shallow grave. The dirt thumped atop the hollow casket, reminding them all that Edward wasn't with them. *Edward, are you even dead?* Abitha wondered, and couldn't help but think of him lying at the bottom of that hellish pit, broken and paralyzed, waiting for thirst and hunger to take him, or worse, for the worms and rats to eat him as he watched.

With the hole filled in, the men began to beat down the dirt with the backs of their shovels. Each blow resounding in the silence. Abitha flinched with every strike, each thud feeling like they were beating Edward into his grave, beating away his very existence. They stopped and Reverend Carter stepped forward, his hat pressed to his chest. "It is done."

People immediately began to break off, to head away, back to their farms, their lives.

That's it? Abitha thought. *It's done? A man's whole life not worth so much as a word?* And again, the need to cry out Edward's name, to shout his praises, overwhelmed her. She heard Edward then: *No, Abi, keep your words to yourself. You are on your own now, you must learn to fit in.* She shook her head. "Wait," she said. No one heard her, and she said it again, louder. No one stopped. "Wait," she called. "Can you all please but wait a moment!"

They stopped as one, all of them setting their eyes on her.

"Can I say a few words? Is that asking too much? Just a few words?"

There came many pitying looks—it was plain she wasn't the only one who felt the funeral too austere—but others didn't hide their ire.

Reverend Carter stared at her as one would a disobedient child, and for a moment Abitha thought he would reprimand her there in front of everyone, but his eyes fell on Edward's grave and he sighed. "Go on then."

Abitha sucked in a deep breath. "I just want it said, here, before everyone, that Edward were a good man. That is all."

She received many odd looks and knew her words had fallen flat. *So be it,* she thought. *The words are for you, Edward, not them.*

They turned their backs and headed away, leaving Abitha alone with a box of clothes in the ground and a stone with her husband's name on it.

She waited until they were over the rise, then knelt down. She dug into her coat pocket and removed a braid of her hair tied into a small bow. "This is for you, Edward. For being a kind and gentle soul . . . for being my friend." She kissed the bow and placed it upon his marker.

She stood, slapped the dirt from her hands, and headed back. She topped the rise and saw the three ministers waiting for her down by the road. Wallace was with them. "Jesus," she said beneath her breath. "Could that vulture not wait one day?"

"Abitha," Reverend Carter called. "A word, if you would."

Abitha strolled up to them, feeling overshadowed by these men in their tall hats and wide, billowing black cloaks.

"I apologize for what I must say here," the minister continued, "on the very day of Edward's burial, but there are pressing matters." He hesitated, searching for the right words. "We need to see to your well-being."

Abitha tensed, realizing that they were deciding her future—her very future—right here and now.

"Wallace and I have been discussing what would be best for you. Given that you are now on your own."

Abitha's blood went cold. *Pay attention, Abi,* she thought. *Be sharp, this is everything, this is your very life.* "I do not see how my well-being is any of Wallace's concern."

Wallace stiffened.

"Abitha." Reverend Carter cleared his throat, his voice becoming as stern as when he gave his sermons. "Listen to me. Wallace is your brother by law, your closest male relation, and as such your welfare falls upon his shoulders. Surely you understand that? And Wallace has stepped forward and offered to help you. If you but give him a chance, I believe you will find his offer most charitable considering your circumstance."

Circumstance? And what is my circumstance? Abitha felt ambushed. These men weren't here to deliberate with her, to have protracted discussion. She was a woman, and women didn't have say in such affairs. They'd come to inform her of what was to be. "I appreciate what you are trying to do, Reverend. But I need time to consider—"

"Abitha," Wallace interjected. "Here, now, listen to me." He was speaking to her as to one of his children. "Edward's gone. You cannot be on your own. So I am inviting you into my home. You can help Charity and Isaac with the chores and—"

"You wish me to be your servant?"

"He's offering you a roof over your head," Reverend Carter stated. "You are still young; there are many men here in need of wives. You would work for Wallace until such time as a suitable husband is found."

"I have a roof over my head. As well as a farm and a field ready to be planted. Why would I leave it to be *this* man's servant?"

The four men looked to one another as though she'd asked why she needed to breathe.

Wallace threw up his hands. "I told you this is beyond her."

"Abitha," Reverend Carter said. "You are in mourning, confused and over-whelmed. We all understand this. But you need to see that due to his debt, Wallace cannot keep both farms. It is obvious that he should forfeit Edward's homestead. It is best for you and the community as a whole. No one wants you left out in the cold."

How did it become Wallace's land? Abitha wondered. *Can they just take it? Nay, that does not seem right.* Something tickled at the back of her thoughts. She tried to focus, to ignore the minister as he rambled on. *The Widow Pratt! Aye, that's it. Widow Pratt did not have to leave her place when her husband died last spring. Why?* Abi didn't know why, not exactly, but something about representing her husband in his absence.

"Abitha," the reverend asked, "are you hearing me, girl? Those are your only choices: work for Wallace or strike out on your own. It is an unforgiving world out there. I would suggest—"

"There is another choice," she said firmly. "*I* can farm my land."

They all appeared dumbstruck.

"But . . . Abitha," Reverend Carter started, "how—"

"No!" Wallace interrupted. "You cannot. That is not *your* land to farm. That is *my* land. It is only by my charity that I let you stay even another night."

"The farm belongs to me so long as I make timely payment. That is the agreement."

"That agreement were with Edward, not you!"

Abitha set eyes on the ministers. "I am a widow now," she stated calmly and evenly, trying to sound confident. She didn't know her rights with any certainty, but felt if she spoke as though she did, she might stand a chance. "Does that not afford me the right to own land and conduct business in Edward's name?"

The ministers appeared taken back, unsure what to say. But she saw it then, on their faces, that she *was* right.

"Well," Reverend Carter started. "Well . . . yes, I suppose that *can* be the case."

"And is that not my duty before God, to fulfill my husband's wishes? To fulfill all of Edward's debts and obligations to the best of my abilities?"

Reverend Carter raised his eyebrows. "Yes . . . but—"

"Nonsense!" Wallace cried. "I shall not listen to this. We all know she cannot bring in that crop. She will lose the property regardless, so why play this game?"

The ministers appeared at a loss as to how the conversation even got to where it was. "One moment," Reverend Carter said, pulling Reverend Collins and Reverend Smith aside, where they continued the conversation in hushed voices.

Wallace stepped right up to Abitha, glaring down at her, his anger palpable. "You best hear me, you ungrateful girl," he hissed. "Edward is no longer here for you to hide behind. You play this game and you will lose everything. Do you understand me? Everything. I will see you in the ground before I concede that land to you."

Abitha turned her back to him, clutching her hands together, trying to hold steady.

The three ministers returned.

"Abitha," Reverend Carter said. "Again, let me emphasize that we all feel your best course is to accept Wallace's charity and live with him until you find a suitable husband. We feel it would not be proper or prudent for you to try and manage Edward's homestead on your own."

Wallace nodded in agreement, a smug smile on his face.

Reverend Carter then looked apologetically at Wallace. "Wallace, as much as we feel this is not the best course, Abitha's words are true. It is the law that she serve as Edward's stead. She is morally obligated before God to do Edward's will as best she knows it. So it must be left for her to decide."

"What?" Wallace cried. "That is utter madness! Can you not see? I will lose my farm, and then where will we all be?"

"I am not disagreeing with you," Reverend Carter said. "But this is our law. Who are we if we do not uphold our own laws?"

"You would have me lose my farm just to placate this insolent woman . . . this *outsider*?" Wallace growled, his face red, furious. "Why . . . that is utter lunacy!"

"Wallace!" Reverend Carter snapped. "Please, calm yourself. Mayhap there are other ways to—"

"The magistrate was right," Wallace said. "You cannot see the forest for the trees!"

"The magistrate? What magistrate?" Reverend Carter slowly narrowed his eyes. "Do you mean Magistrate Watson? You talked to him on this matter?"

"I did, and . . . and, well, see here." Wallace tugged a folded letter from his jacket. "He told me to give this to you." Wallace jabbed the note at Reverend Carter like a knife.

The reverend took the note, unfolded it, his mouth tightening into a thin line as he read, then suddenly he crumpled the note and threw it to the ground. "That man," Reverend Carter said beneath his breath, a noticeable quiver in his voice, but then his brows knotted together and his face was like that when he spoke of Satan himself. "Magistrate Watson likes to bend the word of God whenever it suits him. His say means naught around here. The ruling stands."

Reverends Collins and Smith both appeared unnerved by this proclamation.

"But, Reverend," Reverend Smith started. "Mayhap we should discuss—"

"I said the ruling stands."

Wallace's mouth fell open. "What . . . you cannot! Who do you think you—"

"It is on the account of men like Magistrate Watson, men with weak morals, that I left Hartford all those years ago. I will *never* allow his ilk to assert their influence here. *Never!* My ruling stands. Do you hear?"

"No, no, I do not! Do you have any idea what it is you do to me? Do you?" Wallace was all but shouting at them. "This is *not* acceptable! The magistrate will be hearing—"

"*Enough!*" Reverend Carter shouted. "Check yourself, Wallace Williams! *Now!*"

Wallace grimaced.

"This is the law according to our charter, before God," Reverend Carter declared. "Do you challenge the council's wisdom on such matters?"

Wallace opened his mouth to speak, could find no words, but his eyes found

Abitha, burned into her. "I will come to the farm tomorrow and we will speak more on this matter."

Abitha held his glare. "I am done talking to you," she said, her voice loud and firm, like a sergeant snapping out commands. "Hear me and hear me well, Wallace Williams. You are to stay *away* from me."

All the men seemed shocked by the brass in Abitha's voice, but none more than Wallace.

Wallace's face cinched into a knot. "No! I have put up with enough! I will not tolerate such insolence, not from a woman!" He snatched hold of her, his big callused hand swallowing her small arm. "You are going before the sheriff. He will see you thrashed and in the stocks."

"You will unhand her!" Reverend Carter cried. "Or it is you that will be thrashed."

"What . . . what do you mean?" Wallace stammered, staring at the man incredulously. "Did you not hear her?" He looked from minister to minister. "Has everyone gone mad? No woman is allowed to speak in such a disrespectful manner."

"It is her place to speak up in all matters to do with Edward's holdings," Reverend Carter said tersely. "And if that means standing toe-to-toe with one such as you, then it is her right. Do you understand me, Wallace?"

Wallace started to speak.

"Do you understand me?" Reverend Carter growled.

Wallace said nothing, but he let go of Abitha.

"This matter is closed," Reverend Carter stated firmly.

Wallace looked from face to face, like some cornered mongrel, his breath hissing through his teeth. He began to nod, the hiss slowly turning into a mean laugh. "She will not last through the season. Of course, by then it will be too late. I will have lost my land." Then directly at Abitha: "And you." He smirked. "When you're hungry . . . when you're cold, do not come begging at my door. That door is closed to you forever."

He spun away and stormed off.

"Sir," Reverend Smith said. "I worry about the magistrate. He is not a man to be trifled with."

Reverend Carter let out a long, troubled breath, shook his head. "Why must you do this, Abitha? Is it spite? Is it your pride? No good can come of this. If I were you, I would go home and reconsider, then go to Wallace and beg his forgiveness."

The rain picked up, and the ministers buttoned up their cloaks and left.

Abitha stood there on the roadside watching the dirt turn to mud, shaking her head as the weight of what she'd just done settled on her shoulders, as the dread clutched at her heart. *What are you doing, Abi? Why must you always let your stubbornness get the better of you?*

She looked up toward the gravesite, thought of the plain casket with Edward's clothes in it, and felt more alone than ever in her life.

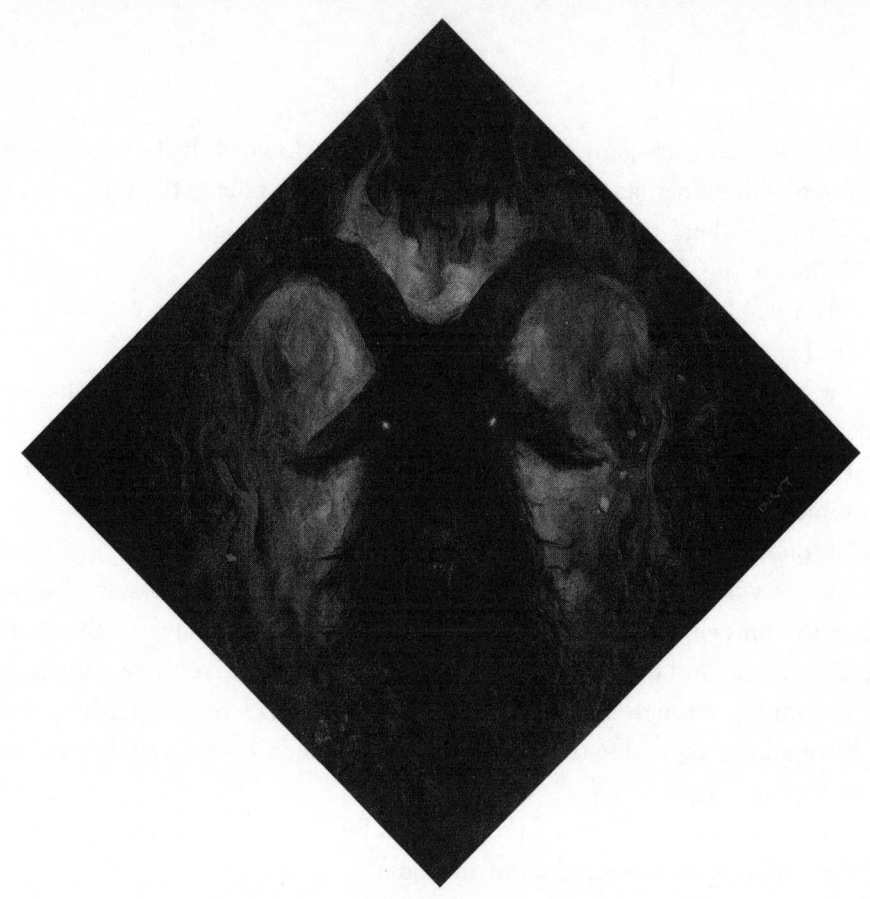

CHAPTER 3

S*creaming.*

Flames licking a night sky. Huts on fire. People running in all directions, their faces fraught with terror. Bodies, so many bodies, limbs torn away, guts ripped open, brains splattered. The air smelling of blood and burning flesh. And the screams, going on and on as though never to stop.

The beast opened his eyes.

"At last, Father. You're awake."

The beast groaned. An opossum stood before him on its hind legs, thin to the point of emaciation, its face that of a human child, a boy perhaps. Its two eyes, small and black, with tiny pinpricks of light at their centers, sputtered like fireflies.

"Who are you?" the beast asked.

"He is awake," the opossum called, his voice echoing up the shaft.

A large raven flew silently into the room, alighting on a rock, followed by a fish. The fish floated in the air, swishing its tail softly back and forth as though holding itself in place against a gentle current. They too had the faces of children, the raven with human hands instead of claws, the flesh blue as the sky.

"Get up, Father," the opossum said. "There is blood to spill."

"Who are you?"

"Have you forgotten us?"

The beast shrugged.

The opossum appeared deeply disturbed by this. "You have known us for a long time. Try now to remember. It is important."

The beast tried to remember, to recall anything, but his mind seemed nothing but tumbling shadows and hollow echoes.

The opossum clutched the beast's hand. "Close your eyes. See us!"

The beast closed his eyes, felt a soft pulse coming from the opossum. The pulse fell in rhythm with his heartbeat and hazy shapes began to appear. Slowly they came into focus and he saw them, little impish beasts just like these, hundreds of them, running through a forest, chanting and howling, their childish faces full of fervor and savagery. He tried to see more, but the vision blurred, began to slip away, then nothing.

The beast let out a frustrated groan, shook his head, and opened his eyes.

The small creatures shared a worried look.

"Do not fret," the opossum said. "It will all come to you soon. You just need more blood. We are the wildfolk . . . your children." The opossum thumped his own chest. "I am Forest." He pointed to the raven—"Sky"—then the fish—"Creek."

"And I am *Father*?"

"Yes," Forest said. "You are the slayer . . . our guardian. It is time to leave this pit. Time to drive the people away before they kill Pawpaw."

"Pawpaw?" The name brought forth an image, a shimmering mirage, that of a giant tree with crimson leaves. "Yes, I know this."

The children grinned, revealing tiny needlelike teeth.

"Hurry," Forest called. "Follow us!"

Sky, the raven, took off, flapping soundlessly up the shaft. Forest and Creek followed, the opossum scampering up the rocks as though weightless, while the fish swam as through some invisible stream, all three disappearing into pale light at the top of the shaft.

Father climbed to his cloven feet and noticed the ground was covered in bones, some fresh but most ancient, all shapes and sizes, tiny skulls mixed with larger ones, even a few crumbling tusks. He took a step and realized that the bones were layers thick, wondered just how deep down into the earth they went.

His eyes shifted to the bodies, the man and the goat, understood that he was now a bit of both. He noticed something sitting upon a stone above the dead man—some kind of egg-shaped fruit, split in half, its meat crimson, the color of blood. Above the fruit, painted in that same blood, an eye. *I know this too,* he thought as he stared into it.

The eye blinked, split into two, four, six—six black eyes like those of a spider, flickering this way and that, searching for something.

Father's skin prickled. He raked his claws across the symbol and the eyes disappeared. He shuddered, suddenly wanting out of this pit, this tomb. He looked up at the slice of pale light far above. *The sun, yes. The sun will help clear my mind.*

He began to climb the clammy stones and a short time later found himself in a cave, peering out into the forest. It appeared to be early, fog lingering amongst the trees, a few birds singing their morning song. He crawled out and stood, sucking in the cool air. It was sweet with woodland spice. Then he smelled something else.

"They stink, do they not?" It was Forest. "The people."

Father nodded. "Did I not drive them from this land once before?"

"Ah, you are beginning to remember, Father. You did indeed."

"And they have returned?"

"These are new people. A different kind of people. They come from far away and know not to be afraid yet. But that is all about to change. Now, do you remember why you drove them away?"

Again, Father saw the tree like a dream in his mind. This time noting the egg-shaped fruit dangling from its limbs, the same fruit as in the pit. "The tree."

All three of their faces lit up.

"Yes!" Forest cheered and pointed at the rocks and boulders above the cave. "See the bones of the grand pawpaw tree."

Father saw only a tower of dark jagged stones.

"Do you not see?"

He stepped back and realized that it was the remnants of a vast tree trunk.

"What is this place?"

"This is our heart and soul, our place of birth and our place of death. This is the house of Pawpaw. Look there." Forest pointed to the top of the stones. "Mother Earth has given us back our Pawpaw." His voice sounded on the verge of tears. "After all these years she has given us another chance!"

Father saw only a struggling sapling, no taller than himself, sprouting out from the top of the massive stone trunk.

"We have our Pawpaw and now we have *you,* our guardian. A clear sign that the time of the wildfolk has returned!"

None of this made much sense to Father, and he started to say as much when a lone ray of sunshine broke through the trees, alighting on the sapling. The light glistened off the leaves, shimmering deep crimson, dazzling Father. A wave of dizziness overcame him and he clasped the dark stone to steady himself, and when he did, he felt a faint pulse emanating from the rocks. He shut his eyes and let out a moan.

"What is it?" Forest asked. "What do you see?"

"Nothing, I—" Heat shot into his hand and then a flash, just a flash, but he saw the massive tree reaching up into the sky, towering above all other trees, its crimson leaves blowing furiously in a wild wind. Fire, smoke, blood, so much blood as to saturate the very ground. He tried to hold the vision, to see more, but the pulse, the vision all faded. "Blood," Father said. "Always so much blood."

"Good," Forest said. "Blood is your language, your soul, your purpose. Mother Earth is showing you that you are her slayer, her champion, her guardian, that you must protect her pawpaw tree."

Sky and Creek, who Father realized seemed not to speak, not with words anyway, nodded.

"The tree, Pawpaw, produced a *fruit*!" Forest said this with all the awe and reverence his small voice could muster. "One fruit . . . but the fruit is full of big magic, and that is how we brought you back. How Pawpaw brought you back. So, listen, hear us. You must not let the tree down. As it grows, so does its magic, so does *our* magic. If we, if *you,* can keep the tree safe, it will give us more of its precious fruit. And with that magic we will, at last, reclaim all that was stolen from us! Do you understand? It is time for you to go forth and drive them back. Time to be the slayer!"

"I am the . . . *slayer*?"

"You *are* the slayer."

Father still felt unsure, but he nodded. "I *am* the slayer."

The faces of the wildfolk lit up.

"Follow us!" Forest called, and the three wildfolk dashed away up the slope, heading toward the foul smells.

Father followed and a short walk later stopped at a cluster of felled trees and burnt stumps.

Forest jabbed a finger at the toppled trees. "See, look! The people, they did this. Closer and closer they come to Pawpaw!" Forest's face twisted into fear, then anger, the two other wildfolk mirroring his expression. "We are out of time," he spat. "We have to stop them, *must* stop them! How long before they set their blades to Pawpaw? How long, I ask you? And the day that happens, we are done, all done. If you cannot understand anything else, understand that!"

Father could clearly see that the line of the felled trees was leading down toward the crimson sapling, felt an instinctive anger building in his heart, his gut. He grunted and started toward the smell.

The wildfolk followed him up to the edge of the field. Father took in the turned soil, the livestock in their foul pens, the structures built from timber.

"Look upon it," Forest hissed. "See how they cut down the trees, dirty our water, burn our nests and burrows. They are a plague killing our magic, our very souls." He shook his small fist. "And now they are here, upon our last sanctuary."

Father watched a thin trail of white smoke drift up from the main structure. He sensed a great sadness, then spotted a woman crossing the yard toward the pens. She was different than the women in his dream, their flesh being copper in tone, while hers was pale. She was covered in clothing, even her hair captured in cloth. He didn't like it, didn't like anything about her, not her smell, her pasty skin, but most of all that she kept these animals in pens, in their own filth. He growled.

Forest smiled at Father. "Yes, there you are. There is our slayer. Now, let us go introduce ourselves to this woman."

Abitha walked into the barn, scattering a handful of hens, the lot of them clucking at her reproachfully as though she had no place there. She strolled up to the mule, leaned her cheek against the animal's neck, and gently stroked its forehead. "All right, Sid," she said, speaking softly. "We can do it. Me and you. But we must work together. All right?"

The mule flicked its ears.

"Good boy. Now, let us get you harnessed up." Abitha stepped over to where the yoke hung on the rail. The yoke was made of wood, iron, and leather and looked heavy. She gave it a tug; it barely budged. She'd seen Edward do this numerous times and it hadn't looked difficult, but then Edward had been much stronger than her. The trick was getting the yoke over the mule's head and onto its shoulders, a trick made doubly difficult by her small frame, her being but eye to eye with the beast. She got a firm grip on the yoke, sucked in a deep breath, and slid it off the rail.

"Shit," she hissed between her teeth. The yoke felt to weigh nearly as much as she did. She struggled not to lose her grip as she waddled toward the mule. With an immense effort she hefted it to her chest and shoved it up and forward, hoping to get it over Sid's head. The mule backed away, causing Abitha to miss her mark, and both Abitha and the yoke tumbled into the dirt.

"God's nails!" she cried, and slapped the earth, sending up a fresh ruckus amongst the hens.

She got to her feet and grabbed the yoke again, lifting it up onto her knee with a loud grunt, then to her chest, almost falling over backward in the process. Again she wobbled toward the mule; again the mule dodged and Abitha fell.

"I cannot. I just cannot!" She felt the sting of tears, got to her feet, and headed out of the barn. She stopped at the entrance and stared at the unplowed field. *Do not leave. You leave this barn now and you might as well just keep going right up to Wallace's door and tell him the farm is his.* She turned, glaring at the yoke. *You have to do this. Have to.*

She marched back, this time backing the mule against the stall, leaving it no room to escape.

"Please, Sid. Now, stand still." She stooped, wrapped her fingers around the yoke. "All right, one, two, three!" She lifted it atop her knee again, then maneuvered forward, keeping a close eye on the mule. "Easy, boy. Easy." She swung the yoke up to her chest and shoved it toward the beast. Sid ducked his head at the last moment, causing the yoke to hit his shoulder. The mule brayed and leapt forward, knocking the yoke onto Abitha. She fell back and the yoke landed on top of her.

Abitha cried out, struggling to get the yoke off her, but she was pinned. She started to call for Edward, his name actually on her tongue, before she caught herself. That was when the tears came.

"Why, Edward?" she cried, all but snarling through her teeth. "Why did you leave me?" She was stunned by the anger in her own voice. "Damn it, Edward, it is so hard alone!" A fresh round of tears burned down her cheeks. "I miss you . . . miss you so damn much," she sobbed. "You hear me? Wherever you are, you better hear me." A sudden wave of regret swept over her as she recalled the last words between them—her accusing him of sounding like her father. The look of pain on his face and him only trying to look after her, keep her safe amongst this clan of vipers. And what she would do now to have him beside her, to hear him fretting so after her well-being. "I am sorry, Edward. God, please tell him, at least give me that, tell him I did not mean it . . . that I love him. Please, God, you owe me that!"

She shoved the yoke, putting all her anger, her sorrow, into it, rolling it off her.

She sat up, cradling her arm, sure it was broken. She flexed it, winced from the pain. It appeared sound, but she knew come morning it would be stiff and covered in bruises.

Abitha heard a meow and felt warm fur pressing against her side. It was Booka, her orange, one-eyed tabby. She'd rescued the cat from a few dogs in the village many months ago and the poor thing's back had healed poorly, was bent and his tail twisted. He pushed his way into her lap, nudging her hand. She stroked his lumpy fur and he began to purr.

Abitha wiped the tears from her cheeks. "I am all right, Booka. I just need—" She heard a sound, a faint thump, and what, a hiss? It had come from farther back in the barn, near the sacks of corn seed.

Do we have rats now? Yet one more trouble, atop all my troubles?

She stared at the seed, knowing it was already April, that she had to get them in the ground and soon, wondering how she would ever do that if she couldn't so much as hitch a mule to a plow. "Just need a little help, that's all," she whispered. But from where and from whom? She had no money to hire anyone and besides, everyone was too busy getting their own seed in the ground.

Another thump, followed by what sounded like a child's giggle, mocking and cruel.

The hens let loose a flurry of clucking and fled the barn, the two nanny goats bleated from their pen, and Sid snorted in his stall. Booka leapt from Abitha's lap, stood staring toward the back of the barn, his fur raised.

Abitha stood up, searching the shadows. She spotted a pitchfork and stepped quietly over and picked it up. She waited, and just when she was beginning to doubt she'd heard anything, the giggle came again, crawling under her skin. She shuddered, leveled the pitchfork in the direction of the sound, wondering if it might be one of the native folk, suddenly aware of just how alone she was.

A large raven strolled from the shadows. It was just a black shape there in the dark, but she could tell it was staring at her. It snickered, sounding uncannily human, causing the hair on Abitha's arms to prickle.

The mule stomped nervously.

Need to get the musket, Abitha thought, and began backing up while keeping her eyes on the strange bird.

A chuckle came from behind Abitha; she spun, pitchfork ready.

An opossum blocked the entrance of the barn, too long, too thin, and grinning.

Abitha caught movement from the corner of her eye—a dark looming figure. Before she could turn, a rough hand clutched her neck and all feeling left her. She dropped the pitchfork and collapsed, her head striking the ground hard. Her vision blurred, and when it unblurred she saw the opossum stroll up, walking on its hind legs like a small person. The raven landed next to it, then something that made even less sense: a fish swam over, just floating in the air beside the others. Slowly their faces changed into those of children, all three smiling and staring at her with small black eyes.

They began to chant, bopping up and down as their words crawled into her head and the world began to spin. *"Blood, blood, blood!"*

Abitha tried to scream, managed only a strangled cry, before *it*, the dark figure, was beside her. It leaned over her, all shadows and colliding shapes, but she saw its eyes, and she saw its horns, and she saw its hooves.

The Devil has come for me! She clawed the dirt, tried to get away, but her body was numb and she could barely move.

It ran long spidery fingers through her hair, down her forehead, then clasped her face between hot, clammy hands. She felt its hunger, its craving.

God save me!

Its hand slid around her throat, tightened, squeezing until she couldn't breathe and her pulse hammered against its fingers.

And still the little creatures danced about, chanting, their black eyes alive with glee.

The world began to dim.

Abitha felt a throbbing, realized it was a pulse, a heartbeat, that it was coming from the thing's hands. The pulse fell in rhythm with her own, as though sharing one heart.

The Devil let out a harsh gasp. Its silver eyes blazed. She felt their heat as it glared at her, into her, and suddenly she shared its heart, its mind, felt its shock, its confusion, felt them blend with her own.

It let out a moan and so did she as the world swam in and out of focus, faded to black, then erupted in a blast of heat and bright flame.

Abitha found herself standing in a circle of huts. They were on fire and people were running and screaming; mutilated bodies lay everywhere. The air smelled of blood and acrid smoke. She saw a shadow—cast long by the flames—of a beast with great horns, standing on its hind legs. The shadow split, tearing into two separate but identical shadows. The two shadows began to tussle, then to tear into each other, clawing and ripping each other apart. She felt every wound as though it were her own flesh tearing.

There came a long cry of anguish and pain; it came from the beast, it came from her, turning into a howl, louder and louder until she felt sure it would rip open her throat.

Thunder rumbled and sooty rain began to fall, only it wasn't rain, but to her great horror, spiders, tiny black spiders—hundreds, thousands, millions, blotting out the very sky. They covered her arms, her legs, her face until she couldn't move. They crawled into her mouth, her nose, her ears, her eyes until she couldn't see, hear, smell, or breathe, and her pulse, their pulse, slowed, faded, then died, and all became darkness, nothing but endless darkness.

Abitha opened her eyes, unsure where she was.

"Spiders," she whispered, sat up fast, glancing anxiously around. There were no spiders, but the barn held plenty of shadows. She blinked, trying to clear her vision. Where were they? The thing, the beast, the little creatures?

She spotted the pitchfork, grabbed it, and staggered drunkenly toward the sunlight—sunlight and salvation.

"Jesus, God! Do not forsake me!"

She made it out of the barn, dropped the pitchfork, fell down, almost impaling herself on its sharp prongs, pulled herself back up, and stumbled to the cabin. She ducked inside, slamming the door and sliding the heavy bar into place. She grabbed the musket, put her back against the far wall, trembling and panting as she waited for *it* to come and bash down her door.

What am I doing in the wilds by myself? Why did I not listen?

Blood trickled into her eye and she dabbed at a small gash on her forehead, found a good-sized knot there. She glanced at the musket, wondering what good it would do against a devil, and snatched up Edward's bible off the mantel, clutching it to her chest like some protective talisman.

A minute crawled by, another, and when several more went by without the foul beast busting through the door, without a thousand spiders swarming up through the floorboards, her breathing began to slow, her thoughts to clear. *What was that? What cursed thing is out there?* She touched the bump on her head. *Am I losing my mind? Seeing things? God, Jesus, help me!* She heard a voice, not that of God or Jesus, but of her mother. *You know what you must do.*

Abitha shook her head. *No . . . I cannot.* Her eyes shifted from the door to the bed, where the corner of a tattered traveling bag jutted out—it was the one she'd brought over from England. She'd emptied it except for one thing: a small tied pouch that had once belonged to her mother.

Leave it, Abitha thought, but she continued to stare at the bag and there was no stopping the memories. She clenched her eyes shut, trying to block them out, trying to stay sane, but her head felt light from the blow and she was growing dizzy and the memories flooded in, so vivid, so real—Abitha there, in her mother's garden shed, but twelve years old, her mother not yet cold in the grave, one more uncounted victim of the plague sweeping through London.

She watched herself digging frantically through her mother's cabinet. It was night and she had but a small candle to see by as she shuffled about bowls of herbs and roots, bottles of dried beetles and spiders, looking for the book. It was here, she knew it. She had to find it now, *right now,* before *he* showed up.

She slid open a drawer, discovered a few books, but not *the* book. She quickly tugged them out, and there, finally, hidden beneath them all, she found it—several dozen sheets of tattered parchment sewn together between two thick pieces of worn goat hide.

She flipped it open, glancing over the hundreds of scribbles, sketches, and marks, some in her mother's sharp penmanship but most by others. Her mother called it her recipe book—an irreplaceable collection of remedies passed down from one generation of cunning women to the next. Abitha's fondest memories were of her mother going over them with her, teaching her how to decipher the symbols and codes, teaching her the most basic potions and ointments.

Abitha reached the back of the book and stopped. The edges of the last few pages were black as though pulled from a fire. These were the ones her mother had forbidden her to look at. Abitha hesitated; she knew that the book contained more than remedies, that her mother's cunning craft was not limited to root medicine, that she had the sight and told fortunes, that it was even rumored on rare occasions she'd acted as a conduit to call dead loved ones to speak with their families. But Abitha felt sure what was written on the black pages went deeper.

She flipped the page and for a moment forgot all about her purpose as she stared at the dark scrawling. She could only decipher bits of it here and there, but enough to know them for what they were—curses, poisons, doors to the dead. She shuddered. She'd never known her mother to stray into such dark places, but everyone had their secrets.

A creak came from the door. Abitha started, slapped the book shut, glancing furtively behind her. He would be here any moment, and anything she didn't hide he would destroy. She would never have another chance. She stuffed the book into her bodice, but she wasn't done. There was one other item that she *had* to save, *had to*. She continued searching, digging through drawer after drawer.

"Where is it?" she hissed, trying to quell her panic. "Think. Where would she have put it?"

Abitha froze.

Someone was there, in the shed with her.

She glanced round.

No one.

She caught a scent, lavender and sage, like the sachet her mother always wore about her neck.

"Mother?"

Abitha stood up, looked about, and saw it, the braid, the item she was searching for. It was just lying atop the desk in plain sight. She knew it hadn't been there before. "Mother . . . are you with me?"

The braid was composed of twelve loops of braided hair woven together to form a chain, each loop a slightly different shade of auburn. A simple copper pin in the shape of a serpent tied the two ends together. Her mother had worn it about her neck—a dangling necklace of shimmering auburn hair—but rarely. She'd told Abi she only used it when she needed the help of her mothers, to conjure, to reach out to the spirits, or perhaps for some particularly difficult bit of root medicine.

Abitha would never forget the first time her mother allowed her to hold it. Her mother had tapped the last loop in the line and told Abitha that loop was hers, that the next was her mother's, then her grandmother's, great-grandmother's and so on all the way back twelve generations. She touched the bottom rung and said, "One day, when you're ready, you will join all your mothers and your hair will be added here."

Abitha picked it up off the potting bench, and the moment she touched the braids, her mother was there in the shed with her. Abitha couldn't see her, but the scent of lavender and sage was strong, as though her mother were standing beside her.

"Be brave, Abitha. Listen to your heart. Learn to trust yourself."

"Mother . . . *Mother?*" Abitha clutched the braids to her chest, began to cry. "I miss you, Mother."

"ABITHA!" Her father stood in the door, his raging eyes burning into her.

Abitha jumped back, crashing into the bench.

"What are you doing here?" he demanded.

67

She slid the braid into the back of her skirt, into her undergarments, hoping he wouldn't notice.

"What have you there?" He stormed over to her. "Give it to me now!"

She couldn't speak, just shook her head.

He grabbed the top of her bodice, tore it open, and the recipe book spilled out, falling onto the ground. His eyes grew even wider and he shoved her away from it like it were a pit viper.

"*What have I told you?*" he screamed. "There is the very hand of Satan! Your mother has played with the Devil and it has cost her her life, her soul. She has cursed us all!"

He knocked over a shelf of jugs and potted plants, shattering them upon the ground. "Look around you at all this wickedness."

He snatched up an oil lamp, twisting the wick off, dumping the oil over the recipe book, then the cabinet and the other books.

Abitha watched, terrified, unable to move.

He grabbed Abitha's candle and set the oil ablaze, the books igniting.

Abitha found her voice. "*No!*" she shouted, reaching into the flame, trying to save the recipe book.

He snatched hold of her arm, dragged her screaming from the shed, into the yard, held her, his hard fingers biting into her arm as the shed burned.

"The Devil took her! Do you not see?" he cried, and began to weep. "Your mother was a good woman. A good wife . . . a good mother. Know that, always know that. But the Devil is tricky. He took hold of her through that book, through her little spells and divinations. She opened the door . . . your poor mother let the Devil in and he took her from us!"

Her father began to bawl, and this frightened Abitha more even than his yelling. She'd never seen the man cry so; it was as though his heart was being torn out.

"How did I not see?" he wailed. "I thought her only doing her medicine. Doing her Christian duty. I were so blind. Now it is too late . . . for her, for us. We are damned." He pointed at the flames. "See him there in the fire . . . the *Devil!* He has your name, Abitha. It is written in his book. The only chance you have is to pray to God every day . . . every day, every moment you can spare. Then, only then, mayhap God will erase your name from Satan's book."

He fell to his knees, tugged Abitha down with him. "We must start now, this very minute. Put your hands together, child. Pray to God. Beg his forgiveness."

She did as she was bid.

"Now, Abitha, promise me . . . swear to me and to God, to Jesus, that you will forsake all of your mother's evil ways. That you shall never tamper with her wicked crafts."

She didn't answer, only stared into the fire.

He shook her, twisted her arm so hard she thought he would break it. "Swear it! Swear it to God!"

"I swear it!" she cried.

"Swear it to me! Swear it to God!"

"I swear to you, Father. I swear to you, God, Jesus. I will never again touch such wickedness!"

And then finally, he let her go, left her there staring into the flames as he gathered all her mother's belongings from the house—her clothes, shoes, combs, even the blankets she'd slept on, anything personal to her—and burned them as well.

It wasn't over for Abitha, no. Each day thereafter, her father forced her, her brothers, to pray, sometimes for hours depending on how much he'd been drinking, how dark his mood, pray to have their names struck from the Devil's book, to have the strength to keep their hands from the wicked crafts.

But he never found the woven loops of braids. Abitha slipped them into an old pouch and hid them away. But all his talk of devils, his endless prayer sessions, did their work, and Abitha didn't open that pouch, didn't dare.

Abitha opened her eyes, found herself back in the cabin. *The Devil is at my door.* She walked over and slid out the bag, unbuttoned it, and took out her mother's pouch. Stared at it.

She'd kept her promise to her father, to God, at least until she'd arrived here, in the New World. Then Edward, or her, needed some small bit of root medicine here or a blessing there. She wasn't a child, she knew well the difference between ointments and charms, and spells and divinations. Were not prayers blessings? But with the burden of Wallace and his demands, they had so little, and when the opportunity arose to barter a few charms, some fortune-telling, or maybe a small spell, for things they were in desperate need of, it was hard to say no. And by then London, the plague, her father, that life, it seemed a distant dream.

She untied the pouch.

Is my name indeed in the Devil's book? She glanced toward the door of her cabin. *Was Father right? Has Satan been waiting for me this whole time, waiting for me to open the door with my dabbling? Waiting for me to untie this pouch?*

She lifted the pouch, shook it. The long chain of braided hair slid out onto the bed.

69

It was her mother's words she heard then. *"Be brave, Abitha. Listen to your heart. Learn to trust yourself."*

What does my heart say? She stared at the serpent-shaped pin. *I'm afraid.* But that wasn't all; she knew her mother was a Godly woman, that she certainly was no pawn of the Devil. *No, no soul was ever more at peace with herself, with nature, with God. And I never witnessed her do naught that were wicked. She died of the plague along with thousands of others, that is all. So I ask you, Father, were they, all those stricken, were they then too pawns of the Devil? Nay, I think not, Father. I think not.*

A creak came from over by the door.

Abitha started. *But that, that thing out there, that is some kind of devil or demon. That I am* sure *of.* And she remembered well her mother telling her of wayward spirits, demons that would plague a soul if given the chance. She also remembered her mother showing her a few tricks to ward them away.

Ash and salt, she thought, but that was just a common folk charm. She knew there was more to the spell, the real spell, other ingredients. *I saw it, aye. In the recipe book. If but only I still had it.* She tried to recall the details. It was there, so close, but no, she couldn't see it.

She looked again at the chain of hair. Her mother had used it when she needed the help of her mothers.

Abitha's hand hovered above it.

"Mother, I need you."

She touched it, a soft caress, and when she did, a lightness swept over her and she caught a whiff of lavender and sage and with it a flood of memories.

Abitha set the musket and the bible on the table, grabbed her largest skillet, setting it down next to the bible, then quickly rounded up the sack of salt and a knife. There wasn't much salt left, but she scooped out two handfuls anyway, tossing them into the skillet. She took the knife and hacked off a chunk of her hair. She spat three times on the hair and dropped it in. Next, she tore out several pages from the bible, touched them to her lips, said a prayer, then tore them to ribbons, crumbling them atop the mix.

She picked up the knife again and hesitated. There was one more ingredient. She held up her finger. *Blood,* she thought, *my blood. Why is it the most powerful spells all seem in need of blood?* She pricked her finger, watched as two drops spattered atop the words of God, staining the paper dark crimson.

She carried the skillet over to the hearth. There were still a few embers from the morning fire. She stoked them to flame and set the mix ablaze, repeating her small prayer over and over until the flames burned out. Then she poured the charred mix into the ash pail, stirring it in with the ash.

The dust made her cough and it was her father's ranting she heard then, felt his eyes burning into her.

"No," she whispered. "No! I will not listen anymore. I care not what promises I made you, Father. The Devil is upon my step."

She heard a thump, started, leapt to her feet, her heart drumming.

What was that? But she knew.

The sound grew louder, a soft clumping like hooves in the dirt.

Abitha snatched up the pail, dashed over to the door, sprinkling a line of the salt and ash across the threshold, then to the one small window, closing and locking the thick batten shutter and spreading a thin trail of the mix along the sill. She grabbed the musket, her hands trembling as she watched the door and waited.

"Be gone, Slewfoot," she whispered. "Be gone."

The hooves continued, circling the cabin; she caught sight of its shadow through the thin cracks in the shutter as it passed.

The hooves came back around to the front and stopped near the door.

"Hello," someone called. "Abitha? Are you there?"

A man! Someone from the village! Oh, thank God!

She dashed to the door, propping the musket against the wall, then lifted the heavy bar free. She yanked the door open.

Astride his white stallion, Wallace Williams stared at her.

71

Wake.

"No."

They are here. You must kill them.

"I am dead."

Smell them.

The beast did, smelled the blood beating in their veins. There were two of them.

You must kill them, Father.

"Father?"

Do you not remember your name?

The beast tried to remember, but all was blackness, then the blackness began to squirm, sprouted legs, so many prickly little legs. "No!" he hissed, seeing that the blackness was alive, that it was a tangled mass of boiling black spiders, millions of them, and they were crawling all over him. He tried to claw them away, only to find he couldn't move, that he was trapped in their wet webbing.

Father gasped, opened his eyes, and sat up. He glanced frantically about for the spiders—there were no spiders, just an opossum, a raven, and a fish, staring at him, horrified.

"You're all right, Father. Just a nightmare."

Father stared at them.

"Do you not know us?"

Father's head throbbed. "You are Forest . . . Sky . . . Creek."

The wildfolk appeared relieved.

Father heard someone yelling.

"A man is here," Forest said.

Father winced and rubbed his temples.

"His blood. It will make the pain go away."

Father nodded, crawled slowly to his feet, swooned, clutched the barn post. He heard voices and slid into the shadows, remembered how not to be seen and was not seen.

He spotted the woman and a man over by the cabin. The woman stepped off the porch and tromped right past the man without hardly looking at him, staring into the barn, her eyes wide with fear. She stopped several paces away. "Did you see them?" she asked the man. "Did you?"

"See who?"

"In the barn, Wallace. Did you see anything when you rode up?"

They were both looking toward Father, but neither could see or hear him, not now, as he didn't want them to.

"I saw no one," the Wallace man said. He dismounted. "What happened, Abitha? Pray tell."

The woman started to say something, then closed her mouth. Father sensed a great distrust between them.

"What happened to you?" the man asked, looking her up and down. "You are a mess. Why, you are bleeding."

The woman, this Abitha, straightened her clothing, pushed the loose hair from her face, then wiped the blood from her eyes and forehead with her apron.

Something jabbed Father's leg. "Kill them," Forest hissed. "Now."

72

Sky landed on the rail near Father, and Creek floated up next to the bird. They too didn't want to be seen or heard by the people, so were not.

"What are you waiting for?" Forest growled.

But Father didn't move, felt if he tried, he might collapse. He studied the woman. *What did she do to me?* The vision returned, just a flash—two shadows fighting. *Was it real? Was it sorcery?* Then he saw the spiders again, brimming about the edges of his vision, thousands of them waiting their chance to pounce, to cover him in their sticky web, to drag him back down into the darkness. He shook his head, trying to clear his mind, trying to focus on the man and the woman.

"Were it Indians?" the man asked. "The Pequot?"

Pequot, Father thought. *I know that name. Yes, they are one of the people. One of the tribes.* He nodded to himself and wondered if the Pequot had been the people in his dream.

"No," Abitha replied. "It . . . it were but an accident. Fell and hit my head. I were dizzy, seeing things not there. That is all."

The man eyed her suspiciously. "That is most troubling . . . and you must admit it is a good example of how this farm is too dangerous for you to work alone."

She flashed him a dark look.

Wallace raised his hands and added, "Abitha, it would be dangerous for anyone. The wilds are no place to be alone. Listen, hear me. I did not come to bicker." He went to a bucket sitting against the well, fished out a cup with a long handle, dipped some water, and brought it to her. "Here, please."

The woman took the cup and drained it, wiping her mouth on her sleeve. "Thank you," she said, but it sounded forced.

"Let us go in the house where we can sit down," he offered. "Where we can talk."

"I am in no mind to talk."

"Very well." He nodded. "Then at least let me bring you a chair? You appear ready to faint."

"Wallace, if you have something to say, just say it." She stared at him, waiting.

Wallace sucked in a deep breath. "In reflection, I will admit that I could've handled some of this business better. It is a trying time for all of us, and none but the Lord are perfect. I am hoping for a new start between us."

She crossed her arms, his words seeming to only put her more on guard.

"The solution to our problems, yours and mine, came to me while Charity was reading scripture to the family last night. It is from Ecclesiastes. 'Two are better than one; because they have a good reward for their labour. For if they fall, the one

73

will lift up his fellow: but woe to him that is alone when he falleth; for he hath not another to help him up.' Do you not see where this is going?"

The woman shook her head.

"It is so very simple. . . . You and Isaac should wed."

The woman blinked at him as though struck dumb.

"Now, this is not a decision I came to lightly. I—"

"You mean *Isaac*? Your son, *Isaac*?"

He nodded.

"You wish *me* . . . to marry *Isaac*? My nephew by law?"

"I do."

"The boy's not but sixteen."

"He's seventeen and soon to be eighteen."

She shook her head.

"Isaac is young," he continued. "I know this, but he is very mature for his age. Do not be hasty, Abitha. There is much to consider. If the two of you marry, then all your troubles be gone. You'll have a strong man to head up the farm and the help of all his family. And here, here is the best part. I have spoken with Lord Mansfield in Hartford. He has agreed to work out reasonable terms so that the farm would eventually be yours."

"You mean it would be Isaac's, and in all but name *yours*."

"And what is wrong with that? Papa always wished to keep everything in the family, because he knew that there are no bonds like those of family."

"And what does Isaac have to say to this? Have you talked with him?"

"The boy will abide. Marriage is not only about love. He will see the opportunity and seize it. And I am sure, with time, the two of you will develop a bond."

"The boy only has eyes for Helen and Helen for him. You know that."

The man looked away.

"Wallace, are you truly willing to marry away your only son to pay off *your* debt? And to a woman you profess to dislike so? Would you destroy the love between Isaac and Helen, condemn them to a lifetime of heartbreak, of unfulfilled longing? Look at yourself, Wallace. Is that the kind of man you wish to be?"

Father sensed the man's growing anger.

The woman let out an unkind laugh. "And there I'd be, no land, no say, beholden to you and your son. No different than a servant . . . worse off even, as at least a servant can leave should things become too bad. No. No. I'll not be yours to be kicked around my whole life."

"Abitha, you're not hearing me."

"I will not marry your son, Wallace. I will not do that to him, nor Helen, nor me."

"You are but a fool then," the man growled, his face reddening, his embarrassment and humiliation palpable. "You know you cannot bring in that crop alone. Do not let your pride bring ruin to us all. Take a minute. Think very carefully before you reply, as I will not ask this again. Now, what say you, Abitha? Will you at least consider marrying Isaac?"

"If you are so sure that I will fail, then why do this? You need but wait 'til fall and it will be yours. You can give it to Lord Mansfield then. I am sure he will work something out with you. Unless . . ." She cocked her head, giving the man a quizzical look. "Aye." Her brows lifted and she laughed. "Why, Wallace, is that worry I see there on your face?" She laughed again, louder. "You're afraid. Aye, afraid that I *will* bring in the crop and then you will lose *both* farms! Well, if *you* believe I can do this, then so do I. Thank you for this. You have given me a breath of confidence when I am in most need of such. You—"

He slapped her, sending her sprawling to the dirt. "I will not allow you to steal my father's farm!" he snarled. "Do you hear me, girl?" He stepped forward, his eyes simmering with rage, his big hands clenched.

The woman rolled to her feet, jumped over to where a pitchfork lay in the dirt. She snatched it up, met the man with wild fierce eyes, bared her teeth. "One more step," she hissed, jabbing the weapon out before her, "and I will stick this in your gut!"

Father smiled.

Wallace hesitated. Father sensed his surprise, his uncertainty.

"You stupid girl," Wallace spat. "You stupid, stupid, girl. You better start practicing your Pequot, because after you're done making a mess of everything, they'll be the only ones who will have you."

The man walked back to his horse and mounted the steed. "This is not over," he called. "Hear me and hear me good when I say I will not let you steal this farm." His eyes bore into her, his voice dropped down to a hiss. "You are alone in the woods, dear Abitha. Vulnerable . . . ever so *vulnerable*. Why, any awful thing could happen to you out here. Do you understand? *Anything*." He smiled then, wide and sinister, kicked the horse, and road away at a hard gallop.

The woman stood there holding the pitchfork in her trembling hands until the hoof clomps faded. Finally, she dropped it, turned and stared into the barn, her chest heaving. But her fear was now replaced with a seething rage. Father could hear, *feel*, her pulse drumming.

75

She headed back into the cabin, returning a moment later marching, almost stomping toward the barn, carrying an iron pail and a long stick of metal and wood, not a spear, but a weapon of some kind. She stopped at the entrance, propped the weapon against the fence. He knew she couldn't see or hear them, yet she was looking right at the three of them.

"This is my goddamn farm! My goddamn barn!" she cried, her voice shrill, cracking as though on the edge of sanity. "Leave at once. I command you! Go back to Hell. In the name of God, in the name of all that is holy, in the name of the earth, moon, and stars, in the name of my mother and all her mothers, in the name of every fucking thing, *BE GONE!*"

She jabbed her hand into the pail, brought out a fistful of white powder, and threw it into the barn.

The powder struck Father, stinging his nostrils, burning his eyes. He flinched, clenched his eyes shut as a host of fiery images assailed him: a wiry man, white as ash, with black lines painted down his face and long silver hair, leaping at him, dousing him in yellow powder. Pain, confusion, a mask, a hundred masks, all staring at him, and the wiry man's laughter ringing in his head. Then the spiders returned, covering him in their sticky web, trying to pull him back down into their prickly darkness.

No! he thought. *No!* He shook his head, shaking the spiders away, forcing his eyes open, setting them on the woman, glowering at this vile, nasty woman. He would have her now, would end her wickedness, her bewitchery, forever.

But the woman wasn't looking at him; she stared up into the sky. "Why, God . . . why do you do this to me?" she moaned, dropping to her knees. She buried her face into her hands and began to sob. "I've had all I can take. Do you hear me? All I can take!"

The woman's emotions blazed so strong that Father felt them burn into him, lucid and visceral. He could all but peer into her soul. He caught a flash of her very thoughts, saw her tying a rope around her own neck.

Abitha wiped the tears angrily from her eyes, looked past him, through him, into the barn. She pushed herself to her feet, took a rope from the fence, then marched into the barn, her face set and grim.

She entered a stall, tossed one end of the rope over the beam, tied it off, then tied a loop into the other end. She tested it against her weight; it held. Then she just stood there staring at the rope, her eyes distant and glazed, as one long minute after another passed.

Father sensed her despair, so deep, so cutting.

Finally, the woman let out a deep gasp as though she'd been holding her breath this entire time, looked at the mule standing there gazing at her, then back at the rope, then back at the mule, then, to Father's surprise, she grinned savagely.

"I am not a stupid girl, Wallace Williams."

Abitha took the end of the rope and fastened it to the yoke. She tugged the rope until the yoke hung at eye level with the mule, tied it off, then guided the yoke over the mule's head, sliding the harness into place. She tied everything down and led the mule out.

"C'mon, Sid, we've some ground to plow."

Father stumbled from the barn, through the cornfield, steering well clear of the woman as she turned the earth with her mule and plow. He didn't care about her, not now. He just wanted the pain, the howling in his head, to end, the spiders to leave him be.

Forest and the wildfolk caught up with him as he entered the woods.

"What is it, Father? What plagues you so?"

Father ignored him, continued on until he arrived back at the remnants of the giant tree, and as he entered the circle of stones, at last, some relief from the throbbing in his head. But the spiders, they were still there, out of sight, but there, waiting; he could feel them, hear them scuttling about.

He collapsed, just lay down in the leaves and stared up at the thin crimson sapling. A spot of sunlight set it to glow and a calmness slowly stole over him.

Forest, Sky, and Creek sat down around him.

"Why is it when I close my eyes," Father asked, "I see masks staring back at me, see spooks cursing me? Why are there spiders waiting to take me into the darkness? Why are there two shadows like mine trying to kill one another? How is it that I feel their pain, that it racks my soul so? Do you know? You must know?"

"It is the people," Forest said. "They have put these demons in your head. Have poisoned you just like they poisoned the land. If you want peace, you must drive them away before they are too many. Make them so afraid that they tell all their kin that this is a place of suffering and death, to stay clear lest they wish to be food for the worms. That is your only chance. Our only chance."

"You said you brought me back . . . back from where? From what? What happened to me? Tell me."

The wildfolk exchanged an anxious glance; Father caught their fear and uncertainty.

Forest started to say something, stopped, seemed to reconsider, then started again. "They killed you. They stole your soul."

"The people?"

Forest nodded. "The first tribes. A long time ago. They slaughtered us for our magic, for the fruit of Pawpaw. You tried to stop them, but it was not to be. There was blood, so much blood, our blood, your blood, and—" He gestured to the blackened bones of the tree. "Pawpaw."

"And you brought me back . . . from the dead?"

"Yes," Forest said, his brows cinched as though considering. "Perhaps part of you still lingers in the land of the dead? Death does not give up its citizens easily. I do not know. What I do know is that if we can keep Pawpaw safe, can pay it proper tribute, soon, very soon, the tree will reward us with more fruit, more magic, and then . . . then we will be able to heal you. Make you whole."

Father stared into the cave opening, wondered if the howling in his head was the cries of the dead. He closed his eyes, let his mind drift, to follow the sounds, seeking a path, some connection with the ghosts of his past. He saw nothing, but there, for a moment, the howling grew louder.

"Father!"

He opened his eyes; the wildfolk appeared spooked, glancing about uneasily.

"It is best not to call the dead," Forest cautioned. "Not here. . . . The worlds around Pawpaw are thin. We must be careful what doors we open." Forest studied him a moment longer. "Father, we lost you, we lost Pawpaw. All because of their greed. The people. We must not allow that to happen again. You are our guardian; you have always been our guardian, the lord of the wilderness, the slayer. Save us and you will save yourself. That is the only path."

Father sensed the opossum was holding something back. *There is more*, he thought, struggling to pierce the hazy shadows of his mind. He stared up into the trees, watched them sway in the soft breeze, watched the sun drift slowly across the sky, hour after hour, until it began to sink from view, trying to let go, to let his mind drift. *The memories are there, so close, so very close.*

A star appeared in the cloudless night, sparkled, another, then another, then a hundred thousand. Father drank in their ancient light. He watched an owl fly soundlessly past. The insects and night creatures began their songs. The moon peeked out from behind the hills, bathing the forest in its silver glow.

Are you not the same moon from my other life? he wondered, fixing on it, trying

78

to push through the thin veil of time, listening again for the voices of the ghosts. And there, faintly, from down in the pit, the calls and bellows of beasts from a distant night. He closed his eyes and the moon was still there, but bigger now. There were shapes in the distance, large and small, just shadows, but he knew them, called to them, but they didn't seem to hear. He called again, a long howl from somewhere deep in his soul, and this time, this time, they called back. Their sounds growing, coming closer and closer until they sounded as though they were in the forest with him.

Father opened his eyes and sat up.

The wildfolk were all staring at the cave, their faces full of alarm.

"Father!" Forest hissed. "No!"

A fog began to drift from the cave; it smelled of things long dead, snaking along, the moonlight setting its twisting tendrils aglow. He heard a howl, another, hollow echoes, as though from a dream. Movement in the fog caught his attention, its tendrils swirling together, forming ghostly shapes, creatures of all sorts and sizes.

"I know you," Father whispered. He saw bears and long-tooth cats, elk and bison, and wolves, dozens of wolves, all trotting along, their feet not touching the ground. The lightning bugs began to chase after them, swarming around them, illuminating their ghostly forms with their golden glow.

"You have awakened the dead!" Forest whispered.

Their howls and bellows echoed around Father, tugging at his heart. The pain, the throbbing in his head, began to melt away. He felt light, so very light, as though he could just float away. He stood, started to follow them.

"No!" Forest cried, dashing in front of Father. "You must not!"

"They're calling me."

"Yes, to join them in the land of the dead."

"They can show me my past. I need to see. Need to find the missing pieces!"

"If you follow ghosts you will become a ghost. Now come back!"

Father gasped as a mighty mammoth came striding from the fog, strolling boldly through the parade of beasts as though lord of all. It thrust its trunk skyward and trumpeted, the eerie blast filling Father's heart and soul. "Yes, yes! I remember this!"

Father pushed Forest aside, broke into a light canter, then a gallop, his hooves kicking up the leaves as he chased after the spectral creatures, disappearing into the fog and trees.

"Stop!" Forest cried, running after him. "It is a trick! Heed me. Father! Heed me!"

CHAPTER 4

Creek nudged Forest.

The opossum sat up quick, scanned the clouds. "Yes, there. I see him!"

A raven flew down through the trees and alighted on a stone by the crimson sapling. It was Sky.

"Well?" Forest asked, but he already knew the answer, could read it on the raven's face.

Sky shook his head sorrowfully.

"Nothing? Tracks? Mutilated corpses . . . anything?"

Again, Sky shook his head.

Creek prodded Forest.

"I know not what it means, Creek. I am as blind as you. Is Father lost in the land of the dead? His soul floating around in purgatory? Or has he wandered a thousand leagues from here? How will we know?"

Sky bobbed.

"No, do not say that," Forest snapped. "He is not with Mamunappeht. How do I know? Because if he were . . . Mamunappeht would have already come for us, for the tree."

Neither Sky nor Creek argued this point, but it didn't seem to lessen their worry. They'd all been searching, scouring every nook and cranny for miles around, all the haunted places where the ghosts might have led Father, searching for going on nearly a month, day after day, night after night. *Summer is almost upon us, and still not a single clue to his whereabouts.*

"I know not what went wrong. Why do you keep asking me as though it were my fault? What is your guess?"

"No, it is not like before. Stop saying that. This is different. It will pass." But he knew that Father was showing all the same troubling signs. *No, Mother Earth, I beg you, do not let it happen again.*

Creek bobbed.

Forest sighed. "Yes, it does keep coming back to that. I can think of nothing else. As much as it pains me to admit, we are not what we used to be. It seems even together, even with our blood mixed with that of the fruit, we did not have enough magic to complete the spell . . . not over such a distance. I agree, he is *not* whole. I fear part of him is still with Mamunappeht."

Sky and Creek winced.

"He spoke of spiders in his head. What else could that mean?"

Again, they winced.

"Tell Father what? The truth? Do you really feel it is as simple as that?"

Forest could see that they did.

"No. He is broken, his heart and soul confused. What do you think will happen if we tell him about Mamunappeht?"

Forest waited, but he could see they knew the answer.

"That's right, he will go to the shaman. Will confront him. Do you feel he is ready for that?"

Neither answered.

Forest sighed. "And if the shaman finds out Father is free, where do you think is the first place he will come?"

Creek and Sky both looked up anxiously at the crimson sapling.

"That's right. It will all be over. That is why, if we ever *do* find Father, we must keep things simple. Let us not muddle his mind with what he was before, with past mistakes and failures. For now, it is blood that he needs. If we want him to be the slayer, he must slay. He must swim in their blood, then he will be strong again, will drive them away." Forest's voice rose, full of vengeance and ardor. "Pawpaw will grow tall, give us such a bounty that even Mamunappeht will cower before us. And . . . and—"

Forest looked up at the thin crimson sapling, no taller than the average man, swaying there in the light breeze, with not a fruit, a flower, not so much as a bud upon its branches. He let out a great sigh. "But first we must find Father . . . find him before Mamunappeht does."

Abitha stared at a small apple tree near Edward's beehives, marveled at the luscious low-hanging fruit. The leaves of the tree were a stunning crimson and she wondered how it was she'd never noticed this extraordinary tree before. The apples were bloodred and without a doubt the most delicious-looking she'd ever seen. Her mouth watered and she walked over, started to grab one, heard a hiss, and yanked her hand back. A silky black serpent with red eyes lay coiled about the limb.

"Hello, Abitha," someone said, a woman's voice, low and soothing.

Abitha searched for the speaker, then realized it was the snake.

"Go on," the serpent said. "Take one. They are for you, my child. They will help you see."

Abitha reached again, stopped. The serpent was gone, but Abitha still heard her voice. *Just be wary of the spiders.*

"Spiders?" Abitha didn't see any spiders.

She plucked the fruit. It glistened with dew, felt firm and ripe, smelled so sweet. Her mouth watered and she took a bite. When she did, the apple twitched. She looked at it, at the gash where she'd bitten. It was bleeding, like an open wound. The blood bubbled, then dark prickly legs began to emerge. They were spiders, tiny black spiders, dozens of them! They spilled out of the apple, onto her hand. She threw down the apple, tried to spit the rest from her mouth, and that was when she felt them on her tongue, her teeth, the roof of her mouth, squirming and twisting, pricking and prodding. She opened her mouth to scream, but couldn't as they were in her throat.

Abitha sat up in bed, choking, coughing as she fought to breathe. She swatted at her arms, her hair, her face—but there were no spiders, only her cat, Booka, staring at her from the blanket.

Abitha jumped from bed, dashed to the door, threw it open wide, letting in dawn's light, washing away all the shadows, all the dark places where tiny spiders might hide. She stood staring out into the yard, watching the hens scratch about as the early light set the fog to glow.

She noticed how dusty the ground was becoming. It was June now, spring rain had given over to the warm days of summer, the land slowly drying up. This brought on the realization that Edward had been gone from her life for nearly two months now. Yet this didn't stop her from looking for him around every corner, expecting to see him out in the field, or to come walking out of the forest at any moment with a bright smile just for her.

"Edward," she whispered, and sat down right there on the doorstep, clutching herself, trying to remember the warm sound of his voice. Then, all at once, she noticed just how bright the morning was. "God's nails!" She leapt to her feet. "Booka, it is Sunday. I must not be late!"

She washed her face in the water bowl, scrubbing away as much of the grime as she could. She grabbed her best skirt, noticed the tattered hem, but slipped it on anyway. *I'll get to that,* she promised herself, then laughed bitterly at the mere thought that she'd ever have time for such things again.

She hurriedly buttoned her waistcoat, grabbed her bonnet, then her breakfast— half a biscuit, hard as stone as she was out of lard—and headed out.

She stopped at the door, where she'd hung the braided chain of hair on a hook. She took time to gently trace her finger down its rungs. She did this each morning, and when she did, it washed away the night fears and a sense of calm stole over her. She allowed herself a moment to breathe.

She stepped out onto the porch still chewing, and Booka began rubbing against her legs, all but tripping her as he tried to keep her from leaving.

"I know, Booka. I do not wish to go either. I've far too much work to do to be sitting upon my ass listening to endless sermons."

She stepped down off the small porch, scanning the sky for sign of rain. The morning sun shone upon the cornfield, revealing the crooked and uneven rows, some planted, others not. Yet Abitha felt a sense of pride. *I did that, Edward. If only you were here to see. You would be so proud. I know you would.* The first shoots were beginning to show, and she thought she might have a crop after all. *Just need some rain.* She'd spent most of the last several days carrying pails of water from the well but knew it wasn't possible for one person to keep this much corn watered.

"It'll rain soon," she told Booka.

The cat responded with loud meow.

83

"Well, at least I have something to pray for in church today."

One of the goats bleated and Abitha glanced toward the barn, searching for any hint of the shadowy devil that had assaulted her. She'd not seen it since it had touched her and wanted to believe the ash and salt had driven it away. But if that were so, why then did she hear sounds late into the night, unnatural sounds, hollow howls and moans? And how many times had she caught glimpse of spectral shapes, ghostly things, there one moment and then gone? And Edward, how many times now had she caught sight of *him* at the edge of her vision? To call his name, only to find no one, nothing. And always that feeling that something was there in the woods, watching, waiting.

"What do you want?" she asked for the thousandth time. "What?"

She turned toward Edward's beehives, searching for the apple tree, the one from her dream, needing to assure herself it was indeed just another of her bad dreams.

There was no apple tree, no serpent tempting her like Eve in Eden. Though Abitha did need remind herself that it had been her mother who'd said that the serpent in Eden had brought not a curse, but the gift of enlightenment. Abitha thought again how strong the sight had been with her mother, how she could reach across the void into the world of the dead and conjure lost souls. *Is that it? Has this devil awakened the sight within me?* Her mother had spoken about how her mother, and grandmother, had had the sight, how all the mothers had. *Why not me then?*

She caught movement near the hives—a man, his back to her, staring at the sprouting stalks.

"Edward?" she whispered, taking a step toward him. "Oh, God, Edward, is that you? Please be you."

This time he didn't disappear, but turned around, and it was indeed Edward. He was there, right there, only—

Abitha clutched her mouth, stifling a cry.

Edward's eyes were gone, leaving behind dark, vacant sockets.

Abitha's knees tried to buckle.

Edward raised a hand and pointed a damning finger at her, began tromping toward her.

Abitha stood frozen.

Closer and closer he came, slowly fading with each step, until he finally disappeared, dissipating like smoke, just a few strides away.

"Oh, God! Oh, Jesus Christ!" Abitha cried and spun away, trying not to stumble as she dashed up the path, suddenly wanting, no, needing to be at church, amongst people, even people she despised. She reached the road, glanced back down at the farm, searching for the man with no eyes.

"Edward," she whispered. "Where are you really?" She thought of his body down in that horrible pit, trapped forever with that devil spirit. *Does it have you, your very soul?*

She thought of the accusing way Edward had pointed at her.

Am I to blame? Was my father right, have I somehow meddled where I should not? Is my name in his book?

Abitha raced through the forest along the two-rut trail to church. The towering trees grew ever denser as she went, leaning in on her from either side, blocking out the sun—a twisted tunnel of branches and leaves and gnarled roots that felt ready to swallow her at any moment.

She kept glancing back, expecting Edward to be there, following her.

About halfway to the village she heard someone speaking. She stopped and squinted into the deep gloom of the woods, searching, only to find that every shape and shadow seemed a devil ready to come for her.

She heard it again, little more than a whisper, but near. Her flesh prickled.

It is just the wind, she thought. *Naught is there.* But something *was* there; she felt its eyes upon her.

"Leave me be," she called, her voice shaky. "Please, leave me be."

She heard what sounded like a growl, but oddly distorted as though coming from beneath the ground. Still, she knew who it was then—the Devil, the very one from her barn.

She dashed away, the growl chasing after her.

She hiked her skirt and ran, but it was right behind her. She felt its hand on her shoulder, then . . . then nothing.

She dared a glance back, sure it would be there, stumbled, fell into the bushes.

Nothing was there. Nothing but the trees.

85

Father sat on the bank amongst the endless bones, watching the giant river drift slowly by. All was gray, the river, the bones, the nearby hills and mountains, the dim smoky sky. The only color a glint of orange in the far distance hinting at some great fire. Ash drifted along on the warm breeze, the air smelling of soot.

He wiped his eyes clear of ash, noticed gray shapes along the far bank. It was them, the ghosts, a giant bear, a few bison, several wolves, and a mammoth. But they were not running as when he'd first heard their call; these were either shuffling listlessly along or just standing in place, staring endlessly at nothing, their eyes as dead as they were.

Father didn't know how long he'd been sitting here, as there was no day or night, not amongst the dead, just endless gray. He picked up a bone, watched it crumble in his hand, and tried to recall how he'd gotten here. He could remember following the ghost, how good it had felt to run with the spectral beasts, to share their song, but it seemed he'd become lost somewhere along the way and now wasn't sure how to get back, or if he even wanted to get back.

They moaned, those in the river; you could hear them as they passed, swirling and bobbing about in the lazy current. A face broke the surface, just for a moment, not one of the beasts, but a person, a woman. She stayed afloat just long enough for Father to see the look of utter emptiness in her eyes.

"I am ready," Father sighed. "Ready to join you."

"No, you're not," a voice said. It was the boar, the one with the small sigil of flame floating above its head, the one with three eyes—the third in the center of its forehead—all of them sad. It lay amongst the bones next to Father. "You keep saying that," it added, all three eyes blinking in unison. "Yet you're still here. Just admit it. You're afraid."

Father grunted.

The boar was as gray as the mud, hairless, missing an ear, a leg, its tail, and all of its teeth except one large tusk twisting up from the corner of its mouth. It appeared to be falling apart, crumbling as though slowly turning to dust. It sniffed at the water. "That's the river Lethe. It is the river of lost souls. Its waters offer oblivion to any who drown in it."

"You have told me that already," Father replied.

"Did I?"

"Yes, many times."

"Hmm, that is disturbing to hear. It seems the longer I lie here the more forgetful I become. I need to go for a swim, now, right now, before I forget that is why I came." But the boar didn't go into the river, instead it just laid its head back down.

"Tell me," Father said. "Why am I here?"

The boar cocked his head. "Now it is you that are repeating yourself. Why *are* you here?"

Father sighed, returned his attention to the river, to pondering what oblivion meant. An hour passed, or maybe a day, or maybe a week.

Footsteps, approaching at a hurried pace.

Father looked around.

"What is it?" the boar asked.

"Someone is coming."

The boar glanced about, sniffed the air. "I do not hear anything."

Father stood, spotted a hazy shape heading toward him. A person, a woman, but he couldn't make out her features. She seemed to float, her feet not quite touching the ground as she drew closer and closer.

"It's her?"

"Who?"

Father pointed. "It's the woman . . . Abitha."

"No one is there. You're seeing things."

The woman walked past, stopped, and began looking fretfully around.

"What are you doing here?" Father growled, but she didn't seem to hear him, her eyes seeing beyond him. Then, as though startled, she darted away.

"You shall vex me no more!" Father snarled and took off after her, but the closer he got, the dimmer she became. He leapt for her, but the instant he touched her, she vanished.

There came a jolt and the ghostly world began to crumble, to spin.

Father was falling, swirling into a storm of gray bones and dust.

The dust slowly cleared and he found himself lying on the ground in a forest, alone.

Abitha entered the village commons and finally slowed down, sparing a glance behind her to make certain that *it*, whatever *it* was, hadn't followed her into Sutton. She saw no demon, but instead Goody and Mary Dibble along with about a dozen other women heading toward her on their way to church.

Abitha quickly wiped the sweat from her brow, swatted the leaves and dirt from her ragged skirt.

"A bit of advice, Abi, dear," Goody said. "If you would leave but a bit earlier, you'd need not worry about turning up here such a sweaty mess. Do you not think so?"

The women looked her up and down, making no effort to hide their disgust at her appearance.

"Your boots, Abi," Dorthy Dodd put in. "Why, just look at them. They're filthy. It is sad."

"If you're asking me," Goody added, "that is the folly of a woman trying to take on a man's labors."

"True," Fanne Howell said. "If you kept your hand to women's work you would not be such a mess."

Others nodded adamantly.

"Aye, do you really feel it is proper?" Goody asked. "You out there plowing?"

"Well, I for one do not think so," Fanne put in.

"Nor I," said Dorthy.

The women encouraged one another, the comments hitting quick and hard as they circled Abitha, talking atop one another, giving Abitha no chance to respond.

"It does not look good upon our community."

"Yes, you are giving all the women of Sutton a bad name."

"Aye, Abi. Why must you be so stubborn? What is it you seek to prove?"

"What you're doing is a sin. Reverend Smith even said so."

"It is high time you give Wallace back his land and come in and do your duty like a respectable Christian woman."

"If you are indeed a Christian woman like you claim, that is, and not some heathen."

Abitha began to shake, felt her face flush, knew she must be scarlet.

"Aye, yours is a sin of pride. That is all."

"Indeed. Poor Wallace. Why are you doing this to him?"

Abitha balled her hands into tight fists.

"It is little more than thievery if you ask me."

"And after all he has tried to do for you."

"Mind your own houses!" Abitha cried. "You are all naught but a gaggle of clucking cunts!"

The women fell quiet, all and one, staring at her wide-eyed and slack-jawed.

"Just mind your own houses!" Abitha stormed away, nearly knocking Goody down as she pushed her way out from the circle.

Abitha entered the meetinghouse, dropping into her usual seat in the last bench next to Helen and the other servants, clutching her hands together, trying to quell her shaking.

Helen looked over, eyes full of concern. "Are you all right?" she asked in a whisper, then glanced behind as Goody and her crew marched in, all giving Abitha reproachful looks.

Abitha kept her eyes forward. *You've gone too far once again, Abi. They'll not let it go. You'll be in the stocks by noon. You know you will.*

Helen reached over and gave Abitha's hand a quick squeeze.

Abitha squeezed back, wishing she could tell Helen how much that simple gesture meant to her at this moment.

Reverend Carter took the pulpit and started the service, then one minister after another droned through their sermons. Abitha tried to concentrate, but her thoughts kept returning to the black pits that were Edward's eyes, to the long walk awaiting her back home through those dark woods, to what Goody and her crew would tell on her.

She caught movement from the corner of her eye, an odd shadow flickering over by the stove, toward the back of the meetinghouse. She did her best to keep her eyes forward, but when she noticed it growing, she turned and stared.

The shadow lengthened, stretched, then coiled, then stretched again, taking on the shape of a serpent. Abitha clamped a hand over her mouth as it began to slither, to crawl up the wall.

A sharp jab struck the back of Abitha's head. It was Deputy Harlow; he'd just thumbed her with the long pole.

Abitha started to protest, to point to the shadow, only when she looked back, it was gone. *A serpent in the house of the Lord. Jesus, please save me.*

Finally, the sermons ended and everyone stood for final prayer, after which the parishioners began to file out. Once in the yard, most of the women formed a circle around the reverend's wife, Sarah Carter. As she did every Sunday, Sarah presided over their concerns and squabbles. Abitha watched her sorting out some minor quarrel between the Pratt sisters, captivated by how commanding the woman could be. Decision rendered, all nodded unconditionally. Her word was law, at least amongst the women, but Abitha could see in their faces that it was more than that, that these women shared a deep-down respect for this rigid woman. Abitha couldn't help but feel it was Sarah, as intimidating as she could be, who kept daily life running smoothly around Sutton, even more so than Reverend Carter himself.

Someone tugged at Abitha's sleeve.

"Thank you, Abi," Helen said, and smiled coyly. "I believe your charm has done its work."

"Oh?"

Helen nodded and whispered. "Have a secret. Swear you'll not tell."

89

"I swear."

"Isaac gave me a kiss."

"Why, Helen, that is wonderful." Abitha smiled, then added, "You best be careful Goodwife Carter not find out."

Helen beamed. "He told me he hopes to marry me one day."

"I am so happy for you," Abitha said, then caught sight of Wallace, his wife, son, and daughter, all staring at her. She met Wallace's eyes and held them, wondering how any man could be so willing to throw away his own son's happiness.

Wallace headed toward Abitha.

Helen saw him and scurried off. Abitha started to follow when Wallace snatched hold of her arm, yanking her around to face him, his thick fingers biting into her flesh. He leaned over her. "You would not look so smug if you knew what lay ahead for you," he whispered. "Reverend Carter is not the end of this. You will soon learn what I mean." He shoved her away and strolled off as though not having a care in the world and rejoined his family.

They were all watching her now, not just Wallace and his family, but so many of the others, and she found no sympathy in any of their eyes, only biting looks of disdain.

Abitha rubbed her arm and turned away, suddenly wanting only to go home. *Devils at home, devil in the woods, devils at church, devils everywhere, is there no escape?* She'd no sooner finished the thought than she noticed Goody Dibble and her crew talking intently with Sarah Carter, Goody pointing repeatedly at Abitha.

When will I learn to keep my big mouth shut? Abitha thought, and started off, hoping to slip away.

"Abitha," Goodwife Carter called.

Abitha pretended not to hear.

"Abitha Williams," Goodwife Carter shouted sternly. "A word."

Abitha halted, stiffened; she didn't know if she could take a public scolding right now, not today. "I am sorry. I did not mean to be profane. It is just . . . well . . . those women, they can be so cruel. I just—"

"Come," Goodwife Carter said, leading her away. "I would speak to you in private."

She walked Abitha to the side of the meetinghouse and set her hard, firm eyes on her.

Abitha stared at the ground.

"Listen to me, Abitha. What I have to say I cannot say in front of the others."

Abitha braced herself.

"What you are trying to do is brave and it is noble and I admire you. I truly do. And I am not alone."

Abitha wasn't sure she'd heard right. "Ma'am?"

"But you are too vulnerable on all sides. Wallace has shown himself devious in the past, and I do not trust him. I believe it is about more than the land with him at this point. I fear he is out to do you harm, to ruin you if he can. And he has powerful allies in this, some men out of Hartford, Lord Mansfield and a judge, Magistrate Watson. They're pressuring Reverend Carter to back Wallace. If you cannot bring in this crop, they plan to turn your unpaid debt into servitude."

"Servitude? I do not understand."

"You will be legally indentured to Wallace. You will be his servant until such time as your debts are paid off. That could be years, Abitha."

"But . . . I thought all debt would be tied to the property."

"Wallace's debt to Mansfield doesn't affect your debt to him. It will still be owed."

"He can do that? Even if I lose the land?"

"I am afraid he can."

Abitha's heart raced. *Oh, Lord, what have I gotten myself into?*

"You should marry as soon as you may. It's your only escape of this."

"It is not so easy as that."

"Nay, I understand. One does not just pick a husband like an apple from a tree. But there are several here in great need of a wife. There is Simon Dibble. He were asking after you. Or mayhap Winifred Howell?"

Abitha tried to hide her distaste.

"I know, they're both much too old and Simon widowed twice now." Goodwife Carter sighed. "There are others, I am sure, but Wallace has made it clear to any would-be suitors that you are his business and to leave you be. None wish to cross him. And for good reason, as you well know."

His business, Abitha thought, realizing what all this truly meant, that should her farm fail, none could marry her, unless they paid her debt in full to Wallace first—then, *only* if Wallace agreed. He had her. He could make her work for him or even loan out her labors. She would all but be his slave.

Goodwife Carter shook her head and Abitha caught the woman struggling with her anger. "Lord forgive me for speaking so, but he is such a foul man. He has let greed and pride corrupt his soul. And, I hate to say this, even think it, but I fear that man is not above bloodshed. I fear he might bring grave harm upon you given the chance. You must stay vigilant, Abi, and do not travel without Edward's musket. I do hate that you are all alone out there. I would—" Goodwife Carter's eyes shifted to something behind Abitha. "Ansel Fitch, come out from there this instant."

The craggy old man slid out from behind a bush, his face flushed red, his bulbous eyes cast downward.

"You have been warned about this skulking around, about eavesdropping on folk. Now be gone before I call the reverend."

Ansel appeared offended. "I was doing no such thing! I was but looking for tracks. Devil tracks. One must always be diligent."

Goodwife Carter didn't bother with a response, just bore into him with her cold stern eyes.

Ansel withered and wandered away, grumbling beneath his breath.

"And that one," Goodwife Carter said. "He will be the ruin of us all. Spreading fear with his wicked tongue. If he truly wishes to find a devil, he need but look to himself." She returned her gaze to Abitha and her eyes softened. She sighed. "Abitha, there is not much I can do for you, but what I can, I will."

The kindness in Sarah Carter's voice was almost more than Abitha could bear. This stern woman treating her like a person, a friend even—it was all she could do not to burst into tears. "Pray for rain," Abitha said, unable to hide the quiver in her voice. "That is the only way out for me."

"Here," Goodwife Carter said. "Something for you." She pulled a bundle from her apron and handed it to Abitha. "This is not charity. Charity is for those who cannot help themselves. You are worth twice many of the men here."

Abitha took a peek. It was a goodly amount of salted fish. The tears began to flow then and she quickly wiped them away.

Sarah Carter laughed behind her hand. "A few tears are good, dear. Now all the nosy-bodies watching us will think I have given you a good tongue-lashing." She caught Abitha's hand and squeezed it. "I will pray for that rain."

Father sat up, tearing away the moss and vines growing on and over him. He searched about for the endless piles of bones but found none. He sucked in the rich fragrance of the pines and ferns, knew he must be back amongst the living. He wondered just how long he'd been away staring at that gray river? He tugged a clump of moss from his fur and concluded it had been a while indeed. *And yet still I have no answers.*

Buzzing filled his ears, and he watched several bumblebees bounce from flower to flower. He found their hum soothing, and there, at the moment, felt he could watch them forever. He drank in the scent of flowers, the sweet warm air, the sunlight flittering through the dense leaves. He plucked a flower, studied it, then crushed it in his fist. *I will know who I am.*

Father felt a presence drawing near. He climbed slowly to his feet, brushing the dirt and bugs from his fur as the tread of feet drew steadily closer.

He noticed a wide trail, crept up to it, hid behind a massive oak, and waited.

She came around the far bend, moving at a steady clip, her eyes darting in all directions.

It's her . . . Abitha.

As she approached, he sensed her dread, her heart drumming in her chest, then smelled her blood, and his hunger returned, swept over him, all but overwhelming him.

She drew even, and he let loose a low snarl.

Abitha snapped her head his way, staring wide-eyed into the woods, then dashed off, running away up the trail.

Father stepped out onto the path, watched her disappear around the far bend. He bared his fangs and started after her, then stopped. *What was that?* He cocked his head, listening.

He waited.

It came again. A yowl, that of a beast, from deep back in the woods. The pitiful sound hit him hard, set his heart to racing, and he found himself torn as to which way to go. He glanced back and forth from the trail to the woods.

There came a sound like distant thunder, followed by another yowl full of pain and anguish.

Father snarled and dashed into the forest, heading toward the yowl at a full gallop, leaping over logs and streams as he flew through the trees. He crested a rise and there, just at the bottom of the slope, one of the new people, a man. He carried a long metal weapon, smoke drifting from the end of its barrel.

Several wolves stood growling, guarding a den on the far side of the bank, another lying on the ground, bleeding from a large hole in its side, its breath coming fast and shallow.

The man jammed a rod down the barrel of his weapon, shouldered it, and, to Father's dismay, sent a blast of thunder and sparks toward the wolves. There came a yelp and another of the wolves fell.

"No!" Father snarled.

The man spun, saw him, his eyes going wide. He jammed a load into the barrel as fast as his shaking hands could move.

Father came for the man, tearing straight through the dense brush and briars, coming at a full gallop.

The man brought the weapon level and fired.

Father felt something slap into his chest, spinning him, knocking him off his feet. He touched the spot where he'd been hit, looked at the black blood, then at the man.

"Devil!" the man cried, and began reloading.

Father pushed to his feet, clomping toward the man.

The man fumbled the load, screamed, and swung the weapon. Father knocked it aside, leaping upon him, clawing and tearing, driving the man to the ground. Father shoved his snout beneath the man's chin, locking his teeth on the man's throat and tearing it open. Hot blood spurted into his mouth and still he didn't stop, wouldn't, allowing the blood to take him, biting and tearing, shredding the man wide open, unleashing all his rage, his misery and anguish. Drinking the blood, the sweet, sweet blood, feeling it course through his body, his heart. He let out a moan, drinking and slurping, only stopping when there was no more blood to drink.

Father sat up, panting and dripping in gore. He felt a slight sting on his chest where the man had shot him, touched the wound. It was all but healed.

He heard a snarl, wiped the blood from his muzzle along his forearm, and looked about. The wolves were creeping over, their ears back, growling.

Father tore a strip of flesh from the dead man and held it out.

A she-wolf, the largest of the pack, crept closer, closer, her hackles up, her lips peeled, snarling. She snatched the meat away, devoured it.

When she returned, Father extended his hand. The she-wolf sniffed it and her fur settled, her ears sat up. She began licking Father's fingers.

The rest of the pack shuffled up, tails down submissively, as one by one, Father fed them strips of the man's flesh. A sense of rightness flooded over him and he realized how good it felt to save them from the man, that some part of him craved this, needed it. *Was Forest speaking the truth? Is this indeed who I truly am then? The guardian . . . the slayer? Is it blood that will heal me?*

"Lewis," someone called from far away.

Father and the wolves all looked in the direction of the sound.

Again, this time closer. "Lewis!"

The wolves began to growl.

"Lewis! Where are you?" Another man crested the rise, a much younger man. He spotted the wolves, then the bloody corpse, then Father. "Oh, God!" he cried, then turned and ran.

Father stood up, started after the youth, and the wolves followed. He began to run, to gallop, and the wolves ran with him. Father topped the rise, spotted the young man fleeing, let loose a howl, and the pack howled with him.

The young man glanced back, his face one of utter terror. He screamed, threw aside his sack, his weapon, lowered his head, and dashed headlong through the forest, barreling through the brambles.

The scream ignited Father's pulse. He grinned, letting the blood take him.

Father chased the youth over one hill and down another, catching up with him in a wide meadow. He did not pounce, not yet, but ran alongside of the youth, savoring the thrill of the hunt as the wolves ran with him. And there, in that moment, he felt whole, complete.

"Yes," he whispered. "This is what I am. The father of the wild things, the warder, the hunter, the slayer!"

The young man saw Father's dreadful grin and screamed, his eyes bulging as he tried to run even faster.

The youth stumbled, went sprawling, and Father and the wolves encircled him.

The youth got to his knees, clasped his hands tightly together before him. "Oh, God, Jesus, please save me!"

Father barely heard the youth over his drumming pulse, drinking in the smell of hot sweat, blood, and fear. He grabbed the young man by the hair, lifted him to his feet.

"I beg of you. Spare me, Satan! Spare me!"

Father thrust his snout into the youth's neck and tore open his throat. Drinking long and deep as the blood gushed into his mouth, coursed down his neck and chest. He let him go and the youth collapsed to the ground, twitching and jerking, clutching the terrible wound.

Father met the hungry eyes of the wolves, nodded, and they set upon the youth, tearing into him, finishing him.

Father watched them feed and again felt that overwhelming sense of rightness. "I am the slayer."

He thrust back his head and howled. The wolves joined him, the forest ringing for miles with their mournful call.

Father started away, and the wolves followed. He began to run, to gallop, and the wolves raced with him through the woods.

95

He saw the first stars above through the trees, spotted the waning moon, and it was not long before the ghosts began to appear, joining them as they ran, their howls melding together, creating a symphony of the living and the dead.

Father crested a ridge and spotted flickering lights in the valley below, made out the shapes of buildings. He stopped, stared. *The new people,* he thought, and felt the hunger return. "I am the slayer."

It was late July, the summer heat at its peak, and Wallace sat in Lord Mansfield's office, glad to be out of the hot sun. Magistrate Watson sat across from him, fanning his round moist face with a hand fan.

"And there is no chance Abitha can bring in that corn?" Lord Mansfield asked from behind his desk.

"None," Wallace said with no hesitation. "I rode by just last week. As you well know we've had next to no rain this summer. . . . The heat has dried up most of her crop. Even if it were to start raining and the small bit left were to yield, I can assure you, it would not bear nearly enough."

Lord Mansfield leaned back, looking relieved. "It appears the good Lord no more approves of this woman's doings than do we."

"She is wretched," Wallace said. "Appears half-starved, gaunt, with dark circles under her eyes. Has taken on too much . . . used herself up." Wallace thought of how she'd looked toiling in that hot sun, drenched in sweat, her hair hanging down into her face, matted and tangled, wearing only a soiled blouse and skirt, no bonnet or shoes, her feet filthy. "Any sane person could see it is a lost cause. But I am afraid her mind is going. I watched her trying to water the field one pail at a time."

The men exchanged stunned looks.

"Poor creature, she has indeed lost her way," Lord Mansfield said.

"She has not even made it to church now for many a Sunday."

"What?" Magistrate Watson gasped. "How is that?"

"Reverend Carter, he has taken pity on her. Has given her leave due to hardship."

"That man has no pity," the magistrate said. "I grant you he is doing this to spite us."

"I can tell you, neither her nor his actions sit well with the village. They fear such heresy will lead to God turning His back on us. There are those who have been unhappy with him for a long time. There is even some talk of ousting him from the village."

"I for one would be glad to see that happen," the magistrate added.

"Well," Lord Mansfield said. "It sounds as though we need no longer worry about the reverend or this Abitha Williams. No, this is a simple matter now; since it is obvious Abitha will fail to make her payment, we need only wait. So here, let us do this, let us extend the deadline. So long as you have the deed to Edward's acres to me by the end of October, then all is as we originally agreed. What say you to that?"

It took a moment for Wallace to speak. "I . . . I say bless you, sir. God bless you."

Lord Mansfield smiled and extended his hand.

Wallace took it and the two men shook heartily.

The doe dashed down into the canyon, racing to make it out of the gully ahead of her pursuers, not knowing her way was already cut off. She spotted three wolves coming for her, kicked, spun, tried to dart up the embankment, only to lose her footing. Before she could find her feet, Father was there—a hard strike to the side of her head, snapping her neck.

The wolves piled on, snarling and snapping as they tore the animal apart, fighting for the choicest morsels.

Father stepped forward and the wolves withdrew, growling, baring their bloody teeth. Father jabbed his hand into the doe's mangled underbelly, forcing his hand up into her chest, probing until he found what he wanted, what he needed. He tore out her heart, held it above his face, and squeezed the blood into his mouth.

Father stepped away, letting the wolves return to their feast. He sat down, his back against a tree, sucking in the smell of blood and gore as the wolves devoured the doe. He closed his eyes and waited for the blood to push away the shadows, the pain. And for a moment it did, and for a moment Father felt whole. He saw visions of a wild forest with beasts and wildfolk frolicking about. He sucked in a breath, caught the faintest whiff of honeysuckle. He nodded, a ghost of a smile on his face, then, there—a black spot on the edge of his vision, another, another, wiggling. The spiders came crawling back and with them the pain. "No!" Father cried, and opened his eyes.

The wolves stared at him, shifting nervously from paw to paw.

"How long has it been?" he asked them. "How long have we been running together, hunting, slaying, drinking the blood of our kills?"

They of course didn't answer, couldn't, just stared at him.

Father felt sure the moon was full when he'd met them, and it was almost full again. *A month then, and still the spiders will not leave me be.* Another wave of pain hit him, that feeling of being fractured, of being torn in two. He winced, climbed to his feet holding his head, began to stumble away, walking aimlessly through the woods.

The she-wolf broke from the pack and followed him.

Father came across a wide path. He studied the deep ruts. "It is one of theirs, isn't it? One of the new people's roads."

The she-wolf looked down the road, sniffed—growled.

"Do you think Forest might have been right after all? That it is *their* blood I need . . . the people."

Father followed the road, the big wolf trotting along beside him, and it wasn't long before he smelled them—their sweat, their rubbish, their waste. The smell growing, gradually becoming overbearing.

The she-wolf sat down, would go no farther. Father sensed her fear, her hatred of the people, much like that of the wildfolk.

"Do not fear, wolf, today is *their* day to bleed." Father continued on his own until he spied rooftops. He stopped at the forest's edge, studying the jagged wall built from felled trees. He heard voices coming toward him and slid back into the brush as a grayed-haired woman led a small child past. The woman carried a pail, and when she reached the thicket, set it down, started picking blackberries and dropping them in.

The old woman drifted deeper into the bushes, loading the berries into her apron as she went, leaving the boy, a child of maybe three years of age, alone by the pail.

Father left the brush, heading for the boy, and with each step felt his pulse quicken, his hunger grow, the bloodlust becoming its own animal.

The boy spotted Father, staring at him, his face covered in berry juice. Father expected the child to begin shrieking, but to his surprise the child smiled.

Father hesitated.

"Baa-baa," the boy called, and pointed at Father. "Baa-baa."

"Baa-baa?" Father said.

The boy's eyes lit up and he giggled. "Baa-baa." He scooped up a handful of the berries and held them out to Father.

Seeing this simple act pricked something in Father's memory. He tried to focus, to find it, but needed more, just a bit more. He extended his hand and the boy set the berries in his palm. The moment the berries touched Father's flesh, the memory bloomed—men and women dressed in buckskin kneeling before him. They offered him berries, circlets of flowers, and necklaces made of beads.

"Jarret," someone called, and the scene began to slip away.

"No," Father growled, struggling to hold onto the vision, to see more.

"Jarret, fetch me that bucket."

Father blinked, the vision gone, but not the feeling in his heart. *What is it?* he wondered. Not the thrill of the hunt, or the rapture of blood, but something deep, an odd exaltation, all so familiar. He looked again at the berries in his hand.

"Jarret!" An old woman came out of the thicket carrying a load of berries in her folded apron. "What is wrong with you, child? Did you—"

She spotted Father, gasped, her eyes bulging, stumbled back, falling into the thicket, spilling berries everywhere. She pointed one shaking finger at Father. "Satan!"

The little boy glanced anxiously back and forth between them.

Father crushed the berries he'd been holding, watched the dark pulp drip from his hand as the good feeling drained from his heart.

The woman struggled to right herself, to free herself of the vines, not taking her wild, wide eyes off him. She began gasping, wheezing, trying to suck air into her lungs.

She knows me, Father thought. *How is it that she knows me?*

He stepped to her and she managed to suck in enough air to let loose a loud shriek.

Father seized her throat. "Stop with that now, or I'll choke the life from your bones."

She hushed.

"Tell me, who am I?"

"W . . . what?" she stammered, quivering uncontrollably.

"Who am I?"

"Why . . . the Devil, of course," she blubbered. "You are Satan. Please do not kill me. Please, I beg of you."

"Satan? What is Satan? Is Satan the slayer?"

She shook her head, confused.

He tightened his grip on her throat. "What is Satan?"

"You! *You are!*" she sobbed, then began coughing, making a horrible retching sound. She suddenly arched her back, began clutching and clawing at her chest.

Father released her, unsure what was happening.

Her face turned red, then purple, the veins bulging from her neck and forehead, her eyes rolling into her head. She convulsed rapidly, then fell back, just collapsed and lay there unmoving.

Father realized the woman's heart had quit. He let out a long, frustrated sigh, then just sat there staring at her.

Nothing, I feel nothing. Where is my hunger now, my lust for blood? Death, only death. Death has no answers. He looked toward the timber fortifications, listened, reached for the people there, felt nothing. *There are no answers here. These people's souls do not sing.* He thought of Abitha, of the connection when he'd touched her. *There's something between us. I know not what, but there is something.*

He heard someone crying, turned to see the little boy, tears rolling down his face.

Father stood, put his hand out to the boy.

The boy stepped back, terrified.

"Baa-baa," Father hissed, and the boy fled away toward the village.

Father picked up the pail of berries and wandered into the woods. He found the road again, but the wolf was gone. Father began to walk, heading west, back to the wildfolk and Pawpaw, back to the small woman who could open the doors to his soul.

CHAPTER 5

Abitha stumbled back up the slope toward the well carrying a water bucket. She used to carry two at a time, but no longer; she was too weak. She paused in the shade of the barn, grateful to escape the blazing midsummer sun even for a moment. She used to scan the sky a hundred times a day searching for signs of rain; she'd stopped doing that weeks ago.

She wiped the sweat from her brow and pushed herself on. Her foot caught in a rut and she stumbled. She heard it then, the tittering, like small children laughing at her, like the day that devil had touched her. For weeks after that incident she'd occasionally heard them, only faintly, but the weaker she felt, the hazier her mind, the clearer the sound became—mostly near the forest. She looked for them, the opossum, the raven, the fish. Knew they were there, waiting, but for what? At first, they'd terrified her, but as the drought dried up her crops, as she felt her sanity melting away, as October approached and so did the day Wallace and the sheriff would come and take her into servitude, these spooks and their taunts just became one more part of her daily torment.

She picked up the wooden bucket, crawled to her feet, and continued on to the well, because that is what she did, all day, every day, the only thing she could do: one pail of water at a time, up and down the rows, all day long, trying to keep the crop alive.

She reached the well, wishing for the hundred thousandth time that it had been dug closer to the field, and hooked the bucket to the rope. She lowered the bucket with the crank until a small splash echoed back up to her. She waited a moment for the bucket to sink, then began to slowly crank the water-laden pail back up. The pulley creaked as she turned the handle, over and over and over.

She used to be able to roll it up in one go, but now she had to stop and rest after every eight or nine cranks. She paused, catching her breath, fearful for the first time that she might not have the strength to retrieve the bucket at all. She was down to two chickens, so had had only an egg this morning at dawn, nothing since, and it was now well past noon. Her hands felt numb, her head light, but the bucket was almost to the top.

"Keep going, Abi," she whispered, sucking in a breath and pressing on, putting her weight into it.

She heard it again, the tittering, then a giggle; it sounded as though it were in the well. There came a tug on the rope, followed by a loud pop, and the crank suddenly lost resistance, spun, sending her to the ground. She heard the sound of the pail banging against the sides of the well as it plunged back down, then a splash, followed by another of those eerie giggles.

"Oh no!" she cried, pulling herself back to her feet. She grabbed the crank, gave it a turn, and to her horror, there was no weight, no resistance at all. She stared at the lever and gasped—the rope had come off the pulley and both the bucket and the entire length of rope had fallen into the well.

She leaned over the edge of the well, staring down into its depths, and saw no sign of the rope or bucket, only darkness. She had only one other rope, and it was worn and frayed and not nearly long enough—and no means to buy another. She glanced at the fields, at the withered crops, and the magnitude of what had just happened began to sink in. *There'll be no more water . . . none.*

Her cracked lips began to tremble. "Oh, God. Why do You vex me so?" She stared at the few rows of corn still clinging to life, her head swimming in the heat. *Why am I still doing this? I've already lost. Just too stubborn and stupid to admit it.*

She tugged herself up onto the lip of the well, leaning over, staring into the damp darkness. *How sweet,* she thought, *to be down there in that cold, clear water.* She leaned farther, sucking in the smell of the wetness, the blood rushing into her head and making her dizzy. Her vision began to blur.

Let go, she thought. *Just a little farther and all is done. And if the fall does not kill me, what then?* She smiled savagely. *Then I will die in the wet and cold, my body slowly going numb.* It sounded good, so much better than dying of thirst, or starving, or working herself to death for nothing. *And my rotting body will spoil the well for Wallace.* She managed a weak laugh, little more than a croak. *He will have to dig another far from here.*

She leaned a little farther, teetering, held back only by her thighs and fingertips.

"Let go," she whispered. "Let go. Let go. Let go." She realized another voice had joined her chant. She saw a fish floating far down in the wet darkness. It began slowly swimming up toward her. She recognized it, the one from the barn, the one with the face of a child. Its small, dark eyes reached into hers. *"Let go,"* it sang to her. *"Let go."*

Her hand slipped and she slid forward.

"No!" she cried, clawing for the well post. She caught hold, almost slipped, then grasped it firmly, tugging herself back from the edge.

She rolled to the ground, her cheek against the earth, panting, each harsh breath blowing up the dry dirt. She felt on the verge of fainting, saw something moving down by the barn, a shadowy shape. It walked toward her. She fought to stay awake. It came closer and closer, until it stood looking down at her. Its form was blurry, but she had no trouble making out its long twisting horns.

"Vex me no more, Slewfoot," she mumbled as the world spun away into blackness.

A meow.

Abitha felt soft fur rubbing against her face. She opened her eyes, blinked. Booka sat staring at her.

A cool breeze blew.

Abitha sat up, tried to steady herself; her head felt groggy. The day was edging toward dusk, the sky overcast. It wasn't raining, but there was a slight mist on the wind. It felt like heaven to her. She wondered what she was doing on the ground, started to get up, then saw it—the bucket.

She rubbed her eyes; the bucket was still there. *But . . . it fell in the well.* She swooned. *Mayhap I dreamed that. Mayhap I am still dreaming.* Then she saw another bucket. *Two buckets?* She got a hand on the new bucket; it was real and it was heavy. She tugged it over, peered in, and then knew she was dreaming, because the bucket was full of wild berries.

She licked her parched lips and plucked out one of the blackberries. It was plump and ripe and smelled luscious, not like the dried-up ones growing along the edge of the cornfield. She thrust it into her mouth. The berry burst between her teeth—sweet and succulent. Abitha let out a weak moan, grabbed another, another, then a handful, until she could push no more into her mouth. She closed her eyes, chewing, swallowing, savoring the sensation of the sweet juice flowing down her throat, satiating her burning thirst.

Her mind began to clear and the world swam back into focus. She felt her strength returning. She started to grab another handful of fruit, stopped. She wiped the juice from her lips and chin, considered the wet stains on her hands. *I am not dreaming. This is real.*

She spotted the rope. It was soaked and lay in a puddle next to the well. It all came back to her, the rope and bucket falling into the well. Someone had just pulled it out. *Who?* she wondered. But she *knew.*

Abitha looked to the barn.

It was there—a shadow standing within the shadows.

A chill seized her; the very air felt alive.

She climbed to her feet, walked to the porch, and retrieved her musket. She checked the primer. "This is my farm," she said beneath her breath and slowly advanced on the barn.

Abitha stopped at the entrance, keeping the musket leveled at the shadow. *It was in the last stall.*

"What do you want?" Abitha asked.

The shape shifted, but didn't answer.

She didn't sense the anger, the malice, not like before, but she felt its need, its hunger, burning off it like a fever.

"What do you want?" she asked again.

It answered in a voice that was soft and low. "Your help, Abitha."

Hearing it speak her name sent a shiver through her. "Who are you?"

The shadow slid out from the other shadows, just a silhouette against the open back of the barn, but she could see that it had the body of a shaggy goat, only it was walking on its hinds legs. Its arms and hands were more like those of a person. She couldn't make out its face, only the glint of its eyes and the horns twisting upward.

"I am not sure."

"What do you want?"

"Answers."

"There is naught for you here. Now, please leave me be."

"I believe *you* can help me." He stepped forward and Abitha fell back a step.

"Why would I do that?"

"Because I might grow angry and kill you if you do not."

Abitha took another step backward.

"I am hoping you can help me see," he said, his voice growing surly. "That is all. Is that so much?"

"See? See what?"

"I know not," he growled. "That is what I am trying to find out."

She shook her head, fell back another step. "I have naught for you."

His nostrils flared. "Why . . . why—" His voice cracked. "Why will no one help me?" He spun away from her and stormed from the barn.

Abitha lowered her musket and watched him go.

He stopped at the edge of the cornfield, looked back at her, and there in the fading light, she saw his face. It was neither goat nor human, but something in between. He didn't appear wicked, like she expected, but maybe sad and a bit lost. He shot her a grave look, then continued away, disappearing into the forest.

Abitha's hands began to tremble. She clutched the fence to steady herself.

Booka leapt up onto the rail and began to rub against her hand.

She stroked the cat. "What just happened, Booka?"

Abitha awoke in her bed, glad to see it was almost dawn. She'd tossed through most of the night, her dreams haunted not by serpents this time, but by horned shadows. Her cat lay curled up next to her. "Am I going mad, Booka?"

She slid from bed and dressed—just her skirt, apron, and blouse. She'd given up on any effort beyond that. She walked to the door, but before opening it, she touched the chain of braids. *Mother, what is happening to me?*

Abitha opened the door, walked out onto the porch in her bare feet, and scanned the barn, the yard, and the field. She found no signs of *him*. She wanted to believe him, the beast, was all in her head, because a touch of madness was better than the Devil living in your barn. Then she spied the bucket of fruit on the porch. *That's not where I left it.*

She plucked out a large blackberry, put it to her nose, sucking in the sweet scent. She opened her mouth, then hesitated.

Is this a trap? she wondered. *Will accepting a gift from a demon give it dominion over my soul?* She heard her father's shrill cry. *"Dare not take food from the hand of the Devil! It is a sin!"* Then her mother's strong voice. *"It would be a sin to let it go to waste. You need the food . . . eat it."*

Abitha nodded. "Lord, if this be a sin, please forgive me." She ate the berry; she ate them all.

The chickens gave her two eggs that morning, so between the berries and the eggs she had much more energy than usual. She laid the musket on the porch within easy reach and set to work reattaching the rope to the pulley, quickly getting it back in operation.

The sky was cloudy, the air warm but with a breeze, yet still no rain. With food in her stomach and the cooler weather, her mind felt clear for the first time in weeks. She tried to tally the stalks that might survive. Even with rain, there wouldn't be near enough. Still, she couldn't quit, because even if she lost the farm, she needed every ear of corn to pay down her debt to Wallace. Even a quarter crop might mean a year off her servitude. *And if it really comes to that, will any of it matter? Probably not,* she thought, *because I will never serve that man.*

She spent the morning the same way she'd spent every morning for the past several weeks, lugging water from the well to the corn. But now, each trip past the barn, she thought of *him.* The odd way he spoke. *What is he? Is he the Devil? Why would the Devil need help from me?* She heard her father's voice. *"Because your name is in his book."* Abitha shuddered.

She kept an eye out for him in the shadows of the barn and at the edge of the forest, keeping the musket close at all times.

The horned beast reappeared late that afternoon, just as the shadows began to grow long. She felt him near as she watered the lower rows and spotted him just a few yards away at the forest's edge, sitting on a stump. She blinked, took a moment to make sure she was really seeing him.

"Hello, Abitha."

"Hello," she replied, glancing back to the musket.

He stood and stepped from the shadows, looked at her with his strange long face, that odd mix of human and beastly features. Yet he wasn't hideous or ugly; she actually found there to be a sort of nobility about him. Especially his eyes, they were somewhat feminine and feline, silver, and shone with a light from within.

"Will you try and help me?"

"Who are you?" she asked, struggling to keep her voice steady. "I will answer your question once you tell me who you are."

"I am called Father."

"Are you Satan?"

"Satan? Again, that name!"

She heard his agitation returning.

"What is this Satan?"

"Why do you torment me so?" Abi asked. "What is it I have done?"

He appeared surprised and genuinely confused. "Torment you? Why, it is you that torments me!"

"What?" she scoffed. "You tried to kill me in the barn."

"If I had wanted to kill you, you would be dead."

"Why did you kill my goat? Why did you *murder* my husband?"

His brows cinched and she sensed his distress.

"I did not do those things."

"You did."

"No. No, I did not," he growled.

"You attacked me. This I know."

He held her eyes for a moment, then looked to the ground. "Yes," he admitted, the fire draining from his voice. "But it was not me. I mean it was, but it was *not*." He shook his head. "I did it because I did not know who I was then."

"Who are you now, then?"

He let out a long breath. "That . . . is what I am trying to understand." His emotions flowed into her along with his words, and she felt his loneliness, his despair. "I have been trying to remember . . . but I need help."

"Well, start with what you *do* remember. Tell me one thing of your past."

He closed his eyes, his brows tightened. "Chaos, so many disconnected pieces. I see sunlight, it is warm, it is good."

Abitha felt it too, the warmth; it was as though his thoughts were pushing into hers. She shut her eyes and saw a blurry image of the sun, only dark orange and impossibly large.

"I am running with the beasts," he said.

She saw this too, felt the joy of running un-winded for as long as the day with all manner of beasts, some she recognized, others she didn't, the song of their wild cries in her ears. Abitha realized she was smiling. Then blood, screams of beasts, then screams of men and women and children. Abitha let out a cry, opened her eyes.

107

His face was in torment, a growl came from deep in his throat. He shook his head back and forth as though trying to dislodge a stinging bee. "No. *No!*"

He opened his eyes, let out a long, sad groan. He was shaking. "It's the same . . . each time I try and look into my past . . . the blood, the death . . . it gets in the way. I cannot see around it to who I am . . . to who I was."

"Unless blood and death *is* who you are."

"No!" he snarled. "No, there is more to me. I know it. I have seen it."

He stood, began to pace. She could see him struggling to control his temper, clenching and unclenching his fist. He sucked in a deep breath, let it out slow. "I need help understanding my place in this world I have awakened into. Is that too much to ask?" He paused. "Perhaps if you help me, I can help you?" He set his piercing eyes on her, peered into her. "What is it that you want, Abitha? That man, that Wallace. Would you like me to kill him?"

Her blood chilled. She tensed. Wasn't that just the way of demons, offering gifts and favors in return for . . . *what*? And this—offering to murder a man? How many sermons had she sat through on the temptations of Lucifer?

"What have I said now?" he asked.

"Is this some trick?"

"Trick? What kind of trick?" he asked, his nostrils flaring.

"Some game for my soul?"

"Your soul? I do not want your soul. What would I do with your soul?" He seemed genuinely perplexed. "What must I do to convince you to help me?"

"How can you expect this of me . . . to just forget that you killed my husband and trust you? It is too much."

"*That* again!" His voice deepened and she sensed his rage simmering. "I tell you it was not how you say." He stepped away from her. "If I could undo this thing I would. I cannot." His anger melted into despair. She felt it in the air and was struck by how human his face was at that moment. "You do not understand. How could you? I am a fool for trying to talk to you." He clenched his hands and stormed away once more, disappearing into the forest.

She didn't see him the next day, but she did sense him; his brooding bitterness hung in the air, becoming palpable anytime she neared the forest.

She paused in her work and stared into the trees, wondered how she was supposed to carry on with the very Devil at her doorstep, then she wondered why she kept insisting he was the Devil. Was it because he had horns and hooves? Had her mother not taught her that there were many spirits living in the forest—some kindly, others wicked? Her mother spoke that the church claimed them all to be devils, but that these spirits were here long before Christianity arrived. Abitha thought how hurt, lost, and confused he seemed, and that didn't strike her as the Devil she'd heard so much about.

Why, he could be a forest god, or some long-lost cousin to the fae, mayhap an elf or goblin, or some unruly soul lost between worlds. She considered this and decided regardless, she needed to find a way to drive him off, some ward or spell of protection, something other than ash and salt. She wiped the sweat from her brow. *But do I dare risk provoking him further? Is he not surly enough? Then what? Do I just lie down and give myself over to him?* She shook her head and tried to recall more of her mother's ways.

Her mother had many rituals, spells, and offerings for these haunts and mystical beings, some meant to ward away the wicked, some to draw in the kindly, and others just to keep impish spirits content. Abitha remembered her mother putting out milk to pacify the wee folk. She'd said if she didn't, they'd become peevish and get up to terrible mischief. Abitha recalled offerings of sweets and sometimes a tiny bracelet or necklace made from flowers, beads, and hair. Her mother adding that it didn't matter so much what it was, but that you were paying them tribute, that spirits and fairy folk were often a haughty pompous lot who just needed to feel important.

Mayhap if I cannot drive him away, I can at least appease him, pacify his tortured soul. She figured it wouldn't hurt to try, then recalled his offer to kill Wallace and wondered at that, as she didn't remember spirits killing anyone back in England. *Well, if I cannot drive him away, if I cannot give him the answers he seeks, then what other choice is left?*

She spent that evening weaving a crown of fresh flowers, dried corn, and a lock of her hair. She also cooked up a small batch of honeycomb brittle, made from Edward's honey.

Come morning, Abitha brought her gifts down to the edge of the cornfield and waited.

She sensed him, sensed his dark mood. *Am I mad? Making an offering to a demon? What good can come of this?*

She spotted a shape farther down field and gasped. It was Edward, there in the trees. His face was obscured by shadows so she couldn't make out his features, but she could see that he was staring into the woods, toward the cave.

"Edward," she whispered, taking a timid step toward him. "What is it? What do you know?" She held up the gifts in her hands. "Is this right? Will this help set you free? Or am I condemning the both of us?" She took another step. "Tell me, Edward. I know not what else to do."

He started to fade.

"No, Edward, do not go!" She started toward him, but with each step he faded until he was gone, nothing, not so much as a footprint.

"Do not leave me," she cried, fighting back the tears. She dropped to her knees and touched the ground where he'd stood. "Edward . . . I cannot do this alone."

Abitha stayed there on her knees, looking back and forth between the cabin and the woods, winding the lock of her hair tighter and tighter around her finger, biting her lip so hard that she tasted blood. Finally, she stood, clutching the gifts to her chest. "Jesus, forgive me," she said, and headed into the woods.

"Hello," she called. No response, but she felt the horned beast near. She moved farther into the dense trees and spotted the creature sitting on a boulder with his back to her like a sulking child.

She sucked in a breath, tried to steady herself, and walked over to him.

He did not turn.

"I have brought you something," she said.

He *did* turn at that, slowly, his eyes falling on the folded napkin in her hand.

"I have a gift. May I give it to you?"

His strange, somewhat human, somewhat beastly face appeared uncertain, his silver eyes narrowing suspiciously. "A gift?"

She unwrapped the napkin, revealing the brittle, laid it before him.

He stared at it, and at first she thought him afraid, then maybe angry, his brow cinching so. Slowly he reached down and picked up one of the candies. He sniffed it, then bit it, just a nibble, closing his eyes as he chewed. He took another bite, then ate it, then both of the others.

"They are good?" she asked.

He nodded.

Encouraged, Abitha held up the crown. "And this."

He cocked his head. "What is this?"

"A crown . . . for you." She held it out. "May I?"

He pondered this for a moment and she felt sure he would refuse, but finally he made a slight nod.

Abitha noticed her hands were trembling. *I have truly gone mad*, she thought, and stepped forward until she stood directly before him. "It sits atop your head."

He tilted his head forward and Abitha pushed the crown over his horns, sliding it down until it rested atop his large goat ears. Her fingers lingered for a moment on his fur, wanting to know he had substance, that he was real. His fur was soft and smelled of earth and leaves.

She stood back, trying to come up with something to say. "You . . . you look gallant and noble . . . like a lord of the forest."

"Do I?" He touched the crown, staring at her with his silver eyes. "A gift, an offering . . . like the berries from the boy in the village." He sucked in a deep chestful of air and she sensed his pleasure. "Yes. I know this."

The air began to stir and Abitha felt tingling in her fingers where she'd touched him.

He let out a gasp. "Do you see them?"

The leaves started to swirl and she heard voices, whispers on the wind, then chanting.

"Do you see them?" he growled.

Abitha stepped back and he grabbed her, snatching hold of her wrist. When he did her eyes rolled upward in their sockets and she *did* see them. People giving him circlets of flowers and necklaces made of beads. She could barely make out the people, mostly blurry shapes, thought maybe they were natives.

"I know this!" he cried, his voice now alive, wild with excitement. "Yes. I know what we must do!" He shook her and the vision faded, the forest returned, but the spectral shapes of the people remained, dancing about them.

He leapt up, tugging, all but dragging her along. His grip hurting her wrist as he led her out of the woods and into the field, into the morning light.

"What is it you most need?" he asked.

"What . . . I do not—"

"The corn. You need the corn, yes?"

"Aye."

"You have made your offering to me. Now ask me for the corn."

What is going on? she thought. *What bargain have I struck?*

He entered a row of dried-up cornstalks, knelt, then shoved her hand into the sandy dirt at the base of a shriveled stalk. He pressed his palm atop hers, pinning it there.

"Now, do it, before the moment is past!" he shouted. *"Now!"*

"Give me corn."

"It is not enough. You must mean it!" He pressed harder, hurting her hand.

"Give me corn!" she cried.

"It must come from your heart!"

111

"Corn!" she cried. "Give me corn, damn you! *Give me corn!*"

"There!" he cried. "Do you feel that?"

And she did, a pulse coming up from the ground, flowing into her hand, their hands, up her arm, into her chest. She felt his heartbeat—it fell in rhythm with hers, then with the pulse, all joined together, all beating as one.

"Oh, God," she cried as the sweet sensation filled her up.

He began to hum, then chant, talking to the earth, to the corn, more sounds than words. The chant found a rhythm, matching their heartbeat, turning into a song. The ghosts began circling them, chanting and dancing to the rhythm.

Abitha realized she was chanting along, the strange sounds spilling from her lips, somehow familiar and comforting. The pulse continued to pump through her, gaining intensity until she felt part of it, felt one with him, with the ghosts, with the earth . . . *the corn!*

She could feel the corn's need, its desperation to live, as though it were crying out to her, begging her to feed it.

She did.

She simply channeled the pulse as one would a stream, as though it were a perfectly normal, natural thing to do, no different than breathing. The magic flowed onto the plant, coursing over it and through it. The stalk sucking it up as though starving for it.

The cornstalk began to quiver, then to hum, and Abitha gasped as the stalk turned green before her very eyes, then it grew tall, and an ear of corn sprouted, followed by another and another. The air was suddenly saturated with the smell of pollen and nectar.

Abitha burst into tears. *Oh, God,* she thought, *I want this. How I want this. God save me, I want this!*

He crawled on his hands and knees to the next stalk, dragging Abitha along, his song taking on volume. And again, Abitha channeled the pulse into the plant, again the stalk flourished, and so did the next and the next. They continued until over two dozen magnificent stalks of corn stood swaying in the breeze.

He released her and she moaned as the pulse slipped away. *More,* she thought. *Give me more!* She fell over, clutching her breast, trying to make herself breathe.

He collapsed next to her, his chest heaving.

The song faded and the ghosts began to drift away.

He smiled at her, positively beamed. "Abitha . . . look what we did!" He seemed as amazed as she did. "Look!"

Abitha couldn't stop staring. There must have been forty ears of corn where there'd been none.

"It felt good . . . right," he said. "I believe this is what I am meant to be!" He grabbed her hand, but gently this time, holding it as though precious. "Praise you, sweet creature. You have released me."

Abitha watched the ghosts drift from the field, until there was only one left, standing alone by the edge of the forest. It was Edward, staring at her with empty eyes. *What have I done, Edward?*

Forest tore off an ear of corn, stalked into the woods. He found Sky and Creek.

"Where is he?"

The two spirits nodded toward the cave, then fell in behind Forest as he stomped onward.

Forest spotted Father sitting upon one of the standing stones, his eyes distant and far away.

"What is this?" Forest demanded, jabbing the ear of corn at Father.

"It is corn."

"You were to drive them away. Instead you are feeding them! Feeding the very ones who would destroy Pawpaw!" Forest threw the corn on the ground at Father's feet.

Father picked it up, admired it. "I did this," he said proudly. "I made the corn grow."

"First you run away," Forest spat. "Abandoned us. Now you betray us . . . betray Pawpaw! Why?"

Sky and Creek nodded along.

"Perhaps you have it wrong, perhaps this woman Abitha can help us all. Have you considered that?"

"We have tried to befriend them before. It never works. They always want more. More and more until there is nothing left for us."

"Why did you not tell me I could make the corn grow?" Father asked, his voice growing stern. "If I am what you say, a slayer, then why is it I have this great gift of life?"

"You are the guardian of the wilderness. There is much you are capable of. And yes, at times you are a healer, but this is not one of those times. Now is the time for blood."

Father touched his crown of flowers. "This has made me feel more alive than slaughter. It touched something deep within." He thumped his chest. "Something primal, something pure." He held up the corn. "I want more of this. To feel the magic of life flowing through me. Filling me up."

"Listen, please hear me. The magic you are using, it flows through the earth . . . a precious, fragile thing. Like a small underground spring. Pawpaw needs every drop to grow, and you, you are stealing it! And for what? For who? For that woman? To feed the very ones that are killing this magic!"

Forest scrambled up the rocks and scratched away a layer of old leaves from around the base of the sapling. He plucked up a bone, another, then a small skull. "Look," he demanded, holding up the skull. "Look!"

Father looked.

"So many of us have given our magic, our very blood, the same blood that runs in your veins, to bring Pawpaw back. Your children have stood right where I now stand and sacrificed themselves so that Mother Earth would give us back Pawpaw. Do you know why?"

Father had no answer.

"Because Pawpaw is the heart of the wildfolk, the heart of our magic, the heart of our soul, and only its seed will bring us back!"

Father's face clouded. He gave the corn a hard look, then let it slip from his hand. Forest could see his confusion, his turmoil. Forest let out a sigh. "There will be a time for this . . . for the healer to return. But it is as I keep saying: first we must save Pawpaw."

Father rubbed his forehead as though in pain.

"Bring her here," Forest said.

Father set cold, dangerous eyes on Forest.

"If you want the torment to end, then bring the Abitha woman here. Pay tribute to Pawpaw with her blood. Honor Mother Earth. It is the only way."

"I am done with blood," Father said curtly, coming to his feet. "There is no peace in slaughter." He lowered his voice as though speaking to himself. "There is more to all this than blood." And with that he headed away, back toward the farm.

"Where are you going?" Forest called, but he knew. "Stay away from her. I am begging you. She will bring doom to all of us. Do you hear me?"

Father continued on.

"Stay away from her!" Forest cried.

Father disappeared into the trees, and Sky and Creek set desperate eyes on Forest.

"I do not know what to do," Forest said tersely.

Forest glared up the hill toward the farm. "The woman is poison. If she keeps this up, he is sure to find out about Mamunappeht, or worse, Mamunappeht will find out about him!"

Creek and Sky began to jitter and twitch, clacking their teeth. Forest felt their dread, their growing panic, how it mirrored his own. He began to pace back and forth in front of the sapling. He stopped. "We will kill her."

Sky and Creek both gave him a surprised look.

"We will kill the Abitha woman. We have to."

"Yes, I know Father will be angry, but what choice have we? It is the only way to keep him sane, from falling back into the hands of the shaman." He kicked the dirt. "This all started when he touched her. There is something odd about her. Do you not sense it?"

He could see they did.

"She's opening doors to his past. We cannot allow that."

"No, Creek, we're not helpless. We are the wildfolk." And he remembered when that meant something, when their numbers seemed as infinite as the stars and how strong their magic was before the people began stealing it.

"We might not be as potent as we once were, but we still have a few tricks. Something besides flinging shadows and haunts at her. We may not be able to slaughter an entire village, but we can certainly find a way to kill one little woman."

Father stopped at the edge of the field. A morning fog clung to the land. He studied the row of corn he'd brought to life. *Who am I?*

He walked into the row, touched one of the cobs, closed his eyes, trying to relive the moment, the connection to his past. *I was so close. If I could but see a bit more.* He concentrated, seeking. *Nothing.*

He heard clatter up by the cabin. *What more can you show me, Abitha?*

Father approached the porch, spied Abitha looking up at the clouds.

"There will be no rain today," he said, startling her. "But it will be here soon. I feel it."

"Truly?" she asked, then looked past him, her eyes narrowing. Forest, Sky, and Creek were behind him. He realized that they'd revealed themselves to her.

"Who are they?" Abitha asked.

"It is hard to say," Father replied. "It can be thorny getting the truth from them."

"We are wildfolk and this is our land," Forest said to Abitha, his small dark eyes glowering at her.

"Can they hurt me? Will they?"

"They keep asking me to kill you. But I do not think they can do much on their own. If they could, I believe you would already be dead."

"Dead a hundred times," Forest spat. "You and all your kind." Sky and Creek nodded in agreement.

"My mother taught me a thing or two about the wee folk," Abitha said, and went back into the house, returning a moment later with three saucers and a pail.

Booka followed her out, sat down, and watched as she poured milk from the pail into each of the saucers. Abitha nodded to the wildfolk. "Goat's milk. It's for you."

The wildfolk exchanged uncertain looks.

"We're not pets," Forest said with a sneer.

"It's so very sweet." Abitha pushed the saucers forward. "Still warm, it is so fresh. Just milked the ladies this morning."

Creek licked his lips and started forward.

"Do not!" Forest commanded.

116

Creek halted, looking wistfully at the milk.

Abitha nudged one of the saucers toward Forest, gave him a smile.

Forest bristled. "Your smile will die when Father comes for your blood."

"If he wanted my blood do you not think he would've had it by now?"

"Soon, we will awaken his spirit, his *true* spirit. And when we do, he will gorge himself on your innards."

Abitha stiffened. "I do not believe that."

The opossum snorted. "You have no idea what you are playing with."

"Then do tell."

"Yes," Father put in. "Tell us. Enough with the games and riddles."

"Games? Riddles!" Forest barked. "How dare you. You would still be rotting away in that smelly pit had we not brought you blood!"

"Blood?" Abitha asked. "Whose blood?"

Forest turned away, didn't answer.

"Whose blood?" Abitha demanded. "Whose blood did you bring?"

Still Forest wouldn't answer.

"Tell her," Father said. "Stop hiding the truth."

Forest spun about. "The goat!" he spat. "I fed him your goat."

Abitha narrowed her eyes. "And . . . and Edward? What about Edward?"

Forest crossed his arms over his chest.

Abitha's hands began to shake. "Did you kill Edward? Was it you? Tell me the truth."

"Yes!" Forest snapped. "I did. I lured him into the cave going baaa, baaa, baaa, and down he fell. It was so easy to trick that stupid man. There . . . there's a truth. Would you like another?"

Abitha's hand went to her mouth, her face suddenly pale. Father felt her hurt like a blow.

"Here's another," Forest growled. "Your sweet devil here, this corn-loving clod . . . well, you should know that he gorged himself on your husband's guts. Now, you think of that the next time you want to give him some of your little treats and—"

Abitha snatched up a saucer and slung it at Forest.

The opossum ducked, the bowl going over its head.

Abitha screamed, grabbed another, threw it as hard as she could.

Again, Forest dodged out of the way, letting loose a nasty laugh.

Abitha snatched up the pail, rushed the opossum, swinging it, trying to smash the creature.

Forest danced around her, hooting at her.

Abitha's foot snagged on the step and she went sprawling, but Father leapt over, catching her before she hit the ground.

"We are wildfolk!" Forest cried. "We are here to eat your guts, you and all your kind. And Father here, he will see it done! That is the truth. The only one that matters!"

"Be gone, you miserable beast!" Father growled. "Lest it is your guts I eat."

The wicked grin fell from Forest's face. He gave Father a vicious sneer, turned, and stormed away.

Abitha sat down on the stoop, covered her face, and began to sob silently.

"I am sorry, Abitha," Father said, taking a seat next to her. "There's so much here I do not understand. But I do understand your pain. I also understand now that I wish you no harm. That was a mistake . . . I was confused. But because of you, I believe I am finding my way. I am hopeful that if we work together, we can both find what we need."

They sat that way for a long time, the occasional bleat from one of the goats and the cat lapping up the milk the only sound, until finally Abitha let out a great sigh. She wiped her eyes and brought a napkin out from her apron. She sat it on the porch between them, unfolding it to reveal three squares of brittle. "These are for you."

Father reached for them, then stopped. *There is more to all this,* he thought. "Abitha, what do you think I truly am?"

She considered for a while before answering. "I know not, but I know what I hope you are. My mother told me of all kinds of nature spirits, of fairies, imps, and forest gods, large and small, weak and powerful. These guardians of nature who awakened in the spring and breathed life into flowers and trees, looked over and protected the land and the people in return for tribute. Of the pagans that celebrated solstice and rebirth with them in grand ceremonies, feasts and rituals in their honor. How they joined together in the circle of death and rebirth. I am hoping that you are one of these, that when you fully awaken, you will bless this land and watch over it. That mayhap you will bless me and watch over me."

Creek and Sky exchanged troubled looks, but Father nodded along, liking everything he was hearing.

Honor and tribute, Father thought, her words bringing back visions from the day before, of the people giving him ringlets of flowers and beads, the reverence they showed him. He thought of Forest talking about tributes to Mother Earth in return for her blessings. His pulse quickened. *It is part of it . . . part of the magic!*

Father picked up one of the candies. "There should be more."

"You want more candy?" Abitha asked.

"No, not the candy. More from you." He felt her distrust return, knew Forest's threats were still fresh, wondered how they would ever get past it. "Why do you make me these offerings?" he asked.

"It seems to help you . . . to appease your tormented soul, but if I am being honest . . . I guess I am hopeful that you will weave your magic and breathe life into my crops."

Yes, you give me something I need and I give you something you need! He set his piercing eyes on her, peered into her. "Abitha, what is it you want out of this life?"

"It's very simple for me. Fresh game, eggs, a garden full of vegetables, a field of healthy corn."

"That is not what you want, that is what you need. You are not made out of needs, you are made out of your dreams and desires. What is it you wish and dream of?"

She started to reply, hesitated. "I know not. After Mother died, all I have thought about is surviving. I have not dreamed since I were a child."

"Then what did you dream of as a child?"

It took her a moment; he could sense her searching down memories long buried.

"You will think me foolish. But I wanted to be a fairy queen, to run barefoot through the woods, to sing like a bird and fly through the trees." She smiled. "To be able to talk to the animals." She laughed. "How my brothers and I used to dart about the yard flapping our arms and squawking like magpies." And he saw the joy on her face as she lost herself in the memory.

"Honor me," he said.

"What?"

"Let me help you with your needs . . . your dreams." He set his palm against his chest. "I feel there is great magic somewhere within me, and with your help, who knows what we are capable of. But I see now to unlock this magic, first you must properly honor me. Offer them to me . . . the candies."

She gave him a confused look. "I just did."

"You must do better."

"I do not understand."

"Your tribute, it must be a *true* offering . . . from your heart. Do you not see? These forest gods that your mother spoke of . . . were they not worshipped? As part of this pact between peoples and nature? Yes, it is obvious."

"Worship? I am not sure that—"

"You still fear me?"

She was silent for a long moment, then nodded. "I am scared, and I am confused, and I am conflicted. I hear my father warning me away, telling me that you will take my soul, then my mother telling me to listen to my heart."

"What does your heart say?"

She met his silver eyes. "My heart wants to believe in you. So very badly."

He reached out and gently touched the top of her hand. He felt her pulse quicken. "Remember how the magic brought our heartbeats together so we could raise the corn. Remember the bliss, the rapture, the joy. How is that anything but good? Perhaps if you believe I am a forest god, then I will be a forest god. Believe in me, Abitha."

"But *who* are you? How can I not be wary, not be fearful that you are devil or demon? That if I give too much of myself to you, that you will own my soul? Is that not fair to say given that you, yourself, know not who you are?"

"If this works, then it will prove that I am more than a slayer, more than some devil. Help me find my true self and I will help you in every way I can. I will give you a field of corn, and who knows, perhaps we will fly together through the forest one day."

She looked out at the corn. "I have heard it told that the Devil cannot deny his name. Is your name Satan, or Lucifer? Swear to me that neither of those are your name. That you are not the Great Tempter."

"Those are not my names. I swear."

She studied his face for a long time. "Do you still not remember your true name?"

He shook his head. "I do not."

"Well, you need a name. I will not call you Father." She looked him over, at his horns, then touched his shaggy fur. "Samson."

"What?"

"It is fitting. I shall call you Samson. After my goat. He was a good goat."

Father wasn't sure how he felt about that.

"It is a strong name. Noble and powerful."

"Sam . . . son," he said, as though tasting the word. "Samson." He looked at her. "Is this who you need me to be?"

"Aye."

"Then, for you, I am Samson, the forest god." And upon that declaration, something stirred deep within his breast. He nodded. "This is right . . . that you should name me." And again, he felt the veil between himself and his past grow thin.

She picked up the three candies, held them out before her on the napkin, then looked deep into his eyes. "In the name of God above," she said, slowly and clearly and with heart, "I make this offering to you, Lord Samson. Please watch over me and my farm, please breathe life into my crops." She raised the candies to him.

Samson took the candies and the feeling in his chest swelled, vitality surging through him. He ate them, one at a time, and with each, the vigor and potency grew within him.

"Yes, this *is* the right path." He felt the air stir, looked out at the rows of withered corn, and it was as though he could hear them calling for him. "It is time to be magnificent."

CHAPTER 6

Abitha came out onto her porch with a glass of milk and Edward's bible. She poured the milk into the three saucers and took a seat. She surveyed the corn, still having trouble making herself believe what she was seeing. Most of the top acres were flush with tall, healthy stalks.

For the last two weeks, she'd made small offerings and gifts to Samson, and together the beast and she had brought the corn back to life. There'd even been rain, not much, but enough that she could finally attend to all the chores she'd been neglecting: the two goats, chickens, her small vegetable garden, and Edward's bees, especially Edward's bees, as Samson seemed most fond of the honeycomb brittle.

She searched for sign of Edward amongst the trees, found none. She'd not seen him since she'd made her pact with Samson. "Did it work, Edward?" she whispered. "Are you free? Are you at peace?"

Booka wandered over, began lapping at the milk, and Abitha opened the bible and began to read.

Sky flew in and landed on the porch, looking longingly at the saucer of milk. A moment later Creek joined him, Booka barely sparing them a glance. Every day Abitha set milk out for them. She could see they wanted it, yet still they refused to drink.

Abitha hadn't seen the opossum since his tantrum, and this was fine with her; she hoped never to see that foul creature again.

She spotted Samson coming out of the woods. He strolled up and took a seat on the porch next to Abitha. That was when she saw the wolves, three of them hanging back at the tree line where Samson had just come out. Abitha started to get up, to get her musket.

Samson put a hand on her shoulder. "They will bring you no harm."

"How do you know?"

"Because I forbid it."

Abitha kept an eye on the wolves and few moments later they melted back into the trees. Abitha let out a breath. "You can talk to them?"

Samson shrugged. "In a way." He peered over her shoulder at the bible. "Those are the words of your god?"

Abitha nodded. "Aye, the reverend has given me leave from church and in return I made promise to read several passages a week. And, if I know him, he will have questions for me."

"What does your god say?"

"He says many good things. But it can all become a bit confusing. Such as how is it that God allows the Devil to harry people so."

"You speak often of gods and devils. What is the difference?"

"That's easy," Abitha said. "Gods are benevolent, looking over their flock in return for their devotion. Devils vex and torment."

"And what if it is not that simple?" Samson asked. "Can a god be both slayer and shepherd? Reward and vex? Does your god only do good?"

Abitha started to say yes, then considered the book in her hand. "No, I guess not. The Lord, God, He has drowned the world, brought plagues, sends those who offend Him to everlasting torment. Mayhap it depends on how one defines good."

"Your god, he is a slayer." Samson appeared pleased to hear this.

"Aye, at times. It is said that the Lord works in mysterious ways." Abitha closed the bible. "As I said . . . it can all be a bit confusing."

"Perhaps not, perhaps a god just has many sides." Samson sounded hopeful. "Hmm . . . you make me offerings, I grow the corn, looking after you in return for your devotion. Perhaps I am a god after all? Your god."

Abitha laughed. "If it were but that simple. God has never been an easy thing for me. Between my mother's pagan teachings and my father's conflicted views on Christianity, I often find myself unsure who God even is."

"Why do you limit yourself to only one?" Samson asked.

Abitha paused, realizing she didn't have an answer. It wasn't something she'd ever really considered. But now, thinking about it, her mother had often spoken of Jesus and the spirit world as one connected thing. "How many gods do you think there are?" Abitha asked.

"Not as many as there used to be," a voice said.

They turned to find Forest leaning against the farthest porch post with his arms folded tightly across his chest, a scowl on his face.

Forest plucked a tick from under his arm and ate it. "And if Father does not change his ways, and soon," he said bitterly, "there will be one less."

Abitha entered the village commons, walking quickly past the whipping post. Esther Hollister was bent over in the standing stocks, her legs trembling as though she might collapse at any moment. Abitha wondered how long the poor woman had been standing there, but didn't dare stop, as she was almost late for church.

"Abitha!" It was Helen; she caught up with Abitha and they walked together.

"Abitha, I must warn—" Helen halted, staring at Abitha.

"What is it? My hair?" Abitha quickly checked to make sure none of her curls had escaped her bonnet.

"You look . . . why . . . downright radiant?" Helen appeared shocked but pleased.

Radiant? Abitha thought, feeling herself blush. *Well, now, that's a first.* She'd certainly made an effort, scrubbing up both herself and her clothes, at last finding time to mend her skirts and other garments. But she knew it was more than that. She was finally getting a full night's sleep and eating as she should. Samson hadn't stopped with the corn, and now there was plenty. Samson had plied his blessing all around the farm, gracing them with a bounty of honey, wild berries, vegetables, and plenty of eggs and goat's milk. But she suspected it might even be a bit more, that perhaps some of Samson's magic was rubbing off on her.

They continued along.

"I was going to say . . . going to warn you that there are many who are unhappy that the reverend has granted you leave these last months. He has not backed down, but it has caused much friction."

"Months? No . . . why, it has only been—" She stopped. "It is but August, is it not?"

"August? Nay, Abi, it is now September."

"September?" Abitha sputtered, trying to understand how time had slipped by so quickly. "Well, I am here now and will be from now on, so they can find someone else to harry. But do tell, who is it that is so upset? Is it Wallace by chance?"

"Indeed, it is. His wife and Charity as well. They've been rousing up the usual group of nosy-bodies, Goody Dibble and her friends. But things are not *as* usual, not since they found old Widow Pratt's body."

Abitha stopped. "What has happened?"

"Have you not heard?"

Abitha shook her head.

"She died while picking berries just outside the walls. And here's what's odd, they found not a scratch upon her."

"She were old."

"Aye, but she had her grandson, Jarret, with her, and he speaks that a horned beast did attack them. So, of course, now most everyone believes it were the Devil that came and snatched her soul. Does not help that old Ansel is on a rage, snooping around, spying on folks, crying Devil every time a cat farts."

"Did Jarret say what this beast looked like?"

"Aye, indeed, over and over. Wakes up at night in fits, screaming and crying. Says it's after him in his dreams. Says it be a big goat, with twisting horns, long sharp fingers, and silver eyes."

Abitha put her hand to her mouth.

"Oh, and hear this. The boy tells that the Devil stole Widow Pratt's bucket of berries. Well, sure enough, her pail was never to be found. What do you think of that?"

"I . . . I—" Abitha could find no words. *What happened? Samson, what did you do?*

"And where is your musket, Abi? You have no business walking that trail by yourself in the first place. No one is leaving the village unless armed these days on account that the wolves have grown so bold. Lewis Ward and his son went out a hunting them a while back and none have seen them since."

Abitha's blood ran cold as her thoughts went immediately to the wolves lingering about her farm.

"Everyone fears the worst for them," Helen continued. "And you can hear the beasts howling nearby, sometimes even during the day now. Many believe it's not wolves at all, but Slewfoot himself. That he is lurking in these very forests, watching us, waiting to—"

"It would not be the first time wolves have killed a stray hunter," Abitha said harshly. "Or that men have ventured into these dangerous woods and not returned. It happens. It is nothing new." Abitha was surprised at the defensiveness in her own voice, then wondered just who here she was trying to convince.

Helen gave her a concerned look, said something else, but Abitha didn't hear her, instead hearing Forest's words, *"Soon, we will awaken his spirit, his true spirit. And when we do, he will gorge himself on your innards."*

"We must not dally," Abitha said, wanting the subject to be over, and they resumed their path. Abitha soon spotted Goody and Mary Dibble along with their usual cohorts standing about the front of the meetinghouse. "Speak of the Devil," Abitha said beneath her breath.

The women hadn't noticed Abi yet, as they were watching Sheriff Pitkin, who stood upon a ladder hammering a wolf head above the doorframe—the grisly trophy still dripping blood.

Abitha hurried along, intent on slipping past as quietly as she could, wanting no trouble from these women today, but Mary noticed her and quickly alerted the group.

All the women turned, setting stern faces full of righteous indignation upon Abitha. Their posture that of open confrontation.

Abitha tensed and sucked in a breath.

"Oh, Lord," Helen whispered. "They have got their feathers a flutter now."

Goody started to speak, but as Abitha drew near, she squinted, as though not seeing right. The other women did as well. Their faces going from contempt to surprise. Abitha knew they must be as shocked by her appearance as Helen and intended to take advantage of their befuddlement to slip past.

Goody stepped in front of her, blocking the way with her bulk.

"Why, Abitha," Goody said, leaning in on the smaller woman. "But if you do not look like a peach this morning. Seems leave from church has done you a world of good. Makes one wonder if you might just be taking advantage of the reverend's grace."

Abitha felt her face flush, felt a volley of profanity upon her tongue. *Mind yourself, Abi*, she thought. *Mind yourself.* "Thank you for your concern, Goody. The good Lord has indeed been most merciful these last weeks. Now, excuse me, I would go now and give my thanks."

Abitha started around, when Dorthy Dodd moved into her path. "Is it fair that one should be treated so specially?"

The women all shook their heads.

"You should know," Dorthy added, "your absence has caused much divisiveness within the fold."

"I am very sorry for this. I am truly am. I do hope to make amends."

The women all began to speak.

"Aye, as Reverend Smith said, your pride, your selfish behavior weakens us all."

"There are those who argue that you are opening the door to Slewfoot himself."

"Aye, much talk indeed."

"It is more than talk, this. Ansel has found evidence."

"Aye," Goody said. "Evidence that the Devil be afoot. And such started about the same time as you saw fit to take over Wallace's farm. What make you of this? Coincidence?"

Abitha forced herself to smile. "I know not. I only know I am humble before the Lord and wish to thank him for all his graces. Now, please. I would be on my way." She could see by their faces that this wasn't the response they were hoping for, and didn't care, just needed to be away before she did something she'd regret.

Abitha pushed her way between the larger women and headed for the steps.

Someone grabbed her arm, tugged her around. It was Goody. "We are not done."

Abitha had spent many years on the streets of London dealing with every sort of handsy folk, so reacted instinctively, sticking a boot behind Goody's heel and giving the larger woman a sharp shove.

Goody tumbled back, fell, landing hard on her rump.

Abitha glared at her. "You heed me well, Goody Dibble. You set hand on me again and you'll find out what it is to bear my sting." Though almost every woman there was a stone larger than Abitha, she looked from face to face, daring any one of them to step forward.

"Sheriff," Dorthy called. "Did you not see that? She did attack poor Goody. You must arrest her at once!"

"Indeed, I did see," the sheriff said as he climbed down from the ladder. "I saw Goody set hands on Abitha. And I for one would think twice before doing such again." He smirked at Abitha. "Perhaps we should all go inside and spend some time with our Lord. I think that would be good for everyone. What say you all?"

The women puckered as though having bitten into something sour. Goody's face blazed with raw hate as she glowered at Abitha.

Abitha spun about and headed up the steps. She entered the meetinghouse and was greeted by hard looks, but these looks quickly turned to dismay, as they seemed to be as stunned by her appearance as were Helen and the women. She caught Wallace staring at her, his mouth agape, looking at her as though she'd returned from the grave. He appeared confused and perplexed, then pained, as though suffering bad indigestion. Abitha imagined she must look a sight different than last he'd seen her. She gave him a sly smile and thought, *Wallace, dear, there are plenty more surprises ahead for you.* She knew it a sin to gloat, but couldn't wait to see his face when she paid him off in full.

Reverend Carter took the pulpit and led the congregation in prayer, followed by his opening sermon. It didn't take the reverend long to speak of the Devil and his temptations, but Abi could only think of the widow, the hunters, the wolves, twisting the hem of her sleeve nervously between her fingers. *Samson, what are you?*

Forest stood on Abitha's porch looking out over the farm, making sure Father was nowhere in sight. Sky and Creek were supposed to whistle if he returned, but he couldn't count on them for much these days, feeling they had no more sense between them than a common chicken.

Forest slipped into the cabin and wrinkled his nose. *It all smells of her.* He glanced about, searching for her work clothes, found them on the bed. He knew she'd be changing into them when she returned; she always did. But this time he intended to have a surprise waiting for her.

He climbed onto the bed and stood on the clothes, closed his eyes, searching using his sight, seeking in all the little hidey-holes and cracks and crevices of the log cabin, the thatched roof, the hollows beneath the floorboards, all the places the venomous ones, the snakes, centipedes, and black widows liked to hide.

Forest knew they had to be there, but found nothing.

"It should not be this hard," he growled. When he was in his prime and Paw-paw was the largest tree in the land and the world was full of magic, he could've probed the entire farm, found every creature on it.

"Mother Earth, hear me. Please, I can only do so much on my own." He tried again, this time drawing on the pulse of the land, but it was so faint, a delicate tenuous thread deep down in the earth. He touched it.

There! A few faint spidery glows flittered to life about the room. And in a hollow next to the cabin, a snake, a copperhead! Not very large, but large enough.

Come to me, he beckoned, but received no response.

He called again, straining as he tried to push his thoughts into their tiny brains.

127

Come to me, now! And a few them *did* hear him, but they stayed put, none wishing to leave their cozy nests.

"Come!" he hissed. "Damn you, come here to me now!" He was shaking, the strain taking its toll, his connection to the magic slipping. The world began to spin and he collapsed.

"No," he groaned. "This cannot be. I cannot be so helpless. How will I ever set them on her if I cannot so much as call them from their nests?"

Forest lay there a long time, staring up at the beams. Slowly he began to nod his head. *There is another way. It will be terrible and painful, but that cannot be helped. Just need a little help.*

After nearly an hour of sermons, Abitha's back was starting to ache; she shifted on the hard bench, but there was just no way to get comfortable. Reverend Carter began reading something from Colossians about giving thanks to God, being fruitful in your every good work, endurance and patience and so on. Abitha heard very little, her thoughts on Samson and his dark deeds, but when the reverend read, "For by Him were all things created that are in heaven and are on earth, visible and invisible," she straightened.

128

There was more to it, but Abitha was lost in her own thoughts. *If God did indeed create all things, then did He not create Samson? Why then is Samson not but one more of God's creatures playing His role in the Lord's grand design?* She considered how a wolf killing to feed the pack didn't make that wolf evil, merely dangerous. And were not angels dangerous? Angels did many terrible things in the name of the Lord. When she made Samson an offering, she wasn't choosing Samson over God, but was simply feeding the wolf. And should she get bitten, then it would be to her own demise, but no offense to God. And who was to say Samson wasn't dispensing God's blessing much like an angel? Had he not brought life to her farm? What evil could there be in such?

Abitha liked the idea of Samson being some kind of hand of God. Had her mother not taught her that many benevolent pagan gods were horned beasts? She'd also combined God and paganism in her practices, saying the more blessings the better.

Abitha twisted the hem of her sleeve ever tighter and wondered if she were but telling herself what she wanted, *needed,* to hear. She shook her head. *Mayhap, but the hard truth is that God has seen fit to turn my world upside down.* She stared into the large judging eye painting upon the pulpit. *Lord, I am doing the best that I can. If this is all but some trial, some great test of my faith, then shame on you for tormenting me so.*

Reverend Carter paused, and the sudden silence pulled Abitha from her thoughts. The reverend seemed to have lost his way and not for the first time today.

"My apologies," the reverend said. "I am not myself this morning. Reverend Collins, would you do us the kindness of finishing today's sermons?"

Reverend Collins took the pulpit as Reverend Carter found his seat. It was then that Abitha noticed his wife was not in attendance. *Goodwife Carter never misses church,* she thought, fretful of what that might mean. Abitha clutched the folded napkin in her apron. She'd brought the woman a handful of honeycomb brittle, a small thank-you for the kindness she'd shown her.

Abitha got her first clue to why Goodwife Carter wasn't in church when at the end of the service Reverend Collins asked everyone to bow their head in a special prayer for Martha—Reverend Carter's daughter—asking the Lord to aid in her recovery.

Once the service was over, Abitha waited outside for the minister, approaching him as he headed home.

"Abitha, you know not how it pleases me to see you here. We need to talk of your absence."

"Worry not, Reverend. I promise you I will be here as required from this day forth."

He appeared relieved. "This is good to hear."

"And I cannot thank you enough for this grace. It has made all the difference and I promise to make it up to you."

He gave her a curious look. "You appear well." It was almost a question.

Abitha noticed Goody and several other parishioners watching them, didn't miss the hard looks given to both her and the reverend.

"Sir. I brought this for you and your wife." She handed him the folded napkin. "It's a small gift, but a heartfelt thank-you."

He peeked under the fold and smiled. "Sarah will be pleased."

"Please tell her how much her kindness means to me."

"I will tell her."

She could see he needed to be on his way. "Reverend, one more thing."

"Yes."

"Your daughter, Martha. Sir, what is it that ails her so?"

"Seems the measles are upon her. We had hoped she would be better by now, as both Sarah and myself were stricken as children and neither of us had such a strong reaction."

"She is getting worse then?"

"I hate to say so, but yes, that is the case. That is why Sarah is not with us today."

"Mayhap there is something I can do to help?"

"You can keep Martha in your prayers. Now, I am sorry for rushing away, but I must go."

"Aye, of course. You will all be in my prayers."

Abitha watched him head away, then started her long trek home. She walked rapidly, lost in thought, not thinking of wolves or devils, but trying to remember how her mother had treated the measles.

Forest peeked beneath Abitha's bed, prowled through her cupboard, the firebox, then over to the old hutch where she kept her clothes. He was searching for just the right spot—a hiding place where his helpers could give her the surprise of her life. He halted suddenly, sniffing. "What is that?"

Forest darted over to the door and wrinkled his nose. "Someone on their way." He closed his eyes, searching. "A man . . . on a horse?"

A wicked little smile spread across the opossum's face and he darted off the porch, into the cornfield, sprinting toward the woods. "Father!" he called. "Father, we have a visitor!"

By the time Abitha started home, Wallace was well on his way to her farm, riding hard and fast. He'd left church before her, mounting up and riding off before she'd even left the building.

What is going on, Papa? he wondered. *She looked . . . what? Healthy . . . vibrant? And that nasty little smile? That were not the face of a defeated woman.*

He crested the hill above the farm, got his first good look at her cornfields, and came to a full halt. "This is not possible," he sputtered. "No . . . no!" The field was flush with corn—tall, healthy corn. He kept shaking his head like a man who'd lost his mind.

He rode down to her cabin, dismounted, all but falling from his horse. His heart drummed. He clasped his cheeks, tugging at his face. "They will take *my* farm, *my* home. I am ruined. I shall lose everything!"

Wallace clutched the horse to keep from sliding to his knees. "I will fix this, Papa . . . I promise you. I *will* fix this." He looked at the barn—was considering burning it down, the barn, the cabin, her mule, goats, and chickens, all of it— when a better idea struck him. *Trample the cornstalks,* he thought. *Aye, just ride the big stallion through the fields!*

He grinned savagely and mounted the stallion. He turned the horse toward the field and stopped.

He was not alone. Someone was there, in the tall corn.

Wallace saw no one, but someone *was* there, he felt it in his very bones. It was then he realized that in his haste to leave before Abitha he'd left his musket behind, that he didn't have so much as a knife on him.

"Hello," he called.

The breeze picked up and the stalks swayed. He thought he caught movement, but it was so hard to tell amongst all the dancing shadows.

"You are to come out this minute," he demanded. "Come out or I will—"

A figure, a man, his face obscured, stood far back amongst the stalks; he looked familiar.

Wallace squinted, then gasped. "Edward?" he called, his voice shaky. "Pray tell, is that you, brother?"

Edward raised a hand and beckoned him forward. Then Wallace caught a glimpse of his face, saw his eyes were but two black hollows. Every hair on Wallace's body prickled. "What deviltry is this?"

The wind picked up and the corn leaves clattered, sounding like laughter, that of children. Wallace shook his head, trying to clear away the eerie sound.

Then Edward opened his mouth, as though trying to speak, but not a sound came from his lips.

"No," Wallace whispered. "You're not Edward." His voice rising, cracking. "Edward is dead!"

Edward's face turned unbearably sad and he began to fade, shifting away with the shadows, disappearing back into the corn as though he'd never been there at all.

Wallace blinked, rubbed his eyes. "No, that were not Edward. You are but seeing things. That—"

The stallion snorted and stomped, shuffling back.

Someone—no, *something*—else was there.

131

Wallace tugged the reins hard, struggling to keep his horse in check.

Far back near the trees, the stalks parted, swishing this way and that as something moved steadily toward him through the corn. Wallace couldn't see it, but he felt it, felt its malice sure as he felt the sun on his skin.

Wallace kicked the stallion, driving his heels into its side. The beast bellowed and leapt away from the field, but not fast enough for Wallace. He continued kicking the beast, pushing it into a full gallop, not daring to look behind, not until he crested the hill, and then he did look, sure Edward would be upon him, only Edward would have long fangs and claws.

No one was there.

Wallace reined up, staring at the corn, his pulse racing, his breath coming hard and fast. He waited for Edward to come crawling out of the stalks, or perhaps a bear, a wolf . . . or maybe the Devil himself, but nothing, nor no one, came out.

What was that, Papa? Pray tell. Were it Edward? Mayhap his ghost? Wallace watched the wind and shadows play their games with the tall stalks, shook his head. *No, no, of course not. I am out of sorts. That is all. That is all!* Yet he didn't go back down to trample the corn, telling himself it would do no good anyway, that the corn was ripe, ready to harvest. Abitha would need only pluck the corncobs up off the ground. Instead, he sat there glaring at the farm, *his* farm, at all the beautiful corn.

"Thief," he spat. "You are naught but a thief, you wretched woman." His eyes narrowed to slits. "I will fix this . . . sure as God is in Heaven I will." He bit his lip as a plan began to take shape, then shook his head. *Nay . . . I cannot. How could I ever do such a thing? It would be a sin. It would—*

He looked at his hands, saw that they were trembling. "Get hold of yourself," he growled. "Do not let shadows and echoes put fear into your soul. You are in the right on this. God knows you are." It was then that Magistrate Watson's words came to him. *"Angels must often do dark deeds in the name of the Lord."*

"Aye." Wallace nodded, his voice swelling with righteousness. "What must be done, shall be done!"

He gave the farm one more long look, searching the tall cornstalks. "If you are there, brother, know this . . . I will right this wrong. I will bring you the peace you crave. This I promise you."

He kicked the stallion and rode away, trotting back down the long road to Sutton, his face a grim mask as he pondered the doing of his plan. The farther away he got from the farm, from the vision of Edward, from the eerie laughter, from the menacing thing in the corn, the better the plan sounded, until finally, without even realizing it, he was smiling.

About a mile outside of town, Wallace spied Abitha heading home and kicked his stallion into a gallop, riding directly for her.

Abitha, her eyes wide with fear, leapt to the side of the road, just avoiding being pummeled.

Wallace laughed and shouted, "Judgment is coming for you!" And rode on.

Abitha, still shaken from her encounter with Wallace, entered her cabin. She paused at the entrance, taking deep long breaths, trying to calm herself. She scanned the room—something wasn't right, but she found nothing out of place. She reached over to where the chain of braids hung by the door, seeking their reassurance, gently running her fingers down the links, and when she did, she saw him, Forest, just a ghostly outline.

"Leave," she said, setting hard eyes on him. And even though she could but barely see him, she could still read his surprise.

He materialized, staring at her in an all-new way. "You *are* one of them. One of the magic folk!"

"Get out."

He headed for the door, taking a moment to study the chain of braids, giving her one more shrewd look before leaving.

Abitha quickly donned her work clothes, stopping at the door to tie her short apron back around her waist. Her eyes returned to the chain of braids, the copper serpent pin. "Is it true then, Mother? Am I like you?" She reached for the braids, hesitated, wanting to take them with her, wanting their comfort, but wondering if she should, if she were ready for such a step. She bit her lip and lifted the braids from the hook, clutching them to her bosom.

"Mother, I am blind, walking a path I cannot see. But walk it I must. Steer my hand true, help me stay clear of the Devil's taint." She touched the braids to her lips, and the faintest whiff of lavender and sage came to her. She closed her eyes and inhaled deeply as fond memories of her mother flowed through her mind, touched her heart. She opened her eyes, slipped the braids deep into her apron pocket, and headed directly into the woods, walking fast.

She heard someone coming along behind her. It was Samson. He caught up with her in a small meadow. Abitha looked deep into his silver eyes, started to ask about the hunters, about the widow. But his face, it was so full of concern, concern for her. *Later,* she told herself. *When there is more time.*

"The Wallace man. He was here."

"I know," Abitha said as she searched through the tall grass. "Would that I could have seen his face."

"It was a most miserable face."

She laughed.

"He intends you harm."

"Aye, he does," she said without looking up. "Ah, here we go." She took her knife and dug out a small plant, shaking the dirt loose. The plant had a knot of long, crooked black roots. She held it up. "Knitbone."

"You eat this?"

"It's for Martha, a child in town. She's suffering from measles. My mother once showed me how to make an ointment from this root. It should help with the rash."

"The ointment will heal her? Like a spell or potion?"

"That's what I am hoping. It should at least lessen the pain."

"The child is from the church . . . the church of the Christ God?"

Abitha nodded absently as she cleaned the root.

"Why does her mother not ask the Christ God to heal her child?"

"She has. We all have. Many, many, prayers."

"And this Christ God does nothing?"

Abitha shrugged. "We shall see. Sometimes God helps, sometimes He does not."

Samson shook his head. "They need a better god."

Abitha chuckled. "Oh, you should suggest that to them sometime. The Puritans believe that God helps according to how worthy one is. That He only rewards the truly devout."

"Heals them? Makes their crops grow?"

"Aye, blesses and watches over them."

"Rewards devotion . . . that makes sense. It is the same with me. In many ways I am like the Christ God, am I not?"

Abitha chuckled. "You two could be brothers, you are so similar."

He tugged at his chin. "The root, let me see it."

She handed it to him.

He sniffed it, closing his eyes. "The smell . . . it takes me back." His brows knotted and he sniffed again. "I see them, the magic folk with their potions and spells . . . hexes and curses. There . . . I am with them. I can see my hands on the sick!" He looked again at the root. "If I can heal the girl, would that not mean I am a god? Like this Christ?"

"Can you?"

"I believe there is a way." He sniffed the root once more, as though seeking. "Their hands joined with mine . . . it is not clear. But I believe that it is *you* who summons the spell. Or perhaps *we* summon the spell together. No, that's not quite right. You summon the spell through me. Yes, yes, like with the corn. You must ask this of me."

He handed her back the root and she looked at him, unsure. "How do I do that?"

He shrugged. "Perhaps the same way you ask the Christ God for blessings?"

She considered, then set the knife and root down. "I can try."

Abitha knelt to one knee, clasping her hands together as in prayer. "Great Lord Samson, in the name of God and all that is holy, I ask thee to please help heal Martha of her ailment. Amen."

They waited. . . . Nothing happened.

Abitha reached into her apron, brought forth the chain of braids. Samson watched curiously as she coiled it around her hand. She repeated the prayer, and as she did, she felt an odd tingling coming from the braids.

Samson's eyes grew wide. "Can you hear that?"

"What?"

"They are chanting. The magic folk are chanting to me. Abitha, you must chant to me!"

Abitha did. "Help us, Lord Samson. Help us, Lord Samson. Help us, Lord Samson." But she now knew from her experience with the corn that it wasn't about the words, that it was something deeper in her that she needed to touch, connect with, release. The words melted away, turning into sounds, seeking, searching, touching her heart, her soul, and suddenly she too could hear them, far away, the voices of women. And as the voices found their rhythm, Abitha let go, opening up to Samson, and more of his vision was revealed. She too saw the shadowy folk, saw their hands on the sickly.

"Ah," he exclaimed. "I know this!"

He acted quickly, grabbing a stick and drawing a circle the span of his arms into the leaves and dirt. Within the circle he drew four symbols, mere squiggles. It seemed not to matter what the marks were, that it was more the act of making them.

"Here," Samson said, moving aside. "Step into the circle."

Abitha did.

Samson picked up the root and knife and handed them to her. "Now we need your blood."

Her eyes widened, but she didn't break the rhythm of the chant.

"It is *your* spell . . . it must be *your* blood. Just a drop or two. Here . . . on the root."

She felt a flash of the old fear.

"We must do this together, Abitha."

She clutched the braids tighter and sensed him reaching out to her, baring his heart and soul. And what she felt was only goodness, only a desire to heal. *Mother, steer my hand true.*

"Let me in," he whispered.

She nodded and Samson stepped into the circle with her. A gust of warmth blew through her and she let go, completely giving herself over to him, becoming part of him, together now they were calling to the magic deep down in the ground. It was then that she heard the earth whisper her name.

She held the root in her open palm, took the knife, and nicked her finger. She let the blood pool, then closed her fingers over the root, clutching it, pressing the blood into it.

She felt Samson connect with the earthly force, saw the strain as he drew it up and out from its lair.

The force swirled around them, stirring up the leaves, then flowed into Samson, setting his silver eyes ablaze. He grasped her hand and it entered her.

Abitha let out a fevered moan as the magic filled her, her eyes rolling upward, her whole body quivering, and for a moment she felt it might be too much, it might break her, drive her mad. But she did not break. She raised the root above her head, thought of healing, of life and health, trying to twist and weave her intentions together with the magic. And as she felt them bind, she pushed, steered, guided the magic, letting out a fierce cry as the magic left her and entered the root.

There came a flash, and for one instant she saw them, twelve women standing around them in a circle, their hands linked, their faces hidden beneath their long loose hair.

The root squirmed in Abitha's hand and she dropped it to the ground, stumbling back and falling to her knees, breathing hard and fast.

The air stilled and they both stared at the root.

The root began to writhe, its shoots wiggling like arms and legs, looking like some shriveled-up little man. For a second what seemed to be a tiny face—eyes, a nose, and mouth—appeared. The mouth opened and a faint wobbly wail came out. The root trembled, then slowly coiled up into a rigid knot.

"Is it done?" she gasped.

Samson nodded. "It is done."

Abitha headed to town for the second time that day, setting a brisk pace down the winding rut road, knowing Martha's condition to be dire and hoping to make it back to the farm by nightfall. She entered the wood, going deeper and deeper into the forest, the tall trees looming overhead, forming an arching canopy like some primeval cathedral, drowning her in their murky shadows.

She'd crushed the root into an ointment, wrapped it in a corn husk, and now carried it in her apron alongside the braid. She also carried the musket, not because she feared the wolves—Samson had shown her they wouldn't harm her—but for Wallace. And here, at this moment, flush with the heat of the spell, she almost hoped to meet him, hoped he would give her cause to shoot him dead.

As she moved down the path, her thoughts kept returning to the root ritual. *He bewitched me*, she told herself. *That is all there is to that.* Only she knew it wasn't. *Did I resist him? Nay, if anything I was eager. Mayhap not at first, but once I got a taste of . . . of what . . . magic?* She couldn't think of a better word for that sensation of potency, of power, of being connected to the pulse of the trees, the sun, the earth itself . . . to *Samson*. It had been seductive, almost sensual, awaking something deep within her. She felt its faint pulse even now, as though some part of the spell still lingered, connecting her to the life all around her. *Do you want more?* it seemed to ask her.

Aye, I do, God, I do.

As though in response, the wind picked up, blowing through the branches and leaves, the sound like whispers, like voices calling to one another, alerting the forest of her coming. She shuddered, tried to ignore them, pretending they weren't there, that they were not following her.

A fresh gust of wind, and the whispers grew louder.

Abitha shook her head, sure it was but a trick of her mind, that she was still delirious from the incantation.

You are falling under the Devil's spell, a voice warned, one that could've been her own or that of the leaves.

"Nay," Abitha replied in a hushed, almost pleading tone. "Samson is not the

137

Devil. He has never asked me to denounce God. Not once. He is full of benevolence and healing. How can that not be God's work?"

And what of my death? asked another voice, one not unlike Edward's.

"It were not Samson! That had been that little imp, Forest. It is not fair to put that on Samson."

The widow . . . the hunters?

Abitha shook her head adamantly. "He was confused. He has changed. I know it, I feel it."

And if it were but that simple, asked another voice, more like her father, *then why does it still nag you so?*

Abitha clapped her hands over her ears and quickened her pace. She could sense them all around her now, their pain, their hunger, their need, so much need.

"Samson," she whispered. "Please be what you seem."

She caught sight of smoky shapes slithering along within the shadows, keeping pace with her. Wondered what they might be—ghosts, feral spirits, demons? Perhaps all of those things?

"Leave me be," she whispered, but they slid closer, snorting and sniffing. And it was only then that she understood what they were truly after. That they smelled the magic in the ointment. She clutched her apron, the corn husk, felt its heat, its promises, felt her own lust for the magic bloom.

She caught glimpses of spectral horns and scales, claws and teeth, heard a low keening, the sound of yearning.

She broke into a jog and still they followed, coming closer and closer.

"This magic is not for you!" she shouted, then tugged out the chain of braids, holding it out as some warding talisman. "Begone!"

But the braids seemed to only further their unrest, their hunger. They swirled about her—their eyes full of sorrow, their mouths full of silent screams—wispy, smoky shapes of no real substance. Yet she could feel them, their fingers like a cold breath as they pawed at her clothes and hair.

What doors have I opened?

Then something else, another presence, something of great magnitude, something savage and dreadful. It seemed to be deep in the ground below her.

The ghost, the demons and spirits, whatever they were, fell away, fell behind. She glanced round, saw their pitiful forms slinking back into the shadows, becoming the shadows.

The presence was with her now. Abitha couldn't see it but knew it was there, just beneath the ground, circling her.

"Who are you?" Abitha asked.

She received no reply.

"I know you," Abitha whispered, and then it came to her. "The serpent . . . from my dreams. It is you. I know it is you!"

The presence began to fade, becoming faint, but just before it was gone, Abitha thought she heard her name. She halted to listen, but heard nothing, no ghosts, no wild spirits, no demons, nothing but the wind.

Abitha made it to Sutton by late afternoon. She tried to keep her eyes forward, fighting the need to glance back every couple of seconds to make sure the things in the wood were not with her. She kept her head down, hoping to avoid being noticed, but she knew there were always eyes watching in Sutton.

Abitha came to the Carters' porch and hesitated. She'd felt confident she was doing the right thing, but now, at their doorstep, she wasn't so sure. So many, like her father, considered root remedies and the cunning crafts akin to witchcraft, and Goodwife Carter had made no secret of her disapproval of Abitha peddling her charms and remedies.

Her daughter could be dying, Abitha reminded herself, knowing the risks Goodwife Carter and the reverend had taken on her behalf, that if not for Sarah's kind words when she needed them most, she, Abitha, would most likely be lying dead at the bottom of her own well.

Abitha stepped up onto the Carters' porch, propped her musket against the wall, and knocked.

A moment later Goodwife Carter opened the door. "Abitha? Why . . . what are you doing here? Are you all right?" Sarah Carter, always so together, appeared disheveled and exhausted.

"Goodwife Carter, ma'am. I heard about Martha. And I thought I might be of help."

Sarah Carter gave her a troubled look.

"You might have heard then, about my mother . . . that she were a cunning woman?" Abitha pulled out the folded corn leaves. "This . . . this is an ointment . . . a remedy. Knitbone root. I've seen her use it to great relief on those afflicted with measles."

Sarah stared at the leaves, her brows tight. Abitha could see her wrestling with her principles.

139

"It is but a root," Abitha said. "No different than any other of God's plants. If the Lord created a plant that helps alleviate the suffering of blisters and rashes, does it not make sense that He should want us to use it? That it is but one more of His many blessings?"

Goodwife Carter seemed unable to make up her mind.

"Surely it would not hurt to try," Abitha said.

A wail came from back in the house. It was the girl. Goodwife Carter hesitated for a moment longer, then bit her lip and opened the door wide. "Come in, Abi. Please."

Reverend Thomas Carter sat in a chair by the fireplace, looking defeated. He stood up when Abitha entered. "Abitha? What—"

"She's come to help," Goodwife Carter said. "Now, worry not. Sit down. Let us do our work."

"But . . ." He eyed Abitha warily. Abitha could see the man knew what she was about.

"Thomas," Goodwife Carter said, and there was a plea in her voice. "Let us handle this. *Please.*"

He started to object, but when he caught the look on Sarah's face—that of a mother out of choices—he closed his mouth. The couple held each other's eyes a moment longer, and Abitha sensed the unspoken exchange going on between them.

Reverend Carter sat back down and stared into the fireplace, his hands clutched together. Finally, he nodded and let out a long, sad sigh that said more than any words could. "I am going to sit here. You just call me if I am needed."

Goodwife Carter turned and led Abitha into a bedroom in the back of the house.

Martha lay clad in her nightdress upon sweat-stained sheets, her pasty flesh covered in clusters of angry red bumps, the fever showing bright on her face. Abitha thought her to be around twelve years of age. She had sandy-colored hair, cut short like her mother's, and like so much about the Carter family, she was plain both in face and form, as though to please God with her humbleness.

Martha let out another moan.

A pail sat by the bed. Sarah dunked a cloth into the pail and gently sopped the girl's forehead.

Abitha laid the corn husk down on the bed and unwrapped the leaves, exposing the gray ointment. She dabbed the ointment onto her finger and began blotting it onto the welts. She started with Martha's face, neck, hands, and arms, then unbuttoned Martha's gown and applied it to any spot where the rash had spread.

Applying the ointment was the simple part; it was the next step that worried Abitha. Samson had told her it was her spell and to cast it with the same chant in which she'd summoned it, to let the chant guide her. She knew she couldn't just start speaking in tongues around the Carters. She also knew that this wasn't just a bit of root magic and there was no telling what might happen when she invoked it. The room could fill with wind and smoke, or she might fall into fits. For all she knew Martha's skin might turn green and start sprouting mushrooms. *Then where would I be?* Abitha thought, but she knew where she'd be. On her way to being hanged as a witch, sure as Monday follows Sunday. And all her labors and trials on the farm would be for nothing.

Start with a prayer, she thought. *Aye, just like in the woods. Cover the chant with a prayer.* She felt that was the right path, and that way if something unexplainable did happen, then perhaps it would be viewed as a miracle of God. She knew this was hopeful thinking at best, that in the end she was placing her trust, her very life, in the hands of Samson, a . . . a *what*? A wild forest spirit . . . the Devil himself? *Aye, a prayer indeed, please. One for Martha and two for me.*

Abitha touched Goodwife Carter's arm. "My mother always combined the Lord's Prayer with her root remedies. She said all healing comes from the Lord, that we are but extensions of his hand. I tend to agree with that. Shall we?"

141

Sarah nodded, seemed pleased with the idea. She clasped her hands together, closed her eyes, and began to pray in a soft voice. Abitha did likewise, whispering her own prayer, slowly letting the words slip into the chant.

Within a few moments Abitha's pulse quickened and something stirred within her breast. A warmth grew steadily, building and building, turning into a sweet, warm pulse, matching the drumming of her heart. A sensual chill coursed from her head to her toes. She struggled not to gasp or moan. And just when she felt her heart might burst, the warmth flowed out from her core, carried along through her veins, pushed along inch by inch by her pulse. It traveled across her chest, down her right arm, and into her hand. Her hand began to throb, as though the warmth needed to escape, needed somewhere to go, and Abitha knew just where.

She clasped Martha's hand, thought of health and healing, and let the warmth flow out of her and into the girl. Martha's eyes flashed open, locking onto Abitha's, and for a brief moment they were connected. Abitha could feel the girl's fever, the painful blisters, her fear, then felt the spell pulsing through the girl's veins and arteries, slowly pushing the fever out. And finally, she felt the girl's great relief. Abitha continued the low soft chant until every last bit of the warmth had passed into the girl, then let go of the girl's hand.

Martha's eyes fell slowly shut.

"Amen," Abitha said, and a few moments later, Goodwife Carter did as well.

Other than the occasional popping from the fireplace in the main living area, the house was quiet. The two women sat in silence, watching the girl. Abitha wasn't sure what she should do next, didn't even know what to expect.

"Do you recall how long it takes for the ointment to help?" Goodwife Carter asked.

Abitha shrugged. "I do not rightly recall. I know that my mother's medicines sometimes worked and sometimes did not. But this ointment, she used it on me when I had the pox, and it did indeed help."

Sarah nodded, studying her daughter, searching for any sign of relief.

"Abitha, thank you for coming here. It could not have been an easy thing for you . . . to bring root medicine into the reverend's house. As I am well aware, both I and the reverend can be more than a little intimidating."

"Goodwife Carter, you must understand, I might not be alive had you not showed me the kindness that you did. That both you and the reverend did."

"Thomas brought me your candies. I was very touched by that." Sarah paused, as though weighing what she was about to say. "Abi, I would tell you something, but it must stay between us."

"Of course."

"I were a lot of trouble as a child back in England. My mother called me her holy terror. Even as a young woman I seemed unable to do as I were bid."

Abitha shook her head. "I find that hard to believe."

Sarah smiled. "It is true. My mother would get so upset with me she would send me to stay with my grandmother for days at a time. And that is the part I wanted to share with you. You see, Granny, she too dabbled in the cunning arts. She were a good soul, a God-fearing woman, but she never let that stop her from helping those she could with her remedies. Like you, she saw it all as God's healing hand. I tell you this not to encourage you, but in hopes that you will understand that it is not me that has issue with your ways, but the village. Too many here are insecure in their faith and feel the slightest temptation will lead them astray, will open the door for the Devil. And mayhap they are right, at least for themselves. Abitha, what I really want to say is . . . I am sorry for being so strict about your charms. It's just . . . well, it is what is expected." Sarah's eyes filled with tears. "God has placed this village in my hands and I want to do what is right, but sometimes it is hard to know what is right. Hard to know when to stand and when to bend."

For the first time Abitha saw past Sarah's stiff, stern exterior and saw the woman, the wife, the scared mother. And for the first time since losing Edward, Abitha didn't feel so alone, felt perhaps she'd found a friend. Abitha fought back tears of her own. She reached out and clutched Sarah's hand. "I am not so good with words, but I will say without reservation that you are the backbone of this village, that Sutton would be lost without your guidance." And what Abitha realized then was that she truly meant it, that indeed, this woman made a difference. That like a good parent, she was stern but fair, lived by her words and led by example. Abitha couldn't imagine trying to walk that tightrope.

Martha let out a low moan.

Sarah stood up, leaning over the girl. "Abitha, is it but hopeful thinking, or does she look a mite better?"

She did look better; the redness was down and the sweat was drying on her skin.

Sarah touched Martha's cheek with back of her fingers. "Why, the fever . . . it is *gone*!"

"Thank the Lord," Abitha said, reminding herself to take every opportunity to inject God's name into the ritual. "He has heard our prayers."

Martha's eyes fluttered open.

"Oh, Martha, dear," Sarah said, clasping the girl's hand. "How do you feel?"

"Thirsty."

Sarah picked up the cup of water from the dresser and handed it to her. The girl drank heartily. Her eyes began to clear.

"Why is Abitha here?"

"She's here to help you get well, sugarplum." Sarah stepped over to the door. "Thomas," she called. "Thomas, come in here."

"I had a strange dream about you, Abi," Martha said. "You were an angel . . . but you had *horns*."

Abitha sucked in a quick breath. She glanced at Goodwife Carter, but she'd not heard.

The minister came quickly into the room.

"The fever has broken, Thomas."

"Oh, thank the Lord," Reverend Carter said.

"Aye," Abitha added quickly. "It seems the Good Lord has heard our prayers."

Martha touched the bumps on her arm. "Mother, the lumps . . . they do not hurt anymore."

It was obvious now that the redness was leaving the clusters of bumps, and Abitha began to fear the healing might be *too* miraculous. She searched the minister's face for any sign of alarm, but found only great relief.

The minister dropped to one knee. "Thank you, Lord," he said. "Thank you for this blessing on our family."

Abitha felt she should leave sooner than later, as Martha kept looking at her in that strange way, making her feel uneasy, fearful the girl would start speaking of horns and hooves. She bid Sarah to follow her as she stepped out of the room.

"Goodwife Carter, if I am to make it home by dark, I should be on my way now. I'll be sure—"

"Nonsense. You will stay the night. And I will send you off with a good breakfast in your belly."

"Thank you. Truly. But there is much that still needs doing this day."

"You must be careful then. Have you not heard that Lewis Ward and his son were found slain by beasts?"

"I shall be fine. Here, I will show you." She led Sarah out onto the porch, picked up the musket, and smiled.

Sarah shook her head. "Then, here, at the very least, let me get Thomas to hitch up the cart. He'll take you home."

"Perhaps it is better if he is not seen with me. I have heard tell that I have caused him much grief."

Sarah sighed. "But we know who the real problem is. Do we not?"

"Have you heard any more from Hartford?"

Sarah pulled the door behind her, then set worried eyes on Abitha.

"Yet another letter," Sarah said, speaking low. "More of the same. Magistrate Watson will not let this matter rest. As you may know, there is long-standing bad blood between the judge and the reverend and—" Sarah hesitated. "Well . . . I am afraid the whole situation has gotten out of hand. The judge has made it clear, *perfectly* clear, that if these matters with Wallace are not settled satisfactorily, he will come down and see to them himself."

"He can do that?"

Sarah nodded. "It is unprecedented, but the judge is not one to let precedent hold him back. The man is not above bending the law as it suits him either." Abitha caught genuine fear in the woman's voice. "Why, I did live in Hartford for a spell; I can attest that he has buried more than one poor soul who dared stand in his path."

Abitha felt her own heart racing. "I am sorry, sorry for all this trouble."

"This trouble has been brewing for a long time now. The judge has been but looking for an excuse to come down and undermine Thomas." Sarah let out a sigh. "I have said too much. . . . You have enough burdens. It is all just so overwhelming sometimes, and there is not near a soul I can confide in. Thomas says that we must trust in our rightness, that the Lord will see us through. So let us hold to that."

They were both silent a moment.

"Goodwife Carter . . . I do not claim to know the workings of God, but I know what I saw in there was the Lord's hand at work." Abitha realized she meant this. "Did you not feel it?"

Sarah bit her lip and nodded, then touched Abitha's arm. "Abi . . . thank you. That was not an easy thing to do. If there is ever anything . . . *anything*. You let me know. You promise."

"I promise," Abitha said, and headed off.

Abitha let herself out of the Carters' picket gate, rounded the hedge, and found herself face-to-face with Ansel Fitch.

"Lord!" Abitha cried, nearly falling into the bush.

"A bit late for you to be in Sutton, is it not?" the old man asked in his gravelly voice. "What business are you about at such hour? Must be something important."

"You would do well not jumping out of bushes upon women touting muskets, less you are wishing to be shot."

He bristled, leaned in on her, all but sniffing as he looked her up and down with those bulging eyes of his. He smelled of sour sweat.

She started to go around him, but he blocked her way.

"I asked you what you were up to?"

"I do not answer to you."

He sneered savagely. "How is it you travel the wilds and are not attacked by devil or wolf? Some spell?" To Abitha's dismay, the old man did actually sniff her then. "I am well aware of your wicked ways, girl. Your vile charms and trinkets. I have a nose for such."

Again Abitha tried to move around; again he blocked her.

"What need has the reverend of a cunning woman, I wonder?"

"You should ask the reverend."

He made a sour face. "I do not like this reverend. He worries if one is a minute late for his sermon, yet allows devils to harry us about our very walls. He should be more diligent."

Ansel moved closer, backing her up; she felt the bush against her back.

"But Ansel is watching. Always watching. The Devil will never get into Sutton while I am on guard. You hear me, girl?"

"Get off me," she cried, and shoved him back. She got around him then, spun and pointed the musket at him. "Leave me be!"

He grinned a toothy smile. "You best be on your guard, Abitha Williams. Ansel sees all and I have my eyes on you."

She dashed away, sprinting for the gate.

"Ansel is watching!" he called after her.

146

CHAPTER 7

Wallace rolled the barrel of honey mead up the ramp onto the back landing of the Black Toad Inn in Hartford and rang the bell. A moment later he was greeted by the gruff voice of Barry Jones, the brawny tavern owner.

"Well, it looks to be Mr. Williams himself." The stout man came out onto the landing, wiping his thick hands clean on his apron. The man had a head of curly blond hair and shaggy muttonchops, lively deep-set eyes that matched his tireless spirit—Wallace couldn't recall ever seeing the man sitting still. But his most distinguishing feature was his teeth: he was missing every other tooth, giving him a fiendish grin. "And look here, you brought me a present." Barry bent over and rocked the barrel, listening to the mead splashing within. "Just the one barrel today?"

"Aye, we are running a bit low on honey."

"Well, you are not alone there, man. Seems to be a shortage of honey and beeswax all over these parts. And good beeswax candles, not the smelly tallow kind, are up six wampum for a dozen down at Seymour's shop. Might not seem like much, but when you're running twenty rooms it can add up fast."

Barry removed his purse from his jacket and began counting out wampum beads, placing the small polished shells into Wallace's hand. Wallace found it annoying to be paid in what amounted to him as little more than Indian trinkets. But currently the milled shells were the only dependable currency in the territory.

Barry placed fifty beads into Wallace's hand, folded his purse, and slipped it back into his vest.

"Fifty-eight is the going price," Wallace said. "You know that. Have to pass along the price of the honey."

"Aye, fifty-eight for a full barrel." Barry thumped the barrel. "This one sounds a bit low."

Wallace flushed. "It is not." But he knew it was, knew he'd added a bit more water than he should have as well, trying to stretch his meager honey supply as far as it could go. Now wishing he hadn't, suddenly sure that Barry would take notice, and knowing if he did, he'd be docking him even further come the next batch.

"Shall we open her up and take a look?"

"No . . . no need for that," Wallace said, trying to sound jaunty to cover his embarrassment. "Mayhap the foam settled. Sometimes they do that."

"Seems yours do that a lot, Wallace." Barry grinned at him; it was not a jovial grin. "Now, you can take fifty or take your barrel elsewheres."

Wallace grimaced, dropped the shells in his pocket, turned, and left. He walked purposefully through Hartford down to the market, to where his real business lay.

He passed the stalls of straw baskets, pots, tools, clothes, and other wares, not stopping once, hardly sparing a sidelong glance despite the seductive smells of candies, fried dough, and grilled brisket. He was looking for someone. He'd worked out a plan to fix things with Abitha, but he needed a bit of help, the kind he couldn't ask for back in Sutton.

He came out on the far side of the market where the Pequot were allotted a few spots to sell their wares and shellfish. There were about a dozen blankets spread out on the grass, displaying various items. Women stood or sat around each blanket, as it was the women who handled sales and most money matters amongst the tribes. The few men who had tagged along lounged about behind them, smoking pipes in the shade of the oaks.

Wallace spotted the person he was looking for—a short Pequot man dressed

148

in English clothes, a vest, knee-length pants, and a tall felt hat, all in a stately forest green. With his short-cropped hair, the man stood out in sharp contrast to the other Pequot, who wore the traditional garb of their clans, their hair long and braided, decorated with beads and feathers.

The man went by the name Jesus Thunderbird, but that wasn't his real name. He'd told Wallace the Pequot called him by many names and not a one of them was very nice, so he'd decided to give himself a proper name, and since a name wields great power, he chose the most powerful name he could think of; thus—Jesus Thunderbird.

Jesus Thunderbird noticed Wallace approaching, pulled his corn pipe from his lips, and gave him a broad smile, exposing the gap between his two front teeth. "Big Boots."

Wallace grimaced. Jesus had a fondness for giving people whatever name suited him, sometimes three or four different ones in any given conversation, but usually sticking to the ones found to be the most irritating.

"Please, it's Wallace. Just Wallace."

"What can I do for Big Boots today?" Jesus said, and winked, producing a few smirks from the stone-faced men around him.

Most of the Pequot knew a smattering of English, but along with his affinity for names, Jesus also loved language. In addition to his native Algonquian, he could speak French, a bit of Spanish, and English—all manner of English: the man could mimic most any dialect, be it Irish, Welsh, Scottish, or even the hoity inflections of the nobility. On one occasion, when General Sir Jonathan Ashley came marching through town with his guards, Jesus pulled off such a pitch-perfect impersonation of the man that the general's own guards thought he'd ordered them to about-face, leaving General Ashley marching down the street alone. The stunt had gone over so well with the townsfolk that they'd actually invited Jesus into the Black Toad and bought him a few pints.

"I've come to make you an offer," Wallace said. "A profitable venture for all of us."

Jesus eyed him suspiciously.

"It is a simple thing, really."

Jesus laughed. "Why do I not believe that?"

"A woman owes me a great debt but refuses to pay it. So I need a bit of help in retrieving what is rightfully mine."

Jesus slid his corn pipe over to the corner of his mouth and blew out a cloud of smoke. "Why do you not go to the sheriff?"

Wallace sighed. "It's complicated."

Jesus shook his head. "Hmm, first it's a simple thing, now it's complicated. Which is it, Big Boots?"

Wallace gave himself a moment before replying, trying to maintain his composure. "It's both. The woman . . . she's a widow, living alone. She lives far outside of town, all but an exile. The point I am trying to make is there is not anyone looking out for her. Like I said, she's on her own. So getting what's mine should be simple."

"And what is yours?"

"Corn. A lot of corn. All I am looking for is a few men to help me haul it off. What I am proposing is that we simply go into her barn one night, load up the corn, *my* corn, and cart it off. You may keep all you can haul away and I'll keep the rest."

Jesus glanced at the other Pequot men; none of them appeared interested.

"I am not stealing," Wallace added, speaking to all of them. "You understand? I am simply reclaiming what is rightfully mine."

"I have a feeling this woman will not appreciate us taking *your* corn from *her* barn. Does this woman have a musket by chance?"

"Mayhap, but I certainly do. And I intend to bring it along."

"Sounds like you are playing a dangerous game, Big Boots."

"I am done playing games," Wallace growled, unable to keep the venom from his voice. "The woman is trying to ruin me."

"I see," Jesus said, and turned to the other men, talking rapidly in Algonquian. Wallace knew a few words and phrases, but the stone looks and headshaking were enough to see that the other men wanted nothing to do with his venture. All but two young men headed away toward the docks.

Jesus faced Wallace. "They say your foray could lead to big trouble with the English."

"And you?"

"And me," Jesus sighed. "See that woman over there?" He gestured to a large Pequot woman standing over one of the blankets. "The one scowling at me. Every day she tells me that I am lazy, that I am a terrible hunter, that I am a terrible provider, that I am naught but a big disappointment. She likes to warn me that if I do not start making a better effort, she will kick me out into the cold come winter. I have very thin blood, Big Boots. I do not want to sleep out in the snow. Mayhap if I bring home a couple bushels of corn, I will not have to."

"And these two?" Wallace nodded to the two young men. "Will they help?"

ABITHA

FOREST

CREEK

SKY

SAMSON

MAMUNAPPEHT

SLEWFOOT

THE WITCH

"This is Nootau and his brother Chogan. They are very brave, but not very smart. They have agreed to come with us."

"Good," Wallace said, feeling relieved, feeling as though his life might not be ruined after all. "I checked on the woman just yesterday. She is still gathering the corn. But most of it has already been harvested and is waiting in the barn. I'd like us to meet up at Miller Bridge tomorrow, just after dark. Can you do that?"

Jesus nodded. "We will meet you there."

Abitha dumped another full sack of corn into the cart hitched behind her mule.

"I think that's enough for today, Sid."

There were several rows left to harvest and still plenty of light left in the day, but there was no hurry now; October was still a week away, no need to work herself to death. She would have more than enough to pay Wallace what was owed in full.

Abitha leaned against the cart, letting that sink in—finding it all but impossible to believe. She watched the colorful fall leaves drifting along in the light breeze, realized she was smiling, and sucked in a deep lungful of the unseasonably warm air, enjoying how good it felt to breathe without feeling she was about to drown from all the worry. But she felt something more; the pulse, the magic in her chest, it was as though Samson had planted a seed there and it was growing, blossoming. She could feel her connection to the earth getting stronger, could feel the hum of it even now coming up through the ground, through her bare feet, making her feel as one with the land. She closed her eyes, drank it in, let it take her.

Sid brayed, bringing her back. She rubbed the mule and smiled. "I know, it's getting near your suppertime." She led the mule up to the barn. Booka met them halfway, leaping up onto the cart and riding into the barn with them.

Abitha unloaded the ears into the corncrib, unhitched the mule, then strolled out into the yard.

She scanned the edge of the forest for Samson's familiar shape. She'd not seen him all day. More and more he was disappearing into the forest, sometimes for days at a time. It dawned on her that she was actually looking for him, and she wondered when she'd gone from fearing him to seeking out his company. She tried to tell herself she was just lonely, but knew it to be more.

She wandered around to the bee boxes. She'd often found Samson there, the bees swarming about him as though delighted by his presence. He said he found their song calming and would sit there for hours pondering his past, his future, who he was, what he was. But Abitha felt he'd been doing too much ruminating of late, that he seemed to be growing ever more despondent.

Something must be done, she thought, and headed inside. She gathered up a handful of brittle and wandered down to the edge of the forest.

She didn't see Samson, but sensed him, sensed his discontentment.

She entered the woods, pushing through the limbs and brambles until she spotted the petrified remnants of the great tree and the small sapling with red leaves. She saw the cave and it was as though a cold shadow fell across her heart. She couldn't help but think of it as Edward's grave, his true grave, of his body lying all alone at the bottom of that dreadful pit. "Edward," she whispered, trying to recall his face, but it was the other that kept coming to her, the Edward with only shadows for eyes.

Abitha shuddered and pressed on, skirting around the blackened pile of stones. She spotted Samson sitting on the ground, behind one of the standing stones, his arms draped around his legs.

"Samson," she called.

He didn't answer. His head was down, his eyes closed. His face appeared pained.

"Oh, but if you do not make for a woeful sight. What are you doing here all alone and with such a long face?"

He continued to ignore her.

She stepped up to him, set her hands on her hips. "Samson. I know you hear me. Now, enough of this. You have done wonders. You are capable of so much more. I know this, I feel it. Now, up with you. There is joy to be found. But not if you sit there moping your days away."

He sighed, opened his silver eyes.

"I have something that will cheer you up." She pulled out the brittle, held it out for him.

He looked at the brittle, then her. "I am sorry, Abitha, but I am in no mood for brittle this day."

"What? Not in the mood for brittle? Lord be, Samson, but you are in a sad state."

He frowned and grunted.

"Oh, Samson, I am sorry you are so tormented. I truly am. I wish I could help you find your answers."

"As do I."

"My mother always said friends and laughter can cure any ill." Abitha sat down beside him, touched his arm. "We are friends, Samson, you and me. Are we not?"

His eyes brightened ever so slightly. He nodded. "Yes. That is one thing I do know. We are friends."

She grinned warmly at him. "Good, we are halfway there then. We just need some laughter. Know you any saucy riddles or rhymes, Samson?"

Samson frowned. "I know no riddles or rhymes."

"Well I do, plenty. And I learned a few new ones from the deckhands on the voyage over. I was right fond of this one."

> *"There were a Scotsman named McFee*
> *Who got stung on his nuggets by a bee*
> *He made tons of money*
> *By producing lots of honey*
> *Every time he went for a pee."*

Abitha gave him a coy smile.

Samson stared at her. "I do not understand this."

"All right, then here be another."

> *"There were a blind lass from Glasgow*
> *Who were sent out a milking the cow*
> *She milked the farmhand instead*
> *Until his cock turned bright red*
> *And now he be too sore to plow."*

Abitha pressed her hand against her mouth, suppressing a giggle.

Samson stared at her perplexed.

"Fine, mayhap such genteel poetry is beyond you. Mayhap it is a song you need, a bit of singing to cheer you up. Here's a little ditty that never fails to make me snicker." Abitha cleared her throat, began to hum, found the melody, and then sang.

> *"On the fourteenth of May, at the dawn of the day*
> *With me gun on me shoulder to the woods I did stray*
> *In search of some game, if the weather prove fair*
> *To see can I get a shot at the bonny black hare.*

153

I met a young girl there with her face as a rose
And her skin were as fair as the lily that grows
I says, My fair maid, why ramble you so
Can you tell me where the bonny black hare do go.

The answer she gave me, O, the answer were no
But under me apron they say it do go
And if you'll not deceive me, I vow and declare
We'll both go together to hunt the bonny black hare.

I laid this girl down with her face to the sky
I took out me ramrod, me bullets likewise
Saying, Wrap your legs round me, dig in with your heels
For the closer we get, O, the better it feels."

Abitha snorted.

"The birds, they were singing in the bushes and trees
And the song that they sang was, She's easy to please
I felt her heart quiver and I knew what I'd done
Says I, Have you had enough of me old sporting gun."

Abitha let out a loud laugh and glanced at Samson; he looked puzzled but intrigued.

"The answer she gave me, O, the answer were nay
It's not often young sportsmen like you come this way
And if your powder is good and your bullets are fair
Why don't you keep firing at the bonny black hare."

Abitha was having a hard time finishing the song between snorts of laughter. Samson too was smiling, but she saw it was at her, not the song.

"Oh, me powder is wet and me bullets all spent
And me gun I can't fire, for it's choked at the vent
But I'll be back in the morning, and if you are still here
We'll both go together to hunt the bonny black hare."

Abitha laughed loud and hard, realized it was more than this bawdy song, it was being able to let her hair down, to be her vulgar, sassy self in front of someone again, even if that someone might be the Devil himself.

"Abitha, please, do not stop. I would hear more."

"But I know no more verses."

"The words . . . they do not matter. It is your sweet voice."

She gave him a bashful smile. "You like my voice?"

"I do. It pleases me more than you could know."

Abitha continued, lightly humming and singing, and at some point, she realized other voices had joined in, the birds, the frogs, crickets, a symphony of calls. She laughed, the song touching her heart, making her feel so light and free, as though she could just run off into the woods and join all the animals living there.

Samson's smile grew; his silver eyes sparkled.

Abitha stood, began to slowly swirl and sway with the song.

Another voice joined. It came up through the ground, from deep in the earth, so very faint. Abitha felt it more than she heard it. *The serpent*, she thought, and glanced at Samson. But he seemed not to notice; his eyes were closed, a peaceful smile on his face.

155

The breeze kicked up and the red leaves on the sapling flittered. Her dream came to mind, that of the serpent offering her the apple, and she shuddered.

I care not, she thought, pushing the fear from her mind. *I am alive, the air is warm, there is a bounty in my field. It is time to find whatever joy I can in this often far too cruel world.*

She drank in the sweet air, Samson's smile, and continued to sway to the song.

Jesus, Nootau, and Chogan leaned against two pull carts, waiting for Wallace in the dark beneath a large willow. The night sky was clear and the moon almost full, giving them just enough light to navigate without their lanterns. *A good night for a bit of tomfoolery*, Jesus thought. *And if there is indeed enough corn to fill both of these carts, it will be a very, very good night.*

Clomping hooves approached and a moment later two men appeared on horseback. For a second Jesus didn't recognized Wallace and his son, then realized they were in disguise. Both wore sackcloth tied off at the waist with a rope belt, their arms and legs bare and what appeared to be black horsehair wigs beneath straw hats.

"What the hell are you supposed to be?"

"What do we look like?"

"Ugly women," Jesus said with a snort.

"No, we're Indians."

The Pequot shared a sour glance with one another.

Wallace and his son dismounted and tied their horses beneath the willow, then removed their shoes, leaving them by the tree. Wallace unhooked a lantern from his saddle and the two of them prissy-toed it over to the carts—two men obviously unaccustomed to going barefoot.

"So you're Pequot now?"

"We cannot afford to be recognized."

"What kind of game is this?"

"No game. The woman knows us, that's all. So we need disguise ourselves."

Wallace held up his lantern to get a good look at the carts. One was a rickety two-man cart that the brothers would be pulling, and the other, the smaller one, a single-man cart that Jesus would be pulling. Jesus had *borrowed* them from his uncle and so long as he returned them before his uncle noticed, all should be good.

Wallace seemed concerned.

"What is the matter?"

"I just hope they can carry enough corn, that's all."

"Where is your wagon?"

"Decided it would be too obvious if I were to show up at the market with a cart of corn same time as some went missing. So, it is all yours."

This made no sense to Jesus. "But I thought that—"

"It's complicated."

"Now it is complicated again."

"There's just a lot more to it. It's about the farm for me, not the corn. Look, you will get your corn and I will get back my farm. That is all you need to know."

Jesus noted the desperation in Wallace's eyes. A voice in his head, one that sounded a lot like his wife, warned him yet again that this wasn't a good idea. *Wallace is not the only one who is desperate*, he thought. *And desperate men take desperate chances, and that is all there is to this.* "And you are sure there is corn?"

"Yes. There is plenty."

Jesus noticed the flintlock pistol in Wallace's belt. "We cannot afford any trouble," Jesus said. "I am already in enough trouble with the tribe, my wife, and the sheriff too."

"No, of course not. That's the last thing I want. We will not so much as wake the woman up. Look, she does not even have a dog. We just quietly slip in, load up the corn, and slip away. You take the corn to your village and no one around here need ever know." Wallace stuck out his hand. "All right?"

Jesus hesitated, feeling sure he would regret this, but clasped Wallace's hand anyway.

"Good," Wallace said, and headed up the road.

Jesus grabbed the cart's tug bar and followed. *You will need to keep a close eye on this one.*

The farm ended up being only a short distance from the bridge. Wallace dialed the wick down on his lantern, dimming the flame. "We'll cut in through the lower field," he whispered. "The soft sod will cushion the cart wheels."

Jesus nodded and followed Wallace's lead. There were no lights on at the cabin and thankfully no dogs as Wallace had said, and they managed to make it down to the lower field without any disturbances. Jesus had greased all the loose parts on the carts ahead of time and they rolled almost silently across the soft earth to the back side of the barn.

They brought the large cart into the barn, pulling it up to the first corncrib. Wallace turned up the wick on his lantern, revealing an entire stall packed waist-deep in large, splendid ears of corn.

Jesus grinned. *This is going to be a good night after all,* he thought, then caught sight of Wallace's face. The man was staring into the adjoining stalls, his mouth slack-jawed, his eyes horrified.

"What is it? What is the matter?"

"The corn," Wallace said. "Look at it."

Jesus did, saw two more stalls just as full of corn as the first, but still didn't understand.

"Too much," Wallace said, shaking his head. "How . . . where? What am I to do?"

Jesus hurried the brothers along. The three of them began loading the big cart as quickly and silently as possible. Isaac joined them, but Wallace only continued to march back and forth between the stalls, muttering and shaking his head.

Once they'd filled the big cart, they started on the smaller one. Halfway through, Jesus noticed Wallace loading more corn onto the big cart.

Jesus darted over. "No more," he whispered. "It'll be too heavy to move."

"We have to get more," Wallace said, his eyes wild, his voice rising. "Can you not see?"

"We will come back," Jesus said. "Make another trip." But Jesus had no intention of returning; at this point he would count himself lucky to get away from this madman with what they had.

"No, it is not enough," Wallace said, and continued to pile the corn onto the cart.

"Stop," Jesus said. "You have to stop."

Wallace pushed past him with another armload of corn.

Jesus, seeing the big man wasn't listening to him or anyone, leapt to the front of the cart and grabbed the tug bar. He waved the brothers over and the three of them began pulling the cart away from the stall. Even with the three of them, they could barely get it to move. The axle groaned and creaked. Jesus could see the wheels bowing from the weight. He tried to steer it around the smaller cart, felt the load shift, then came a loud crack as the left wheel splintered, then shattered, toppling the cart and spilling corn everywhere.

158

Wallace stared at the corn, his eyes bulging. "No, God in Heaven. No. *No!*"

Isaac grabbed Wallace by the arm. "Father, we must go!"

Wallace shook his son away. "No! We cannot leave it! Why . . . she could take it in tomorrow. Then all would be lost. You hear me? All *lost!*" He glanced wildly about, his eyes landing on the lantern. He snatched it up, then shoved over a bale of hay, kicking the straw onto the corn. He grabbed a handful of the dry straw, lit it, and tossed it onto the hay, setting it to blaze.

There was plenty of dry hay and stacked timber around, and Jesus could see the whole barn was about to go up in flames. "No," Jesus said, trying to stomp out the fire. "You promised. No trouble!"

Wallace knocked the smaller man out of his way, his eyes blazing like the fire, and continued lighting the bales of hay.

"Damn it," Jesus said, dashing back to the smaller cart.

Wallace kicked another of the flaming haybales over onto the corn. Flames were already brushing the ceiling. The goats began bleating and the mule brayed.

Jesus and the two brothers grabbed the tug bar on the small cart and headed from the barn.

"Leave it!" A woman stood blocking their way, a musket leveled at Jesus's chest. Jesus and the brothers did as they were told, dropping the cart tug bar. The woman saw Wallace, shifted her aim, and when she did, Jesus and the brothers dove into the adjoining stall. They scrambled over the corn and leapt out the small window, landing atop one another in the goat pen.

There came the loud blast of the musket, followed by a lesser blast, which Jesus concluded must be Wallace's pistol. He had a moment to hope the two had killed one another before a dark shape appeared before him and the two brothers.

At first Jesus thought it was one of the goats, that the goat was walking on its hind legs, but when the light from the fire illuminated the creature, Jesus felt his blood turn to water.

The thing was made of horns, shadows, and fur, fur that twisted and swirled, drifting off it like black smoke. With arms and hands like that of a man, only with jagged claws curling out from its fingers. It set eyes on them, eyes that burned silver, almost blue, burning into each of them. The creature snarled, revealing its fangs.

"*Hobomok!*" Nootau cried.

Hobomok! Jesus thought, the name like a knife to his heart as he wondered how it could be that the very lord of death and misery was here before him.

The beast cocked its head and spoke in a low gravelly voice. "Hobomok?" A confused look came over its face and it said it again, slowly, as though trying to decipher the word. "Hob . . . bo . . . mok?" For one moment it appeared afraid, it grasped the sides of its head as in pain, then its eyes narrowed, seemed to burn. "Hobomok," it hissed, as though the word scorched its tongue.

It grabbed Nootau by the neck, yanking the man to his feet and slamming his head against the fence post.

Jesus and Chogan both let out a cry and scrambled across the mud, trying to get their feet under them. They reached the fence, tumbled over, and took off running.

Jesus knew the devil was right behind him, but when he glanced back, the demon stood just where they'd left it, staring at Nootau's lifeless body.

Jesus ran for all he was worth, no longer caring about the corn, his angry wife, his uncle's carts. His whole life he'd heard tales of the wicked Hobomok and wanted only to be as far away from this devil as he could get.

159

Morning found Abitha sitting in the blackened dirt, covered in soot. The fire was out, but the barn still smoldered, the heavy smoke drifting across the field. She'd managed to rescue the mule and the goats, but the corn was burned and ruined.

She knew she should be crying, but only felt numb. She stared at the lower acre—there were still a few rows of corn left, but not nearly enough. Wallace would be back with the sheriff in less than a week It was over. He had won.

Who the hell did he think he were fooling with that ridiculous getup?

She spat—her saliva grimy with soot—and wondered what she would do now. Should she try and prove it was Wallace? It certainly looked bad—her crops being burned just as she was about to pay off her debts. Any sane soul would see it was him. Or would they? She knew she would need more than her word, more than circumstance. He didn't leave so much as a boot print. How was she supposed to convince the sheriff that this was Wallace's doing when she had one dead Pequot and two Pequot carts in her barn? She shook her head. *He set those men up. That devious son of a bitch set them up. People are quick to blame the Indians to begin with. Always a hell of a lot easier than blaming one of your own.*

If I'd only been a better shot, she thought. *I'd at least have had the pleasure of watching him die.* She realized nothing was stopping her from going over to his farm and shooting him now. She chewed that thought over for a while, savored it; it was all she had at the moment.

Booka rubbed up against her and meowed. Abitha absently stroked the cat.

Samson came out of the woods, crossed the field. He walked around the burned-out barn, taking a long, hard look at the dead Pequot man before coming over and sitting on the grass next to Abitha.

He didn't speak, just sat there staring at the barn, rubbing his forehead as though it ached, looking spent and weary.

Sky swooped down, perching on Samson's shoulder. Creek appeared and began swimming in slow circles around all of them.

Forest crawled out from under a nearby log and joined them. He plucked a weed and began chewing the stem. "You should kill him," Forest said. "The big man."

Abitha nodded. "I should."

"We can help. All of us. Father too."

Sky and Creek nodded eagerly.

"Get your musket," Forest urged. "And your long knife. Does he have a family? Friends? Neighbors? We can kill them as well." The opossum was smiling. "Father is very good at killing once you get him started. Someone just needs to get him started."

And there, at that moment, while staring at the blackened husks of the corn she'd all but died for, while watching the remains of her barn smolder, the one she and Edward had built together, Abitha thought it sounded like a good idea, a *very* good idea.

"Who is he?" Samson asked.

"Who, Wallace?"

"No, the dead man."

Abitha's gaze shifted to the body lying facedown in the goat pen. She sighed. "I need to bury him."

Forest shook his head. "Dump him in the woods for the worms and the beetles and the boogers and the bears."

"Who is he?" Samson asked again.

"A Pequot Indian," Abitha said. "This used to be their land, but war and disease decimated them a good many years ago. They're scattered about this area, but I believe most live in a village many miles north of here."

"He called me Hobomok. Have you heard the name before?"

Abitha shrugged. "Nay, not that I can recall."

Forest, Sky, and Creek froze.

Samson set stern eyes on Forest. "What is Hobomok?"

It took Forest a moment to reply. "It means spirit of death. They thought you a devil, that is all. They think we are all devils. It means nothing."

Samson stared at Forest as though trying to pierce the creature's soul. He shook his head, then pressed his palm against his temple. "Last night . . . after killing the man . . . the spiders returned. They lurk in the shadows . . . haunt my dreams. I see masks . . . and the man with the painted face. They will not leave my head. It is growing unbearable."

Forest shared an anxious look with the wildfolk.

"I will never be whole," Samson continued. "Not until I can see past the shadows. Perhaps these Pequot have some answers?"

Forest stiffened. "The only thing the Pequot have for you are tricks and traps, the kind you can never escape."

"I am already in a trap from which I cannot escape."

"You can escape; you choose not to. You need but pay tribute to Pawpaw, honor Mother Earth with blood. We have been around this."

Samson didn't reply, just stared out toward the barn, to where the dead man lay.

Forest began pacing back and forth, a thunderous frown on his face, and after a minute he stopped, sighed. "Father," he said sternly. "I beg you do not go to the Pequot. It will not end well for you or for us if you do. I cannot force you to play your role. I can only hope you will find the truth in my words. But if . . . if you will not help us, then please, I beg you by the moon above, do not betray us so."

Still, Samson did not reply.

Forest studied Samson for another long moment. "I do not know what more to say to you. We are all struggling here. All our lives, our very world, are at stake." And with that, Forest left, looking deeply troubled as he wandered across the field, disappearing into the woods.

Abitha thought how nice it would be to just trot off into the woods like that. To never have to come back, never have to deal with the farm, the corn, with *Wallace,* ever again.

"I am going to try and get away," she said absently, more to herself than to Samson. "To leave before they come for me. Before I am sentenced to serve Wallace and his family." She nodded as though trying to convince herself. "Might be able to scrape together a few things to sell. Make enough to buy passage down south . . . somewhere the winter is not so harsh." She scanned the farm, trying to calculate what she had left of value. "There's Sid . . . the two goats . . . chickens . . . the plow blade—"

A bee landed on her arm; always seemed to be a few buzzing around Samson as though he was some succulent wildflower. She gently blew it away. "And the bees. I have several healthy hives. They'll certainly fetch a goodly price. With wax and honey in demand the way it is, probably will get more wampum for them than all the rest of it together." She considered the wagon. It was beside the barn and the bed had sustained some fire damage, but the rest of it appeared in decent shape.

"Abitha, what is wampum?"

"Huh?"

"Is it something you eat?"

"It is a shell. It's milled into beads, a very difficult and time-consuming process from what I hear. People use it to buy things with, you know, like currency, like money . . . like—" She trailed off, not knowing how to explain the concept of currency to a forest creature and not being in the mood to give a lesson.

Samson grunted. "So, you trade things for the wampum. Such as the corn and beeswax. Yes?"

"Aye."

"Then you trade the wampum for other things?"

"Yes, that's pretty much how it works."

"And you need wampum to trade to Wallace for the land."

She looked at him sharply. "Can you make wampum, Samson? Is there a spell for that? If you could, then . . ." She began to get excited. "Why, if you could, then

I—" She leapt to her feet, dashed into the cabin, returned a moment later with Edward's leather pouch. She dug around and pulled out a cracked wampum bead. It was broken, worthless.

"Here." She sat it in his palm. "Make more . . . as many as you can!"

Samson closed his hand around the fragment, shut his eyes, appeared to be concentrating. He frowned. "Place your hand atop mine."

She did.

"Do you feel anything, Abitha?"

After a minute, she shook her head.

"Nor do I."

She let go and Samson held up the shell. "It does not have a voice. Not like the corn, or the knitbone, the goats, or the bees. I believe it is on account that it is not alive, nor does it want to be. It does not even have a ghost. I am sorry, Abitha, I have no connection to it."

"Oh," she said, not hiding her disappointment.

He continued to study the bead, his brows furrowed, then his eyes brightened. Samson stood, walked over to the porch and picked up her broom. He held the handle out. "Hum for me."

163

"Hum? What do you mean?"

"Like the song you sang the other day, but just hum."

"Samson, I am sorry, but I just cannot. Not this day."

"Trust me, Abitha. Close your eyes and hum. Think of sunlight and flowers."

Abitha started to protest, but caught the fervent look on Samson's face.

"Abitha, trust me."

She let out a sigh, cleared her throat, and began to hum softly. She closed her eyes and tried to picture flowers in her mind, found it all but impossible as her mind kept turning to the blackened husks of corn. Then Samson joined her, adding his warm voice, and the flowers began to bloom and blossom, a kaleidoscope of colors spinning about in her mind's eye. She felt the pulse beneath her in the ground, it moved toward her, seeking her out, found her, touched the magic within her, and all at once she could actually smell the flowers. The humming grew, louder and louder. She opened her eyes and gasped.

Bees, hundreds and hundreds of them, swarmed around her and Samson.

"They are here for you, Abitha. You are their queen. Now, what would you have them do?"

Do? she thought. *Naught. Ah, Samson, you are trying so hard, but this is not what I need. What I need is . . . what I need is . . . Oh, mercy, yes. I see!*

She began to hum again, to sing along with the bees, thought of honey, of large copious amounts of honeycomb dripping from the broom, pushed these thoughts into their song. And her humming and theirs intertwined, became one melody. The bees began landing on the broom handle, began to weave the song, the magic, into honeycomb.

It was more than the bees, more than her; she felt Samson harnessing the magic, drawing it from the earth itself, channeling it through her. She could actually see it—tiny golden sparkles—swirling in the air with the bees.

And again, that rush, an almost carnal lust drumming from her core, threatening to consume her as his magic mixed with hers, her chest fit to burst with the rapturous force of it, as together, they wove comb after comb.

Sky and Creek joined the bees, flying in circles, laughing along with Abitha.

Samson propped the broom against the fence and the bees continued their magic, the honeycomb growing along the posts and rails. The golden honey sparkling in the sunlight.

"Samson, how much can they make?"

He shrugged. "It is your spell. How long can you sing for?"

All day, she thought. *I can sing all day.*

CHAPTER 8

I cannot do it alone," Forest said, glowering at Sky and Creek. "You must help if we are to be rid of her."

Neither of them would make eye contact.

"This is not something you can hide from." Forest scrambled up the black rocks and stood beside the sapling. "Look," he demanded, tapping one of the shriveled leaves. "Look!"

They looked and winced.

"Pawpaw is withering before our eyes. Why is that? You both know. Abitha is stealing the magic. Did you not see her with the bees? Feel the magic growing within her? Abitha is not what she seems. I fear she is like the magic folk of old, like the shaman. And like them, now that she has had a taste, she will want more and more until all is lost. Her sight has already grown so strong that she can see us whether we wish her to or not."

"Yes, it is Father's fault! He's the one empowering her so. But she is learning how to manipulate the magic. There is no telling what she is capable of with his help. She might send us all up in a ball of flame next."

Sky and Creek flitted about as though they wanted to be anywhere but here.

"You heard Father. The spiders are back. You know that means Mamunappeht is getting closer. You know this is the woman's doing."

"No. It doesn't matter whether she means to or not, Creek. She is still doing this. Every time they work one of their spells together, it is like sending smoke signals to Mamunappeht."

"What foolish thing will they do next, I ask you? What door will they open? What do you think will happen if the magic man finds out that Pawpaw has returned to us?"

Sky and Creek met his eye then; both appeared horrified.

"Listen to me, both of you. We must kill her as soon as we can. Before the shaman finds us, before they starve Pawpaw."

"How?" Forest smirked. "Together, that is how. Lend me your magic, help me call forth the venomous creatures. Let them do their work and there will be no trace of our hand in this deed. It will work. I know it will!"

166

The two exchanged a painful look, but nodded ever so slightly.

"Good. Tonight then . . . we set them upon her tonight."

The day was drawing to a close, the setting sun coloring the sky brilliant orange.

Samson perched upon the blackened remains of the barn roof. He watched Abitha, had been watching her all day as she went about her task of cutting the honeycomb from the fence and storing it in her cabin.

Hobomok. The word came to him like a whisper on the wind. He shut his eyes, reliving for the hundredth time the shock of hearing that word, how it had burned into him, how in that moment his mind had felt it would split in two. They were back, the spiders. With his eyes shut he could just see them, tiny flickering hairs at the edge of his vision. How they made his head ache. "Leave me be," Samson growled. He spotted Sky and Creek over by the cabin, watching him, looking nervous, and he wondered yet again what it was they were hiding from him.

Abitha dropped off another load of cut comb, returned, washing the stickiness from her hands in the water pail. She began counting, using her fingers. She smiled. "Samson, I've added up what I have in the cabin. Why, there's almost more than the wagon will hold. Edward was getting a full string, over ninety-six wampum a pound, and that was last year. I've heard they're paying more than double that now. You know what that means, Samson? Do you? It means Wallace can go diddle himself, it does, because this is my land now!"

She let out a laugh, then whooped, a wild grin on her face. She snatched up the broom from the fence, pulled off a bit of the remaining comb, and put it in her mouth, licking her lips loudly. She began to spin about with the broom as though it were her dancing partner, spun until she fell on the grass, then just lay there laughing, sounding elated and exhausted.

Samson felt Abitha's spirit, her fervor, how the magic was drawn to her, how it bonded with her, how strong it was becoming within her. He closed his eyes, drank it in, trying to channel it to open his last memories, but it was the terrified faces of the Pequot men he kept seeing.

Hobomok, Hobomok. He couldn't stop hearing the name. *Am I truly the spirit of death? Am I?*

Abitha lay in the grass watching Samson, disturbed by how troubled he looked. *You have done so much for me, Samson. How I wish I could help you.* She found her hand in her apron pocket, upon the chain of braids—she kept them with her at all times now. *Mother, if you were but here. You would know what to do.*

A bee drifted by and Abitha began to softly hum its song, calling it to her, delighted when the bee responded, began to circle her face, then landed right on the tip of her nose. She marveled at their connection; it wasn't as though she could actually talk to them, but more a projecting of her feelings and desires onto them. It made her feel one with them, one with nature itself.

She gently blew the insect away and sat up. It was growing dark and she needed to pee. She climbed to her feet and let out a groan as she tried to stretch the soreness from her back. She then headed around the cabin for the privy, or what Edward liked to call the small cabin. And, as was Edward's way, it was built like a small cabin, solid and secure to keep the wind out and so you did not need worry about a bear or a pack of wolves joining you while you were about your business.

The privy sat at the bottom of the slope, farther away from the cabin than Abitha would've liked, especially in the heart of winter, but it needed to be downhill from the well, and Edward had said the soil was right in that spot.

As she approached, a rabbit darted out from the side of the outhouse. It ran directly at her, dashing by as though something terrible was after it. Abi glanced about for predators amongst the nearby trees.

She reached for the door and stopped. Something was wrong; it took her a second to figure it out. *Where are the flies?* The air around the outhouse was usually humming with them. She lifted the latch and opened the door, saw nothing but shadows, started to step in, then stopped. Someone was there, next to the privy.

A figure, a man, drifted out from the dark. His face a cluster of dancing shadows, with pits where his eyes should be.

"Edward?" She gasped, fell back a step, her hand to her mouth.

Edward stood staring, not at her, but at the privy. He raised a hand, pointed inside, and his mouth opened into a silent scream.

Abitha glanced back, realized the shadows within were alive, the floor of the outhouse a boiling mass of oily shapes. She heard a hiss, saw Forest hanging from the ceiling beam, his black eyes gleaming.

"Kill her," Forest whispered, and something struck her ankle, another strike, then two more.

Abitha stumbled back, tripped, fell hard onto her rump, and that was when she saw them—snakes, five, maybe six. Tangled amongst them dozens upon dozens of spiders and centipedes. And like a dam breaking, they gushed out, slithering and skittering, racing one another for her, all of them coming for *her!*

Abitha tried for her feet, but they were on her and she let loose a scream as they slid, crawled, and skittered up her legs. There came a sting, a bite, another, then dozens. She screamed again, gained her feet, only to realize she could no longer feel them, her legs going numb, sending her tumbling back to the ground. She clawed and slapped and still they assailed her.

"What is this!" Samson roared. He leapt past her, grabbing Forest and yanking him from the outhouse, slamming the possum to the ground. And just like that, the spell was broken, the snakes and spiders all losing their fire, falling away, scattering into the grass and underbrush.

Abitha moaned; her attackers were gone, but the searing poison continued to crawl slowly up her legs.

Samson dropped next her, clutched her hand. His face mortified.

"Help me, Samson."

"I . . . I do not know how?" He grabbed the earth, her hand, began chanting, but nothing was happening.

The poison continued to spread. Abitha knew she was running out of time, knew if it reached her heart it would be all over. She thought she saw a ghost there in the shadows, not Edward this time, but her mother. She jabbed her hand deep into the pocket of her apron, clasped the braids, pulled them out, pressed them to her lips.

"Aye, Mother, I *can* do this. I must."

She clutched the braids in one hand, Samson's hand in the other, closed her eyes, and focused inward. She knew what she was seeking—the pulse, the glow, the magic that had been lurking within her ever since Samson first touched her, growing with each spell they cast.

And it was there, in her heart, waiting. She felt its hunger, how it wanted her, and she was afraid. She saw them then, the shadowy shapes of twelve women, their faces hidden beneath their long auburn hair. The scent of lavender and sage grew strong in the air, and a sense of calm stole over her.

The magic, the power, it is part of me and I am part of it. She set it free and it bloomed and it was at that moment she felt something else, something below her in the earth, something that knew her name. *The serpent!*

"She is here!" Samson whispered.

The pulse grew stronger, drumming in her chest, spreading, coursing out along her veins and arteries, seeking the poison. And when the magic, her magic, found the poison, she did not fight it, no, but bound it with the magic, the two becoming part of the same. It was her poison now, and she simply pushed it from herself the way one would exhale a breath of air.

She felt a cold dampness along her legs, opened her eyes to see the venom sweating out from her pores. She let out a long groan and fell back on the grass, panting.

Creek and Sky stared at her, stunned.

Samson's eyes were full of wonder. "Abitha, there is more to you than you know."

Forest coughed, rolled over, started crawling away.

"You!" Samson snarled, leaping up and seizing the opossum in both hands. "You are done!" He began squeezing, crushing the spirit.

Creek and Sky flew at Samson, biting and grabbing, tugging his fur, trying to make him release Forest.

Abitha felt the presence in the earth move, felt its displeasure. "No!" Abi cried. "Samson, you must not! Do not let the Devil take you! It is over, done. *Release him!*"

Samson glanced back and forth between Abitha and Forest, his eyes full of fury. Abitha felt sure he would crush the opossum; instead he let out another loud snarl and slung the opossum to the ground.

Forest lay there wheezing.

"You are to leave here!" Samson commanded. "If I should see you again, it will be your end. Do you understand me, foul beast?"

Forest tried to get up, couldn't. Creek and Sky flew over, and with their help, Forest made it to his feet. Slowly they walked him away. Just before entering the woods, Forest stopped, looked back. "Father," he called. "Pawpaw is starving. . . . You must bring it tribute and soon. If you do not heed me, the tree will die . . . and with it . . . your soul."

Samson turned his back on them.

"I tried everything to save you, Father. To save us all. I am sorry I failed you, that I failed Mother Earth. One day, and very soon I fear, you will understand. Only then, it will be too late."

The wildfolk headed off, disappearing into the dark shadows of the trees.

Abitha steadied herself against the well and took a deep drink from the bucket. Her legs were still quivering, dotted with small welts and bite marks, but there was no pain. She searched for Edward down by the trees, found no sign of him. *You saved me, Edward,* she thought, and wondered just what that meant. *Are you truly still here? Please tell me. Or have I gone mad? You must show me what is real.*

Samson stared at her, not hiding his awe.

Night was upon them, and the fireflies flittered about the grass and bushes. The air felt alive, like a storm was brewing.

"Abitha, Mother Earth, she was here. She came for you. I am sure of it. Did you not feel her? You must have."

"I felt many things," she said, as thoughts of her dreams, of the serpent offering her the apple full of spiders came to her. She realized she was still clutching the chain of braids. She touched them to her cheek, savoring their comfort a moment longer before putting them away, back into her apron. *Do not judge me harsh, Edward. I am trying to do what is right . . . only it is so very hard to know what is right. If you are there, you see this; you must.*

Samson began pacing back and forth. "You have such a connection, I feel it. Perhaps, if *you* ask Mother Earth the right questions, she will show you." He shook his head. "No, show *us*." He pulled on his chin, nodding to himself. "Yes, *us*." His eyes suddenly filled with excitement. "That's it! That is the key! *Together!*

All the magic we have done together has proved fruitful. If *we* ask her, perhaps then she will reveal who I am. Will give me some clue. Yes? *Yes!*"

His blood was up; she could all but hear his heart thumping.

"Abitha, now is our chance. Let us dance, you and I. Let us stir up some big magic this night. Let us call the moon and the stars to show us who we are. What say you, Abitha? Will you help me find my truth?"

She had no idea what he was leading her into, but she also knew he wasn't asking, not at all.

He seized her arm, squeezing a bit too hard. "Will you?" He didn't wait for her to answer but dashed off, returning with her broom, handing it to her.

"What is this for?"

"Abitha, I once asked you what you wanted. Do you remember?"

She nodded.

"You said that when you were a child you dreamed of being a fairy queen, of running barefoot through the woods with the animals. To sing and dance with them. And to—"

"—to fly with the birds," she finished with a grin.

He took her hand. "Abitha, it is time to fly."

She laughed, a giddy sound, the sound of someone who has had too much to drink. "I cannot fly, Samson."

"Have you tried?"

"Samson, I cannot fly."

"Sky and Creek can fly, can be seen and not seen. You have pushed poison from your blood, have healed the sick, raised the corn."

"It was more than me."

"I know." His silver eyes lit up, and for a moment she felt the old fears. "You have called her here. Her magic is all around us. Why, you are brimming with it. Do you not feel it? Let us seize it before it slips away again."

It was true, she was flush with the magic, almost buoyant. *Almost as though I could fly*, she thought. *Or at least float.* A wave of excitement coursed through her.

"It is time to see just what you are capable of." He pushed the broom at her. "Let us go for a ride, you and I."

She started to resist, she was so weary, dizzy, almost feverish from the day, from the venom, and this all sounded like madness. But when he touched her, she felt his fever, felt the pulse grow, both within her and about her. Her body began to tingle.

He smiled and started to spin her in a slow wide circle, first in one direction, then back in the other, almost a waltz. She kicked off her shoes, the grass, still warm from the day's sun, feeling delicious beneath her bare feet. The humid night air was intoxicating, going to her head.

"Set yourself free, Abitha. Set us both free."

"Aye," she replied, her clothes suddenly feeling heavy and confining. She tugged off her blouse, throwing it into the air with a laugh. She felt lighter, light as a feather. She slipped off her skirt and apron, falling over in the process, rolling across the soft grass, savoring the feel of it against her bare skin.

The magic began to swirl around them, in the air and in the ground. She couldn't see it, but she felt it dancing along every inch of her nakedness.

Samson pulled her to her feet and the dance began again. The fireflies, moths, and bats joined them, drawn in by the magic, fluttering and swimming about in ever-tighter circles.

Abitha began to hum, to sing a song without words, the crickets, frogs, and toads all lending their voices. The night felt to her a living thing; she felt its breathing, its pulse. She moaned, drinking in its intoxicating sweetness, laughed, then sang, then laughed some more. She'd not slept for going on two days now, and she let her delirium take her.

The air grew dense around her, almost a thing you could swim in. She saw it then, the magic, a shimmering haze flowing around her, her hair floating in its current.

Samson released her and she spun slowly about, circling him.

He held out the broom. "Do you still wish to fly, Abitha? With the bats through the night?"

She looked at him, understood this was no jest. She nodded. "Oh, yes."

"Ask the broom."

"The broom?" She laughed, the sound echoing in her own head. "Why not?" She sauntered, almost glided over to him, clasping the handle just above his hand. She had no idea what to do next, then she did. The earth told her as it always did. She closed her eyes and let the broom *feel* her desire, sent it a vision of her sailing through the night, as did Samson, the two of them together, their hearts as one. The shimmering haze began to swirl around the broom, tighter and tighter, weaving together as Abitha and Samson pushed it, channeling the magic into the broom. The broom shuddered and she felt a throbbing through the handle. The throbbing slowed, becoming a pulse, matching that of her own, that of Samson's.

Samson let go and stepped back.

The broom was buoyant and Abitha found it took some effort to keep it from drifting skyward. She glanced at Samson and he smiled.

"What now?" Abitha asked, and the broom responded, tugging her gently. She followed its lead as they drifted in a wide circle, slowly spinning. Her whole body, her heart and soul, felt so light, so incredibly light. And at some point, she realized her feet were no longer on the ground.

"Oh," she whispered, "this is magnificent."

The oddly paired partners drifted down to the forest's edge, then slowly back up to Samson. Samson caught the broom, steering the handle down so that the broom was horizontal, floating between them at waist level.

He took a seat on the sweep and extended a hand out to Abitha, his silver eyes aglow. He seemed as drunk on the magic as her. "Are you ready?"

She hesitated a moment longer, savoring the excitement and fear. She started to take a seat behind him.

"No, it is your spell. You should lead."

"Oh," she said. "Wonderful, steering a broom. How hard can it be?"

She took a seat in front of him, sitting sidesaddle, all but in his lap. She clasped the handle, gripping it firmly as though for dear life. He slipped an arm about her waist. He smelled of honey and dry leaves, his fur warm and soft.

"Are we ready?" he asked.

She heard distant thunder. "Nay, but we are going to do it anyway. Are we not?"

He laughed. "We are."

"Do you know what you're doing, Samson? Are you going to get us killed?"

"Me, no. I have no idea. It is your spell. It is up to you not to kill us."

"Oh, then we are doomed for certain."

He laughed again, the sound music in her ears.

Her foot left the grass and they began to drift aimlessly, like a boat without a rudder, floating only a few feet above the ground. She would have thought sitting on a broom unwieldy, but she hardly needed even hold on, the two of them connected and both lighter than the air.

"Tell it where to go."

She did, simply by willing it. She set her eyes and thoughts on the cornfield, and the broom responded, slowly at first, but as their connection grew, they gained a bit of height and speed. They glided toward the field, then out over it, circling the farm until soon she no longer felt she was willing the broom, but that she herself was flying, and like a bird, she went where she pleased.

173

She flew higher, well above the tallest tree. The moon was full and bright and she could see for miles in all directions, could see the distant outline of mountains toward the north, lightning far off to the south, and the flickering lights of the village to the east. She circled in ever-widening circles, picking up speed. She swooped down, flying just over the cabin and the remains of the barn. Several bats joined them, playfully flittering in and about.

She flew upward again, the warm night air blowing through her hair. She saw the stars glittering off a nearby lake, swirled down until she was flying level with the lake, dipping a toe into the water as they skimmed across the surface. She laughed and Samson laughed with her.

"Such a wonderful dream," she said.

He leaned forward, his chin on her shoulder. She glanced at his face, so wild, strange, and savage, yet somehow beautiful. She felt the thrum of his heart join that of hers and the broom, all pulsing together as one.

"It is time," he whispered into her ear. "To see what we can find. Ask her, ask Mother Earth, ask the moon and stars to show us our true selves."

She felt his need, his want, but now also her own want, and as it grew, as it filled her up, she ached to satisfy it. "Show me, Mother Earth . . . show me who we are."

He sat his hands atop hers. "Allow me."

She didn't want to relinquish control, she wanted only to fly all night, fly the world around and never come back. But she yielded to him.

His grip tightened on her hand and they plummeted down toward the trees. She let out a cry, certain they would crash into the pines and oaks, but instead they flew through them, the leaves buffeting against her cheeks and toes. Deeper and deeper into the forest they went, faster and faster until the trees were but dark blurry shapes shooting past them, and at some point she realized they were going through them as though they were ghosts.

It became dark; it was only them and the warm wind howling in her ears. Slowly the moon returned, only larger, orange, and muted. They began to slow, the trees coming into focus, different now, with foliage she'd never seen before, giant ferns and palms. The air itself felt different, heavier, denser, like in the wake of a thunderstorm. A thousand sounds, cries, calls, howls rang out from the thick woods all around them.

"Where are we?"

"Long ago."

It was night, yet the forest was alive with lights, radiant flowers of all varieties, and insects, and—she blinked—winged creatures, little winged people. *Fairies,* she thought, sprites and pixies, and so much more. Some small, the size of insects, others the size of hawks and eagles, with bird wings, insect wings, bat wings, all sharing a sparkling luminescence. She saw hundreds of creatures like Creek, Sky, and Forest, with their childlike faces and animal bodies. They began to fly along with Abitha and Samson, following them through the trees, singing and giggling. Other creatures followed on the ground below them, the deer running along with great cats, and giant bears, huge lizards, tiny horses, and so many other beasts she had never seen before.

They flew upward, above the treetops, speeding up, leaving all the creatures behind. A universe of stars exploded above her as they shot through the night, everything blurring together then going dark.

Again, they slowed, again the world came back into focus, this time to a landscape of giant volcanoes, tendrils of lava squirming down from towering peaks, forming rivers of fire. A meteor streaked across the sky, another, then another. Lightning flashed and thunder boomed. The air smelled of sulfur, of ash, of stagnant swamps. The sky above, utterly black, not a moon or star to be seen. Then one star appeared, sparkled, followed by another, more and more, popping open like eyes, then Abitha saw to her great horror that they *were* eyes, a hundred, a thousand, a million eyes, and all of them, every one, staring at her.

"Who am I?" Samson screamed into the firmament.

The heavens did not answer.

"Who am I?" he cried.

And then, for one second, Abitha saw herself through the eyes, through all those millions of eyes, and when she did, she understood something of great magnitude, yet so simple. *All the eyes, they are one. They are all one.*

"Who am I!" Samson screamed. "Answer me! I demand an answer!"

And the heavens began to laugh, like all was a big joke. The laughter growing and growing until it thundered all around them.

"Stop!" Abitha cried, clasping her hands to her ears, squinting her eyes shut, trying to block it all out. "STOP!"

And then suddenly, she was falling away into endless darkness.

175

C H A P T E R   9

Abitha awoke in the middle of the cornfield. It was morning. She sat up and quickly realized she was nude and her hair was full of leaves. She tugged out a leaf; it was bright pink and unlike any leaf she'd ever seen before. She glanced around, looking for Samson, found only Booka staring at her reproachfully.

"Do you know where my clothes wandered off to?"

The cat meowed.

Abitha stood and stretched, savoring the feel of the morning sun on her bare skin. She was surprised at just how wonderful she felt, how sharp and clear her mind, her senses alive as though she'd been reborn, every sound and smell crisp and distinct.

She dug her fingers into the soft plowed earth, felt the connection. *I am part of you, you are part of me.* And this thought tickled something in her mind, the dream; only she knew it wasn't a dream. She had flown through the sky on a broom, through worlds both wonderful and terrible, had looked into the very face of God, and she wanted to do it all again. But there was more, something she wanted to remember, something very important, like a word on the tip of her tongue, some great truth, but here and now, she couldn't remember.

She marched back toward the cabin, her one-eyed tabby trotting along behind. Halfway there she spotted her broom. She picked it up, examined it—it was just a broom.

She passed the blackened remains of the barn with hardly a glance. *It can be rebuilt.* She spotted the dead man. *I will bury that one by the road for all to see, as a reminder that I will not be tread upon.*

She plucked up her clothes from the yard and dressed. Found her apron, checked to see that the chain of braids was still within the pocket before tying it back around her waist. It was Tuesday, or at least she hoped so. It felt like she'd been gone a week and but a moment at the same time. She needed to hitch Sid up to the wagon, load up the honey, and get it to Hartford—a trip that would take all day and then some. As she was sure Wallace wouldn't give her a day's grace, but would be here the first of October—just three days hence. She was also sure he'd be bringing the sheriff and some deputies in tow to escort her to town.

Good, she thought, *the more witnesses the better.* She realized that she was look-ing forward to the encounter, looked forward to staring Wallace down. *And why not?* she thought. *I am the girl who looked into the eyes of a thousand gods, am I not?* A most fierce grin crept across her face.

Wallace reined his stallion up at the top of the hill above Abitha's farm and waited for the sheriff's wagon to catch up. Reverend Thomas Carter rode on the bench next to the sheriff, with two deputies, Samuel and Moses, seated behind them in the bed.

Wallace caught the sour look on the reverend's face. The two hadn't exchanged a single word the whole ride out here. *What's the matter, Reverend?* Wallace thought. *Being set to right by Magistrate Watson not sitting so well on your stomach?* Wallace smirked.

They'd brought along the wagon to haul Abitha back into town, as she'd be staying in the jail for a few nights while Magistrate Watson, back in Hartford, finished sorting out the legal arrangements and set the term for her debt to him. Once that was done, she'd be released to Wallace to serve out her sentence as his indentured servant. The judge said she was looking at a minimum of three years, that he was going to see if he could work a few angles to make it closer to five or six. Magistrate Watson also made it clear that if the reverend were to give Wallace any trouble, he'd personally come down and set the arrogant fool straight. Would even bring down the militia if need be.

Wallace wouldn't have to wait on the judge to take possession of the farm, that was done and signed by the ministers of Sutton. It was his again—at least until he turned it over to Lord Mansfield—they were here only to evict her. He'd made sure all the steps had been done right, leaving her no loopholes, not this time. The sheriff even had a signed warrant for her arrest.

And the best thing to Wallace was that Abitha going into servitude would strip her of all her widow privileges. How could she be Edward's representative if there was nothing left to represent? That charade was over and done now. It was time to put this insolent woman back in her place.

Wallace wondered if she'd put up a fight, would rant and rave and throw a fit. He rather hoped so. After all the grief she'd caused him, he wouldn't mind seeing her get a sound beating. The minister might be soft on her, but the sheriff wasn't and wouldn't stand for it. He'd have her in the stocks in no time.

Wallace smiled, thinking how a few nights in the stocks would be good for her, settle her down before he brought her home. *Yes, Papa, she is a wretch. Had she not tried to drive a wedge between me and Edward, had not tried so hard to steal your land from the family, then I could've found sympathy for her. But my hard heart will not prevent me from doing what is right by God and Edward. And the good Lord willing, under my hand, she'll become a proper Puritan woman one day and a good wife to some Godly man, that I promise you.*

Sheriff Noah Pitkin pulled up alongside of Wallace. The Pitkin clan was one of Sutton's founding families, and Noah had all but inherited the position of sheriff from his father. He was lean, well-built man in his late twenties, with a sound reputation with both sword and pistol.

"What's that?" Sheriff Pitkin asked, pointing. "There, on the bank. Is that a grave?"

A simple marker stood at the head of a mound with the words cut into it: BE-WARE ANY WHO WOULD TRESPASS HERE.

"What does that mean?" the minister asked.

"It means the woman has fallen under the spell of madness," Wallace said, then added, "I must give you all fair warning, she does still possess Edward's musket."

The reverend looked nervously down at Abitha's farm.

"Are you having second thoughts, Reverend?" Wallace asked. "You can sit this one out if you like. No one here will think less of you."

The reverend bristled. "This is my duty. I will see it is done proper."

The sheriff kicked his mount forward and the wagon followed his lead down the short trek to the cabin.

Wallace dismounted, bringing his leg down easy, trying to hide the pain. He still couldn't believe the woman had shot him, catching him midthigh. The wound was healing well, the ball having gone clean through, but he knew it would be a long time before he could walk without pain again. His own shot had gone wide, and now he found himself glad of it. *This is going to be a glorious day.*

Reverend Carter stepped down off the wagon and stood staring at the remains of the barn. "Lord, what has happened here?"

"As I mentioned, Abitha's sanity is in question," Wallace said. "She most likely burned it down herself, just for spite. I wonder what other acts of her wrath we might yet uncover?"

The sheriff dismounted and the deputies unloaded, looking about warily.

Sheriff Pitkin pulled his pistol from his belt, handed it to Deputy Harlow. "This is just in case. You understand?" The deputy nodded, holding the pistol at the ready.

The sheriff started up the steps to the porch, when Reverend Carter caught his arm. "Noah, please, allow me. It might go easier if I were to talk to her first."

The sheriff chewed that over for a moment, then stepped back, allowing the minister to proceed.

The minister knocked on the door. "Abitha, it is me . . . Reverend Carter. I am asking to come in so that we might speak."

They waited, but no one answered.

The minister shrugged, then knocked again.

"Is it me you're looking for?" came a bold voice from behind them.

The men started, turning quick, the deputy leveling the pistol.

Abitha stood several paces away by the well. Her hands set on her hips. She set her brilliant green eyes on the deputy. "I am unarmed and you have five grown men here. Do you really need to be pointing that at me?"

Wallace frowned; this wasn't the woman he'd expected to find. No sobbing bride of failure here. This woman was aglow, radiant, her hair wild and unbound, her eyes and voice clear and even.

"Put the pistol away," the sheriff said.

The deputy lowered the pistol but didn't put it away.

Abitha smiled, strolled boldly up to the sheriff. "Sheriff Pitkin." She extended her hand. "It is a pleasure to have you as my guest here this morning."

The sheriff appeared thrown off by her candor and, to Wallace's chagrin, took her hand and shook it.

She then, in turn, looked each of the deputies square in the eye, nodded to them. "And you, Samuel and Moses, you are welcome as well."

The minister stepped down from the porch. Abitha greeted him, setting her hand atop his forearm. "How is Martha? Still doing well, I hope?"

Reverend Carter nodded and smiled. "Yes, Abitha. She is doing well. Better than well. She is back on her feet and helping her mother again."

Abitha returned his smile. "It does my heart such good to hear this."

What is going on? Wallace wondered. *This is not some social call.* He cleared his throat, preparing to speak.

Abitha's eyes locked on his. "How's the leg, Wallace?"

Wallace's words caught in his throat. "Huh?"

"I hear tell you injured yourself. Dropped your fork while eating your mince pie, was it?"

Wallace glared at Abitha.

"Need be careful with utensils," she added. "They can be dangerous in the wrong hands."

"Abitha, your barn?" the minister asked. "What has happened?"

"You should ask Wallace," she said.

Wallace fumbled for words. "I . . . I . . . know not what you mean. Why would I know anything?" *What is going on?* a voice inside of him cried. *She is turning everything around. Get hold of yourself, take control of this now!* "Abitha," he said as sharply and sternly as he could. "We are not here to play your games. We are here for my corn. Do you have it?"

"Some men raided the barn several nights ago," Abitha said, speaking to the minister and the sheriff. "You will find one of them buried at the top of the road there. A Pequot man. You might have noticed his grave on your way in."

"Yes," Reverend Carter said. "We did. I wanted to ask—"

"Yes, yes," Wallace said impatiently. "No one cares about some dead Indian. The corn. Where is my corn?"

"Sadly, your corn is gone, burned along with my barn. And now I have no corn to pay you with."

There you go, Wallace thought, *things are finally back on track.* Still he didn't like her tone, as though she had not a care in the world. "I am sorry for the loss,"

180

he said. "It would've been nice to have concluded this business in a way Edward would've liked. But sentiment is not a luxury I can afford. And now I am put in a position to do what is best for our family and the community . . . and even you, Abitha." He nodded to the sheriff. "Noah, would you do me the favor of reading her the warrant."

"Oh," Sheriff Pitkin said, as though he'd forgotten the business at hand. He tugged out two folded notes from his vest, shuffled between them, opened one, and cleared his throat. "Abitha, I am sorry it has come to this." He held the paper up. "This is a warrant for your arrest."

"For my delinquent debts, correct?"

"Yes." The sheriff held up the second note. "And this is the eviction notice. You'll find it is signed and in order. There are details here pertaining to the agreement struck between Wallace and your late husband, Edward, as witnessed by the ministers. Here, allow me to explain it to you as simply as I can. The—"

"Edward owes Wallace fifty bushels each year," Abitha said. "For five years. Due by October first each season. If payment is not met, then the farm will, upon Wallace's request, revert to Wallace in full. Is that simple enough?"

Sheriff Pitkin raised his eyebrows. "Why, yes. Yes, that is it exactly."

"Is this not the first?"

"What?"

"Today? What is the date?"

"Yes, Abitha. It is indeed the first."

"Then it is due today. Am I correct, Sheriff?"

"Well . . . yes."

"Then I am not delinquent as of yet. Correct? There is still the rest of this day to make good on my payment."

The sheriff let out a sigh, looked to the minister.

Wallace felt his temper rising. *Why are they letting her get away with such insolence?*

"Abitha," Reverend Carter said. "You have everyone's sympathies here. But please, let's not prolong this. It is plain to all that there is no payment. Why not—"

"Enough of this nonsense," Wallace snapped. "We are all busy men, Abitha. I will not stand here and allow you to waste everyone's time. Look here, woman. It is simple . . . you cannot make your payment, so now you must serve out your debt to me. Do you understand? You are working for me now. So this insolence . . . it will cease as of now. *Right now!*"

Reverend Carter held up his hands. "Wallace, please. There is no need—"

Abitha laughed, loud and strong.

The men exchanged an uneasy look.

She has lost her mind, Wallace thought, feeling relieved. *They will see the truth of her now.*

"Apologies, Reverend Carter," Abitha said. "I did not mean to interrupt. It is just that Wallace, he tends to be easily confused. Wallace, when did I say that I do not have payment?"

"What? Of course you do not have payment. You just said so."

"Not true. I merely stated I do not have your corn."

What is she getting at? Wallace wanted to laugh in her face, but there was such confidence there, such arrogance and what? *Glee?* Yes, most certainly. The face of someone about to play a winning hand.

Abitha reached into her apron, the deputy leveling the pistol when she did. She met the man's eyes and waited.

"Put it down, Samuel," the sheriff ordered.

The deputy lowered the pistol and Abitha slowly removed a worn leather pouch. "On Edward's behalf, I owe Wallace fifty bushels of corn today. At the current market price, that equates to two fathoms of wampum. You can double-check that figure if you are in doubt, but I were in Hartford just two days ago and had it confirmed."

She untied the strap and opened the pouch, revealing it was indeed full of the milled purple beads. "This will cover most of what I owe." She held the pouch out to the minister. "Reverend Carter, would you be so kind as to take this into your custody until it is fully accounted for?"

The minister, his face one of stunned disbelief, accepted the pouch.

Wallace realized he was trembling, that somewhere, deep down, he was screaming. "Where . . ." he said, barely able to get the words out. "Where did you come by this?"

"Gentlemen," Abitha said, ignoring Wallace. "There is a bit more unfinished business at hand. I am in need of a few witnesses. If you do not mind, would you allow me to show you something?" She headed up the steps and into her cabin.

The men exchanged curious looks, then followed, leaving Wallace behind.

What now? Wallace thought. *What further deviltry does she hide?* A bee buzzed round his head and he swatted angrily at it as he followed after the men.

Wallace stepped into the cabin and his breath left him. There, on the big table and along the counter, was row after row of neatly stacked honeycomb wrapped in linen; the air was saturated with the sweet smell of the honey.

"Why, Abitha!" Reverend Carter exclaimed. "You have been very busy. How did you ever manage this?"

"This is the fruit of Edward's labors, not mine. As you know, he has been bee-keeping for years, but this year . . . it were as though something got into the bees. I like to think it were Edward's spirit. That he is looking over me. As you can well see, the bees have been most fruitful."

Several bees hummed around the honey, and a couple began to circle Wallace, but he barely noticed, his mind still trying to comprehend how this was happening to him.

"I am grateful that you've come all the way out here today," Abitha said. "It makes this whole business much easier for me. This"—she gestured to the honeycomb—"is my last and final payment. And I just need you to witness that I have produced it and am now giving it to Wallace . . . that my debts to him are paid in full."

"No," Wallace said. "I refuse to accept this. How do I even know what this is worth?"

Abitha pulled a note from her apron, unfolded it, and handed it to the minister. "This is the receipt from Seymour's shop. You will find the amount of wampum paid listed, but also the amount paid per pound. He paid me top price, said it were the finest comb he'd seen in years. Based on that, I took the liberty to calculate how many additional pounds were needed to pay off the lien. My notes are there, at the bottom. It came to just under forty pounds. You can all see the amount here far exceeds that."

183

Reverend Carter examined the note, then looked around the cabin. "Yes, Abitha, indeed, it is plain you have paid your debt and then some. It is fair to say that this matter is settled."

No! Wallace thought. *No, no, no! This cannot be happening.* "*No!*" Wallace cried. "I refuse to accept this . . . this . . . *honeycomb*! The deal was for corn. You *must* pay in corn. If you do not have the corn, then you must forfeit!"

"Wallace," Reverend Carter said. "You're not making sense. Now calm yourself, please. Payment can be in any reasonable means or currency. That is well-established practice."

"Can you not see her wickedness? See how this knave is playing all of us?"

"Take your payment, Wallace," Abitha said calmly. "And get off my land. Now. Right *now*."

"Insolent cur. How dare you speak so to me!" He stepped toward her, raising a hand to strike her, but the sheriff caught his arm mid-swing and shoved him back against the wall.

"Enough," Sheriff Pitkin shouted. "You will be civil or I will see you in the stocks. Do you understand?"

"Wallace," the minister said. "Let this go. You have been paid well. More than fair. God is watching you, judging you. Do not let greed steer your character."

Wallace glanced from face to face, could see that they all thought him—*him*, not *her*—mad.

How did this happen? How did she twist everything around?

He glared at Abitha and she met his gaze and held it. And it was then, there, while staring into her vile green eyes, that he saw her for what she truly was.

Oh, Papa, look! There is true deviltry at play here. The corn, all that corn. The strange visions of Edward. The honey . . . so much honey. An impossible amount of honey. And these men . . . she has them under her spell, just like with Edward. Papa, there can be but one explanation. "Abitha . . . have you made pact with the Devil? Have you practiced witchcraft here?"

And Wallace saw it, a flash there upon her face—*guilt*. It was so obvious now.

"You have! Oh, Lord. You have!" He leapt and grabbed her, pinning her against the cupboard. "Tell them!" he cried. "Tell them now how you bewitched Edward! Turned him against me!"

Sheriff Pitkin and the deputies grabbed Wallace, dragged him back, and threw him up against the wall.

"Wallace!" the minister cried. "You will cease this at once!"

"She is a *witch*! A *witch*! Pray tell you see it!"

"I see only a man who has lost himself to madness."

They dragged Wallace from the cabin and tossed him off the porch and into the yard.

Wallace clambered to his feet. "She has you under her spell!" he screeched, jabbing his finger wildly at them. "I tell you, she is in league with the Devil!"

Abitha walked out on the porch, and when she did, Wallace felt a sharp sting to the back of his neck. "Ah!" he cried, and swatted. It was a bee. He looked from the crushed insect to Abitha. "You have been found out, witch!" he shouted. "And I shall make it my mission to expose your wickedness for all to see!"

He grabbed the reins of his steed and pulled himself up into the saddle. "Hear me now. All of you. As I will give you but this one warning. I go to Hartford this very day to report this wicked woman. So you better consider your position well. Are you on God's side or that of the Devil? Because when the Magistrate Watson hands down his verdict, all those who side with this witch will also be found guilty."

He saw it on their faces then, the fear, and it did him good. "God is coming to Sutton. Time to choose your side!"

Wallace kicked the horse hard and galloped away.

"We made it back, Sid," Abitha said to the mule. She pulled the wagon up to the lean-to she'd constructed and hopped down. She unhitched the beast, gathered up her musket and bag, and headed toward the cabin.

She spotted Samson sitting in the shade of the porch, staring off at the far hills, his brows tight.

"It's done!" she called, putting down the gun and dashing over. She took a seat next to him and clutched his arm. "I dropped off the remaining honey and met with the ministers." She removed a rolled piece of parchment from her bag and held it up. "Here it is! All signed and witnessed. The property is mine, clear and clean!"

He looked at the parchment, but his deep silver eyes seemed distant.

"Samson, my thanks to you is not enough. You have done more than save me here . . . you've given me the strength to stand on my own. Giving me back my dignity . . . the means to . . ." She felt the sting of tears and had to stop lest she start crying.

He gave her a warm smile, but she could see something was troubling him.

"What is it?"

"Would you like me to kill him?" Samson asked. "The Wallace man?"

Abitha let go of his arm.

"You need but ask," he added.

She saw something in Samson's eyes then, something hungry, something that wanted out. It startled her.

"He's not finished," Samson said. "He intends you harm."

"Aye, I know," she said.

"You might not have another chance."

She sensed it, his need, almost a craving to kill Wallace. She shuddered, not liking this side of him. She'd come to love him, to trust him. And how was it she ever came to trust such a beast? Because up until now, all their work had been of a Godly nature. Murder was the Devil's work, and once she crossed that line, what else would *she* be willing to do?

"No," she said. "I just cannot do such a dark deed."

He appeared troubled by this, stood, and began pacing. "Do you still think me a devil?"

She studied him for a moment, watching as a couple of bees buzzed around his horns. "Samson, you have proved your heart is good and that your nature is Godly. But there is more to your nature . . . we both know that. I have put my faith in you, Samson . . . and I believe that you are *no* devil."

He snorted, his eyes searching the tree line like some hunting cat.

What has gotten into him? she wondered. *Why is he in such a dark mood this day?* She watched as he began clenching and unclenching his long fingers with their clawlike nails. "What do you think, Samson? Do you feel you are a devil?"

He started to answer, then stiffened, sniffing the air. His eyes shot to the trees and Abitha saw them—three figures.

She tensed. "Indians."

"The Pequot?" he asked.

"Aye, I am almost certain."

Samson took several steps toward them, and they faded back into the woods.

Abitha grabbed her musket and stood beside Samson. "I am willing to bet Wallace sent them here."

"No," Samson said. "They're here for me."

"You?"

"Yes . . . for Hobomok." He started down the hill, heading for the woods.

"Wait, where are you going?" Abitha called.

"To find Hobomok," he called back, and disappeared into the woods.

Wallace walked almost the complete perimeter around Sutton before finding Ansel Fitch, finally spotting the old man over by the south wall rooting about in a bush with a long stick.

Wallace watched the man probe and prod, poking his nose into bushes and stumps, surprised at just how spry he was for a man of his years.

Ansel squatted and plucked up a leaf, bringing it to his nose.

Wallace sighed. *Do I truly feel this stewed prune can help me?* Wallace considered leaving; the only thing keeping him from doing so was the fact that it was this *stewed prune* who'd called out the Muford widow for witchcraft several years ago—it was his evidence, his testimony that had seen her hanged.

Ansel's head jerked up as Wallace approached, and his eyes narrowed, regarding him suspiciously.

"What are you doing out here?" Ansel asked.

"I could ask you the same thing. But I know well what it is you're about."

"You do, do you? Well, just let me show you something." Ansel pointed his stick at some tracks in the mud. "What kind of tracks do you see?"

"Those are goat tracks. Probably one of Goody Dibble's; she often lets them graze out here."

"Aye, and if you were the Devil, how would you cover your comings and goings?"

Wallace shrugged.

Ansel grinned, tugged a piece of parchment from his coat, and unfolded it to reveal several drawings of hoofprints; they were of various shapes and sizes.

"See this one." He pointed to one larger than the rest. "This one I drew from prints I found next to Widow Pratt's body. Some say her heart gave out, but I think you and I know better. Now look here." He pointed to the mud again. "See that set there? Are they not the same?"

Wallace felt the hair on his neck rise. "Aye, they are indeed."

187

"Slewfoot is a clever one. He thinks no one will notice if he walks along the beast trails. But old Ansel, he is clever too, does not miss a trick."

Wallace smiled. "I know. That is why I've sought you out."

Ansel gave him a quizzical look. "What do you mean?"

"I know exactly where the Devil be. I just need a little help proving it. Do you know anyone who can help me with that?"

Ansel stood up straight, his bulbous eyes all but dancing. "I most certainly do."

"Good, then let me tell you a story."

The Pequot men ran through the forest and Samson followed. It was a game and Samson played along, staying visible to them but never quite catching up. They knew he was there, he could sense it, could tell they wanted him to follow, that they were leading him somewhere. They traveled throughout the day, moving briskly, the men darting and dashing through the woods along streams and animal trails.

It was almost dark when Samson first sensed the village, smelling it long before he saw it. It was the smell of people, of their fires, their food, their sweat and blood.

He spied torches ahead, twinkling between the trees, came to the edge of the woods and watched the men disappear into the village. He listened for a while to the sounds of children playing, infants squalling, people bickering, others laughing, and somewhere someone chanting softly.

Samson left the cover of the trees and strolled into the village. He didn't bother to hide himself, wanting to be seen, needing to know how these people would respond to him. He was struck by a sudden familiarity, as though he'd done this before.

One by one, the inhabitants saw him, and he had no problem reading their fear, their horror, as they grabbed children and ducked into their huts. Soon there was no one to be seen, the entire village falling quiet, until the only sound remaining was the soft chanting.

The chanting grew louder. Samson followed the sound to the far side of the village, to the base of a rocky cliff. There, on a ledge high above, stood a man silhouetted against the night sky.

He knew this man.

Samson climbed the steep cliff with the ease of a mountain goat. When he arrived at the ledge, the man was gone. He noticed smoke and a faint light emanating from a cave in the cliff face.

Samson entered the cave, found that it was more of a tunnel. He followed it several dozen paces, tracing his hand along the hundreds of cave paintings, before it opened into a small cavern about the size of one of the huts.

The walls of the cave were covered floor to ceiling in skulls and masks of all sizes and shapes. All intricately decorated with sigils, feathers, and bones. They were strung together by long strands of woven reeds, grass, and hair, giving Samson the impression of a spider's lair. Again, Samson felt an overwhelming sense that he'd been here before.

A fire burned within a circle of stones at the chamber's heart, and there, on the other side of the flames, waited the man.

The man sat cross-legged upon a blanket, softly chanting, his face covered by an eyeless white mask carved from wood into the shape of a circle, like the moon. The man appeared ancient, yet neither feeble nor frail, but wiry and alive. His leathery skin was dusted in ash, his silver hair snaking down his back in two long braids.

The man lifted the mask, revealing a ghostly white face with dark lines running vertically down his features. It was the face of the magic man from Samson's visions.

The man's eyes were black smudges of paint, and when he stopped chanting and opened them, they gleamed out from their shadowy sockets.

The man stared at Samson. "You are lost. Are you not?" The man's voice surprised Samson; it was that of a young man.

"I am."

"Come . . . sit with me. I have much to show you."

CHAPTER 10

Wallace approached Abitha's farm through the forest, followed by his son, Isaac, and Ansel Fitch. It was nearing noon and the woods were alive with the shrill calls of insects and birds. The warm humid spell had continued into October and the air was heavy and still.

They came to the tree line above the farm and stopped. It had been a long hike; Wallace's clothes dripped with sweat and the bullet wound in his thigh throbbed.

"What exactly is it we're looking for?" Isaac asked.

"It will be the kind of thing you know when you see it," Ansel said. "Some unnatural act that the three of us can swear to. Some odd display, something to present to Magistrate Watson."

Yes, Wallace thought, *and it shouldn't take much.* He'd already spoken with both the magistrate and Lord Mansfield and knew it wouldn't take much at all.

They spotted Abitha right away, hammering boards to a post, rebuilding a shelter for the livestock. Her hair was loose and wild, she wore no bodice, no shoes, only a loose blouse, apron, and single skirt. The blouse was untied at the neck, exposing her cleavage, the sweat causing the thin fabric to cling to her chest. Wallace watched the shape of her small breasts as they swayed back and forth while she worked, and it wasn't long before he felt a stirring in his loins.

There, Wallace thought, *the very Devil tempting me through her wiles.* He glanced at Ansel and Isaac, could see she had the same effect on them, Isaac appearing embarrassed and Ansel all but leering.

"See how wantonly she dresses?" Wallace said.

Ansel nodded, not taking his eyes off of her. "Aye, this is not a Godly woman, that much is clear to see."

They found a vantage point that gave them a good view of the farm and waited, watching Abitha's every move, but as the hours dragged by Wallace began to fear they'd come all this way for nothing. Ansel now sat upon the ground, his back against a tree, his eyes half-closed. Isaac too had found a comfortable spot and was fighting to keep his eyes open. But Wallace stood, leaning against a large maple, watching Abitha's every move like a bird of prey.

Wallace caught movement from the corner of his eye, thought he saw someone down near the bottom of the field, but when he looked, no one was there. *Edward? Is that you? If so, rest easy, brother. I will not let this wicked woman steal Papa's farm.*

191

Abitha set down her hammer and went to the well for a long drink, after which she took a seat in the shade of the porch. She picked up a circular object and began to work on it, weaving flowers and other small items together.

Wallace squinted. *What is that?* His heart raced. He nudged Ansel.

"Look," he whispered. "See there. What is it that she makes?"

Ansel and Isaac got to their feet.

"It is but a wreath of flowers," Isaac said.

"No," Ansel said. "It is some kind of talisman . . . mayhap a pagan crown."

Abitha's bent, one-eyed cat came out from under the porch and yowled at Abitha.

"That is a most foul beast," Wallace said.

"It could be more."

"What do you mean?"

"Her familiar."

"Familiar?" Wallace asked. "I know not what that is."

"Her spiritual guide . . . an imp or demon sent by Satan to assist her. That would explain why it is so tortured-looking."

The orange cat strolled over and took a seat next to Abitha. Wallace watched the feline paw at the straw Abitha was weaving with.

"Look there," Ansel said. "Do you see? The creature . . . it helps her! Do you see?"

"I see," Isaac said, his face horrified.

"Ansel," Wallace asked, "do you feel the crown will be enough? To convince the judge?"

Ansel considered. "I think it might. Magistrate Watson has presided over several cases of witchcraft, including that of Widow Muford. He is well versed in the deceitful ways of Satan. I am sure he will see it for what it truly is."

"Then come first chance, I shall retrieve it."

A short while later, Abitha laid the crown back on the porch and returned to her work.

"You two stay here," Wallace said, and headed down.

He took the long way around, coming in from behind the cabin so as not to be seen. Giving the beehives a wide berth, he came up along the side of the cabin and peered around, saw Abitha by the barn hammering a plank into place, her back to him.

Wallace stepped out and hurried over to the porch.

The cat leapt to its feet at the sight of him, arching its back, hissing and glaring with its one crooked eye.

Wallace fell back, horrified, then saw just what Abitha had been weaving, that along with the flowers and seeds, there were small bones, beetles and strands of hair, her own hair.

No one can dispute such deviltry, he thought, and pushed himself forward, forcing himself to snatch up the loathsome object.

"What are you doing?"

Wallace spun around, almost dropping his prize.

Abitha stood a few paces away with the hammer in her hand, glaring at him.

Wallace held up the crown. "This is your undoing, witch!"

"Thief," she said. "A swindler, an arsonist, a bully, a liar, and a *thief*! Your father would be so proud of you." She spat on the ground before him.

He felt his face flush, his temper burn. It was more than her words, more than the way she was speaking to him—it was her sneer, her contemptuous little sneer.

He stepped forward, fist drawn.

She raised the hammer. *"Leave!"* she shouted. *"Now!"* There was no fear on her face, none, and that was the final insult.

He slapped the crown down and lunged at her.

Abitha tried to strike, but he came in hard and fast, punching her in the chest with the full might of his arm, knocking the hammer from her hand and sending her tumbling to the ground.

She managed to get to her knees, gasping and coughing, trying to breathe.

"Witch!" he cried, grabbing her by the hair. She weighed nothing to him and he spun her like a rag, tossing her into the fence. She slammed into the post and landed in a crumpled heap.

"I have had enough of you!" he shouted.

She looked up at him, and he saw it, what he'd wanted, what he needed—the fear. *Oh yes, she is afraid now—terrified.* He drank it in and laughed.

She tried to crawl away, but he caught her by the ankle and spun her yet again, slamming her back into the post. Abitha let out the most pitiful cry.

He laughed some more and reached for her again, when Isaac dashed between them, grabbing Wallace by the arm, trying to hold him back.

"Enough, Father! You will kill her. Now stop!"

Ansel ran over and plucked up the crown, holding it as one would a deadly snake. "Lord, this is indeed deviltry!"

Wallace shrugged the boy off, shoving him out of the way. "God has revealed the witch to us! It is our duty to be His sword, to slay Satan wherever we find him! We have our proof! Let us end this now!"

Wallace picked the hammer up from the dirt and started toward Abitha, then heard—no, felt—a strange humming. He blinked, trying to figure out where it was coming from, realized it was coming from inside his head.

It grew in volume.

Wallace dropped the hammer, clapped his hands over his ears, and the hum traveled into his skull, into his teeth, vibrating through his entire body.

Abitha was staring at him, her eyes blazing, both her hands on the ground, her fingers digging into the grass, and he saw that it was *her* . . . she was *humming.*

Something struck him on the back of the neck, just a thump, like someone had tapped him, then came the sting.

"Oww!" He swatted it; it was a bee. Then another, on his cheek, followed quickly by two more, then three more, then ten, twenty. The air suddenly full of them, stinging his face, his arms, the pain overwhelming, blinding; they were in his shirt, his pants.

Wallace screamed and fled, flailing frantically at the air. He dashed right into the fence, hardly feeling the impact over the unbearable pain. He found his feet and ran as fast as he could into the woods—running and running through the underbrush, heedless of thorns in his mad scramble to escape his tormentors.

There came a sudden pounding from the front door. Reverend Thomas Carter opened the door to find Wallace glaring at him, his face swollen and covered in red lumps. Ansel and Wallace's son, Isaac, and at least a dozen other men and women from the village stood in his yard behind the huge man, their eyes full of alarm. They all began talking at once, speaking over one another. The minister could decipher little, but the two words he clearly heard over and over were: *Abitha* and *witch*.

No, not this, Reverend Carter thought. *Not here.* His chest tightened; he'd seen the havoc witch hysteria had brought upon Hartford many years back, knew where it led. *Lord, give me strength.* He raised his hand. "Stop," he commanded. "Please, one at a time."

"It's Abitha," Wallace proclaimed in his loud brash voice. "She is cavorting with the Devil!"

Reverend Carter wanted to grab the man, beg him not to do this, not to play this dangerous game.

"We have the proof," Wallace said, pulling Ansel forward.

Ansel unfolded a cloth, revealing a circlet of dried flowers as though it were Satan's very crown. "We found her making this!" the old man proclaimed, his bulbous eyes bulging as he held the circlet up so all could see, holding it by the cloth, careful not to let it touch his bare skin.

"It is but a wreath of flowers," Reverend Carter said. "I do not understand."

"Look closer," Wallace shouted, now speaking more to the crowd than the reverend, his voice alive with theatrics. "Bones and hair . . . *her* hair! She does consort with a familiar spirit! We did witness this, the three of us, myself, Ansel, and Isaac here."

"Aye," Ansel said. "They did consort indeed . . . Abitha and her imp! Whispering and conspiring with one another. And then, this." He shook the circlet again. "There, before our eyes, they crafted this together. A horrifying sight to behold."

The crowd fell back, staring warily at the circlet.

"Familiar spirit?" Reverend Carter asked. "What manner of creature do you speak of?"

"The imp has taken the form of a cat," Ansel said. "A bent and crooked beast with but one wicked eye. And when it set that evil eye upon me, I felt a chill to my very bones and could not move until I spoke the Lord's name."

"What say you, Reverend?" Wallace challenged. "Why do you stand mute? Why do you not cry witchcraft in the face of such evidence?"

The crowd grumbled, nodding their heads in agreement.

Reverend Carter struggled for the right words, knowing all too well how any and all could be swept up into such hysteria.

Wallace's eyes bore into him. "And this?" he cried, jabbing at his own face. "What of this? I am covered head to foot in welts." He turned to the crowd. "She did this. Set her bees upon me! Isaac and Ansel as my witness."

"You were at her farm?" Reverend Carter asked. "But why?"

"We are beset with demons and you worry on trivialities," Wallace challenged, not hiding his scorn. "Why is that? Why do you defend her so?"

And here it comes, the reverend thought. *How quick the fingers are to accuse.* "I seek only full knowledge of circumstance. As to make a fair assessment. It is well known that you have an ongoing feud with Abitha."

"You dare imply my motives are anything other than protecting my children and this village from the Devil's hand?"

195

"I am well versed in the severity of your claims. That is why we must be prudent. We all know where this can lead if we are not deliberate in our proceedings."

"She did curse Wallace," Ansel said. "After which the bees attacked him in a most unnatural way. As though possessed and under her spell. How is it Isaac and myself stood beside Wallace and did not suffer the same affliction, less it were some kind of witchcraft?"

An uneasy rumble drifted through the crowd. A few carried bibles and they thumped them to their chests. More people joined them, curious to see what the commotion was about.

Sheriff Pitkin and Deputy Harlow arrived, the sheriff carrying a pike. They pushed up through the crowd.

"What is it, Reverend?" Sheriff Pitkin asked. "What brings such trouble?"

Once again, the crowd all spoke at once.

The sheriff thumped the pike loudly on the minister's step until they quieted.

"Reverend, what is the trouble?"

"Wallace, here. He brings forth a charge of—"

"It is Abitha Williams!" Wallace cut in. "She has been witnessed using black magic."

The sheriff set hard eyes on Wallace, appeared ready to reprimand him for interrupting, then saw the big man's swollen face and winced. "What has happened to you?"

"That is what I am trying to tell you. Abitha is using black magic."

"And we are to believe you?" Sheriff Pitkin asked. "All here are well aware of your vendetta against that woman."

"We have witnesses—*proof*! Hear this." Wallace pulled his daughter forth from the crowd. "Show them, Charity."

Charity appeared frightened and nervous.

"Go on, child," Ansel said. "Abitha cannot touch you here. You are beyond her reach."

Charity held out a napkin. Ansel took it from her and unfolded it, revealing a small clump of dried rose petals wrapped in twine, holding it up for all to see.

"More of her witchery!" Wallace said. "Tell them, Charity."

"Aye, it were Abitha that did make it for me. She told that if I wear it always about my neck . . . then I would be rewarded with Cecil's love. But when Father arrived home, vexed as he were, and began to speak ill of Abitha . . . it—" There were tears in her eyes. "It did burn me such that I had to tear it from my breast."

Many in the crowd gasped, sharing wary glances between one another. Reverend Carter could see the seeds of suspicion growing; there were plenty here who had solicited Abitha's remedies.

"I see," Sheriff Pitkin said. "Mayhap we should—"

A cry came from behind Wallace and the crowd parted to reveal young Mary Dibble beating at her apron. "It burns me!" she cried. "Take it from me!" She tore off her apron and flung it upon the ground, stumbling away from it. The circle widened, all eyes staring at her apron as though it were full of spiders.

"What is it, child?" her mother, Goody Dibble, asked.

"There, in the pocket. A charm. Abitha did give it to me. Promised me many suitors, she did. But I knew it not to be deviltry. I swear it! She did trick me with sweet words."

Ansel knelt down and gingerly slipped his hand into the apron pocket, sliding out a dried rose, wrapped in red twine. He left it on the ground in front of the crowd.

Reverend Carter met the sheriff's eyes; he could see the man was unsure what to do.

"Please, punish me not!" Mary cried. "I beg of you. I were under her spell. I swear it before God!"

"Fear not," Ansel said. "It is but your pure flesh repulsing her black magic. Now that her witchcraft has been exposed, her witchery can hide no longer from any who are innocent at heart and righteous with the Lord."

"It bites like a hornet!" Jane Foster screamed, clawing at her neck, tugging out a small pouch and throwing it on the ground next to Mary's apron. Followed a moment later by fearful cries from Rebecca, and the Danforths' servant girl, Helen. Rebecca tugged a bracelet of twisted rooster feathers from her wrist, while Helen yanked another of the pouches from about her neck. Both threw them on the ground by the apron.

The crowd stepped farther back from the pile of charms.

The sheriff looked to each woman in turn. "And these, they are all from Abitha?"

They all nodded adamantly.

"She tricked me, too!" Charity shouted, stepping forward. "Spoke to me in a forked tongue. She did try to corrupt me with promises of love and admiration. I see that now that her spell is broken."

"Aye, as do I," Helen cried.

"As do I!" Jane cried.

"The Devil's hands have been lifted from my eyes!" Charity shouted. "I denounce her! I denounce her and all her deviltry!"

"I denounce her!" Helen cried.

"I denounce her!" Mary cried.

"I denounce her!" Rebecca cried.

"Aye, I denounce her and her deviltry!" shouted Jane.

"Reverend," Wallace called. "What do you intend to do?"

The reverend was certain that Wallace had orchestrated this tragedy, yet could find no recourse, no way to hold the man accountable. He realized that there was nothing he could do for Abitha at this point other than try to save her from the brutality of a vigilante execution. They were in Sutton, not in Hartford; the law was a tenuous thing out here, most small villages preferring to handle such matters on their own—quickly and often brutally. "We will arrest her," Reverend Carter said, barely able to get the words out. "We will have a trial like rational men of God. The Lord shall decide her fate." He caught Wallace's smile, realized that he had played right into the man's hands.

"Now, there is the first sensible thing you have said," Wallace stated. "I will ride to Hartford this minute."

And before the reverend could respond, Wallace was away.

197

Oh, dear God, Reverend Carter thought, realizing he'd just invited the wolves to Sutton. He started to shout after Wallace when a sudden cry came from behind him. It was his wife, Sarah. She was clutching their daughter in her arms. Martha's face had gone deathly pale, her eyelids drooping. She seemed unable to stand.

"What is it?" Reverend Carter asked.

"I know not, husband! She just collapsed."

The reverend help lay Martha on the porch. Martha's eyes fluttered open, met his, then opened wide. He could see the terror in them.

"What is it, child? What plagues you so?"

She seized his arm. "Am I touched by the Devil then?"

The crowd drew silent, pressing forward to listen.

"No, child. Of course not."

"She put her hands on me. Abitha did. Stood at my bedside, Father. You and mother saw her. You saw her! What has she done to me?"

"She has done naught impure. Only an old remedy. Mother and I would never allow anyone to sully you. Now hush. We can speak more on this later." Reverend Carter glanced about at all the wary faces and gave the sheriff a dire look.

Sheriff Pitkin turned, facing the crowd, and thumped his pike. "Hear me, all of you. I assure you that Abitha will be arrested this day. Will be held accountable. But let me make it clear here and now that I will tolerate no disorderliness from anyone. Now disperse . . . the Lord does not look favorably upon idle hands and wagging tongues."

The reverend watched the crowd drift away, painfully aware of the whispering and talking behind hands as they cast suspicious looks upon him and his wife.

"Samuel," the sheriff said. "Go hitch up the wagon. I will fetch Moses and meet you at the stables. We shall go right away."

Samuel took off at a run.

Sheriff Pitkin met the reverend's eye. "I want to get Abitha before some of these fools decide to take matters into their own hands."

"Agreed."

The sheriff headed quickly away.

"I fear the worst," Sarah said.

Reverend Carter set his hand atop hers, his thoughts straying to Magistrate Watson and his soldiers here in Sutton. "As do I."

Using the broom as a crutch, Abitha hobbled across her porch, grimacing against the throbbing pain in her right knee. She'd not been able to walk on that leg since Wallace slammed her into the fence and feared it broken. She tugged along a bundle of blankets behind her, dragged them down the steps to the wagon and tossed them into the bed atop some cooking gear, her musket, her clothes, a few tools, and a scattering of other belongings.

Her two goats were tethered behind the wagon, but she'd set the chickens free, as she couldn't catch them, not with her leg in the shape it was in. She glanced around the homestead trying to remember if there were any other items of value she'd overlooked. She checked her apron for the dozenth time to make sure she had the chain of braids. She clutched it, desperate to feel that her mother was here with her in any way.

"You've won, Wallace," she said, with no emotion at all. "The sweat, the blood, the tears . . . have all been for naught."

Her cat sat on the porch, watching her with his one sad eye. "Come along, Booka. It's time to go. They'll be coming for me sooner than later."

She considered yet again going into town and facing Wallace, but knew there was no fighting this, even with the reverend and the sheriff lending her their testimony. She'd cast a spell in front of three men, and they would swear on God's name against her. Nothing could save her from that, not amongst the Puritans.

Why did I call the bees? she wondered for the hundredth time. *Such a fool.* But she knew why: because he would've killed her otherwise—there'd been nothing but murder in his eyes. *God be damned, why did I not listen to Samson and kill that foul man? Why?*

She scanned the edge of the forest. *Where are you, Samson? Where did you go?*

"Come, Booka," she said, limping over to the porch.

Booka meowed and came to her, rubbing up against her hand. She felt the cat's bent spine, recalled how she'd thought his back broken when she'd rescued the poor thing from those dogs. He'd certainly appeared lifeless. But it hadn't been magic that saved Booka, just goodly care and tending.

She lifted the cat, cuddling him, pressing her face into his soft fur. The cat began to purr, and she allowed herself a moment to savor the simple love of this broken cat, as it seemed the only comfort left to her in this world.

She heard them then—several horses and a wagon heading her way.

"God's nails," she snarled, dropping the cat and limping quickly back to the wagon. She tugged the musket and a few loads of shot out from the bed, checked the primer. There'd be no running now, not for her. She propped herself against the porch post and waited, hoping to Hell it would be Wallace coming for her. If the last thing she did was shoot that foul beast of a man, she'd die happy.

Sheriff Pitkin appeared at the top of the yard. He waited, watching her until a wagon and two deputies pulled up behind him. She could see the men were armed with muskets and swords.

Sheriff Pitkin tugged his pistol and cutlass from his belt, handed them to one of the men, then started down the short trek to the house. He stopped about sixty paces out. "Abitha, I am here to arrest you on the charge of witchcraft. I implore that you come along peacefully."

"I shall not."

"I am not armed." He put his hands out where she could see them.

"Makes no difference. Come another step and I'll shoot you."

"Abitha, you'll not stand a chance against the three of us. Now put the gun away."

"I'd rather die here and now than be tortured and strung up by a pack of liars and pious denigrates."

"Abitha, please. Let us do this easy. You'll have an honest trial. I promise you this. And you know me to be a man of my word. It will be a lawful proceeding and you'll be given a chance to state your piece. Now, what say you?"

"I say I am no fool. Now get off my land. I do not want to shoot you, Noah Pitkin."

"You will not shoot me, Abitha. As I know you are no murderer. Now, I am doing all that I can so that you may keep your dignity. Please, put down the musket and surrender to me." He resumed walking slowly toward her.

"There is no dignity in being tried as a witch. We both know that." She jabbed the musket at him. "I *will* shoot you, Noah."

"No. Such a thing is not in your heart." He took another step and another.

Abitha pulled the trigger, and there came a thunderous report, the kick of the musket knocking her down. She heard a cry and sat up.

"Damn your hide!" the sheriff yowled. "Damn your hide!" He sat on the ground, holding his ear, blood dripping between his fingers.

Abitha pulled the rod from the musket, grabbed another load of shot, and began to ram it down the muzzle.

"Get her!" the sheriff shouted, and the two deputies came on at a full run.

Samuel reached her just as she finished loading the shot, wrestling the musket from her hands. The musket went off, punching a hole in the side of the wagon. He tossed away the musket and drove his fist into the side of her head, knocking

200

her onto her back. Moses arrived and the two of them began kicking her soundly. A boot connected with her cheek. She cried out, trying to cover her face with her arms, caught a blow against her ribs, and all the air left her lungs.

"Enough!" Sheriff Pitkin cried, but the deputies continued to beat her. "Leave her!" he shouted, shoving the two men back.

Abitha curled up, choking and gasping, clutching her side as she tried to suck air back into her chest.

Sheriff Pitkin, his hand pressed against his ear, gave Abitha a pitiful look. "Damn it, Abitha. It need not be this way." He tugged out a pair of shackles from his belt and tossed them to Moses. "Bind her and let us be on our way."

Samson sat in the dirt in front of the low-burning fire. The man sat across from him. The flames cast their shadows high up along the cavern walls, sending them dancing across the multitude of masks, a hundred hollow eyes watching them impassively.

Samson stared at the man and the man stared at the fire.

"Who are you?" Samson asked.

"Is that the question you came here for?"

"I have many questions. But first, you will tell me who you are."

The man chuckled. "I'll never forget the first time I saw you all those many, many summers ago, the way you strutted around like a god."

Samson narrowed his eyes. "How do you know me?"

"Ah, are we getting closer to the right question?"

"Stop the riddles. It is most annoying."

"Life is nothing but riddles . . . we spend our whole lives puzzling them out. Sadly, as soon as we find the answer, the riddle changes. Does it not?"

"I am not here to play games. Answer me now or—"

"Or what? What will you do?"

"Perhaps," Samson growled, "I will break your bones and eat your flesh."

The man laughed. "Hear yourself and you might find the right question."

"Who am I?" Samson asked.

"There is the question! The only one that matters. And I will be glad to help you find the answer, but let's return to your first question." The man leaned closer to the fire, and in the harsh under-light, Samson could now see that the dark lines running vertically down the man's gaunt features were scars, noticed something else, that the man's skin, it was made up of tiny bumps and scales, realized that perhaps he wasn't even a man at all.

"You still do not remember me?"

Samson squinted at him. He did. He knew he did, but like so many of his memories, just scattered pieces that he couldn't fit together.

"The Pequot think me a magic man, a shaman; they call me Mamunappeht. But that is just a name. But these—" He gestured to the rows of masks. Well over a hundred of them lined the walls. "They are who I truly am. Each one contains a spirit, a soul." He smirked. "In a way I am their guardian. Like you, they were tortured souls all. I have given them a place to harbor, a sanctuary to escape their torment. They live with me, in me. I am but the sum of all of them."

Samson glanced around at the masks. Most were small, childlike, some tiny, no bigger than a mouse, a few larger ones, near the size of a bear's head. He wanted to dismiss the man's claim, but as he stared at them, he heard a distant whisper, then many whispers, the voices of ghosts, building, circling around them, turning into a wind that finally blew through him. He felt their woe, their sorrow. He shuddered.

"I am not of the Pequot," Mamunappeht continued. "I am much older than the Pequot, I came over with the great ice. But the Pequot are foolish enough to allow me to stay here in return for paltry charms and piddling tricks. I help them where I can. But it is too late for them." He snickered. "I grow weary of this guise and have hopes to move on, as is my way. Mayhap there is a place for me amongst these new people, the ones from across the great sea."

Samson barely heard him; he was staring at the masks, drawn to one in particular.

"Ah," the shaman said. "You have found it. Mayhap you're not as lost as you think."

The mask was built upon a burnt and blackened skull, that of a great stag, framed in fur. Charred antlers twisted out from its forehead and long knots of hair hung between the horns, woven together, forming a web. Symbols covered the mask. Samson recognized one of them—an eye painted between the empty sockets. It was the same as the one on the wall back in the pit where he had awoken.

"Go on," Mamunappeht goaded. "Take a closer look."

Samson stood. The skull hung at eye level. He approached it warily, felt the sensation of someone, or *something*, watching him from within and stopped.

"Do you feel fractured, a bit broken? As though parts of you are lost?"

Samson nodded absently.

"Well, the pieces are there . . . before you."

"What do you mean?" Samson asked, not taking his eyes from the mask.

"Do you not recognize *who* you are looking at?"

Samson cocked his head. "I know it . . . it is—"

"Yes, that is *your* head there on my wall."

"No!"

"All the missing pieces are waiting for you within. Look closer. The skull will show you because the skull is you."

Samson did look closer, taking another step, then another, even though every bit of him cried out not to, that this was a trick or a trap, that this man was not to be trusted. *I have to know,* he thought. *Just a peek.* A light flickered, only a spark, deep within the sockets. Samson flinched and fell back a step.

"Are you afraid . . . of *yourself*?"

Yes, Samson thought. *I am.*

The spark turned into a warm light, like late-afternoon sun, beckoning him in. He stepped forward, just a few inches away now, could make out blurry shapes moving within the sockets.

People, he thought. *Are they dancing?* He wanted to see them, needed to. Samson leaned forward, eye to eye with the skull, pressing his forehead against the mask, trying to focus on the shapes. A flash, a touch of vertigo, and the eyes of the mask were his own, as though he were looking out from within the skull, but it wasn't the cave he was seeing, it was as though he were transported. The people were now dancing before him like in his dreams and visions, only this seemed so very real. He felt the warm sun on his skin, inhaled, sucking in the smell of flowers. He could see so much more than in his dreams. The people had built a tall horned statue out of wicker and saplings, had adorned it with flowers. They paraded past, carrying baskets of fruits, nuts, vegetables, and wild game. They gave him looks of naked adoration, great smiles full of love and devotion. He basked in it, flooded with the joy of their reverence. Relief pulsed through Samson. *See, Abitha, see! I am not a devil. I am a nature god after all. At last I know.*

And then, as though the mask had been playing a cruel joke on him, the scene changed. The air warped, twisted, then untwisted, and all at once his statue was burning, the air full of smoke. The piercing sounds of screams came to Samson. Huts on fire, the flames licking a night sky. People running in all directions, their faces fraught with terror. Bodies, so many bodies, limbs torn away, guts ripped open, brains splattered. The air thick with the smell of blood and burning flesh and the screams going on and on as though never to stop. Samson saw a shadow cast long by the flames—*his* shadow, as he slaughtered the men, women, and children.

"No!" Samson flinched. "No, this is not me. I do not wish to be this. I will not." Samson let out a great moan, tried to close his eyes, to shut out all the pain and suffering, but could not.

The shaman sighed loudly, and the vision faded. Samson found himself back in the cavern, only now he was looking down at the shaman from out of the skull. Samson tried to come forward, could not, realized he was trapped within the mask. "Let me out. You will let me out, now!"

"I am sorry for you, beast. Sometimes it is best not to have all the answers. But you are no great riddle. You have known all along what you are. Have you not?"

Samson realized he was weeping.

"Do these names sound familiar? Hobomok, Atlantow, Chepi, Matanto, Okee, Widjigo?"

They did, each one hitting Samson like a punch to the chest.

"Or as the Christians call you . . . the beast, tempter, Father of Lies, Satan, Lucifer, on and on. So many names, but they all mean the same thing. And you know what that is . . . do you not?"

"I am no devil."

The shaman shook his head. "Even the Devil does not wish to be the Devil. So sad. It would be so much easier if you could wallow in your role. But who wants to be the harbinger of death and devastation?"

"No!" Samson cried. "I know compassion. I have empathy. I am one with Mother Earth. I am her hand. I give birth to her seed. I am good and I am *just!*"

Mamunappeht laughed. "Oh, you are such a tragedy. Who do you think turned you into the Devil?"

"What?"

"Yes, Mother Earth and your little imp friends, the Pukwudgie. The ones who call themselves wildfolk. They did this to you. They are the ones who infested you with demons. Do you not feel them, the demons, fighting for your soul? Of course you do."

No, never. It is a lie, Samson told himself, then thought of the two shadows fighting in his vision, the pain in his head, the struggle in his heart as though being torn apart. And now, here within the skull, he felt them, felt their hunger, a brooding presence, drawing closer.

"You were not always the Devil; you were once a great forest spirit and the wilderness was your kingdom. It is the wildfolk who twisted you, they who set the demons to you, they who begged Mother Earth to make you so."

Lightning flashed, thunder boomed, and another vision assailed Samson. He saw a hundred, maybe even a thousand wildfolk, their tiny black eyes aglow, their hands covered in blood. Saw the massive Pawpaw towering above them, its leaves on fire, its trunk slashed, blood oozing from the wound. And before them, on the ground, a body drenched in blood—*his body*.

"No," he groaned.

"Who brought you blood? Who set you to murder, goaded you to slaughter all the people? The very people who worshipped at your feet. Who drove you to madness? See the wildfolk for what they are!"

Samson did, could not help it as the mask threw more memories at him. Forest pushing him to be the slayer, to murder—blood, always more blood. First the people, then Abitha. How they tried to keep his hand away from the healing crafts, his magic away from nature, from breathing life into Abitha's crops.

"They feed . . . *thrive* on human suffering. Can you not see that?"

And it was Abitha Samson saw now, how the wildfolk harried and tortured her at every chance. Killing her goat, her husband, giggling as they terrorized and tormented her, breaking her well and then trying to murder her with the spiders and snakes. The vision faded and Samson groaned.

"Now, who are the true devils, I ask?"

"Why would they do this to me?"

"It does not matter now, all that matters is that the creature you once were is gone forever, lost."

"It does matter. Why?"

"Is it not obvious?" Mamunappeht smiled. "They did not, do not, wish to share this great land. They were jealous, angry that you dared to help the people. And when you would not drive the people away, would not go against your *own* nature . . . they *changed* your nature." The shaman sadly shook his head. "Punishing you by twisting you into a devil . . . a vessel for their demons. You are their slave, you are Hobomok, lord of misery. You are pestilence and plague, war and strife. You bring ruin to all you touch. See it! *See it!*"

And Samson did, over and over, as the mask showed him preying upon one village of people after another. He remembered, until all the memories blurred into one long river of blood and death and screams.

"No! No!" Samson cried over the screams, trying to flee it all, but could not. The mask held him, bound him within, and there was no escape. And he felt them again, the demons, the ones set upon him by the wildfolk, they were with him now, in the skull. He felt their anger, their hunger. He dared not look at them,

205

would not look at them. Felt sure if he did, they would reclaim him as their own. "Set me free! I beg you!"

"I can free you from the mask, if that is what you want. But I cannot free you from your demons; their magic is too strong, even for me. They will be with you wherever you go. You know this. There is no returning to what you once were."

Samson groaned.

"Now, tell me, is that what you truly want? To be set loose again? For me to hand you back over to these wildfolk, these devils? Have you not had enough of murder and blood? Do you wish to be their slave forever? To have to watch as they drive you to kill and kill and kill? What of this woman? The one on the farm. Do you not care for her? Love her? If you do, why would you do this to her?"

The screams intensified. And Samson saw a vision of Abitha lying on the ground covered in blood, clutching a great wound on her chest. "No, not Abitha . . . I would never—"

"*You* would never, but your demons surely will, come their first chance. You know this. How will it end? Not well for her. And it will not stop with her. Once you begin, once the demons have full possession of you, you are very good at being Hobomok."

"I am not Hobomok," Samson moaned.

"There is another path, an escape. I saved you before, remember?"

Samson's vision twisted and he found himself lying on his back, his eyes blurry with smoke and tears. The smell of blood and wailing in the air. Mamunappeht was there, kneeling beside him, his hand on his chest, chanting while the huts burned. Then they came, the spiders, and with them a great wave of relief. "Yes," Samson whispered. "I remember. You brought the sleep."

The shadows began to flitter within the skull, his skull, to roll in, and he saw the spiders again, crawling all around him, all over him. The screams slowly faded; the world within the skull dimmed until all was darkness.

"Yes," the shaman said in a low lulling tone. "Back into the arms of sleep. You would be there now, if not for your little imp friends waking you and setting you upon the world once more. But this time your sleep will not be disturbed. This I promise you."

"Is there no other choice?"

"Only the spiders can keep the demons at bay. I am sorry."

Samson heard voices flitting about in the dark with him. It was the demons, they were calling him, but the spiders had created a wall, a barrier between them, and they sounded far away.

206

"I cannot keep you here against your will, not for long, your demons are too strong. So, you must make a choice. You can shut your eyes, shut it all out, sleep and find peace, or leave this sanctuary and return to murder and strife. Which will it be?"

The spiders began to retreat, and little by little the screams returned, building. The moans of the demons grew louder, closer.

"I can make it all go away," the shaman said. "Just ask."

The screams intensified and Samson felt them, the demons, right behind him in the skull, felt their breath on the nape of his neck.

"Sleep," Samson whispered.

"Ask me. You must ask or the spell will not bind."

"Yes . . . *yes!* Please. Give me sleep. I beg you!"

The spiders rushed in, and this time Samson didn't resist but welcomed them, and the shaman spoke true as their embrace took him away, floating off into silence and darkness. He felt the demons withdrawing, fading, until they were gone, completely gone.

Samson smiled, and from somewhere far, far off, he heard Mamunappeht laughing.

Samson's eyes grew heavy. He shut them and let himself drift into that utter and complete blackness.

Peace. Peace at last.

207

CHAPTER 11

Abitha awoke to the sound of men's voices. She found herself in darkness so it took her a moment to remember that she was in the sheriff's cellar—the cellar often seconding as a holding cell, as Sutton didn't have a real jail. The sharp pain in her leg brought it all back to her. *This is real,* she thought, *no dream, no nightmare to awake from. I will be tried as a witch and hung as a witch, and that is all that is left for me now.* She closed her eyes, wanting to go back to sleep, wanting to wake up again someplace else.

She slipped her hand into her apron pocket, found the chain of braids, clasping it as though it were her mother's very hand. She started to slide it out, wanting to feel its soft touch against her face, when a knock came from the door, and she quickly shoved it back down into the pocket.

There came the clank of a key in the lock and the thick door opened. Soft morning light spilled into the dank cellar. Sheriff Pitkin stood in the entrance, a bandage wrapped around his ear. "Abitha," he called in a kindly voice. "Come. Let's get some breakfast in you."

Abitha tried to stand but fell back, the pain in her leg too much.

Sheriff Pitkin put an arm around her and gently lifted her up. "All right, we'll take this slow. Now, keep your weight off that leg." He all but carried her up the short run of steps into his kitchen, seating her at the table, where a biscuit and a cup of tea awaited her.

Deputy Harlow stood by the back door, his posture tense, his hand on the hilt of his sword. Abitha met his eye. "What are you so afraid of, Sam? Think I might turn you into a toad?"

Samuel's face went pale as though he was thinking just that.

The sheriff poured himself a cup of tea and took a seat across the table from her. He nodded to the biscuit. "I fixed that myself. Tastes better than it looks."

Abitha poked the biscuit. "This is kind of you, Sheriff. But my stomach is not in the mood for food for some reason."

"You should try," Sheriff Pitkin coaxed. "It will be a long day."

Abitha nodded, picked up the biscuit, and took a bite, chewing without tasting, trying not to think of what lay ahead. While she ate, Sheriff Pitkin sipped his tea and stared out the window. The sheriff appeared tired, weary, as though wanting nothing to do with this mess. Abitha thought how Sheriff Pitkin had always been kindly to her, had always made her feel welcome since she'd first arrived in Sutton. He seemed to live outside the righteous nature of so many of the sect. The kind of man who only wanted to get along. She guessed that might be one of the reasons Reverend Carter had assigned him to the post. She noticed a fresh spot of blood on the bandage. "I am sorry about your ear," she said.

He shook his head. "I am just glad you are not a better shot."

"What do you mean? I were aiming for your ear."

He mustered a small smile and sighed.

When she'd finished her breakfast, he helped her up and led her to the door. He removed a set of manacles from a hook on the wall. "I am sorry, Abitha, but I am required to put these on you."

She extended her wrists, and he clasped on the cuffs. He slipped his pistol into his belt, then helped her down the steps and to the street, where his two deputies awaited them by a wagon.

"Do we really need the wagon?" Samuel asked. "Not going very far."

"Yes, we do," the sheriff said. "I'll not have her suffer the pain of walking on

209

that leg of hers, nor having to hobble through that group of leering loons. . . .
Someone might get it in their head to do her harm."

"She's a witch. What does it matter?"

"It matters because I say it matters."

Samuel shrugged.

They loaded Abitha and rode the few short blocks to the meetinghouse. A
crowd awaited them; they were indeed leering, several coming forward to meet
them. Abitha saw many carried sticks or held rocks.

The sheriff pulled out his pistol, cocked it, held it where all could see. "I will
shoot the first person who throws stick or stone. You know me to be a man of my
word. So, who will be the first?"

There were many hard looks exchanged, but it seemed none wished to be the
first, and the sheriff steered the wagon right up to the entrance, parting the crowd.

People stared at her as though she had sprouted horns. Many carried bibles,
clutching them to their chests like a shield to ward away her wickedness. Abitha
felt like screeching at them, vexing them all, and if she had a little more spirit left,
perhaps she would've just to see the terror on their faces.

210

Abitha was brought into the meetinghouse. The pulpit had been replaced by two
tables; behind one were three chairs that Abitha assumed awaited the magistrate.
Twelve chairs lined the far wall on one side of the magistrate's table; on the other
side, a lone chair. Sheriff Pitkin led Abitha to this chair and seated her, then nodded
to his deputies and they opened the meetinghouse doors.

Twelve men filed in, all ranking members of the village, taking their seats in
the chairs across from Abitha. Several gave her curious glances, but none would
hold her eye for long.

Ansel and Wallace came in together, Ansel carrying a large satchel and a sack,
the two in deep discussion. Wallace's family, his wife, son, and daughter, followed
along behind them. Ansel went to one of the tables, set down the satchel, and
began unloading a few papers.

Wallace and his family took a seat on the front bench. Abitha thought nothing
of this until several more women and girls trickled in and also took seats in the
front row. She understood then, a chill pricking her arms: these women, these
girls, they'd all solicited spells and charms from her in the past.

The rest of the benches quickly filled up as more and more people entered.

Apparently, the usual seating arrangement not applying, as people sat where they wanted, regardless to standing, even men and women together.

Reverend Carter, his wife, Sarah, and their daughter, Martha, came in and sat a few rows back. Reverend Carter and his wife appeared nervous and upset; they both cast sympathetic eyes Abitha's way.

Those without seats stood in the back. People talked in hushed voices, but their faces betrayed their excitement as they waited for the magistrate to arrive. And it was the waiting, the sitting there before this mass of callous onlookers, that ate at Abitha, their endless staring and whispering behind hands becoming more than she could bare. She dropped her eyes to the floor, trying not to hear them, and there, amongst the entire village, Abitha found she felt completely alone, more alone than ever in her life. So much so that it actually came as some relief when Deputy Harlow stepped in and announced the arrival of the magistrate.

All heads turned to the door.

There came some clamor outside and five soldiers armed with swords, pistols, and pikes marched into the room, their heavy boots clomping loudly as they took up positions along each wall. A moment later two men entered carrying an ornate chair. This was set behind the larger of the tables.

A tall, wiry man entered, dressed all in black like a minister, only he was armed, wearing a thick leather belt cinched high on the waist, from which hung a sword and pistol. His dark, piercing eyes darted about the room, quickly taking it all in, coming to rest on Abitha. His intense glare seemed to take her measure in a heartbeat and dismiss her as fast. He cleared his throat loudly. "I am Captain John Moore, appointed first council to the magistrate," he announced to all in a commanding voice. He glanced back out the door. "All rise for Magistrate Lord Cornelius Watson."

Everyone stood with the exception of Abitha as a middle-aged, doughy-looking man of average height entered the building. He marched directly up the center aisle, glancing neither left nor right. It was obvious the man was bald beneath his white powdered wig, as the wig had slid to one side, revealing his shiny pate. Abitha was struck by how clean and crisp his cloak and hat appeared, as though just fresh from the tailor, making the village folk look shabby by comparison.

The magistrate tossed his richly oiled satchel upon the large table, and one of the guards helped him remove his cloak, revealing a long billowy robe. Magistrate Watson pulled a cap from a pocket, straightened his wig, and placed it on top.

The guard slid out the ornate chair, and the magistrate took a seat and began rummaging through his satchel. He first pulled out a gavel, then a pair of spectacles, placing them on his bulbous nose. He picked up a piece of parchment and began to read it over.

"Captain," Magistrate Watson called, and the tall man came to his side. Together they examined the parchment. After a moment, the captain waved Wallace up. Wallace shared a warm handshake with both men, quickly falling into confidential conversation, and it became apparent to Abitha that they were all well acquainted. Captain Moore then called Ansel over, and again warm handshakes all around. At one point all four of them looked at Reverend Carter as though taking his measure. Ansel said something behind his hand and the men's eyes shifted to Reverend Smith. There came a round of agreeable nods.

"Reverend Smith," the captain called. "Would you come here, please."

Reverend Smith came forward.

"We would like you to serve as second council to the magistrate. Is there any reason you need excuse yourself?"

Reverend Smith appeared surprised, started to reply when Reverend Carter stood up. "What is the meaning of this?" he demanded. "You are well aware that I am head minister in Sutton, and as such, it is my place to serve as second council."

Magistrate Watson smiled as though he'd been looking forward to this. "Yes, it would be your place . . . if not for the fact that suspicions have been cast on your role in this mischief. Thus, the court has deemed you *unsuitable*."

Gasps shot round the room.

Reverend Carter appeared a man struck a weighty blow; his face turned ashen and he seemed unable to speak. Finally he uttered, "By the court you mean you, *you* have deemed it so, Cornelius." There seemed to be more he wanted to say, but instead he shook his head bitterly and sat back down. The two men glared at one another, neither making the least effort to hide his disdain for the other.

"Now," the magistrate continued. "Reverend Smith, please, is there any reason you need excuse yourself from serving on the council?"

Reverend Smith shook his head. "No, sir." He stole an uneasy glance to Reverend Carter. "I am agreeable to help as I best can."

"Good," Captain Moore said. "Take a seat here." The captain indicated one of the chairs next to the magistrate.

Reverend Smith nodded and took the chair.

"We are ready then?" the magistrate asked the captain.

Captain Moore nodded.

Magistrate Watson struck his gavel twice, and the murmuring died away.

"Reverend Smith," the magistrate said. "Would you please open the proceedings with a prayer."

Again Reverend Smith appeared taken aback, again he cast Reverend Carter an uneasy glance as this was an obvious snub, but he quickly composed himself, stood, and led the congregation in a short prayer. Once the prayer was concluded, Captain Moore took a piece of parchment from Magistrate Watson and walked round the table to stand before the room. He faced Abitha and cleared his throat. "Abitha Williams, widow of Edward Williams, please stand."

Abitha sucked in a breath. *Lord, here we go,* she thought, and pushed herself up, bracing herself against her chair, being mindful of her injured leg.

"You stand here before the Lord," Captain Moore stated loudly. "Charged with consorting with the *Devil* . . . the grand enemy of God and mankind . . . consulting with a familiar spirit and . . . affliction with black magic and witchcraft."

The charges came as no surprise, but hearing them announced so forcefully before all cut Abitha to her marrow. She clutched the chair and struggled not to let her knees buckle.

"Abitha Williams, how do you plead to these charges?"

Abitha closed her eyes for a moment, sucked in a deep breath, opened her eyes, and locked them on the captain, meeting his fierce gaze with that of her own. "I am innocent to all. I have not now, nor ever, consorted with Satan."

"Very well," Captain Moore said, sounding unsurprised. "You may be seated."

Abitha sat back down.

"The court calls forth Ansel Fitch to present evidence."

Ansel nodded, shuffled a few pieces of parchment back and forth until he found the one he was seeking. He cleared his throat and stood. "It is well known amongst all that Abitha peddles in the Devil's wares. Potions, charms, spells. I have a list here." He held the parchment up. "Sworn to by over a dozen members of this congregation, as to witnessing such insidious behavior. And that, sir, is just the beginning. Only the tip of the blade. For it is attested to, and seen by my own eye, that Abitha Williams did and does consort with familiar spirits of the Devil."

A murmur drifted through the crowd.

"If it pleases his magistrate, I would call forth my first two witnesses."

Magistrate Watson nodded.

"Wallace and Isaac Williams, please rise."

Wallace and his son stood. The swelling had gone down on Wallace's face, but numerous bumps and scabs still stood out prominently on his pasty skin.

"Wallace Williams," Ansel said. "Will you, in your own words, tell the court that which you, young Isaac, and myself did witness there at Abitha's home?"

"I will," Wallace stated. "Well . . . it is pretty simple. Having knowledge of Abitha's deviltry and her grievances against myself and my family, I felt it necessary to bring witnesses to her homestead. And it is to the good of all that I did, for what we saw was beyond that of my worst fear. She, Abitha, was upon the porch whispering and conspiring with an . . . with an *imp* . . . her familiar, the very minion of Satan. And what we saw . . . why, it were the two of them, together, making a crown. Not any crown, but a witch's crown."

"It is a lie!" Abitha shouted. "They are trying to—"

"Silence, woman!" Captain Moore commanded, striding over to her, his hand on the hilt of his sword. "You shall not speak unless asked to. Is that clear?"

Abitha glared at the man but held her tongue as she struggled to calm herself, reminding herself nothing she said would matter, that this was all for show. But it was just more than she could bear, and she began to tremble.

"Wallace, a moment," Ansel said, and proceeded to don a glove. He reached into the sack he'd left on the table, withdrawing the circlet Abitha had been working on and holding it up for all to see.

Again, the crowd murmured.

"Is this the crown, Wallace?"

"It is."

"Is this it, Isaac?"

"It is," Isaac said.

Ansel placed the circlet on the table.

"There is more," Ansel continued. "For Wallace, overcome by what he saw, did confront Abitha on her deviant behavior. A most reckless act to be sure, but one predicated on his outrage at this woman for inviting Satan into our community. Upon which she and her imp did cast a spell on him. This, I swear, I saw for my own eyes, as did young Isaac here."

Isaac nodded. "She called forth her bees, set them on my father. And they did attack him in a most unnatural manner."

Captain Moore held up his hand. "And what say you to this, Abitha?"

"I say Wallace Williams trespassed on my farm, assaulted me, and broke my leg. I say it is well known that I keep plenty of bees on my land, and when Wallace attacked me he disturbed them. That is all there be to that."

"Then why is it that no other were stung that day?" Ansel asked. "Young Isaac and myself were there beside Wallace. Yet neither of us suffered a single sting."

"I know not. But I do know, as do many here, that Wallace has been trying to steal my land. That he burned my corn and barn, all in an attempt to gain my property. Does his motive not play some role in his accusations? Does he not deserve some scrutiny for his desire to ruin me?"

"Wallace is not on trial here, woman!" Ansel barked. "He did not cast a spell. Did not conspire with the Devil's familiar. It were you! Only *you!*"

"No!"

Ansel spun, returned to his table, grabbing the sack and dumping out the remaining contents—a few sheets of rolled parchment and about a dozen charms and totems. Using his gloved hand, he picked up a handful of the charms. Held them up for all to see, then out toward Abitha. "Did you make these?"

"I did."

"Are they not the hand of the Devil?"

"They are not. They are but common charms and blessings. Each delivered with the Lord's prayer. Such as many here have made."

He approached the six women and girls seated in the front row, held out the charms. They all cringed.

"Charity, would you hold these?"

Charity looked at Ansel, mortified. "Please, sir. Do not make me touch it again."

"Jane, Mary, Rebecca, Helen, Lydia, would any of you hold these?"

They all shook their heads, clutching their hands to their chests and adamantly refusing.

"And why not? Why are you so afraid of mere charms and blessings?"

"Because it burns me!" Charity cried.

"Aye, yes!" the other women and girls agreed. "It burns our flesh."

"Your magistrate," Ansel said. "This is no exaggerated claim. Upon public revelation of Abitha consorting with the Devil, the moment her black magic was called out, these very charms spontaneously burned these innocents here before you. Not one, but all of them. Before many witnesses. How, I ask you, could such a thing be? For six honest and pious members of our church to be afflicted all at once if not witchcraft of the highest order?"

"Abitha," Captain Moore called. "If these are but charms as you have claimed, why then do they burn them so?"

Abitha shook her head. "They do not burn them. They are but saying such because they are afraid. Afraid to be accused of consorting with me. Afraid to admit that they solicited such charms. That is all."

215

"Not true," Charity cried, shaking her head adamantly. "Not true. She *lies!*"

"Aye! Aye, not true!" the other girls cried, their eyes darting about fretfully.

"These girls have sworn before God." Ansel held up the parchment. "Given accounts on how you tempted and seduced them with fanciful promises, tricking them to partake in the Devil's magic."

"Aye!" Charity Williams cried. "She did. I swear to it. She spoke to me, whispered in my ear at night while I were sleeping. I swear it. I *swear* it!"

"Aye!" Mary cried. "In a dream." And then they were all nodding and agreeing, all clutching their skirts and wringing their hands.

Abitha sneered at them. "And I swear before God that I have never dealt in any form of deviltry."

"Then what is this?" Ansel snatched up a sheet of parchment from the pile and unrolled it. He held it up for all to see. There came gasps all around. Women covered the eyes of their children. It was one of Edward's drawings. The last one he did—the nude of Abitha.

The picture hit Abitha like a punch to the chest. She clutched her hand over her mouth, fighting back the tears.

"What is this if it is not deviltry? Here is proof that you bewitched Edward, seducing him with your womanly wiles! Now, look closer, one and all. See that this profanity is scribbled over the very words of Edward's own father . . . over his Godly lessons, no less. I ask you, who but a witch could force a man to do such a profane act? She has damned poor Edward's soul! Has claimed him for her master, Satan!"

"Blasphemy!" someone cried.

"Hang her! Burn her!" others shouted, the room taking up the call.

Magistrate Watson beat his gavel, but the crowd didn't settle, not until Ansel held up his hand and shouted, "There is more!"

Slowly the room quieted.

Ansel put away the drawing and walked over to Abitha. "Do you swear, here and now, that you have not consorted with the Devil's minion?"

For a moment Abitha didn't know what to say, could only stare at Ansel, confused, for she could think only of Samson, that somehow Ansel knew of him.

Ansel nodded to Deputy Harlow, and the man brought forward a cage covered in cloth. He set it down on the table and Ansel removed the cloth, revealing Abitha's cat in a small hutch. The animal appeared terrified, hunched down and cowering, its one eye darting fretfully about.

"Oh, Booka!" Abitha cried. "Oh, you poor thing."

"Do not say that name in this place!" Ansel commanded. "It is the name of a known demon."

"It is the name of a common pixie. And that . . . that is but a common cat, you half-wit!"

Magistrate Watson slammed his gavel. "You will not speak the name of any demons in this place. If you do, you shall be gagged. Is that understood?"

Abitha didn't respond, just stared at her cat, wanting only to set the terrified animal free.

"Your Honor, this wicked beast is the familiar which Wallace, Isaac, and myself witnessed whispering and casting spells with Abitha."

"It is but a cat," Abitha said, shaking her head. "A poor sweet cat. Not anything more."

"Goodwife Dibble," Ansel called. "Please stand."

Goody Dibble stood.

"Goody Dibble, is it true that you witnessed this very beast killed by dogs in Sutton?"

"Yes, sir. It is true. Seen it with my own eyes, I did."

"Did you see Abitha take the corpse home with her?"

"Aye, she wrapped it up in her apron and took it off."

Ansel pointed at Booka. "Goody Dibble, is this creature here the same beast that you saw killed by the dogs?"

"Aye," she said, staring wide-eyed at the cat. "There is no doubt." She pressed her knuckles to her lips. "That there is the Devil's work!"

"Indeed, it is," Ansel agreed.

"Wallace, Isaac, is this the imp you saw conspiring with Abitha? Helping her make the witch's crown?"

"It is," they both said.

"It is but a cat!" Abitha cried again. "Not anything more."

"It is the Devil's minion!" Ansel shouted, stepping toward the cage and jabbing his finger at the cat.

The cat cowed and hissed, and Charity cried out. "It sets its evil eye upon me!" She clutched at her throat. "It hurts. It hurts me so!"

The other girls looked horrified at Charity, then at the cat, then Mary clutched her own throat. "It hurts me!" Jane glanced back and forth at the two girls and she too cried out, followed by the remaining girls, until all six of them were clutching their throats begging someone to make the cat stop.

Fearful cries burst forth from several in the crowd; a few stood and rushed out. The room erupted in cries and shouts of "Witch!"

Magistrate Watson beat his gavel. "Remove that foul beast!"

Captain Moore stepped over, grabbed the cloth, and slung it over the cage, covering the animal and handing it to the deputy, ordering the man to take it outside. As soon as the cat was gone from the room the girls all dropped back into their seats, gasping, shivering, and holding themselves as though suffering from a grave fever.

Magistrate Watson continued to beat his gavel until eventually the room quieted.

Ansel pulled out a chair from behind his table and set it in front of the magistrates. He strolled back and forth in front of the congregation, hands clasped behind his back. Finally he stopped, setting his eyes on Martha. "Martha Carter," he said in a gentle voice. "Would you please come forward."

Martha flinched, her face that of a frightened rabbit; she looked anxiously to her parents.

"Just a few questions," Ansel added. "There's naught to be afraid of. You've done no wrong."

The room came alive with whispers. Reverend Carter and his wife exchanged a concerned look and the reverend stood. "I request a private word with the magistrate, if he would."

"Request denied," the magistrate replied.

"Then I must state that Martha has not been well of late. She has been very confused and—"

"Need I remind you," Magistrate Watson interrupted, "Sutton is under assault by the very Devil, and her aid is essential. Is there any reason the court should be aware of that you would not wish your daughter to help us?"

Reverend Carter started to say more, then a look of extreme frustration crossed his face and he sat back down.

Martha gave Abitha a quick terrified look, appeared afraid to move.

Ansel came to her. "Fear not." He spoke in a low, reassuring voice. "She cannot harm you. Not ever again." Martha stood, and Ansel led her to the chair.

"Martha," Ansel said, keeping his voice gentle, coaxing. "Is it true that Abitha came into your house and did visit you at your bedside?"

"Yes," she said in little more than a whisper.

"And that she did enter your house at the behest of your mother?"

"Yes."

"Martha, I know this might be hard for you, but would you please tell us all you remember of this visit?"

Martha's eyes dropped to her hands. "Well," she started. "It is hard to speak of." She glanced back at her parents. "Mayhap as my father said . . . I were ill . . . confused . . . and do not remember so clearly."

"Martha," Ansel said, his voice becoming firm. "Keep your eyes on me. This is not about your mother or father . . . this is about God and the Devil. This is about a war for your soul. You must state true, lest you give Satan dominion over you. If Abitha has infested you with her demons, we must find out or we cannot protect you."

Martha began to tremble, to visibly shake.

"I were very sick. And . . . and—" She began to cry; her voice cracked. "I know not how or why, but when I did awake—" She pointed at Abitha, her voice becoming hysterical. "She, she stood there beside me! She had hold of my hand and I did see many things! Many awful things!"

"What did you see?" Ansel demanded. "Tell us, child!"

"A dark shadow with horns!" she cried. "It did stand behind her!" She began to bawl. "And it touched me . . . through her . . . and I have feared since that it lives here!" She clutched her chest. "I am afraid!" She dropped to her knees. "Afraid that it will come back and demand payment. Will demand my soul. Please do not allow it to come back. Please, please save me from it!" She jabbed a finger at Abitha. "From her!"

"Enough!" Reverend Carter shouted. "Enough! This is too much. She was overcome by fever. Had nightmares. That is all!"

Sarah Carter rushed to Martha, held her. "You are safe, child. None shall harm you."

Shouts and cries erupted all around the room. The atmosphere had changed from one of curiosity to outright terror and hostility. The people no longer bothering to hide their cutting glares and curses. Abitha felt sure, if not for the guards, they would take her and stone her this very minute. And then she wondered if that wouldn't be a mercy.

Abitha caught Ansel share what appeared to be a conspiratorial look with the judge. The judge's lips tightened and he nodded.

Magistrate Watson pounded his gavel. "Silence. Now!"

Ansel slid another chair around and set it next to Martha. "Goodwife Carter," he said. "Would you please take the chair."

Sarah appeared not to understand, but she took the chair, putting an arm around her daughter and holding her tight.

219

"Goodwife Carter," Ansel began. "Did you invite Abitha into your home?"

"I did."

"Did you invite her to use magic upon your daughter?"

"Abitha's mother were a cunning woman. And Abitha knows many remedies. It is common practice to—"

"Sarah, a simple question. Did you invite Abitha to use magic upon your daughter?"

"Not magic, but an ointment. That is all. You must understand, it were dire. We feared the child might be dying. I was desperate to—"

"Martha, did your mother ask you to keep this visit secret?"

Martha kept her head down, not looking at her mother. "Aye."

Reverend Carter stood up. "I do not see the reason for such a question."

"Reverend Carter," the magistrate called. "You will stay seated and be quiet lest you be taken from the room. Is that understood?"

The reverend sat down.

"Goodwife Carter," Ansel went on. "It seems that you and Abitha have had a history of secrets."

"This is not true."

"Not true? Did you not exchange things, secret things, with Abitha after church? Hidden things in baskets and folded napkins?"

"No! I mean yes, but not like that. It were but some food. She—"

"Did you and your husband not encourage Abitha to craft her dark magic on the Sabbath?"

"What? No! Of course not."

"No? Yet it appears in the church records that Reverend Carter has repeatedly allowed Abitha to skip church."

"That is true, but it were on account of her hardship. You must understand that she—"

"Did you allow Abitha to sell spells and potions in the very house of the Lord?"

"I did not. I strictly forbid it."

"So, you admit that you were aware that Abitha peddled her magic during church."

"I forbade it once I found out."

"So, you admit you found out she peddled witchcraft and chose to keep this a secret."

"N-no," she stammered. "Th-that is not what I said at all. You twist my words."

"Did you encourage Abitha to conjure the Devil in your house?"

"No!"

Reverend Carter stood up. "This is an outrage! How dare you ask such a question!"

The congregation exploded in shouts, cries, and demands to hand over both Abitha and Sarah.

Magistrate Watson beat his gavel, and the guards quickly moved forward between the crowd and those up front.

"Court is adjourned," he shouted. "All those not part of these proceedings are hereby ordered to leave at once! Now out!"

Abitha awaited her sentencing in the small room at the back of the meetinghouse. Two of the magistrate's guards leaned against the wall by the door, staring at her glumly.

One of the guards, a burly middle-aged man with a patchy beard and leathery face, going by the name Garret, began to pace. "Ah, cannot believe I got dragged into this mess. My brother is getting married this week and it will be a party not to miss. The lot of them will be getting soused on my father's good cider, and me—me, I'll be here tending this wench. Just cannot believe my luck." He threw up his hands. "And to add to it. Y'know, it were supposed to be Robert, not me. It being his turn."

"Yeah, well," the second guard, a fellow named Jacob—a clean-shaven, slender young man—responded. "I do not think Robert went and got snake-bit just to shuck his duty."

Garret snorted. "Knowing Robert, he probably did."

"Well, you've done this sort of thing before. Have you not?"

The older guard nodded. "Aye, I had to go down to Wethersfield few years back. Now, that were a bit of nasty business. They must have poked and prodded and stabbed and burned that poor woman for two weeks and still she would not confess. And you know what?" He chuckled. "After all that, they put her in the water. Y'know, to see if she'd float. 'Cause a witch, she will float on the surface on account that the water is pure and so will reject her . . . at least that's what they say. Anyway, the poor woman sank like a rock, she did, and by the time they drug her out . . . why, she were not breathing no more. So, I guess that means they tortured and drowned an innocent woman. But did you hear anyone apologizing? Trying to make amends? No, sir, the magistrate were back in Hartford that same day, going about business as though nothing ever happened."

Jacob shook his head. "Why . . . that's not funny. That's just terrible."

"I guess it is."

"You do not think this case will go two weeks, do you?" Jacob asked. "I do not much like leaving my Isabel alone that long. She's got eyes for our neighbor, Daniel. And there's no telling what trouble she might get up to if I am gone so long."

Garret snorted. "That there is a sad predicament. Jacob, my boy, mayhap you should invest in a chastity belt for that one." Garret laughed, but his friend didn't appear to share his humor. "Anyway, it's hard to say how long. Depends on if they want to drag a confession out of her or just hang her straightaway. And if they do want a confession, it depends on how stubborn she is. How much pain she's willing to endure." He looked at Abitha. "Hey, lass, you do us a favor, hear. When they ask for your confession, just say yes. All right? Save you and us a whole lot of grief, it will."

Abitha turned away, faced the wall.

"I am telling you it will end the same way regardless."

There came a knock at the door. They were ready for her. The guards led her back to the main room.

The meetinghouse was full, every eye on her as she was seated. A moment later the twelve men of the jury entered and took their seats across the room, facing Abitha.

Magistrate Watson entered. The guard pulled out his chair, and he took a seat behind the large table between Reverend Smith and Captain Moore. The judge replaced his cap, then took a moment to pick something from between his teeth before grabbing the gavel and hitting it twice. "Court is in session." He looked to the jury. "Do we have a verdict?"

John Parker stood holding up a small piece of parchment. "We do."

Magistrate Watson nodded, and John brought him the note. The magistrate put on his spectacles, reviewed it, and handed it to the captain.

Captain Moore came around the table and stood before the room. He cleared his throat, and the room went dead silent. "Abitha Williams, you have been charged with consorting with the Devil, consulting with a familiar spirit, affliction with black magic, and diabolical influence upon the innocent. The jury, on this date of October fourth, 1666, finds you guilty on all accounts."

A satisfied murmur flowed through the crowd.

The captain held up his hand, and the crowd quieted. He continued. "Abitha Williams, you have brought down the Lord's Holy Anger. According to the law of God and the established law of this commonwealth, you deserve death and as such are sentenced to death by hanging."

Abitha heard the words; they came as no surprise. Yet still the weight of them was too much to bear, and she thought she might faint. She felt numb, no longer even in the room; her vision blurred and the commotion about her became muffled, sounding far away. The bang of the gavel brought her around. People were arguing. She blinked. Sarah Carter stood; she appeared anxious and confused.

Magistrate Watson struck his gavel until the room returned to order.

"Goodwife Carter," Captain Moore said. "Please come forward."

Sarah hesitated, glanced desperately at her husband.

"Goodwife Carter," the captain said again, more forcefully.

Sarah approached the large table and stopped before the magistrate.

Magistrate Watson handed Captain Moore a sheet of parchment. The captain read it aloud. "'Sarah Carter, based on the sworn testimony of your peers and statements made in these proceedings, including those of your own daughter, the court has found evidence to accuse you of aiding a known witch and familiar in the corruption of a child. How do you plead?'"

"*No!*" Reverend Carter stood and shouted. "This is not right!"

Sarah shook her head. "No . . . no! I did no such act!"

"If you wish to discredit me, Cornelius Watson," Reverend Carter cried, "then I challenge you to do so, but for the love of God, not by such underhanded means!"

The meetinghouse erupted with cries and shouts, with everyone talking at once.

Reverend Carter headed for the judge. Two guards intercepted him, struggling to hold him back.

"If you have cause to hate me," the reverend cried, "I beg you. Do not take it out upon my family!"

"Remove that man at once!" Magistrate Watson shouted, jabbing a meaty finger at the reverend.

The guards wrestled Reverend Carter away, dragging him down the aisle to the door. There, the reverend snatched hold of the frame and shouted, "The governor will hear of this, Cornelius! I will be bringing forth a full report! Heed me, you *will* be held accountable!"

And there, for the first time of the entire trial, the magistrate's smugness fell away and Abitha caught a glimpse of doubt on his face.

The guards removed the reverend and the judge pounded his gavel, kept pounding until at last, the room quieted once more.

"Sarah Carter, how do you plead?"

Sarah met Magistrate Watson's eyes. "Innocent. I am *innocent!* I would never

223

allow harm to my child. *Never!* I am a devout woman . . . a child of Christ, and I am *innocent!*"

The magistrate gave her a pitying look and shook his head. "Sarah, none here are perfect. We have all sinned. The charge before you is not witchcraft, but aiding a witch and her familiar. There is room for leniency from the court should you show proper contrition. If you confess here and now to your role, the court has agreed to give you clemency. You will be spared a trial, spared further interrogation. But this can happen only . . . *only* with your good and honest confession. So, Sarah, please take a moment to consider carefully. The eyes of the Lord are upon you."

"I need not a moment, not so much as a second, as my answer is honest and true, and will always be the same. I am innocent of these charges!"

Magistrate Watson appeared genuinely pained. "You leave me no choice, as it is my sworn duty to protect this community from Satan. I must order that you be held and interrogated until we can be sure of your guilt or innocence."

He gathered his papers and stood. "Captain Moore, you are hereby authorized to take charge of Sarah Carter and to extract from her the truth by whatever means you deem necessary. Do you accept this charge?"

Captain Moore set his hard eyes on Sarah. "I do."

Magistrate Watson struck the gavel. "This session is closed. This matter to be settled by other means."

Abitha sat in the back room of the meetinghouse, twisting her shackles mindlessly back and forth, staring blankly at the wall, feeling nothing. After about half an hour, there came a sharp bang on the door, startling her from her trance.

"They're ready for her," someone called.

Am I to be hung here and now? Abitha wondered. *So soon?* She tried to steady herself, to quell the rising panic.

Abitha's two guards, Jacob and Garret, stood. Garret, who looked to have weathered more than his share of hardship, leaned over, putting his leathery face directly into hers. "You listen to me. . . . Witches and devils, they do not scare me much. I've been this world round and seen my share of real spooks. I've fought pirates all up and down this coast, the Iroquois and French in Canada, Powhatan in Virginia. I've been shot, stabbed, stuck with arrows, cursed, burned, and buggered. I do not like Puritans and all their priggish swill and I sure as hell do not like witches. So, you're going to do as I tell you and not give me any shit. Is that understood?"

Abitha nodded.

"Good." Garret grabbed her by her upper arm, lifting her to her feet. Jacob opened the door and they led her back into the main room, where Sarah waited with a guard on either side of her. Sarah's face was vacant, as though she were in shock.

The guards escorted the two women from the meetinghouse. Abitha winced, fought not to cry out as she hopped and limped along on her injured leg.

Even though it was nearing dusk, a small crowd lingered. When they saw Abitha, they fell in step, following her and the guards as they headed down the river road.

Abitha's injured leg buckled, causing her to stumble and fall. She landed on her hip and hands, the shackles twisting and biting into her wrist. She cried out, the pain in her leg excruciating.

"To your feet," Garret growled, grabbing hold of her arm and tugging her back up.

She tried to walk, could not, her injured leg simply unable to bear her weight, and again she fell. Garret let out a curse and this time both guards grabbed an arm, lifting her, all but dragging her along.

Even though the crowd didn't jeer and taunt, it was on their faces, in their eyes, an almost gleeful bloodlust. She was no longer one of them, no longer a person at all. She was a condemned witch, a tool of the Devil.

They approached the old common stable, going around to the side, to the corral.

There were already a few people there, lined up along the fence. The small crowd joined them and they all watched as Garret removed Abitha's shackles from her wrists.

A grand oak tree grew just outside the far end of the corral, its broad branches overhanging the fence. A line of twine hung from one of the limbs, a sack hanging from the twine. Abitha couldn't make sense of it until they marched her into the corral and she saw what it was.

"Booka!" she whispered. "Oh, no!"

They'd bound the cat in a sack and hung him by the neck. The cat was dead; there was at least that mercy, his suffering done. But she could see by the way the cat's tongue jutted from his mouth and his one sad eye bulged, it hadn't been an easy death.

"That's your kitty, aye?" Garret said. "A real fighter, that one, had to about beat the life out of it just to get it strung up. Then the foul thing twisted about so, I thought sure it would tear loose. Took a long time to die. Screeched like a demon the whole while. I'd be the first to say it were *truly* a demon if I were inclined to believe in such malarkey."

"Oh, Booka," Abitha said, dropping to her knees.

"I hear tell you brought the wretched beast back from the dead. Like to see you do that now. Go on, give it a go."

Booka, she thought. *You poor, sad cat.* And as bad as she felt, she found she still had room to hurt even more.

"No sorcery today, aye?" Garret said. "Did not think so. I believe your witching days be done."

Garret left Abitha laying in the dirt and shoved Sarah along toward the big oak. That was when Abitha realized there were two freshly constructed crates, or cages, sitting on either side of the corral. They were built out of splintery slats and raw timber. She tried to understand their purpose, as they couldn't be for her and Sarah Carter—they were far too small for a person.

Garret lifted the lid on one of them. "All right, in with you."

Sarah stepped back, looking at the cramped cage, horrified.

"You can get in yourself, or we can put you in. It's your choice."

Sarah shook her head, took another step back.

Garret shoved her forward, knocking her down. She landed hard against the cage. Several gasps came from the spectators, then a couple of cheers.

Garret grabbed Sarah by the back of the neck, shoved his face into hers. "One more chance. You get your priggish ass in there, or we're going to toss you in. You understand?"

Sarah let out a weak cry but nodded.

"Good." Garret let go of her.

Sarah placed her hands on the cage, swung a leg over, and stepped in. She had to pull her legs in to her chest in order to be able to sit down.

"Now, if you do not want to be knocked in the head, lean over."

Sarah hunkered down as he lowered the lid, but still it wasn't far enough. She had to lean over to the point where her head was between her knees.

Garret sat on the lid. "There, now, is that cushy enough for you?" He wrapped a short bit of chain around the lid and attached a lock, locked it, putting the key away into his pocket. He peered in between the slats. "You just let me know if there's anything I can do to make your accommodations more pleasant."

A clod of manure hit the ground in front of Abitha, startling her. She looked over at the fence to see young Cecil Cadwell smirking at her. She glared at him, but even as she did, he picked up another. "Witch," he yelled, and threw it. This one striking her on the shoulder.

Abitha let out a shocked cry.

Cecil picked up another clod and Abitha looked to the adults, hoping someone would put a stop to it, but found only fear and hatred.

"Witch!" Cecil cried, and threw the clod, hitting Abitha on the leg.

Two of Cecil's friends joined him, all three of them gathering up clods and throwing them at Abitha.

Abitha couldn't get to her feet to get away, not on her injured leg, could only put up her hands, trying to block the manure. The clods struck her, one after another, one hitting the side of her head.

Abitha let out a yelp and looked to the guards, certain they wouldn't stand for this. Jacob, the young guard, started forward, but Garret put out a hand, held him back. Garret caught her eye and gave her a malicious grin.

Another clod hit Abitha, then another, and another. *"Stop it!"* she screamed.

"Whore of Satan!" a woman yelled; it was Goody Dibble. "You will vex us no more!" She picked up a clod and lobbed it. Her daughter, Mary, joined her, then several others did as well.

Abitha began to crawl away toward the stables, but turning her back only seemed to encourage them. Suddenly they were all throwing clods of dirt and manure—the men, women, and children. Their faces contorting into masks of rage and hate, looking like monsters, their eyes wild, their mouths twisting into vicious snarls as they pelted her.

"Witch!" they cried. "Satan's whore!"

All Abitha could do at that point was hunker down, covering her head with her hands and arms. Then something struck her back, something hard, not a clod, but a rock. Abitha cried out. Another rock hit her hand, another her arm. Then a stone hit the back of her head, the pain all but blinding her. She screamed, struggled to crawl again, but found herself dizzy, unable to see straight.

"Stop this!" someone cried in a booming voice. "You will stop this at once!" Reverend Carter stood behind the crowd, his eyes burning into them. "Hear me, all. . . . Any caught harassing these women will spend the night in the stocks. Am I understood?"

Several in the crowd appeared cowed, a few even left, but most of them met the reverend with open looks of contempt.

"Make way," the reverend called, pushing his way up to the corral. He carried some bedding and a basket. He opened the gate and started toward the women.

"No, sir," Garret said. "Captain's orders. There's to be no bedding, nor food, no visitors until he says otherwise."

"But my wife has not eaten since morning. Be a Christian soul, allow her but a bit of bread. I beg of you."

Garret strolled over. "Reverend, you do not want to be giving us trouble." He set his hand on the hilt of his sword. "I've got strict orders to see that you, especially *you*, are to have no discourse with the prisoners. Now turn yourself around and get home, before you find yourself in a box next to them."

"No," Reverend Carter said, looking levelly at the guard. "This is Sutton, and outside of that court, *I* am the authority." The reverend started past, made it one step before Garret struck him in the chest, knocking him down, the bedding and basket spilling to the dirt.

"I told you we have orders—"

Reverend Carter leapt at the guard, driving a knee into him, snarling as he pummeled him with hard powerful strikes.

Sarah screamed.

"Oh, Lord!" Abitha cried.

228

Three more guards rushed over. One got an arm around the reverend's neck, yanked him off of Garret.

Garret got up slow, spat out a mouthful of blood, then drove his fist into the reverend's stomach, once, twice, a third time. The guard let go of him and the reverend dropped to his hands and knees, coughing and choking.

Garret kicked the man in the ribs, sending him over onto his side, then proceeded to kick him over and over.

"Stop!" Sarah cried. "Please, please, stop this!"

Garret didn't, not until he was out of breath and Reverend Carter lay groaning in the dirt.

"Take him to the sheriff," Garret said, gasping.

Two of the guards grabbed the reverend and dragged him away.

"Norton," Garret called, wiping the blood off his lip. "Come here." One of the guards, a big dulled-eyed oaf with a thick neck and slouching shoulders, came lumbering over. "Put the witch into her cage. Think you can do that?"

"Oh, aye, sir," Norton said. "You can count on it." The man talked in a slow, clumsy manner, as though words were hard to come by, and Abitha guessed he might be a touch feebleminded.

Norton grabbed Abitha by the arm and dragged her across the corral. Abitha let out a cry as her leg twisted, but the big guard didn't seem to care, didn't even seem to notice as he dumped her in front of the cage.

"Get in," Norton ordered.

Abitha looked at the tiny cage with horror, knowing there'd be no way to get in without bending her injured leg.

"Get in."

Abitha clasped the cage, tried to pull herself up, but her leg gave out and she fell back down with a cry.

The big guard grabbed her, slapping one hand atop her shoulder, jamming the other between her legs and lifting her up as though she weighed nothing, and then dropped her into the cage.

Abitha landed hard, fighting not to cry out as the splintery planks dug into her flesh.

Norton grabbed her legs and proceeded to situate her, forcing her knees into her chest. Abitha let out a scream as he bent her bad leg, but he didn't stop, not until she was all the way in. He then dropped the lid on her, knocking her in the back of the head and forcing her all the way down into the cage.

Garret came along and locked it, then strolled over to where the reverend had dropped the basket. He reached down and picked up a roll, wiping away the dirt. He brought the bread over to Sarah's cage, held it up. "Right nice of your husband to bring us a snack." He took a bite. "This is really good. Did you make this, Sarah?" Garret took his time, eating the entire roll, chewing loudly, smacking his lips. "Just so you know, Goodwife Carter. The captain, he'll be coming to visit you tonight. He'll be seeking your confession. The captain is a very persuasive man, if you get my meaning. Now, if I were you, I'd take some time and consider what you might say to him to avoid yourself a whole lot of unnecessary suffering."

Garret strolled away, joining the other guards near the gate where they were getting a small fire started.

The crowd lingered for a bit, but after a while got tired of watching two women sweat in their cages, and most of them began to drift away.

Abitha's injured leg throbbed. She tried to maneuver into any position to take some of the pressure off, but found it almost impossible to even move in her cramped confines. And despite the sun going down, the night remained warm and humid, especially pressed so tightly within the cage. Sweat trickled down her back, into her face, stinging her eyes. The smell of manure filled her nostrils. Her head ached, and

229

she felt dizzy, kept swooning. She touched the knot on the back of her head where the stone had struck her, and her hand came away bloody.

Sarah began to weep. Abitha could see her fingers clutching the slats. Abitha looked at her cat, his one bulging eye staring endlessly at nothing. Her own tears began to flow then, and she turned away.

"Samson," she whispered. "Are you there? Can you hear me?" She slid a hand through the bottom slats, pressing her palm against the ground. "Samson," she whispered. "Samson, I beg of you, come to me. I'll give you whatever you want. Whatever you need. Just take me from here."

She closed her eyes, began to hum softly, trying to make the connection to the earth, to the serpent, to Samson.

"Please hear me."

She felt no pulse, no magic, no response, not from the earth or from within her own heart, nothing at all. It was as though part of her had died.

She reached into her apron, searching for the chain of braids, and for one horrible moment thought them lost, then—*there*. She let out a gasp of relief as her fingers found the comforting softness of the hair. She slipped the braids out, clutching them to her chest. "Mother," she whispered, pressing the braids to her lips and nose. "Mother, hear me. Please hear me. Mother—"

"What have you there?"

Abitha started, bumping her head against the slats.

Garret stood staring in at her.

Abitha tried to slip the braids out of sight, but Garret shoved his hand through the slats and caught her wrist, twisting it painfully, revealing the braids. He grabbed them with his other hand and tried to tear them from her grasp.

"No!" Abitha snarled. "It is mine!" She felt the braids slipping, tearing, and bit him, chomping down as hard as she could into his thumb.

Garret let out a cry but didn't let go.

Something hard struck Abitha against the side of her head. There came a blinding flash of pain, causing her to swoon, and she felt the braids slip from her grasp. "No!"

"What is that?" Norton asked. He stood beside Garret, a small wooden bludgeon in his hand, the two of them staring at the woven hair.

Garret held up the chain of braids, looking at the serpent pin with utter disgust. "Witchery!"

"Please," Abitha begged. "It is naught but a weave of hair. It is all I have left in this world. It hurts nothing. Please allow me to keep it. *Please!*"

Garret wiped the blood from his thumb, spat at her, walked over to the fire, and tossed it in.

"NO!" Abitha screamed. *"No! No! No!"* Her scream turned into a wail as she watched the braids, that of her mother, of all her mothers, ignite and burn. The fire darkened, a reddish smoke spiraling up from the flames, then a moment later, both the hair and the smoke were no more.

"Mother," she whispered, between sobs. "Mother." There came no scent of lavender and sage, no sense of her whatsoever. "Please . . . do not leave me."

231

C H A P T E R   1 2

Forest lay curled into a tight ball within a small crevice amongst the blackened stones of the ancient Pawpaw. He could feel the faint pulse of the sapling through the rocks, feel it growing weaker by the day.

"I am sorry," he whispered to the sapling. "I have failed."

He heard a clatter of small stones, knew who it was. "Leave me be," he growled.

They did not leave him be; instead Sky and Creek began scratching and pawing at the cluster of sticks and stones that Forest had piled up in a sad attempt to barricade the opening of his hideaway.

He could feel their fretting.

Done with them, he thought. *Done with all of it. Our time is over. It is the time of the people now.*

There came a furious flurry of pecking and scratching. The sticks and stones crumbled inward and daylight flooded in, causing Forest to shield his eyes.

"You're wasting your . . ." Forest trailed off as he read the terrible news on their faces.

"No! He did not. The Pequot. Why?" But Forest knew why. "That fool. That thickheaded ass. Why does he not ever listen?"

Forest climbed out from the hole, looked up at the sapling, hoping against hope that he would find a fruit hanging from its branches, even just a bud. Instead, to his horror, the small tree was shriveled, almost all of its leaves now gone. He let out a long groan, the sound of a soul who has given up all hope.

"Yes, I know he'll find the magic man, or I should say the magic man will find him. Either way, that demon Mamunappeht will see him back in the skull, I'm sure of it." He shook his head sorrowfully. "It is over, can you two not see that?"

He saw what they were asking of him, knew what they wanted.

"No, we cannot bring him back again." He pointed at the tree. "We have no fruit. No magic. We're too weak. You both know this."

"But there *is* no other way. What would you have me do? Stroll into Mamunappeht's very lair and steal Father's skull?"

And Forest saw that was indeed what they wanted. "No, no, no," he groaned. "If he has Father now, then he knows about us. He will have traps set everywhere. We would be handing ourselves over to him, to a fate worse than any death. This is no common shaman we are talking about, this is a powerful demon!"

Creek and Sky clacked their teeth angrily.

"So many ifs. And we do not know *if* Father can even kill Mamunappeht!"

They began darting round and round the sapling, forcing Forest to face the truth, the only one that mattered—the tree, it was *dying*.

Forest groaned, crawled to his feet, gave the sapling one last wistful look, then headed north, toward the Pequot village, and Sky and Creek followed.

233

Someone kicked Abitha's cage, jolting her from her stupor. She blinked; the guards had lit torches and placed them around the corral. Abitha had no idea what time it might be other than it was night. She kept drifting in and out of consciousness, the intense muscle cramps, ache in her leg, and sweltering humidity keeping her from any actual sleep. Her clothes were soaked with sweat and clinging to her skin, but at the moment, it was her enormous thirst that tormented her most. She'd not had a drink since the sheriff gave her tea the previous morning.

She heard approaching voices, peered out of her cramped cage, saw Captain Moore strolling into the corral. Two guards followed him, carrying a small table and a chair. They placed them in the center of the corral.

The captain carried a bag; he dropped it on the table. The contents clanked, sounding like tools and knives and God knew what else. He removed his jacket and took a seat in the chair. "Garret, bring out Sarah."

"Aye, sir," Garret said, and both he and the big guard, Norton, walked over to Sarah's cage. Garret produced the key, unlocked the chain, and lifted the lid.

"Get out," Garret ordered.

Sarah slowly stood, wincing as she tried to straighten. She appeared dazed, her face drawn, her lips parched, her clothes dark with sweat. She'd lost her cap and her short cropped blond hair lay matted to her skull. She clutched the lid to keep from falling over as she stepped out of the cage.

The guards prodded her toward the captain, and when she didn't move fast enough, Garret gave her a shove. Sarah stumbled but managed not to fall, staggered over, and stood before the captain, struggling to stay upright.

Captain Moore poured water into a cup and handed it out to her. She looked at it warily.

"Take it."

She did, drinking it down greedily.

There was movement over by the fence and Abitha realized several men from the village had followed the captain down. Ansel Fitch and Deputy Harlow were amongst them, their faces leaving little doubt they'd come in hopes of seeing a good show.

"Sarah Carter, you have been accused of aiding a witch and her familiar. There is overwhelming evidence of your guilt. Yet due to your standing in the community, Magistrate Watson has shown you great leniency. He has not condemned you . . . *yet.* He has given you time to consider what you have done and to do the right thing for the good folk of Sutton. If you give testimony and confession to your involvement, you will be set free of this cage . . . you will be spared an interrogation. Your crime will carry a sentence of one year in Hartford jail, nothing more. If, on the other hand, you choose to lie to the court and thus to align yourself with Satan, then, come tomorrow, you are to be hung alongside the witch. Do you understand this?"

Sarah lifted her head. "I understand that I am innocent of these charges. Guilty only of trying to aid my daughter in her time of need. I understand that my only judge is God, that He sees into my heart and knows I am innocent."

Captain Moore let out a long, loud sigh. He took a sip of water, then reached into his bag and removed a bundle wrapped in cloth. He set this upon the table and unrolled it, revealing an assortment of serrated knives and long needles.

Sarah's eyes locked on the knives and she began to shake.

"There are other ways, tried and proven ways, to find out if one is in league with Satan. I would prefer a simple confession, but if one is not forthcoming, then you leave me with little choice." He walked his fingers across the tools, coming to a stop on a thin blade with a jagged hooked tip. He plucked it up, stood, and walked over to Sarah. He held the instrument out so that Sarah could get a good look at it.

"Sarah, witch-hunters have prescribed searching for a mark upon the body . . . a devil's mark. And if any such marks are found, the mark is to be cut and pricked to see if the mark bleeds, to find out if the mark is numb or alive. This can be a very painful procedure. Before I subject you to such suffering, I will ask you again . . . Sarah Carter, have you aided a witch and her familiar?"

"I am innocent," she said, her voice trembling.

"Very well. Garret, Norton, you know what to do."

"Aye, Captain," Garret replied, a sordid grin pushing at the corner of his mouth.

Norton clutched an arm and held her while Garret came around behind and began unlacing her bodice.

"No," Sarah protested, tried to turn away. "Please, do not."

Garret grabbed a handful of her hair, gave it a hard yank, bending her head back. He pressed his lips next to her ear. "You behave and do as you are told and this will go much easier on you. You understand me?"

Sarah closed her eyes and nodded and Garret let go. He removed her bodice, then grabbed her blouse, tugging it over her head, leaving her exposed.

Sarah covered her breasts with her arms. Her eyes cinched tight, as though trying to block out what was happening to her.

"Jacob," Garret ordered. "Gather those torches there."

"Aye, sir."

"There now, hold them so we can best see."

The younger guard did as he was bid. The flame leaving not a shadow for Sarah to hide her modesty within.

Garret began examining her, starting with her back, jabbing and prodding his thick fingers into her flesh, up her spine, searching for bumps, moles, warts, birthmarks, and any other peculiar marks. He prodded her neck, throat, behind her ears, through her hair. "Open your mouth and stick out your tongue, lass."

Sarah did as she was bid, and he jabbed his dirty fingers into her mouth, under her tongue.

"Lift your arms," Garret said. "Higher, up above your head."

Sarah looked at him fearfully. She glanced at all the guards staring at her, over to the faces lining the fence. The fine folks of Sutton weren't outright leering, but close; there was little doubt that this was just the sort of show they were hoping to see.

When Sarah didn't lift her arms, Garret jabbed a knuckle sharply into her ribs. She let out a cry.

"Plenty more where that came from," Garret growled. "Now arms up."

Captain Moore watched impassively while twiddling the hooked blade between his fingers.

Sarah slowly raised her arms, exposing her breasts to the guards, to the captain, to the good and pious folks of Sutton.

"That's better," Garret said, staring at her chest. He grabbed a breast and tugged it roughly upward, then to the left and right, then the other one, searching for any marks. He then prodded under her arms, digging with his fingers, making Sarah wince. Garret snagged the top of her skirt and tugged it down. It slid down her legs, pooling around her ankles, leaving her fully exposed.

Sarah had held back her tears this whole time, but she now began to cry.

"Oh, hush with your blubbering," Garret said. "We've all seen diddle-bits before. Yours are not anything special." He knelt to one knee and proceeded to examine and probe every inch of her, all the way down to her feet. When he'd finished, he stood and faced the captain.

"Three. She's got three marks." He poked the side of her left breast sharply. "See that dark spot. Mayhap the Devil's teat. Mayhap just a mole. Not for me to decide." He slapped the inside of her thigh. "A mark of some sort there. And here." He spun her around and tapped what looked like nothing more than a blotchy birthmark on her back, just beneath her shoulder blade. "This one. This one looks suspicious to me."

"Yes," Captain Moore agreed, holding up the jagged blade. "I see. Let's start with that one then. Hold her."

Sarah took a step back, horrified. The two guards caught her, pinning her between them. "We got her, Captain."

Captain Moore took the knife and jabbed it into the center of the birthmark, puncturing well beneath the skin. Sarah let out a cry, but the captain didn't stop. He twisted the hook this way and that, causing her to scream. Only when a steady flow of blood began to run down her back did he stop.

Sarah slumped and, if not for the guards propping her up, would've collapsed.

"Guess not that one, aye, Captain?"

"No. Have to be thorough, in case it is some kind of bewitchment."

"Of course, Captain."

Captain Moore worked his way around, from the mole on the side of Sarah's breast to the mark on her inner thigh. Each mark produced its share of cries and blood. Frustrated, the captain finally quit. He withdrew the blade from Sarah's flesh and nodded to the guards. "That is enough for now."

The guards released Sarah and she crumpled to the ground, sobbing.

The captain wiped the blood clean from the blade and laid it back amongst the other instruments. "You can get dressed, Sarah."

Abitha found herself shaking, clutching hard to the slats of her cage. She glanced to the small group of men at the fence, gawking and exchanging lively whispers as Sarah struggled to put her skirt and blouse back on. And through her rage, Abitha found her voice. "God sees you!" she cried, her voice cracking. She caught their guilty looks. "God sees your leering, sees your lewd thoughts. God is judging you now!"

"Silence, witch!" Ansel shouted. "Who are you to speak of God?"

A few of the men looked away, uneasy, but none left.

237

"Sarah," Captain Moore said, "it seems we made no progress this night. A lot of suffering for naught. Please, let us end this torment. Just a word from you. What say you, Sarah? Did you lend hand to the Devil?"

Sarah met the captain's eyes. "Nay, I am a good Christian woman and serve only God." She looked to the fence, to the faces there. "Hear me now, all of you. I serve God. Only *God!*"

The captain nodded to the guards and they dragged her back to her cage, locking her in. He then grabbed his jacket and bag. "Sarah Carter, your life is in your own hands now. You have but until tomorrow to make your confession and to ask for redemption. I bid you all good night." And with that he left the corral.

Forest, Sky, and Creek perched on a ledge, peering down on the Pequot village as the sun slowly began to rise. They didn't wish to be seen, so were not, but they knew such tricks were useless against the shaman.

Creek and Sky pointed to the cliff.

Forest could just make out a cave. He felt a chill and glanced at his companions, tried not to think of their fate should the demon shaman catch them. He didn't know how many more of the wildfolk were left in the world, hoped there to be a few clusters of them scattered here and there about the land. They used to call to one another, sending out soft songs, mere whispers on the breeze, the light wind carrying the songs for leagues. But not any longer, as the shaman might hear and come for them.

Mother Earth, I have wronged you and I have wronged Father. But I beg that you do not let my wrongs keep you from helping Father, from saving the wildfolk. Allow me this one chance at redemption. Please, Mother Earth, we are the last, do not abandon us.

Forest looked down at the village, at the Pequot people milling about, and let out a long sigh. "Are you ready?"

Sky and Creek didn't look ready, but they both nodded.

"All right."

Sky and Creek let themselves be seen and took off, flying and swimming through the air. They swooped down into the village, began flying around the huts. It didn't take long for the cries and shouts of the people to echo back up the valley. Forest paid them no mind, his attention fixed on the cave.

Mamunappeht appeared, spotted the spirits, and ducked back into the cave, returning a moment later with a sack and a long stick. There was a net on the end of the stick.

Creek and Sky saw him too and shot away into the woods.

The shaman scrambled down the steep ledge and disappeared into the trees after them.

Forest headed for the cave. He had no idea how long he would have; Mamunappeht might catch the two spirits right away, might not catch them at all. Either way, Forest was under no illusions: he was going into a trap, and if he failed to free Father, he would never come out again.

"You are a clever one, demon," Forest hissed. "But not as clever as you think. There are still a few tricks you do not know about." Forest grinned fiercely, showing all his little needlelike teeth.

The sun slowly rose, bringing the oppressive heat with it, and Abitha drifted in and out of a sweltering daze. The unseasonably hot weather refused to lift, and all was a fever dream of cramps, pain, thirst, and hunger. At times she noticed people staring at her from the fence. At one point Wallace was there, gloating, but it was hard to say if he was real or a dream as she also saw Edward and her mother; even her father made an appearance. But not Samson, never Samson, no matter how many times she whispered his name.

Abitha was hit with a shock of cold. It took her a moment to understand that she'd been doused with a bucket of water—wonderful cool water. A weak cry escaped her parched throat and she began licking the droplets from her hands and arms, sucking it from her blouse and hair.

There came a rattle as Garret unlocked the chain and lifted the lid. "It's your big day, witch," he said. "Time for you to put on a show." He nodded to Norton and the huge guard grabbed the side of the cage and flipped it over, sending Abitha tumbling out.

She let out a howl, feeling as though her tendons had been torn from the bone by the sudden jolt. She lay on her side, clawing at the soft dirt, trying to bear the pain, trying not to scream.

They left her there, and after a while Abitha managed to sit up, clenching her teeth as she worked to unbend her neck and back. She could no longer feel her legs, felt sure she could no longer move them either. She began rubbing them, trying to get the blood flowing, trying to slowly straighten them.

239

Sometime around noon they began to arrive, the men, women, and children of Sutton. Soon, every spot along the corral fence was occupied. Aside from a few children running about and laughing, people were quietly talking amongst themselves, their faces full of anticipation. Abitha could do nothing but sit in the dirt, in her filthy rags, the entire village staring at her.

Captain Moore arrived, giving the corral and guards a quick inspection. Abitha watched one of the guards testing the rope, grasping the noose and pulling himself up to see if it would bear his weight. It did.

A table was brought in, along with two chairs, set up facing the noose. One more chair was brought in and set beneath the noose.

Garret and Norton removed Sarah from her cage; her blouse was stained with dried blood. Abitha met Sarah's eyes, but there was nothing between them other than sadness and hopelessness. They dragged Sarah across the corral and sat her in the chair. She didn't look at the noose, wouldn't, only stared at her feet.

"Out of the way!" someone shouted, and the crowd nearest to the gate parted. The guards dashed over to open the gate and in strolled Magistrate Watson, carrying a bible, his plump face pink and sweaty. Reverend Collins and Reverend Smith followed the judge in. But Abitha saw no sign of Reverend Carter.

The judge pulled the captain aside, away from the ministers. He spoke in a hushed tone, but Abitha managed to catch some of it.

"Still no confession?" the magistrate asked.

Captain Moore glanced at Sarah. "None. The woman is unmovable."

The judge appeared deeply troubled. "Reverend Carter is not the sort of man to take lightly. He *will* make good his threat to bring this before the governor. We're talking about the wife of a prominent minister here, Captain. Think how it will look should we not get that confession." The judge wiped his hand across his mouth. "The governor will request a full accounting, I am sure. He has made it his business to stick his nose in such affairs as of late." The judge shook his head. "Mayhap we have gone too far, but we must see this through now . . . we *must* have her confession."

The captain studied Sarah and frowned. "There are still ways, sir. But they are not easy ways." Captain Moore lowered his voice, spoke in some detail, but Abitha could hear none of it.

Magistrate Watson clapped the captain on the shoulder. "I am hopeful it will not come to that . . . but let us see how it goes."

A guard came in carrying the magistrate's large ornate chair, placing it at the table. The judge set down his bible and dropped into his chair. He invited the two ministers to sit next to him.

The magistrate put on his spectacles and took a moment to arrange a few papers. Finally, he glanced up and stared at the two women, making no effort to hide his disgust. "Well, they certainly look a mess." He shook his head. "Reverend Smith, would you do us the favor of a prayer?"

The reverend nodded and stood. He asked everyone to bow their heads and gave a short prayer.

The guards took up places on either side of the women.

"Sarah Carter," Magistrate Watson bellowed, talking so everyone could hear. "You stand before us accused of aiding a known witch and familiar in the corruption of a child. A severe charge that carries a severe punishment. But there is still hope for you." He studied her. "If you but admit your role, the court in its mercy has found room to grant you a reprieve. We but need your confession and your sworn oath never to involve yourself in witchcraft again. If you can show us the proper contrition, show a genuine desire to protect this community from Satan's evil influence, you shall be spared. Sarah Carter . . . will you now confess?"

The crowd stilled, not a sound, as though no one dared even to breathe.

Sarah stood; she appeared scared, her hands quivering, but still she met the magistrate's eyes. "Sir, I . . . I cannot confess to a crime I did not commit. I beg you to please understand that to do such would be to consign my soul to perdition."

A murmur went through the crowd.

Magistrate Watson frowned. "Sarah," he said, his voice becoming stern, pressing. "Look there at that noose. If you do not confess, then I will be left with no other choice but to charge you with lying to the court to protect a known witch and thus entering a covenant with the Devil. Such charge brings with it a sentence of death. Now, this will be your last chance. Do . . . you . . . *confess*?"

"I confess only to my love and faith in the good Lord above."

The magistrate's face reddened. "Sarah Carter, you *will* confess."

Sarah just stared at him.

"You *will* confess!" he demanded, spittle flying from his lips.

Sarah slowly shook her head.

Magistrate Watson slammed his palm on the bible. "There are other ways!" His eyes shifted to Abitha. "Captain, see to the witch."

Abitha flinched.

Captain Moore strolled over, almost as though the scene had been rehearsed.

"Abitha," the captain said, speaking in a slow, deliberate manner. "*You* . . . have been found *guilty* of witchcraft and condemned to death. For that there is no reprieve. But . . . I would like to offer you a choice . . . a quick merciful death, or a slow . . . *bad* death." He studied her. "I have decided that you are to be hung from your ankles until you expire. As you can imagine, this is not a peaceful way to die. The convicted can linger for days as the blood pools in the brain, until eventually the pressure becomes unbearable, the pain excruciating. I have seen prisoners scream themselves into insanity. You can avoid this, you can choose a quick snap of the neck instead, an almost instant death. It is in my power to grant such a mercy. I would but ask one small thing of you in return."

The crowd waited in silence, but Abitha knew what was coming.

"For you to show some contrition by allying with the Lord and the good people of Connecticut. To state it plainly and clearly before all . . . that this woman, Sarah Carter, *did* aid you and your imp. That is all."

"No!" Sarah cried out. She started toward Abitha, but the guards grabbed her, held her. "Abitha, for the love of God, do not do this thing. Do not condemn me so! Please! I beg of you!"

Captain Moore stepped forward and drove his fist into Sarah's stomach, doubling her over. The guards dropped her to the dirt, where she lay gasping and groaning.

241

"Abitha," Magistrate Watson said. "You have this one last chance to save your-self so much needless suffering. What say you?"

Abitha sucked in a deep breath. *Such a simple thing to say,* she thought. Only it wasn't. If she said nothing, Sarah would die martyred, her name in good standing, her death a blight upon the face of all of Connecticut. If instead she accused her, Sarah's name would be forever tarnished, and her husband, her daughter, they would pay the price, and God only knew who would be next after them.

Abitha noticed Magistrate Watson fretfully squeezing his hands together. She understood his desperation, the pressure he was under, but then she saw another face, there in the crowd, that of Wallace, and what struck her odd was that Wallace too appeared nervous and anxious. She wondered why that was, when he should be gloating; then, she understood, almost laughed at how obvious it was. An upstanding Puritan woman, the wife of a minister, was about to be hung on account of Wallace. A woman who would rather strangle to death than confess to a lie, and that held weight. Such a thing wouldn't look good for Wallace or the judge. But especially not for Wallace, as there would always be those who doubted him, who knew of his underhandedness. *They might not hold my death against you, Wallace Williams, but by God, they would that of Sarah, of a woman only guilty of try-ing to save her daughter.*

242

"Abitha Williams," the magistrate called. "We await your reply."

Abitha barely heard; she was still staring at Wallace. *Is he praying?* She could see his hands clasped, his lips moving ever so slightly. *Why, yes, he's praying.* Their eyes met, and when they did, she gave him a vicious smile. *Nay, Wallace, I will not answer your prayers.*

"Abitha, I will ask you but once—"

Abitha turned her smile, that fierce, wicked smile, on the magistrate. "It were not Sarah Carter that aided the Devil, good sir. Nay. It were that man yonder!" She pointed at Wallace. "It were his greed that brought the Devil into the fold, his deceit and wanton ways. Tell them, Wallace Williams!" she shouted. "Tell them how you have played them all with your lies, how you have made pact with the Devil so that you could take Edward's land!"

Nervous murmurs fluttered through the crowd, and Wallace went pale, sud-denly looking as though he were the one about to be hung.

"I ask who here is not aware of his underhanded ways? Who—"

"Shut her up!" Magistrate Watson cried.

Captain Moore drove his boot into Abitha's gut, kicking all the air from her. Abitha rolled into a ball, gasping and clutching her chest.

Magistrate Watson's face grew redder still. "Satan shall not win this day. Captain, a word."

The two men began an intense discussion. The magistrate nodded his approval to something and Captain Moore strolled quickly away. He enlisted a few men from the crowd and disappeared into the stables, leaving everyone wondering what was going on. The men returned a few moments later carrying an old wooden door.

Jesus, Abitha wondered, *what is this to be?*

Upon the captain's orders, two guards grabbed Sarah, dragged her to the middle of the corral, and forced her down on her back. The men then placed the heavy plank door atop her, pinning her to the ground, leaving only her head visible.

Sarah's eyes darted about, confused and horrified.

Magistrate Watson strolled over, peered down at her. "You will confess, Sarah. You must. It is the only way to keep Satan at bay. I care not how long it takes. You *will* confess."

"Where's my husband?" Sarah cried. "Thomas! *Thomas!*"

"Your husband is in the stocks. If you wish to see him, simply confess. Do it now and I will take you to him myself."

"No. No. *No!*"

A small retaining wall of stones wrapped around one side of the stables. The judge nodded to the men waiting there, and they lifted out a few of the larger stones and carried them over.

"Let us start with six," the magistrate said.

The men carefully laid six of the heavy stones on the door.

Sarah let out a cry.

The judge paced slowly around the trapped woman, his hands clasped behind his back. "Do you confess, Sarah Carter?"

"No!"

Magistrate Watson held up two fingers, and the men laid down two more large stones.

Sarah let out a groan, her face turning red from the strain, the veins bulging from her neck and forehead.

The magistrate stood watching, waiting, his face glistening with sweat and frustration. "Let us end this, Sarah. Please, I beg of you, confess."

Sarah shook her head, and he let out a huff and threw up his hands. The judge tromped back to the table and sat down heavily in his ornate chair. "Some cider," he demanded, and one of the guards brought him a large mug. He sat there sipping his drink, glowering at Sarah, listening to her rasping gasps and waiting.

243

The crowd waited as well, silently staring as Sarah fought not to suffocate under the immense weight as the muggy day dragged slowly on. Legs grew tired, and many began to sit on the ground along the fence.

After what must've been an hour, perhaps a little more, the judge stood and wandered back over to Sarah.

"You can lay out here all day and night, slowly dying beneath the weight of your own guilt, or you can simply confess and be done with this. The choice is yours."

"I cannot," she gasped between rapid shallow breaths.

"Just a few words and you can go to your husband."

She shook her head.

Magistrate Watson's face tightened. He held up two fingers, and the men laid down two more stones.

Sarah let out a sharp scream, her breathing becoming ever more labored, as though each breath were taking her last bit of strength. Abitha knew the woman couldn't last much longer.

The judged paced back and forth, his agitation growing with every step.

Sarah's lips quivered. Her eyes bulged, her mouth gaped, rapidly opening and closing. Her face was now purple, her left eye bright red; bloody tears streamed down her cheeks.

Oh, for the love of God, someone stop this! Abitha thought, and turned away. She searched the crowd, hoping to find some outrage there, some desire to end this senseless torment. A few were crying, but most watched grimly, their faces stolid and righteous. There were some, yes, like Goody and Ansel, whose faces betrayed their inner vileness, but most appeared transported, almost in rapture, as though sharing this moment with God Himself, their hands clasped to their breasts, staring upward into the firmament, their lips moving in silent communion with their Lord and savior. Abitha could see that these people believed, truly believed, that they were doing God's work here this day. And there was something about these people that horrified Abitha even worse than those whose faces were lined with cruelty. As at least cruelty was a thing that could be pointed out, confronted. But this belief, this absolute conviction that this evil they were doing was good, was God's work—how, she wondered, how could such a dark conviction ever be overcome?

There came a commotion from near the gate. "Let me pass!" someone shouted. "Let me pass!" A girl pushed her way through the crowd, shoving past any who tried to stop her. The girl came running into the corral. "Mother!" she cried. "Oh, Mother. Enough!" She dashed over and slid down on her knees next to Sarah.

244

Captain Moore started to intercede, but the judge raised his hand, shook his head.

Martha clasped her mother's face between her hands. "Mother, please, please. End this! *End this now!*"

Sarah shook her head, said something—barely a whisper.

"Yes, you can!" Martha cried as the tears streamed down her face. "You have to! Father has lost his mind to all of this . . . I am alone. Do not leave me! Please, I beg of you! I love you!" She let out a sob. "I . . . I love you, Mother."

Sarah turned her head, looked at her daughter for a long, long moment, and again she whispered something.

"She says *yes!*" her daughter exclaimed. "She will confess. Remove the stones so she can speak. Do it *now!*"

The men looked questioningly at the magistrate.

His face lit up. "Yes, here, remove the stones. Be quick!"

The men rushed in and gently rolled off the stones; Sarah sucked in a deep breath.

Magistrate Watson knelt beside her, his face bright with hope. "Do you confess, Sarah Carter . . . to the charges brought against you this day?"

Sarah sucked in a few more breaths, coughed violently. "Yes," she sobbed. "God forgive me . . . I confess."

The judge leapt to his feet. "It is done!" There was absolute glee in the man's eyes.

They lifted the door off Sarah, and she curled up into a ball, hitching and coughing and wheezing uncontrollably.

Abitha stared on in shock. Seeing these fanatics break this Godly woman somehow seemed a worse crime to her than even seeing her hung. "Oh, Sarah, what have they done to you?"

"God has won the day," Magistrate Watson proclaimed, all but dancing. "Bear witness, all, to this great victory over Satan!" He marched over to Abitha and spat in her face. "When you are in Hell, be sure to tell Lucifer how the good people of Sutton overcame his wicked designs this day!"

Hard hands fell upon Abitha; Norton and Garret grabbed her arms and dragged her to the end of the corral, to the large oak. Garret kicked her prone, pressing her down with a heavy boot, while Norton bound her arms to her sides, the ropes biting deep into her flesh. Then they bound her skirt, legs, and ankles together, pulling the ropes so tight that Abitha felt sure her very bones might snap. They secured one

245

end of a rope around her ankles and tossed the other over a thick low-hanging limb. Then slowly they tugged the rope, lifting her up off the ground feetfirst.

Abitha spun and swayed back and forth, her world suddenly upside down, the blood rushing into her head, her face tight from the pressure. Her vision blurred, then cleared, and even as she spun, she could see the crowd, catching quick glimpses of their faces, and again she saw their righteousness, their rapture. They were, after all, doing God's work this day.

She watched Captain Moore put shackles on Sarah and take her away. And as her mind tried to sort through her pain, her grief, her sorrow, she couldn't help but feel that Sarah had somehow abandoned her, that they had all abandoned her.

Samson, where are you?

As the rope bit deeper and deeper into her flesh and the pressure mounted inside her head, drumming along with her racing heart, Abitha cursed them. "He will come!" she cried. "He will come. The Devil will come for all of you!"

CHAPTER 13

A shadow deep in darkness—the darkness only the dead know.

A whisper . . .

Another.

"I do not hear you . . . I will not hear you."

The whispers became words—distant but urgent. *You must wake.*

"No, I will not awake, not again . . . never again. Leave me be."

Father, you must wake.

"No. I am dead. And dead I shall remain."

They have your precious Abitha.

"No . . . no more. I am done."

Abitha will die. All your children will die unless you wake . . . now!

He tried not to hear the name, but it pricked him like a knife. "Abitha?"

She suffers. Oh, how your pet suffers. She cries out your name. Do you not hear her? Listen.

The shadow opened his eyes, saw two specks of light floating in the dark, moved toward them, and found himself peeking out through eyeholes. Before him was a cavern lit by a small fire, the walls covered in masks. It was all very familiar. He flinched as pain, suffering, guilt struck him, as a wave of remorse engulfed him. He pulled back, searching for the darkness, for the sweet arms of the spiders.

A face moved into his line of sight, peering into the mask. An opossum, but with the face of a child. He knew this creature.

"Do you remember me?"

"You are one of the demons."

"I am Forest, your child," the creature said. "Now, what is your name?"

"I . . . I am Hobomok . . . the Devil. I am murder and blood. I am misery and torment."

"Look around these walls. Whose heads do you see here?"

"Leave me be!"

"Stop hiding and look!"

"No," Samson whispered, yet he did look, glancing from mask to mask, noting the various shapes and sizes.

"These are *our* kin," Forest said. "The wildfolk . . . *your* children. Mamunappeht has made trophies of your children's heads, prisoners of their souls. Now tell me *who* is the *real* devil?"

"You! *You* are! It was you that poisoned me with your sorcery, twisted me so, infested me with your demons! The mask has shown me the truth! You tricked me to slaughter them, the tribes, the people. It is you and the wildfolk that are the true devils! I saw it!"

Forest cinched shut his eyes as though in great pain, then slowly reopened them. "Please . . . please listen to me." There was such sorrow, such deep remorse in his tone, that Samson did listen.

"I have done you a great wrong. One that I will never be able to atone for. I can claim it was for the sake of the wildfolk, for Pawpaw, for Mother Earth, but my truth is I have allowed my need for vengeance, my hate, spite, jealousy, and more than anything . . . my *fear* to lead me. And lead me it did, led to ruin for all of us." He was silent a moment. "Once you are free you can judge me as you will, exact your rightful vengeance. I am at your mercy. But first, for the sake of Pawpaw, we *must* get you out of this devil den."

Forest grabbed the skull, began to tug.

Samson felt *them*, the demons, the ones within the skull with him, felt them stirring. "No," Samson said. "This is my sanctuary. You will plague me no more. Go! Leave me be!"

Forest tugged and pried and shoved, but the skull didn't budge. He tried again, his face twisting into a knot of frustration with the effort; yet still the skull held.

"What deviltry is this?" Forest growled, glancing fearfully back toward the cavern entrance. He tried again, slamming himself against the skull, over and over, yet still the skull stayed on the wall.

"No . . . no!" Forest panted, shaking his head. "He will not win . . . *must* not." He shot another fearful glance down the tunnel, then a cold determination set upon his face. "We will do this here, then," he whispered, and scrambled up the wall, out of view. The skull trembled and Samson felt the creature tearing away the webbing, trappings, and the mask from the skull as though from his own head. Forest tossed the mask away and suddenly Samson felt untethered, his mind sharper, the world before him clear.

"The skull showed you *a* truth," Forest said. "That which the mask wanted you to see. But sometimes there are many truths."

The demons! Samson thought, suddenly feeling their hateful eyes on his back. *They're awake!*

"It is time for you to face yourself."

The demons behind Samson growled. Samson tried to close his eyes, tried to shut out the pain, the guilt. *No. I want to sleep . . . sleep.* He pushed back from the eyeholes, began to drift away. The spiders, they were there waiting for him. *Darkness, sweet darkness.*

"Father!" Forest said, smacking the skull. "Stay with me!"

"No! I will hear no more of your lies!"

"The skull does not lie. Cannot lie, because the skull is you. Look, see for yourself! The stag!"

"The stag?"

"Yes. The stag. Now look, remember the land. See it as it was before the people arrived. See your story."

The mere suggestion sent the visions; it was as though removing the mask from the skull had freed his mind, his soul, and his memories, *all* his memories, were his once more. He saw the land; it was the place he and Abitha had visited together upon her broom, the world of wildfolk, giant beasts, and magnificent forest. "Yes, I know of this place."

"Good. Now seek. See who you were then."

249

A great golden stag strolled out from the trees, an imposing beast with sprawling antlers. It stood proud and majestic. There was no confusion; the moment Samson saw the beast he knew who it was. "It is me," he whispered, and upon that declaration his view shifted to that of the stag. "I am the stag."

"Yes."

Samson, the great stag, tromped through the forest as though he lorded over all, the giant beasts giving him a wide berth. The wildfolk followed in his wake, some flying on tiny wings, others darting and dashing, skipping and leaping. All laughing and singing, snarling and growling, tussling and playing, dancing and rutting, as they frolicked through the ferns, flowers, and towering trees of the great virgin forest. Samson smiled.

"Earth was our mother," Forest said. "And you were our father . . . the great forest lord. You were the heart of the wilderness, of the wildfolk. You were loved and you were feared. You were life and you were death, doing what was needed to preserve the balance. All part of the cycle of nature, of death and rebirth, of winter and spring."

"Yes, I remember." Samson began to cry as the memories overwhelmed him.

"The best of times," Forest said. "Sadly, one cannot know the best of times until they are gone, until they are lost. How I would give the rest of my days to have just one of those days back." Forest sucked in a deep breath. "Nothing lasts forever, not even the moon and stars. Now see the first people. See them invade our land."

Forest needed only speak of it and the memories flooded in. The people arriving, coming down from the north during the time of great ice, from a land far away, a type of creature none had witnessed before—animals that covered their skin in the hides of other animals.

Samson saw how pitiful they were, these small clusters of nomadic people searching for a home. Saw the wildfolk harrying them, the people seeing him, the golden stag, for the first time. How terrified they were.

Then as timed passed, he saw them kneeling before him, just as the shaman had revealed, saw again the wicker statue of the great stag adorned with flowers and bowls of fruit. The people paying him tribute and him blessing them in return, bringing fertility to their crops and wombs. He felt a flush of joy.

"As their numbers grew," Forest continued, "as the people flourished, they wanted more . . . they *always* want more. They're wicked, greedy creatures."

Samson witnessed their small villages spring up about the land, watched the people living off the forest, struggling to survive in a harsh, unforgiving world as any creature might. "I see no wickedness, only creatures trying to claw out a space for themselves."

"There is more."

A memory flashed—the wicker stag burning, men with their faces painted like the shaman, like Mamunappeht. And above them, Mamunappeht, standing upon a cliff, laughing.

Samson heard the demons growl behind him in the skull. "No more, I have seen enough. I—"

"See the truth, Father!" Forest snapped. "Mamunappeht had discovered the power of Pawpaw. He lusted for its fruit. You were in his way, so he gave the people a taste of our magic, showing them the wonderful things they could do with it, the miracles they could perform." Forest grimaced. "They craved more, as Mamunappeht knew they would. He showed them how the magic was in our blood and they came after *us*!"

"I do not believe you."

"You are the master of your own memories now. See for yourself. It is all there for you to find. They had fire, they had weapons and traps. The wildfolk were no match."

Samson saw crazed men with painted faces hunting the wildfolk with nets—brutal and ruthless. Saw the wildfolk in cages, their dead bodies drained of their precious blood. Samson tried to look away but found it impossible to turn from his own memories. He felt the demons within the mask growing restless.

"Devils! Devils everywhere!" Samson cried.

"No, not everywhere. You, you, Father. You are no devil. Look, see what I did to you!"

Samson saw the great Pawpaw towering above him, its bloodred leaves shimmering against the glow of the full moon. Hundreds of wildfolk circling the tree, circling him, dancing and prancing and chanting. The smell of blood hit him. The wildfolk were cutting themselves, gathering their blood in a large bowl. Forest stepped forward, his fur stained bright crimson. He brought forth nine of Pawpaw's fruits, sliced them into halves, squeezing the bloody pulp into the large bowl, mixing it with theirs. The wind picked up as Forest held the bowl out to Samson, beckoning him to drink. Chanting, all of them chanting for him to drink. The wind began to howl and Samson drank, the blood going down his throat like fire.

"The potion was meant to give you strength to fight the demon, Mamunappeht, to drive him away, to save the tree. That is what I told you then. But it was more."

Again, Samson saw the burning statue, just as the shaman had shown him, the air full of smoke and dreadful screams. He smelled the blood, saw the mutilated

251

bodies—hundreds of them, men, women, and children. Saw the raw looks of terror as they ran, ran away from *him—him!* "No," Samson moaned. "No!" And the demons within the skull moaned with him.

Forest shook his head. "I want to tell you that what happened that night—the spell sending you into that frenzy the way it did. That it was not deliberate, that I did not will it so. And for so long I told myself this, believed it, but I see now that I . . . that all of us, the wildfolk, that we were so full of hate and vengeance that we put that hate into that potion . . . put that poison into *you*. You were the lord of the forest, the balance, and what we did was so against your nature, against Mother Earth herself, that it tore your soul apart." Forest paused, his eyes distant. "We paid for our offense. We all did, but none more than you."

And suddenly, Samson felt as though he were actually there, on the ground amongst the burning huts and mutilated bodies, as the cries and acrid smoke drifted around him. He tried to get up, could not. His head felt as though it were splitting, his heart drumming. Again and again he tried to stand, but it was as though two of him were wrestling for control, fighting, tugging, pushing until finally utter exhaustion set in and Samson just lay there panting. A cloaked figure approached, leaned over him, and chuckled. The figure pushed back its hood, revealing a painted face with dark scars running down its features. "Mamunappeht," Samson whispered as the scene faded.

"Yes, the true demon," Forest spat. "He'd been skulking in the shadows, biding his time, his play."

"Sleep . . . he brought me sleep," Samson whispered. "Peace, sanctuary. The spiders." And with that, Samson saw them again, the spiders. "Sleep . . . give it to me."

"No!" Forest shouted, and slapped the skull. "Are you not curious as to why your own head is here on this wall? Why the great Pawpaw is now but a charred ruin?"

"No," Samson whispered. "No more!"

"Well, you will know! You will know all of it! After Mamunappeht put his spell on you, he chopped off your head, your very head, and burned your body. Your skull here is testament to that! With you out of his way he came for the tree, for Pawpaw, for us. The wildfolk gathered before the tree. We made our stand, and there we paid the price for our wrongs, our sin against you and Mother Earth, for we were no match for Mamunappeht and his frenzied disciples. They slaughtered us!" The fire went out of Forest's voice. "But the tree was not to be his. No, Mother Earth would never allow such. The sky began to howl and thunder and a blast of lightning struck the tree, igniting its trunk . . . burning it to the ground." Forest was weeping now. "Mother Earth took Pawpaw from us, from *all* of us."

Samson groaned, and the demons within groaned with him.

"Father, it is time to—"

A clack echoed down the cavern.

Forest glanced behind, then back at Samson, his face frantic. "Father, the pit, the eye, you remember?" He spoke rapidly. "When we brought you back, I now know what happened. Why you are so tortured! Your soul, it was shattered by the potion, by our blood magic all those years ago. So, when we brought you back in the pit, you were not whole; part of you was left behind, here, in this skull." Forest rapped the skull twice. "There was never a chance for your heart and soul to come together and heal!" Forest glanced fretfully toward the tunnel. "Hear me, understand. You must understand. You are here, in this skull, all of you, all the pieces!"

The demons in the skull began to hiss and stomp, coming closer and closer.

"It is up to you, only you, to find them and bind them. Find the stag, Father. Free yourself! There'll be no more chances. Come out now, or the last of the wildfolk, your children, Abitha, your very soul will be lost forever! Face yourself! *Now!*"

Mamunappeht appeared in the cavern entranceway. In one hand he held a staff with a web-shaped net strung between the forked tip. The web glistened as though sticky. In the other hand he held a sack. Something was squirming within.

"I'm so glad to find you here," the shaman said to Forest. "You and your friends." He shook the sack, and Samson could hear Sky and Creek whimpering. "I'd feared all your kind gone." Mamunappeht smiled and entered the cavern. "Feared my days all but over. But not anymore. No, your blood and the blood of your brethren will see me through, will bring these tired old bones back to life." He grinned savagely. "And it seems this day is full of gifts. Your friends shared a secret with me. Though I will admit it took a bit of pain and sorcery to pull it out of them."

It was then that Samson noticed the bloodstains seeping through the sack.

"But what a secret it was!" Mamunappeht continued. "Well worth my effort." His eyes narrowed to mere slits. "I have won, little beast. After all these years, it's mine. The pawpaw is mine. There will be no stopping me now. I will rule the land, the forest, the people, *all* the people. They will learn to kneel before me."

Forest jumped to the floor, darted left, then right, tried to leap past the man, but the man moved uncannily quick, intercepting Forest and catching him in his net. Forest screamed and flailed as though the net burned him, but couldn't escape. The shaman slammed Forest to the ground, planting his foot atop his neck, pinning him to the dirt.

"Face the demons, Father," Forest cried. "Face them now!"

Mamunappeht chuckled. "The stag cannot hear you. He is gone and this time for good. Where I am sending him there will be no coming back."

The shaman withdrew a knife.

"Stop!" Samson shouted. "Stop this!" He pressed forward, pushing his face against the skull from within the skull. His demons began to howl, the sound cutting to Samson's core, and he wailed with them.

The shaman stared at the skull, shocked. "No!" he cried. "You cannot be awake!" His eyes alighted on the crumbled mask in the dirt and his tone changed—low, deep, soothing. "Sleep! You must sleep. It is your only salvation."

"Father!" Forest screamed. "You must—"

Mamunappeht pressed his foot harder, choking Forest's words away. The shaman reached down with his free hand and picked up the mask, placing it back on the skull. And when he did, all became muffled and the spiders came rushing in, like a wave of shadows, smothering Samson in their soothing embrace.

Samson's vision dimmed and the demons within quieted, drifting away from him.

"*Sleep.*" Samson heard the words from somewhere far-off—so sweet, so seductive. "*Only sleep will stop the murder, the misery. Only sleep will stop your pain. Now sleep.*"

Samson struggled to stay awake, but the shaman's words were like hands tugging him down, deeper and deeper into the darkness, the sweet, warm darkness.

"Sleep," the man purred. "Only sleep will stop Hobomok."

Hobomok. Hobomok. The word echoed about in the skull, *Hobomok,* pricking at Samson, then stabbing at him, slowly mounting in volume. *Hobomok. Hobomok. HOBOMOK!*

I am not Hobomok.

Samson felt them return, the demons; they were right behind him in the skull. He could feel their hunger, their growing fury, feel their hot breath on his neck. They began to growl, snarl, then rage, and as they raged, the spiders began to fall away and Samson could see once more, see the skulls of the wildfolk, see the shaman, the gleeful sneer upon his face as he squeezed the life from the opossum.

It is you . . . you that are the Hobomok. Not I!

And with that Samson turned and faced his demons.

He saw a great stag, glowing brilliant gold, and another great stag, with smoke rising from its charred fur, its head but a skull. Their hands about each other's necks as they struggled to strangle the other from existence.

"We are one," Samson said, and reached for them. The moment his hands touched them, there came a brilliant flash of heat and light and pain, and all three howled. A multitude of memories, feelings, emotions rushed in, colliding, swelling inside the skull, inside him, swirling together and pressing, pushing, until finally, slowly, their howls came together and the three voices became one, the three souls one.

Samson blinked, not knowing where he was, then the cave swam back into focus and he realized he was still within the skull. He saw Mamunappeht wrestling with Forest, trying to slice open his neck.

"Hobomok," Samson growled, and pressed against the skull, harder, then harder. He felt a small pop, felt the skull crack, followed by a stab of pain to his forehead, and suddenly he could hear Forest screaming and snarling.

Forest bit Mamunappeht. The shaman cried out, then stabbed Forest in the chest—once, twice.

"*NO!*" Samson howled, pressing harder; it felt as though his own skull were splitting. There came another crack and a pop followed by searing pain, yet still he pressed on. The mask began to tremble.

The shaman looked up, brows knotted. "Stop!" He stabbed Forest once more, then leapt over, slapping his hands on the skull, trying to hold it together.

Samson pushed and pressed, felt another snap, another. The skull began to crumble beneath the shaman's hands. Samson felt himself growing, expanding; there came a great release and the pain disappeared. The darkness, that feeling of being within, of being trapped, evaporated, and he was there, in the cavern, lying on the ground amongst the shattered remains of his own skull.

Mamunappeht fell back, his eyes full of dread and confusion. "*No!*"

Samson's heart drummed. He stood, sucked in a chestful of air, and let out a long deep growl. He set his eyes on the shaman. "I am the shepherd and I am the slayer. I am life and I am *death!*"

The shaman jabbed his hand into a pouch strung about his waist, pulled out a handful of yellow powder, and flung it into Samson's face. He began shouting a barrage of jumbled words at Samson, scoring symbols in the air with his finger.

The powder stung and Samson stumbled back into the wall. The world blurred, then slowly came back into focus, and when it did, the shaman was crawling up the wall, his arms and legs split in twos, then fours, giving him eight limbs, his eyes to four, then six. He cackled as he scuttled across the roof of the cavern.

Samson tried to keep him in his sight, became dizzy, almost falling into the fire. Something struck him in the back of the neck—a deep searing pain.

Another wild cackle from the shaman.

Samson spotted him; he held a small spear, the tip black and sticky. Samson grabbed for him but fell, landing in the fire. He rolled out of the flames and again the shaman jabbed him with the spear, the tip going deep into his side. Samson let out a groan; his legs buckled and he collapsed, falling against the wall, amongst the masks and skulls, the shaman's cackling echoing in his head.

"The masks!" someone cried. "Destroy the masks!" It was Forest. Samson looked at the skulls, not understanding.

"Smash the skulls!" Forest screamed.

Samson slammed the side of his fist into the nearest mask, the skull beneath shattering like an eggshell. A plume of black smoke escaped along with a mournful wail. It dissipated as it drifted upward, fading away, but not before Samson glimpsed a face in that smoke—that of a wildfolk.

The shaman's cackling ceased. "No!" he shouted.

Samson smashed four more in quick succession; when he did, his vision and his mind became a touch clearer.

Mamunappeht clutched his head and let out a scream.

Samson pulled himself up onto his feet, smashed another and another, all that he could reach, and with each one felt his legs growing steadier beneath him.

Mamunappeht lunged for Samson, trying to jab him again, but this time he wasn't so quick, and Samson managed to knock the spear away.

Samson shoved the shaman back and stumbled around the room, smashing every skull he came to, dozens and dozens of them, and with each skull he felt his mind clearing, his strength returning.

The shaman let out a long wail and slid down the wall, landing in a heap next to the fire. His array of limbs slowly returning to their original form. And with each mask that Samson smashed, the shaman aged. His hair fell out along with his teeth, his limbs withered, his skin wrinkled and turned sallow, shriveling up until dry as parchment.

Samson smashed the last mask, and when he did, the shaman let out a final moan, a weak, frail sound, and crumbled into a heap of dust and bones.

Samson stood to his full height, his heart drumming with vigor, the pain, the spiders, the torment, all gone from his head and heart. He spotted Forest on the ground, the dirt dark with his blood. Samson dropped to one knee next to him, setting his hand on the creature's arm.

Forest looked up at him. "You just might make a good devil yet." He grinned, then the tiny sparks in his eyes flittered out and he stilled.

Samson heard a muffled whine coming from the wiggling bag. He tugged it over and opened it. Creek and Sky came tumbling out. They saw Forest and went to him, both of them trying to get him to wake up. But he didn't wake and Samson knew he never would.

Samson scooped up Forest's body and carried him from the cave. Creek and Sky followed him.

Ghostly clouds drifted across the night sky and the early moon cast all in its murky glow.

Samson climbed atop a large boulder overlooking the valley and set Forest's body upon its crest. He spotted the village below, threw back his head, and howled, the haunting sound echoing up and down the hollow.

Faces peered out from the huts below, terrified faces. Samson smiled. "I am the shepherd and I am the slayer. I am life and I am death."

Abitha hung upside down. She was not asleep, not awake, but somewhere in between, fading in and out of darkness.

Thunder rumbled in the distance.

Abitha opened her eyes, hoping for rain, some relief from the stifling heat. It was night again; they'd lit torches and placed them all around the corral.

Abitha tried to swallow but couldn't, her throat and tongue swollen. She could barely breathe, knew she was slowly suffocating. Her head ached, her face throbbing from the pressure. But at least her arms and legs had gone numb, the rope bindings so tight as to cut off the circulation. Blood ran from her nose into her eyes, making everything appear red and fuzzy. She could hear the guards, make out their shapes over in the stable. A few appeared to be sleeping. The scene faded in and out.

Something flew past her face, the lightest touch, like a feather. A black shape landed on the post next to her. It had the face of a child. "Sky," she tried to say, but no sound came from her parched and swollen throat. Sky was smiling at her. A kindly smile. He nodded his head up and down.

Samson? she thought. *Samson is coming.*

Her vision blurred, went dark, then returned, but the raven, it was gone, and she wondered if it had been real.

Someone was there, hard to see, a tall dark shape. *Samson? It's Samson. Oh,* she thought, *at last.* Only it wasn't Samson. It was Norton. He stood staring at her, swaying slightly as though drunk, his eyes bleary, his face blank, his mouth half-open. He held something in his hand—something familiar. He stepped closer and held the item up: something on a rope.

Oh, God, Abitha thought, and managed to let out a weak groan. It was her cat, Booka. He dangled the dead animal in front of her.

"Witch," Norton spat. "I am not afraid of you. You hear me?" His words were slurred, his breath smelling of rum. He took the cat and tied it to her so that it hung against her face. "You two can go to Hell together. You hear me?"

She didn't answer, couldn't. The world was fading again, just the drumming of her pulse in her ears, fading . . . fading . . . then blackness.

Blackness.

Pain, stabbing pain. The blackness dissipated like smoke. Abitha found a face staring into hers; it came slowly into focus. It was Garret. He was crouched down before her. He held a long knife in his hand. He grinned. "See there. Told you she's not dead."

"She is," Norton said.

"She's not. Here, I'll show you." Garret jabbed the knife into Abitha's cheek. Abitha flinched. "See there."

Norton squinted. "Oh . . . damn."

"Well, how long is this going to take?" a paunchy guard named Richard asked. "I am tired of sitting around this dung heap of a village."

"Hard to say. I've seen them last four or five days."

"F . . . four or five days?" Richard stammered. "God . . . and we have to stay here until she dies?"

Garret nodded. "Captain's orders."

"Sure, easy enough for him, he's not the one having to sleep out here on the ground. Nay, him and that lump-of-lard magistrate, they're all comfy over at Ansel's house, drinking their goddamn cider." Richard jabbed Abitha, sending her spinning. "Do us a favor, woman, and hurry up with the dying. I've better things to do than sitting around watching you expire."

"Do you really want her to hurry it up?" Garret asked, a sly grin on his face.

Richard squinted at Garret. "What do you mean?"

Garret glanced back to the barn. "I mean, Jacob is asleep. So, if she were to *expire* right now, say . . . mayhap . . . if she were to suffocate on her tongue or such, there'd not be any questions, that's all."

Richard glanced around, nodded. "True."

Garret put away his knife and pulled out his handkerchief, wadded it into a ball, and held it in front of Abitha's face. "She does not appear to be breathing well. Does she?"

"Not at all," Richard added. "Why, looks to me that she's suffocating."

"How about you, Norton?" Richard asked. "Does she look like she's suffocating to you?"

Norton glanced back and forth between the two men; his brows knotted up. "Huh?"

Richard nudged him, winked.

"Oh," Norton said. "Oh . . . yeah. All right. Yeah, she's suffocating."

Garret clutched the back of Abitha's head and shoved his entire handkerchief into her mouth.

Abitha tried to pull away, but Richard grabbed her, held her tight as Garret clasped his hand over her mouth and pinched her nostrils shut.

"Time to go to sleep," Richard said.

Abitha saw a dark shape come up behind Norton. There came a thud and Norton collapsed to his knees. The dark shape had long horns and held a tomahawk. It struck Norton again and Norton fell over face-first into the dirt.

Samson! Abitha thought.

Samson stood there, somehow bigger, his horns no longer those of a goat, but now magnificent black antlers, his eyes no longer silver, but gold, and they gleamed in the torchlight. He grinned at the men.

Garret leapt to his feet. "What in the Hell?" He grabbed for his sword, but before he could get it half out of his scabbard, Samson knocked him in the face with the tomahawk, sending the man reeling to the ground.

"Devil!" Richard screamed, fumbling for his pistol as he stumbled backward toward the stables. The weapon went off, a blinding blast kicking up the dirt right in front of Abitha. Richard turned and ran into the stables, not stopping, but running all the way through and out the other side.

Jacob awoke, jumping to his feet, staring at Samson, his eyes wide with terror and disbelief.

"The Devil has come for you!" Samson roared. "For your blood and for your bones!"

Jacob turned and fled, following Richard from the stable.

Garret struggled to get to his feet. Samson strolled over, swung his tomahawk high over his head, and brought it down in the middle of Garret's back. Abitha heard the man's spine crack. Garret cried out, fell forward, and lay still.

259

Samson lifted his head to the sky and howled.

Abitha would've grinned if not for the handkerchief in her mouth, if she could but stay awake, but the darkness took her once more.

Abitha sucked in a deep breath of sweet air. Another. Coughed. *I can breathe,* she thought, and opened her eyes. Samson's face swam into focus. She found herself lying on the ground, cradled in his arms. She lifted a hand to touch his face and realized her bindings were gone, that the pressure, the terrible pressure was gone, that she was free from the ropes, from the tree. She touched him. "You're real."

"It is good to see you again, my friend," Samson said. There was a faint smile on his face, but his golden eyes were solemn. Again, she noted how different he was, his face, closer to that of a noble stag, but it wasn't just his appearance that had changed, but also his manner, a sureness that wasn't there before.

She tried to sit up, but a blinding pain stabbed at her legs. She winced and looked down at her twisted limbs.

"I am a bit broken, it seems."

"Yes."

Sky flew past and landed on the fence post; a moment later Creek appeared, swam up, and floated next to the raven. They both looked at her sadly.

Abitha heard a muffled cry, saw Garret trying to crawl away, but it seemed something was wrong with his back. He was whimpering like a child. She felt no sympathy, none at all, only an overwhelming desire to go over and finish him.

Samson followed her glare. "Abitha, what do you want?"

She managed a smile. "This again?"

"I see vengeance in your eye."

It is so much more than vengeance, she thought, knowing it was deeper, something on some primal level, a need not just to kill this man, but to hear him scream as she butchered him.

"You can have it," Samson said. "Their blood. If that is what you want."

Her eyes returned to Samson.

"Abitha, I know who I am."

Yes, she thought, *I can see that.* It was part of why he looked different. The confusion, the torment, it was gone from his eyes.

"I am the Father of the wildfolk, the guardian of Mother Earth. I am the shepherd and I am the slayer. I am life and I am death."

She nodded. "Aye, my mother spoke of you. You are the great horned god."

"We do not always get to choose our own paths. But you, Abitha, you do get to choose."

Samson reached over to where Norton lay upon the ground beside them and pulled the man's knife from his belt. Samson ran the sharp blade across his own palm, and Abitha watched, mesmerized, as his black blood pooled in his cupped hand.

"My blood offers you a choice." He dabbed the tip of his finger into the blood and wiped it down her forehead and along the bridge of her nose. When he did, her pain receded, not much, but enough to clear her head. The blood did more, it opened her senses to the night, and she became aware of a presence—something not of this world, something savage and dreadful—circling her, slithering in the earth beneath her. *The serpent*, she thought. It seemed to be waiting to claim her. This terrified her, yet at the same time, some part of her wanted it to take her. She felt its promise of power and prowess. *Why be the rabbit*, it seemed to ask, *when you can be the wolf?*

"I can carry you away from here," Samson said. "And you can continue your life the best that you are able . . . a cripple for the rest of your days."

Abitha shuddered.

"There is another choice. You could take my blood and walk by my side."

She stared at the blood in his hand.

"But you must know that if you take this blood . . . there'll be more blood. Mother Earth resurrected me to protect her, and I intend to slaughter any who threaten her or her children. If you walk with the beast you become the beast. That is the choice before you."

Abitha heard men shouting in the distance, knew they'd be coming for her soon. She thought of those men and what they'd done and felt her rage returning. Norton grunted, appeared to be coming around. She looked at him, then her eyes found Booka's corpse, and the hatred blazed in her chest, so much so she began to tremble. *And how*, she wondered, *would I be able to live with such hatred? Day after day, eating away at my very sanity until the moment I died.*

Samson studied her quivering hands. "I am not the tempter, nor would I deceive you. This has to be your decision. It has to come from your heart or the spell will not bind. And once you cross that line there is no return. My blood will run in your veins. You will be one with the serpent and the beast." He nodded toward Norton. "You will be at odds with your own people, your teachings, with your Christ God. It is not an easy thing to turn your back on—"

Abitha laughed. "You think me worried about my soul?" She laughed again, loud and fierce, locking blazing eyes on Samson. "I've no soul left," she growled. "They've crucified my fucking soul!" Her voice cracked and hot angry tears began to flow. "This is about blood. This is about hunting Wallace down and killing him even if it takes my last breath. Two eyes for an eye. If I can kill him twice, three times, four times, I'll do it, and each time I will dance a jig of joy upon his bloody corpse." She wiped the snot from her upper lip. "I want to burn them to the ground. All of them. All of it. Their church, their commandments, their covenants, their rules, edicts, and laws, their fields, their homes, and most of all their fucking bonnets and aprons. I want to hollow them out, make them know what it is to lose everything, everything, to lose their very soul!"

Samson showed no surprise at the venom in her reply. He simply nodded as though expecting nothing else. He extended his cupped hand of blood to her. "My blood is the first step. Drink."

Abitha seized his wrist and despite all her bold words, there, at the last, she hesitated. "I have no choice," she whispered, almost pleading. "You understand? My soul will never be at peace, not so long as such evil as these men walk the earth." At this point she was talking more to herself than to Samson. "Abitha is dead, they killed her, all that is left is wrath and malice . . . my restless soul. Do you understand?"

Again, Samson nodded.

Abitha felt the serpent respond to her need for vengeance; it was as though she were calling its name. Something else responded as well—there, in the shadows, the ghostly shapes of twelve women appeared. They stood, silently watching her, their faces obscured by their long hair.

The serpent closed in, closer and closer, its lethal promise igniting something deep within Abitha's breast: the primordial need of every creature that has ever been hurt by another—*the need to bite back.*

A hard grimace set on Abitha's face. "If it is a witch they want," she hissed, "then a witch they shall have."

Abitha drank the blood, lapping it up with a burning thirst until every last drop was gone. The blood flowed into her, became a rush of heat pulsing through her entire being. The numbness left her arms, her hands, her feet. Her legs began to burn with agony as though all the old wounds were fresh. She saw why—that they were healing, the broken bones mending, the gashes and welts disappearing. She clutched them, cried out, and just when she felt sure she could bear the pain not a moment longer, that it would break her, the pain began to subside, little by little, until finally it was gone. She gasped, wiped the tears from her eyes, and saw that her legs were all but healed. She rubbed them, overcome with relief.

Samson took her hand, placed it on the ground, pressing his atop hers. Mother Earth, the serpent, was there, calling to Abitha louder than ever, circling restlessly just beneath her. The serpent's voice multiplied, two, four, more, becoming a chorus, and it was then that Abitha realized that it was not just one serpent but hundreds racing round and round her. One of these broke away—it came for her.

"Mother Earth has sent you something wild and deadly," Samson said. "Are you ready?"

Abitha looked up into his golden eyes. "I am."

"Call it."

Abitha closed her eyes, felt the earth quake beneath her hand. "Come to me," she whispered, and that was all it took to break the thin barrier between the spirit world and her own. She felt the heat as the errant serpent left the earth and slithered up her body, coiling around her. She couldn't see it, yet it was there, constricting, tighter and tighter. But Abitha felt no fear; it told her what it wanted and she wanted the same.

"Come to me," she repeated, and it did, entering first through her mouth, her nose, her ears, then through the most private places between her legs, flowing into her. She let out a moan of sheer joy, of fulfillment, but then her senses opened and the smell of blood, that of the guards, filled her, all but overwhelmed her. She could actually hear the beating of their hearts. A hunger like none she'd known set upon her, and when it did, it was as though she split in two. Her eyes flashed open and fell upon Norton. It, the serpent, tried to lunge for the guard, while Abitha strove to stay put, causing her, them, to fall over. She, it, they, began to fight for control, writhing on the ground. A roar filled her head as she struggled to hear her own thoughts. She, they, cried out, growling and howling like squalling cats.

"Finish it!" Samson cried. "Quickly, or it will destroy you! Only blood will bind you. Kill him, kill the guard! Complete the spell!"

Abitha, the serpent, their eyes returned to Norton, and this time Abitha allowed their shared desires to align, and the roar, the tug-of-war in her head, began to subside. *Kill him!* the serpent thought. *Yes, kill him!* Abitha thought. *Kill him,* they thought together. *The knife,* Abitha thought. *Yes, the knife,* the serpent agreed. Abitha, the serpent, they sat up, grabbed the knife, crawled over, and plunged it into Norton's neck.

Norton's eyes popped opened, wide with terror. Abitha, the serpent, they fed

263

on his fear, and together they let out a fierce howl, and together they drove the knife into the man's chest, again and again until the blade pierced his heart.

Norton let out a final strangled cry, then his heart ceased to beat. When it did, the serpent's voice and Abitha's became one, *they* became one—one mind, one soul, one heart, and that heart strummed with venom.

All at once the world opened to Abitha; her senses sharpened and it felt as though a shroud had been lifted from her head.

Mother Earth, the hundreds of serpents in the ground below, swam together, becoming one again, slithering away, deep down into the earth.

Abitha's pupils dilated, revealing all the secrets hidden by darkness, every sound coming to her sharp and clear; the night creatures seemed to be singing just to her. She heard them then, the men; they were coming, and then another sound, growling—she realized it was coming from her, from her own throat.

She met Samson's eyes, found a fire there. A small smile creased his face and he nodded.

Abitha slid Norton's cutlass from its scabbard and stood up, her legs solid beneath her.

There came the strong scent of lavender and sage, and one by one, the spectral shapes of the women walked over to her, until all twelve women stood around Abitha in a circle. And as she looked to each one, they pulled back their hair, revealing their faces, faces so like her own, until finally—

"Mother."

The women began to chant, their voices echoing as though from far away. Her mother pulled a strand of her own hair taut and bit it off, the others following her lead. They wove the locks into loops, the loops into a chain, until there, in her mother's palm, lay a chain of twelve braids.

Abitha reached for it, sure it would disappear, that they all would disappear, but the braid, it was real, and she took it. Then with the cutlass she trimmed off a lock of her own hair, twisting it and using it to bind the twelve, making thirteen and forming a loop. She slid this over her head, down onto her shoulders, wearing it like a necklace as she had seen her mother do.

Her mother smiled, as did each of her mothers.

Abitha smiled back, and then one by one they faded, yet she still felt their power, their love, and knew they were with her, part of her, and she a part of them.

Sky and Creek began to laugh and Abitha joined them, laughing wildly and wickedly.

A scent struck Abitha: it was fear. She stopped laughing, spotted Garret frantically crawling away, trying to find a place to hide in the stables. Her eyes narrowed and her lips peeled back, exposing small fangs. She lifted her head to the sky and howled long and loud, wanting them to hear—the men, the women, the children—wanting them to know that the beast was coming for them.

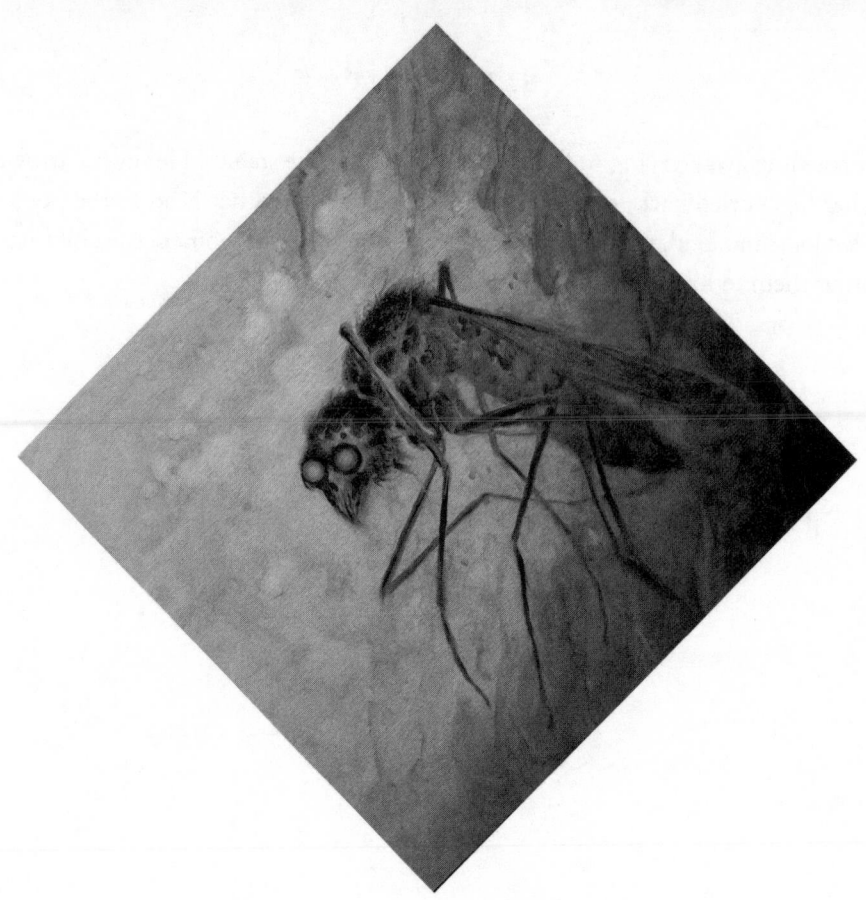

CHAPTER 14

Say that again," Captain Moore demanded.

Jacob shook his head. "It were a demon, I tell you. A horned beast."

The captain, Jacob, and Richard stood on the porch of Ansel's home. They'd gathered arms—swords, pistols, and muskets.

"And you, Richard. You saw it too?"

"Aye," Richard replied. "It's true. Horns, hooves, it had a tail. The damned beast had a fucking tail."

"But it carries a tomahawk?" Captain Moore asked.

"Aye."

"What devil carries a tomahawk but an Indian? Are you sure it were not one of the savages?"

"Does an Indian have a swishing tail and horns?"

The captain smelled rum on the guard's breath. If it were Indians dressed as demons, he didn't think these men would know the difference, not in the dark like this.

A howl pierced the night—long and terrible, causing the hair on the captain's arms to stand on end.

Magistrate Watson and Ansel both came out onto the porch.

"What was that?" the magistrate demanded, his voice little more than a squeak.

"It sounded ungodly," Ansel added, his bulbous eyes searching the shadows.

"It is but savages," Captain Moore grunted. "A few young renegades causing trouble is my guess. I have dealt with such before. There is no real danger. They just want to prove their bravery to one another. A few well-placed shots will scatter them, send them back into the forest." The captain started off the porch.

"Captain, where are you going?" the magistrate asked.

"To the stables."

"No, that will not do," Magistrate Watson said. "I need you here."

"The threat is out there, sir."

The judge glanced fretfully out at the night. "Well . . . what about the prisoner? I must insist on a guard for the prisoner."

"You mean Goodwife Carter? Why, she can barely stand. What do you think she is going to do? Sir, we're already shorthanded and—"

"You *will* leave a guard," the magistrate insisted.

Captain Moore struggled not to set the judge straight, knowing it was fools like him that got good men killed. "Go inside," he said tersely. "Lock the doors. I will leave a guard."

The captain handed Jacob a musket. "Jacob, you're to stay with Magistrate Watson for now."

Jacob's face showed great relief. "Oh, aye, sir. I can do that."

"Richard, you're with me."

"Do not go far," the judge said. "I am a magistrate of the territory. You're under orders to keep me safe."

Captain Moore didn't bother with a reply but headed off with Richard. The captain was glad to be out in the dark, away from the house. He'd been through enough Indian skirmishes to know it was better to be amongst the trees, where one could maneuver, than locked up in a box. He headed for Sheriff Pitkin's home, hoping to round up a few more men.

They found the sheriff on the porch, musket in hand, looking down toward the stables.

"You heard it?" Captain Moore asked.

"Hard not to," the sheriff replied. "Bet they heard it all the way to Hartford. Any idea of what is going on?"

"Most likely savages causing trouble."

"Savages?" Sheriff Pitkin said. "That's hard to believe. We've not had Indian problems around here for at least a decade."

"All I know for certain is that whoever it is, they injured, or mayhap killed, two of my guards."

"Makes me wonder if Abitha had a Pequot lover. Would explain a lot."

"It were a demon," Richard put in. "A foul beast with horns and hooves, I tell you."

"Is that so?" the sheriff said.

"It sure as hell is."

"Sheriff," Captain Moore said. "I need you to round up your deputies and a few sure men and meet me at the stable. Can I count on you for that?"

"You can," Sheriff Pitkin said. "As fast as I am able."

"Good," the captain said, and headed off with Richard toward the old stable.

"Oh, Jesus! God! Fuck!" Garret growled through his teeth as he clawed at the dirt, struggling to drag himself into the stable. *The goddamn Devil himself is here!* He tried to kick, to propel himself along, but his legs wouldn't respond. "I am broken," he whimpered. "Broken but good. Fuck!"

A howl tore open the night, piercing Garret's very core. He glanced back, froze. The witch, she was up, standing beside the Devil. And what? A raven and a fish? No, no. Not either, but some kind of floating demons with the faces of wicked children. And all of them were staring at him, glaring at him. "Oh, sweet Jesus, God!" he cried, and redoubled his efforts. He crawled into the stable, trying to hide amongst the haybales and sacks of seed.

"Garret," someone, or something, called.

Garret curled up into a ball behind a bale of hay, clutching himself, clenching his eyes shut, trying to block it all out, trying to disappear.

"Garret, where are you?" It was her, the witch. "You owe me something."

He heard footsteps.

"There you are."

Garret opened his eyes and there she stood, only it wasn't the helpless miserable wretch he'd been kicking around. No, the thing before him appeared anything but. Her feet were feet no longer, but split, her toes clumping together as though forming hooves. Her body lean, her tattered skirt and blouse spattered in blood. But it was her eyes that he found most disturbing, the pupils but slits, like some wild beast, only filled with hatred, all but gleaming with venom and fixed upon him. Then she smiled and he saw her teeth, her small, sharp fangs.

Garret began to shake, pissing himself and bawling. "Oh, Jesus!"

"You killed my Booka," she hissed. "I loved my Booka."

"Nay, it were not me. It were . . . *Norton*. Norton that done it!"

"You owe me a life."

"Mercy, I beg of you."

"I know not the meaning of that word." She pushed a sack of seed over on top of him.

Blinding pain shot up Garret's back. He cried out, struggling to free himself, but the weight of the seed was too much; he couldn't move.

Abitha picked up one of the lanterns. Held it up so that he could see.

"N . . . no! No, Abitha. *No!* I beg you. Do not, please . . . *do not!*"

"I am not Abitha. Abitha was murdered. I am the witch, and the witch cares not for your tears." And with that, she smashed the lantern against the post next to him, the oil splashing all over the hay. The oil ignited and a robust fire bloomed.

"No!" Garret screamed. *"NO!"*

The hay and seed quickly went up in flames and the fire began to spread. Garret fought to get out from beneath the sack, pleading and begging someone to help. But no one heard him; he was alone.

Captain Moore and Richard moved cautiously toward the edge of town. As they approached the stables, they heard screaming and noticed a bright red glow.

"The stables are afire!" Richard said, and started forward.

"Wait," Captain Moore said, grabbing the man. "Could be a trap." He led them to a cluster of brush; there he scanned the houses and trees on all sides, looking for any sign of an ambush.

The screaming continued.

"We have to do something," Richard said.

The fire was growing, the whole stable now aflame, lighting up the sky and surrounding woods.

The captain spotted movement—two shadowy figures heading toward town along the far edge of the woods. It was hard to tell who or what he was seeing in the dark, then part of the stable roof collapsed, sending up an explosive fireball, giving him a good look. It was her, the witch, and to his shock, she was walking fine, moving along at a good clip. *How?* he wondered. *Her leg, it was broken.* Then he caught a glimpse of the other figure and forgot all about her. It was indeed a horned beast.

"See!" Richard exclaimed. "See there. I told you!"

The captain squinted, trying to understand what he was seeing. *No*, he thought, *it is but a man.* He'd seen plenty of the Indians wearing outlandish outfits into battle—masks, horns, and hides, and covering themselves in paint. "It is a disguise, a getup meant to frighten us. That is all."

"We shall see," Richard said, raising his rifle.

"Wait," Captain Moore said. "Need to find out how many there are." He noted that they weren't making signals or looking for others, and this wasn't the way warriors acted when coordinating an attack. He now felt certain that the man must indeed be her lover. It was the only thing that made sense; with her husband dead and needing help on the farm, why wouldn't she take a savage to her bed? "They're alone," he said, and raised his musket. "On my order . . . *fire!*"

They both fired, the blast thundering in the night.

It took a moment for the smoke to clear. And when it did, they saw the witch helping the man to his feet.

"There," Captain Moore said to Richard. "Your demon appears to be but a mortal man after all."

Richard didn't appear convinced.

The witch and the man slipped into the trees.

The captain tugged out his pistol and rushed forward, but when he arrived at the spot found no sign of either the witch or her companion. A moment later Richard caught up with him—and right on his heels, Sheriff Pitkin and two deputies, all armed with muskets.

"Did you see them?" the sheriff asked.

"Yes," Captain Moore said. "Indeed. It is just the witch and some renegade savage. He's hit. They'll not get far."

"Captain!" Richard called. "There!"

The captain saw them hurrying through a small clearing, just a glimpse before they disappeared back into the woods, just enough that he could see the man was limping.

"We have them," the sheriff said. "These woods are backed by the river. They'll be trapped."

The men entered the woods.

"You're shot!" Abitha said. "Oh, Samson. No!"

Samson stopped, looked at the hole in his side. "Yes, it appears so."

"We have to get you somewhere safe."

"I think I'll be all right," he said, sounding unconcerned.

"What do you mean? You've been shot in the chest."

"Yes, and here as well." He pointed to his thigh. "I have suffered worse. Does make it hard to walk, though."

Abitha stared at him, horrified.

"It will heal; the question is how long will it take. I'll probably not die. It seems I'm very hard to kill."

This did nothing to calm Abitha's concern. She started to say as much when they heard the men moving in on them through the woods.

"Abitha, my blood brings many gifts. It's time you began to understand what you are. The wilderness is your home. . . . You have many friends here."

She wasn't sure what he meant. Sky? Creek? But they could do so little.

The stables were fully ablaze now, and though they were well within the trees, flickering beams of light penetrated the darkness. Samson led her around a large clump of brush, pulling her down within the shadows. He placed her hand on the ground. "Feel Mother Earth . . . hear her."

Abitha did and felt the pulse; it flowed through her and all the living things around them. The voices of the forest began to open up to her: the frogs, the birds nesting in the trees, the spiders, the insects. *Oh,* she thought, *so many insects. So many hungry insects.*

"Call them," Samson said.

"What?"

"Call them."

Abitha closed her eyes and spoke, not with words, but with her heart, her soul. Found it to be an easy thing now that Samson's blood ran in her veins. Found she was wed to the wild, their language one.

"Hello, I am here," she said, and when she did, their song grew louder.

She called to them: the cicadas, the moths, the beetles and fireflies, the little gnats and mosquitoes, the thousands and thousands of little mosquitoes. And they responded, their tiny voices swelling, coming together like a song, filling the woods with their melody as they flew to her, swarming and swirling together like a growing storm cloud.

Another insect, some kind of beetle, hit Captain Moore in the eye, then something flew into his mouth. He spat. "So many damn bugs this night," he said, all but shouting to be heard over the din of cicadas and locusts. He'd never heard such a racket.

"There!" Richard shouted. "Someone is over there."

The captain looked, tried to make sense of what he was seeing. It looked like a fish, a flying fish. He raised his rifle and another bug hit his face, another, then another. Something small flew into his eye. "Gah!" he snarled, trying to wipe his eyes clear. The fish was gone.

Richard let out a cry, and the captain saw that all the men were plagued by the insects, wiping their faces and eyes as they stumbled along. *What is going on?* he wondered.

Captain Moore saw her, the witch, just a glimpse. Was she smiling? "There!" he shouted. "She's just there." He took off after her, the men following. Then a great cloud of smoke rolled over them, engulfing them. Only, he too quickly realized, it wasn't smoke, but mosquitoes, thousands upon thousands of mosquitoes. They set upon him, driving into his eyes, his ears, his nose. He couldn't breathe without inhaling them. He screamed, as did the others, and when he did, they entered his mouth. He stumbled, dropped his musket, wiping his eyes, choking and spitting out a soggy clump of squirming mosquitoes.

Someone bumped into him, one of his guards, impossible to tell who, the man's face a mask of swarming insects. The man dashed past, clawing at his eyes, trying to rake the bugs away. Then *she* was there, just a blurry shape, but he knew it was her, the witch. She struck the guard, a flash of her blade, and the guard spun, clutching his throat, and fell to the ground.

Captain Moore pulled his pistol from his belt and fired, the blast lighting up the scene for a mere second, but long enough for the captain to see that he'd missed his mark, to see that two of the men were cut wide open, to see the witch dash away, agile and fleet as some deer.

Someone grabbed him; he cried out, tried to strike them with his pistol. "Stop," the person cried. It was the sheriff. "We must go!" the man shouted, then fled. The captain tried to follow, but lost sight of the sheriff almost immediately.

Captain Moore stumbled along in what he hoped was the right direction, trying to reload his pistol as he went, trying to do so by touch alone. He could actually feel the mosquitoes squirming in his eyes, in his nose and ears. Their incessant high-pitched buzzing drowning out all other sounds, as though they were screaming just at him. He tripped over a log, or stone, or who knew what, fumbled his pistol, dropping the shot. He didn't bother to look for it, just pressed back to his feet. Then, all at once, the bugs let up, drifting away. He could see the stable burning in the distance. "Oh, Lord. Thank you! God, Jesus. Thank you!"

He started forward, but someone—something—was there, a blurry shape in his path. He wiped frantically at his eyes.

The something spoke. "I would like to offer you a choice. A quick, merciful death, or a slow . . . *bad* death."

His blood went cold. It was her, the witch. He could just make her out in the light of the flames. She stood holding a cutlass, her teeth bared.

"Witch!" Captain Moore cried, and snatched out his knife, but she was fast, moving in, slicing his wrist, all but severing his hand. He cried out, dropping his blade.

273

"A slow death then," she said, and slashed him across the stomach.

Searing pain spread through the captain's gut. He let out a cry, clutching at the wound, then screamed when he felt his innards, his very intestines, spilling out in a warm gush into his hands.

"Oh, God! Jesus Christ!" Captain Moore wailed, and crumpled to the ground.

She grinned at him. "That should take a while. Do you not agree?"

And somewhere in his intense agony, her words got through to him. He knew then that she wasn't going to finish him. And he'd seen enough gut wounds in his day to know it was his end, only it might take days, but he *would* die, he would most certainly die, and in the worst kind of pain.

A raven flew in and perched on the witch's shoulder, then a fish, just floating there next to her, all watching him moaning and wailing and rolling in the stink of his own foul bowels.

The witch turned and walked away, and when she did, the bugs returned, setting to the captain, crawling beneath his clothes, into his eyes, his nose, his ears, into the deep wound across his stomach, squirming their way into the stinking pile of his intestines, biting and stinging and pinching. His wails turned to screams, to shrieks, screeching until he could screech no more.

Abitha saw Sheriff Pitkin engulfed in a cloud of mosquitoes, his arm across his face, his hand out, staggering blindly through the trees. His weapons were gone, as were his hat and one of his boots.

Abitha spoke to the insects, asked them to return to their night, and they did. She stepped up to the sheriff. He sensed her and frantically wiped his eyes.

Abitha set her blade against his neck and he froze.

"Thank you for the biscuits and tea," she said. "That were kind of you."

He looked at her, his eyes bleary with tears and bugs.

"What?"

"Do not follow me," she said. "If you follow me, I will kill you."

She left him there and headed back toward the village. She strolled past the stable; it was fully engulfed in flames, great clouds of smoke billowing skyward, the fire lighting up the entire village in its eerie red glow.

There were about a dozen people milling about, many holding buckets of water, probably in hopes of saving their stores of feed.

It is far too late for that, Abitha thought. *You'll soon know what it is to be hungry this winter.*

They saw her and she smiled at them, and when she did, they froze, their faces full of bewilderment and horror. Then she stomped her foot and hissed, laughing as they fled in terror. Abitha continued on, heading into the village, walking boldly down the main street, heading for Wallace's homestead.

At some point she noticed she was injured, a long slash along her arm. It must've been one of the guards. There was pain, but not like she would've thought from such a wound. She noticed something else: her feet, they kept changing. No longer feet at all now, but hooves. Abitha lifted her skirt and saw her legs; they too were changing, somewhat goatlike, with a soft coat of fur, giving a light spring to her step. She wondered if Samson's blood was turning her into something like him. She touched her head, and yes, sure enough, two bumps were sprouting there that she suspected would soon turn into horns. *And what do you think of that?* Abitha asked herself. "I think it is wonderful."

She glanced around for Samson; they'd become separated in the woods. She didn't see him but knew he wasn't far. She spotted a man in the stocks, there in the village commons. It was Reverend Carter.

She approached and he lifted his head, looked her up and down. "Abitha?"

"Abitha is dead. I am the witch."

He nodded. "I see."

His clothes were torn and filthy, his face gaunt and haggard, covered in dark bruises, a nasty wound across his forehead. His eyes were unbearably sad. He cleared his throat. "Pray tell then. Is it true that they did crush her, my Sarah, and that she did confess?"

"Reverend, I am sorry. But yes, it is true."

He nodded, looking pained.

"Do not dare judge her harshly, Reverend. Few have ever borne so much suffering as did she. It was only for her daughter that she gave in. It was love, not pain, that broke her."

He looked past her, his eyes going wide. "Is . . . is that the Devil?" He opened his mouth to say more but uttered not a sound.

Samson walked up and stood next to Abitha.

"Aye," Abitha said. "He set me free."

Reverend Carter just stared, unblinking, his mouth agape.

Abitha lifted her blade and chopped into the plank of the stock, hacked it once, twice, and on the third strike, the wood gave way. She kicked it loose, freeing the reverend.

The reverend seemed to barely notice, just continued to stare at Samson.

"I hope there is something left for you in this life," Abitha said, and turned and headed away.

Abitha took the south road out of the village, along the river, at first walking, but as she grew accustomed to her new feet and legs, she began to trot; soon she was galloping down the road. And for a moment, she forgot about her anger, her venom, of her need to claw Wallace's eyes out, and just enjoyed the simple pleasure of the warm wind in her hair, the song of the night, and the beauty of the moonlight bathing all in its warm autumn glow.

She arrived at Wallace's homestead in short order, it being only about a mile from town. When Samson finally caught up, she could see he was still limping, but not so bad as before.

"Your wounds," she said. "Are they better?"

He nodded. "Yes, a little."

275

She glanced at the slash on her arm. It was beginning to heal.

Samson inspected it as well. "You are not immortal by any means, Abitha. But my blood is potent, and if you are careful, you could live a very long time, perhaps even a few centuries." He looked up toward Wallace's cabin. "Are you sure you want to risk that?"

She followed his eyes, saw a shape moving around inside and forgot about the moon, the wind, living for hundreds of years. Her pupils dilated and she saw only red.

CHAPTER 15

Wallace concluded grace, and his family commenced to eat. It was just his wife and daughter tonight, as his son was away visiting Helen and her family.

"We are truly blessed," his wife, Anne, said, looking over the bounty of food before them.

Wallace nodded as he forked a large portion of goat meat onto his plate. He took a scoop of beans, taking a moment to savor the aroma of honey wafting up from them, then took a bite of the meat and began to chew. The meat was succulent.

Wallace glanced at all the honey lining the shelves, at the food before him. *Edward's honey, Edward's goat, Edward's corn,* he thought, and no matter how he tried he couldn't help seeing his father's stern, judging face. *Do you not think I would trade it all to have Edward back, Papa? I stopped the witch, I saved Sutton from the very Devil, that is why I've reaped these prizes. Was it not you, Papa, who always told me that God rewarded the righteous?*

"Father," Charity called, and when he didn't answer, she said it again, louder and more forcefully. "Father!"

He looked at her crossly, annoyed to be pulled so rudely from his thoughts. She seemed a different person this night, seemed to think her position elevated to that of an equal, perhaps more. Evidently the recognition and praise, the status she'd received from the magistrate for her testimony, going to her head. *She just needs to be reminded of her place*, he thought, yet found himself oddly cautious. And why was that? He knew why. Because she'd been so convincing at court, how easily she'd played the part, saying and doing whatever was needed to sway the jury against Abitha. Why, even Wallace found himself believing at times. What then, if she turned that tongue on him, especially after all the accusations Abitha had spewed?

"Father, what is that racket?" she demanded.

"Lower your voice, child," Wallace said, striving to keep his tone calm. "It is not your place to speak to me in such a manner."

Charity scowled at him. "Do you not hear it?"

"I said lower your voice. This is my house and you will show me the proper respect. Do you understand?" But then Wallace did hear it; it sounded like the night bugs had all gone insane, and their incessant screeching was getting into his head, making it difficult to control his temper.

Charity rolled her eyes. "I but asked a simple question."

Wallace started to give her a proper reprimand, when he caught a warning glance from Anne, causing him to bite his tongue.

"Charity," Anne said, speaking gently but firmly. "Enough now. The bible demands that you be obedient and respectful to your parents."

Charity crossed her arms over her chest and just sat there glaring at the both of them.

This will not do, Wallace thought, barely able to contain himself, knowing that just a week ago, he'd have given the girl a sound beating for such sass. *Something will be done*, he assured himself. *Just not now. I can ill afford more controversy at this time.*

Wallace returned his attention to the food, quickly shoveling a forkful of beans into his mouth before he said something he'd regret. He began to chew only to find the beans crunchy.

Charity opened her mouth to say something more, and it was at that moment a large bug flew straight down her throat. Wallace, however, missed this, as he was staring at his plate, trying to make sense of what he was seeing. There were little black shapes in his beans, and they were—moving. *Beetles!* he realized, and spat. He looked to Anne, ready to chastise her for failing to properly sift the beans, but she was staring at Charity.

Charity let out a strangled cry and stood up, clutching her throat—the very same act she'd put on during the trial.

"Charity!" Wallace shouted. "I've had enough of your games. You're fooling no one with your charades. You will cease this mockery this instant or I shall beat you into obedience!"

But Charity didn't stop; she continued to gag, her face turning red.

Anne leapt up, knocking over the pitcher of mead as she rushed to her daughter.

"Damn it!" Wallace cried. "Now look what you've done!"

Charity's eyes grew wider still, and she pointed and jabbed wildly at something behind Wallace.

"Enough," Wallace shouted. "The witch is dead. That show is over. Do you hear me?"

"I hear you," came a woman's voice right behind Wallace.

Abitha? Wallace wondered, and spun, barely recognizing the feral woman before him. This was not Abitha, couldn't be. Then he saw her cloven feet and understood, realized that he was seeing her true self, the witch fully revealed.

He spotted the cutlass in her hand and grabbed the steak knife. He lunged for her, but she was quicker and sidestepped, sending him sprawling to the floor, losing the knife. Before he could even get a knee up, she was on him, hacking repeatedly into the back of first one leg, then the other. The blade cutting deep into the muscles and tendons behind his knees.

Wallace let out a howl, tried to roll away, and she drove her hooved foot into the back of his elbow. There came a dreadful crack and his arm dangled, broken and useless. He reached for the knife, and her foot, her terrible cloven foot, landed on his splayed hand, stomping it over and over again, the bones snapping and popping. She didn't stop, not until his hand was nothing but a mangled lump of flesh.

Wallace screamed and bawled, unable to even crawl away, his limbs all but useless. And through the tears he saw it, the beast, the Devil himself walk right in through his front door, a tomahawk in his hand. The Devil stepped over him, plucked up the leg of goat, sat down, and began to gnaw on it.

Anne thrust herself between the witch and Charity, but Charity was still gagging, her face turning purple. Abitha walked calmly over to her.

"No!" Anne pleaded. "Please, not my daughter."

Abitha knocked her aside and grabbed Charity by the neck. "You are a liar, Charity Williams," Abitha hissed, and snatched hold of her tongue, pinching it between her long-clawed fingers. Blood began to flow. "Should I tear your lying tongue from your mouth?"

"I beg you, no!" Anne cried out.

Abitha reached into Charity's mouth, deep into her throat, and plucked out a large beetle, tossing it aside.

Charity let out a loud gasp, coughing and gagging as she sucked air back into her lungs.

Abitha shoved her against the wall and Charity crumpled to the floor, clutching her throat, heaving, trying to catch her breath.

Wallace watched helpless as Abitha pointed her cutlass at Charity. "The Devil has come for his due."

Anne crawled to the girl's side, cradled her. "No, no more! Please. I beg of you!"

Abitha pointed to Samson. "Look, Charity, look what your lies have brought into your home."

Charity began to bawl.

"I'll not kill you this day, child. That would be too easy." And with that, Abitha set the blade to the girl's forehead and began to saw.

Charity screamed as Abitha slowly carved two deeps cuts across her forehead, forming a bloody *L*.

"*L* is for the Little Liar."

The girl wailed as the blood ran down her face.

"I want you to live knowing what is waiting you at the end of your life. This scar will always remind you that there is no redemption, not for you, child. The Devil, old Slewfoot himself, has already claimed you for his own. If you do not believe me, just ask him." She inclined her head toward Samson.

Samson stopped eating for a moment and grinned. "Yes, yes, you are indeed mine, child."

"No!" Charity sputtered between sobs. "Mother, Father . . . *save* me!"

"There is no saving you, Charity Williams. You are damned. Now leave here, both of you!" Abitha banged the side of her cutlass against the post once, the noise resounding like a gong. "I'll not tell you again."

Anne and her daughter scrambled to their feet, rushing for the door, leaping right over Wallace in their haste to flee.

"Wait!" Wallace cried, then screamed. "Stop, do not leave me here! Please . . . do not leave me!" But they were gone, and if he could've looked out the door, he would've seen them running away as fast as they could without so much as a glance back.

Abitha walked around him to the shelf, picked up one of the pots of honey; she seemed lost in thought. Wallace dared not guess what she might be contemplating.

"Abitha . . . listen." Wallace spoke, trying to get the words out between gasps of pain. "Anything . . . you want. I . . . will do anything you ask. I will recant . . . all, everything. I will swear it were all lies. I will admit that I coerced my daughter . . . anything you want. Anything."

But he could see Abitha wasn't listening. She replaced the honey gently, almost tenderly, back on the shelf, then set her hand on a timber beam, closed her eyes, and began mumbling, no, humming softly. It was as though she were in a trance.

There came a strange clacking sound, followed by popping and snapping, like that of splintering wood. For a moment, he thought the log planks and beams of his home were splitting, that they were going to collapse in on him. Then he saw what it was—beetles, dozens and dozens of them in all shapes and sizes, coming out of the timber. He knew what they were, wood beetles, but what he didn't know was that hundreds of them lived in the timbers of his cabin and that they had incredibly powerful mandibles designed solely to chew long tunnels through very hard wood.

The beetles began to crawl toward him, but it wasn't until one crawled up on his arm and bit him that he fully appreciated his predicament.

He squirmed, flipping the beetle away, but just as quick another was upon him, another, and another. They dropped from the beams above him, crawled out of the floorboards around him. They bit him and he screamed and writhed, trying to dislodge them. Then they began to not just bite but to *burrow,* to actually burrow into him. He could see and feel them digging into his flesh.

"Oh, God!" he howled. "Get them off me!" He flailed about, his broken limbs all but useless.

The Devil left the cabin and Abitha followed after, stopping at the door, watching him, a small smile on her face.

Wallace realized his only chance was to get out of the cabin and began to squirm his way toward the door. More and more beetles fell upon him, digging into him. He felt them *inside* of him now. He whined and yowled and just when he thought he might make it to the door, Abitha pulled it shut with a solid slam, leaving him all alone with the beetles.

"*NO!*" Wallace wailed, screaming and shrieking until finally one of the beetles burrowed into his throat, and then he shrieked no more.

Ansel, the guard Jacob, and Magistrate Watson all stood on Ansel's porch staring north toward the fiery glow, listening for more gunshots. A smoky haze drifted through the village. Small clusters of people shuffled about; no one seemed to know what was going on or what to do.

"The stables are burning," Jacob said.

"Let's just hope the fire doesn't spread," Ansel said.

"Guard . . . there!" Magistrate Watson cried, pointing to a figure weaving its way toward them. The magistrate ducked behind the door as the figure approached.

Jacob raised his musket, then lowered it. "Richard?"

Richard made it to the steps, then collapsed onto the porch. Jacob set down his musket, going to the man and propping him up.

"What happened?" Jacob asked.

Richard tried to reply but was having difficulty breathing. A strange rasping sound coming from his throat. That's when Ansel noticed the deep wound to his chest.

The magistrate peeked out from behind the door. "What has happened? Is it Indians? How many?"

Richard said something, but it was little more than a whisper.

"Speak up, man," the magistrate demanded, walking over and kneeling beside the man. "Speak up!"

"Devils," the man said weakly. "The witch . . . devils . . . demons." He coughed, spattering blood onto the magistrate's cheek.

Magistrate Watson jerked back, yanking out his handkerchief and wiping the blood frantically from his face. "Did you hear that? Did you?"

Ansel nodded, his face pale.

"Witches and devils! We need leave. *Now!*"

The guard coughed violently, tried to say more, then went limp, staring up at nothing.

"Richard?" Jacob called, shaking the man. "Richard . . . *Richard!*"

"He's dead," the magistrate said. "Now let's go. Hurry, man."

When the guard didn't move right away, the magistrate grabbed his jacket and gave him a sharp tug. "Now, I said. That is an order. Load up my wagon and let's be off."

"But, sir," Jacob said. "The captain . . . we should wait for the captain. He might need—"

"Captain Moore can take care of himself. Now let's move!"

"We cannot just—"

"Soldier," the magistrate growled. "Your job is to keep me safe. Now I am ordering you to load up my bags."

Ansel glanced back to the billowing smoke, to the dead man, and decided it might be prudent if he left with them. "Yes, we must get Magistrate Watson out of here. It's too dangerous. Jacob, you get the wagon hitched, and I'll assist the magistrate in gathering his belongings."

The guard reluctantly complied, dashing off to gather the horses. Ansel followed the magistrate in and helped him pack, bringing the two bags out onto the porch.

"My chair, do not forget my chair."

Ansel nodded, running back in and dragging the heavy chair out. Jacob was there waiting with the wagon when he returned, and Ansel was surprised to see Sarah Carter in the wagon bed. The captain had put her in the cellar, but in all he chaos, Ansel had forgotten she was even down there. She lay in a crumpled heap, her hands in shackles, her breathing raspy, avoiding everyone's eyes.

Ansel helped the magistrate up onto the seat of the wagon.

"Why is she here?" the judge asked.

"Sir?" Jacob replied.

"The woman."

"Why, she's our prisoner. It was you that said we're responsible for bringing her to Hartford."

"There is no room."

"But there is."

"Where will you put my chair?"

Jacob appeared dumbfounded. "Can we not send for it later?"

"No!" Magistrate Watson cried. "That chair is an heirloom. I will not risk losing it. Now get rid of that damn woman, load it up, and let's be off."

Jacob appeared ready to strike the man; instead he darted to the porch, hefted the chair, and brought it over. Ansel helped him lift it up onto the wagon bed.

"Careful," the magistrate barked. "That chair came all the way from England."

"Sit up, woman," Jacob said. "Now." When Sarah didn't move, he climbed up and gently pushed her farther back in the bed to make room. Sarah let out a cry, clutched her chest. Ansel guessed she might have several broken ribs from the pressing.

"Why are you dillydallying?" the judge cried.

Jacob returned to the chair and shoved it roughly into the wagon.

"I said careful!" the magistrate shouted. "If that chair is damaged, it'll come out of your wages, by Heaven."

Ansel climbed up and took the reins.

Jacob pulled his own horse around and mounted up.

Ansel snapped the reins and they took off at a fast trot, Jacob following them on his horse, his pistol cocked and draped across his arm.

They were heading south to Hartford and away from the stables. Ansel realized they'd be going right by Wallace's homestead and wondered if they should stop and warn the man.

Sheriff Pitkin sprinted into the village, running directly to the meetinghouse. There he found a small cluster of people gathered. He grabbed Felix James. "Ring the bell!" he cried. "Quickly. Do not stop until everyone is here." He turned to the group of anxious faces. "Go. Gather anyone you can find. Tell them to bring muskets, swords, axes, and bring them here. Now!"

"What is happening? Indians?" So many questions all asked at once.

"Enough, quiet!" Sheriff Pitkin shouted. "We are under attack. It is the witch. She has friends with her." This was met with shocked looks of horror. "We'll make our stand here . . . in the meetinghouse. God will protect us, but we must do our part. Now go! *Go!*"

The bell tolled, and in short order, the people of Sutton began to gather inside the meetinghouse. The sheriff did his best to organize them, first steering the elderly, the women, and children into the center of the room, setting a barricade about them with the benches.

Reverend Collins and Reverend Smith arrived.

"Reverends," the sheriff called. "Get anyone who cannot wield a weapon praying. God needs to be in the house." Both ministers gave him a horrified look but nodded, gathering people into a circle and leading them in prayer.

As more men with muskets arrived, the sheriff began to set up defenses, lighting a ring of torches around the meetinghouse so that they could see any who approached.

The meetinghouse had only four windows, two on each side, and he placed several men at each, as well as a handful at the door behind a barricade, giving them instructions to space out their shots to ensure some were firing while others reloaded.

He glanced around, trying to think of anything else they could do to strengthen their position. *But just how does one defend themselves against a witch?* he wondered. *We pray,* he thought. And as he walked from window to window, searching the shadows for any sign of the witch or her tricks, he prayed, whispering right along with the ministers. Hoping that God would be their shield against the Devil and his wickedness.

Ansel kept glancing behind, sure she'd be there—the witch, her imp, chasing the wagon with burning red eyes and howling for vengeance. He shuddered, then heard the meetinghouse bell begin to toll far back—confirming that the trouble was behind him—and let himself relax somewhat.

Good luck, Sutton, he thought. *Perhaps if you had been a little more accommodating to an old man and his talk of devils, you'd not be in such a predicament.*

They crossed the Williams's bridge, which meant they were coming up on Wallace's homestead. Ansel weighed if he should stop and warn the man or not.

"Why are you slowing down," the magistrate barked. "Do not slow down until I tell you."

"Sir, Wallace—"

"Not until I tell you!"

Ansel started to snap the reins when something—what looked to be a fish—flashed in front of the horses. It, the fish, screamed and both horses veered sharply left, and the next thing Ansel knew, they were crashing through the underbrush. The wagon struck something solid—a log or boulder—and both Ansel and the magistrate flew from the seat.

Ansel flipped at least once and landed on his back in a bush. He lay there a moment waiting for the pain to hit, as there was no way he could've escaped such a wreck without at least a few broken bones. But no pain came. He sat up, and other than some scratches, seemed fine.

The magistrate, however, wasn't so lucky, and lay in a heap, wailing.

Ansel crawled to his feet and even in the dim moonlight could see the magistrate's legs were twisted and mangled. Ansel stepped over him, looking to the wagon, hoping to set the horses free so he could be on his way. But the whole of it, the horses, the wagon, they were impossibly tangled in the brush. The wagon a complete loss. He spotted Sarah, somehow still in the bed, sitting up, looking dazed.

Jacob reared up and hopped down from his horse, dashed over to the howling magistrate. "Hold tight, sir," Jacob called. "We will get you bound up and away in short order. Ansel," Jacob called. "Here, a little help, please."

Ansel didn't hear him; he was looking at the two shadowy figures walking toward them down the road. His blood turned cold. One of them had horns. "Oh, Lord. Oh, Lord."

"Ansel," Jacob called. "I need your help."

"The Devil!" Ansel cried, his bulbous eyes ready to pop from their sockets.

"What?" Jacob looked up, saw them as well. "Lord Jesus!" He let go of the magistrate, yanked his pistol from his belt, aimed, and fired.

And there, in that flash of gunfire, Ansel saw all he needed to see. He leapt over to the guard's horse, grabbed the reins, and swung up into the saddle.

"My musket," Jacob shouted.

The musket was on a sling on the horse, but Ansel didn't hand it to the guard. He didn't even consider handing it to the guard—his only thought was escape. He kicked the horse, shouted, and galloped away. He heard the guard calling after him, then came a long, terrible scream. Ansel tried not to hear that, but it dug into his head. "Oh, no! Oh, no!" He kicked the horse again, and again, racing away as fast as he could, not daring a glance back, not wanting to see, not wanting to know, only wanting to get away.

Abitha watched Ansel ride off. "You cannot hide," she said, then looked down at Jacob's young face, at all the blood pooling beneath his body, and felt only sorrow; he'd been kind in his way. Her eyes shifted to the man moaning in the brush. "Hello, magistrate. How are you doing this fine evening?"

Magistrate Watson clutched his twisted leg, trying to press the protruding bone back beneath the flesh. He glared at her in horror and pain.

"You do not appear to be enjoying yourself."

"Stay away from me," he whimpered.

Sky flew in and landed on a branch next to him, and Creek circled about play-fully, both of them giggling.

"Demons!" the magistrate cried. "Away, all of you! I am a man of God. Touch me and suffer God's wrath!"

Abitha grabbed him by the hair and jerked his head back, pressing her cutlass against his throat. "You enjoy giving people choices. Not very good ones, I would add, but when you are making up your own rules, I guess you can do as you please. Fair is fair, so here, now, I shall return the favor." She released him, stepped over, and pulled a knife from Jacob's belt, held it out to the magistrate. "Take it."

He looked at it as though it were poison.

"Take it. I'll not ask you again."

He took it.

She smiled. "I need assurance that you'll not condemn another soul. So, I can either gut you and slowly tear out your entrails . . . as I believe that would provide ample assurance, or . . . you can cut out your own foul tongue from your own foul mouth. Which choose you?"

The magistrate looked at the knife, swallowed, and shook his head. "No, please. I beg of you, mercy."

"This is a mercy. Trust me."

"I swear, swear to God . . . I swear to my soul, I will quit this business. I'll step down from my post as of this minute. I will grant a full pardon to all." He began to bawl.

Abitha pressed the blade against his gut. "Your Magistrate, I am about to start cutting you open. I will only stop once you begin slicing your tongue." She jabbed the blade into his stomach, just far enough to draw blood.

"All right . . . *all right!*" he cried, and grabbed his own tongue, held it out be-tween his fingers, then hesitated, unable to do it.

Abitha jabbed the blade deeper into his gut. He howled and began to saw, hacking and sawing, trying to force the blade through the stringy meat, gurgling as hot blood spurted, filling his mouth, as it ran down his throat, gagging, all while trying to scream. With a final hack, he severed his tongue. Holding it up for her to see while he sobbed and retched.

Abitha removed the blade from his gut, reached down, and snatched the tidbit from his hand. "Thank you." She tossed it over her shoulder and turned away. She stepped back up onto the road, then heard laughter, realized there was a woman in the wagon bed.

"Sarah?"

287

"So, you're a witch after all," Sarah said with a sneer. "Look at you there, dancing with the very Devil." She laughed again; it was not a cheerful laugh, but that of a person losing her mind.

Abitha stepped toward her.

"Stay away from me!" Sarah cried, and broke into a coughing fit, clutching her ribs.

Abitha stopped.

Sarah held up her shackles. "I deserve this, all of this, because the Devil came knocking at my door and I let him in."

"Sarah, that is not fair. You did not—"

"How could you do this to me?" Sarah cried, clutching her chest. "To my family? You bewitched me!" She ran her fingernails across her chest, leaving bloody gouges. "Damn you, Abitha Williams! Damn you! I hope you burn for all eternity!" She began to cough again, a brutal retching sound that slowly turned into a cackle, then to laughter that was akin to screeching.

Abitha said nothing, just turned and headed away, at that moment wanting only to escape this tragic, broken woman. *And whose poisonous tongue was it that* *condemned this poor woman so?* She looked toward town, could see the slight glow from the distant fire. Abitha began to walk.

Samson joined her. "You're going back, are you not? After that man."

She nodded. "His name is Ansel. It is the final name on my list."

"It will be dangerous."

"I have no choice," Abitha replied, and took off at a trot, quickly picking up speed. It seemed that each kill further bound her to the magic, transformed her a bit more, and she found herself galloping down the road at a pace near that of a horse. As the hunt took her, it was the serpent's pulse she felt drumming in her chest—the venom and the bloodlust. The night called to her and she answered, howling to the moon as she bounded down that dark and lonely road.

CHAPTER 16

Abitha spotted Ansel just as he galloped through the village gate into Sutton. She raced after him, letting loose a screech, wanting him to know she was there, that she was coming for him.

He glanced back, his eyes bulging with terror as he kicked his horse harder.

They raced down the rutted path, past the rows of thatched-roof houses and gray wattle fences.

Abitha saw the ring of torches posted about the meetinghouse ahead, knew where he was going. "No," she growled, and pushed herself even harder, her fleet hooves kicking clumps of dirt into the air.

They entered the square and she could see the horrified faces lining the meetinghouse windows, see the dozens of muskets pointed her way, and understood she had to get to Ansel before they came in range.

She screeched again, a long, hair-raising yowl, and as she had hoped, Ansel glanced back in openmouthed terror, causing the horse to veer, slapping into one of the torches. It didn't stop the horse, but it slowed it down *just* enough.

Abitha bounded forward, using all her newfound strength to hurtle herself through the air. She had the satisfaction of hearing Ansel's scream as she struck the tail end of the horse. The horse spun and stumbled, crashing to the ground, sending both Ansel and Abitha tumbling across the yard.

Abitha sat up and for a moment couldn't find Ansel, then she spotted him on the far side of the horse, crawling toward the meetinghouse.

Men were shouting Ansel's name, telling him to get clear.

Abitha rolled to her feet and leapt for him, and that was when the night came alive with thunder and white smoke.

Hot heat slapped into Abitha's chest, hammering her backward. Another blast kicking the dirt up all around her, and more rounds struck her, knocking her off her feet and flat on her back.

Abitha tried to sit up, couldn't, her entire chest burned and ached as though her very heart was being crushed.

"Ansel!" they shouted. "To us! Hurry!"

She forced her head up. Ansel was on his feet now, hobbling his way to the meetinghouse door.

"No," she growled, clawing at the dirt, fighting to rise. Another volley and something hot struck her side. She bellowed.

"Hold fire!" someone was shouting; it sounded like Sheriff Pitkin.

Abitha realized a man was standing over her. All was blurry, but she could make out his boots, his black jacket. She raised her arm as to ward off a blow, but no blow came; instead strong hands grabbed her beneath her arms and began to drag her away.

More cries from the meetinghouse, followed by more shots. They were shooting at the *man*. Abitha blinked, trying to clear her vision, saw that it was Reverend Carter, his face grim and set, barely flinching as the bullets zipped about them.

The reverend dragged her behind a giant pair of oaks.

The musket fire continued for a few moments more, spattering bark off the trees.

Abitha tried to sit up, started coughing.

"Lie still," the reverend said. "You need to lie still."

Abitha glanced at her chest, saw six large holes. She heard a strange sucking, wheezing sound and realized it was coming from her. *Oh, I've been shot but good.*

Sky flew in, perched in a tree, joined a moment later by Creek, both watching Abitha with woeful eyes.

"Abitha?" It was Samson; he came and knelt beside her, his face grim.

The reverend gave Samson a wary look but didn't flee.

Samson looked over her wounds, and Abitha didn't like what she saw on his face. He laid a hand on her chest and began to hum softly, and she felt him reaching for her, into her, connecting with her, then their souls were as one and she could hear her own heartbeat, how it was growing fainter and fainter. She felt a wave of sorrow wash over Samson.

"I am dying," Abitha whispered.

Samson continued humming. He closed his eyes, began conjuring his own blood, that which was mixed with hers. She could feel it stirring within her as he tried to hasten its healing hand, but it wasn't enough; she was sure she would die before his blood could restore her.

"Please, Abitha. I cannot do this without you."

She tried to join him, to call her own blood, her own magic, but felt dizzy, unable to concentrate. She thought she caught sight of her mother, but she seemed so far away, everything seemed so far away.

Samson's cadence changed, he was calling to Mother Earth, trying to summon her aid. Abitha sensed his growing desperation and despair.

She coughed, spitting up blood, and it was then that Samson grabbed the reverend's hand, placed it atop Abitha's. "Call your God," Samson said. "Call all your gods. Death is here, I can feel it. She needs all the help, all the blessing, all the magic we have."

The reverend took her hand and squeezed it between his. "Abitha," the reverend said. "It is time to pray, time to call the Lord back to you. Abitha, let God back in."

"I . . . never turned him away," Abitha gasped, and coughed. "It was He . . . that turned His back on me. I will always have room . . . for God . . . in my heart."

The minister began to pray.

And there, with her vision fading with every breath, Abitha managed to be astounded by the impossible: a Puritan minister and the Devil praying together, praying to Jesus and Mother Earth and who knew what else, all in an effort to save her. She would've laughed long and loud if she but could; instead she coughed and spat up more blood.

And as death's darkness swam in, she saw them, the eyes, popping out from the void. First one appeared, two, a hundred, a hundred thousand. The same eyes from when she'd flown through the night with Samson, through the very fabric of the universe—the eyes of a hundred million gods. And the truth she'd seen, it was so clear to her now. *All the eyes, all the gods, they are all part of the same. Mother Earth,*

Christ, all the religious sects across the globe, the sun, the earth, the moon, the planets, the stars, man and beast, gods and devils, all of existence. All of it, one thing!

One by one the eyes began to shut, their light to fade, and just before the last eye closed, just before total darkness took her, Abitha had a final thought. *God, I am you, and you are me.*

Abitha's eyes fell shut; her breathing imperceptible.

"Hold on," Samson whispered, and a tear fell from his eye and landed on Abitha's face. But it was no magic tear; she didn't suddenly suck in a deep breath of life and give him her warm, vibrant smile. She just continued to fade, her heartbeat growing fainter and fainter.

Again, he tried to summon Mother Earth, digging his claws into the dirt. He could sense her power, her pulse; it was there, deep in the ground, but the Mother of all Mothers simply wasn't responding. "Why?" he growled. "Why do you turn your back on me now?"

A shot rang out, another, slapping through the tree limbs. Sky cried out and leapt into the air, cawing as he circled. Creek fell to the ground, flopping about. He'd been hit.

Samson snarled, stood to his feet.

Creek flipped back up into the air, swimming back and forth, hissing angrily, a big hole in his tail.

Samson, the rage boiling up from his gut, from his heart, stepped out from behind the trees, set his golden eyes on the meetinghouse. He could see them, their terrified faces peering out from the windows, their damnable weapons pointed at him.

Another shot, this one hitting a branch near Samson's head. Samson sucked in a great chestful of air and started forward. "I am the shepherd and I am the slayer. I am life and I am *death!*"

The Devil, the very Devil stepped out from behind the giant oaks.

A collective gasp went up inside the meetinghouse. Sheriff Pitkin tried to order the men to fire but found no air left in his lungs.

"If it is a devil you seek, then it is a devil you shall have!" the beast shouted in a booming voice, his words rumbling through the meetinghouse like low thunder, through each person, cutting them to their very core.

Every gun facing the oak trees fired, filling the air with dense white smoke. And even though they couldn't see past the end of their muskets, they continued to fire.

"Cease fire!" the sheriff cried, wanting to conserve the little powder and ammunition they had.

The shots tapered off, and when the smoke finally cleared—nothing, no sign of the beast.

A clamor arose from the west windows.

"Sheriff," Felix called. *"Sheriff!"*

The sheriff dashed over, and he was there, the beast, standing at the edge of the trees.

The men let loose another volley.

"Where is he?" the sheriff asked. "Anyone see him?"

"There!" Felix called. "By the well." The men fired.

"Is he down?" Sheriff Pitkin called.

"I think so," Felix said.

"Nay, he's here!" Charles cried from the other side of the meetinghouse, and the men there fired.

"Is he down?"

"I know not," Charles cried. "One minute he is there, then he is gone."

The sheriff spotted the Devil back on his side of the meetinghouse, just strolling along the tree line. The creature was oddly dim and shadowy, grinning at them and waving his tomahawk. Then he was gone. "He is playing us! Hold fire until he comes closer."

The men shifted nervously about at the windows, jerking their muskets this way and that, as though something might leap upon them at any moment. The room smelled of gunpowder, sweat, and fear, all the bodies heating up the meetinghouse, stifling the air. The children were crying, as were many of the adults, and the room filled with the sound of their fervent prayers.

"I warned you," came a shaky voice. It was Ansel, pulling himself up from behind the pulpit. "I warned all of you. But did anyone listen to poor old Ansel? Nay, you snickered behind your hands at me. I saw you. Do not think I did not. Now, look what you have wrought. What your lack of vigilance has done!"

"Enough," the sheriff commanded.

"You have brought the Devil down on yourselves!" Ansel shouted, his bulging eyes darting every which way. "This is your fault!"

293

"You are to shut your mouth!"

"You, and you, and you!" Ansel cried, jabbing his gnarled finger from one soul to the next, each person flinching, withering beneath his accusing glare.

Sheriff Pitkin stepped over and drove his fist into Ansel's gut, doubling the man over, dropping him to the floor.

The sheriff readied himself to follow through with another blow, when he heard chanting. It was coming from outside. He jumped over to the nearest window and leaned out as far as he dared.

He spotted the demon amongst the trees, well out of effective range. The beast was kneeling, its hands on the ground, its claws digging into the earth.

"What is it doing now?" the sheriff whispered, not truly wanting to know.

The chant grew louder; it was in his head now, shifting into a wail, taking on a wobbling echo, sending shivers up and down his spine. *God,* he thought, covering his ears. *Make it stop.* And when the sheriff felt it could get no worse, other voices joined in, as though in answer, and together they made a song—that of singing banshees.

The song emanated from deep in the woods, but it was coming closer and closer. He could see the leaves rolling like in a wind, only there was no wind. And then, from out of the trees stepped a huge beast, some kind of bear, but unlike any bear the sheriff had ever seen—skeletal, with ragged shards of flesh trailing from its body in long wispy tendrils. It was quickly joined by a large cat, like a mountain lion, but with long savage tusks, a lumbering elk, more bears of all sizes, several horned stags, then a handful of tiny horses. All of them cadaverous, ghostly and pale, looking as things dug up from the grave.

The menagerie entered the meetinghouse yard, turning shades of red as they passed through the ring of torches. The flames billowed in their wake. And still they sang their song, wailing and howling. The sheriff felt his knees grow weak. He wanted none of this, he wanted to run and never stop until that awful song was far, far behind him.

Men began to weep, some to wail, several leaving their posts, crumpling into shivering heaps on the floor, weapons forgotten, their hands clasped tightly over their ears.

"Hold your place!" Sheriff Pitkin shouted, and the sound of his own voice gave him some resolve, thinking, hoping that if they could but hold out until morning, that the daylight might bring them salvation.

He thrust his musket back out, set his bead on the nearest beast—the giant bear—and fired. He hit it, he was sure; there was almost no way to miss. But the creature didn't stop. Other men began to fire as well, but still none of the creatures fell or even slowed.

The sheriff rammed in another shot—fired, but to no effect.

The beasts began to gallop, circling the meetinghouse, and it was then that the sheriff saw that they were not bound to the earth but were flying through the air.

The men were all firing as fast as they could, volley after volley. The meetinghouse was dense with smoke, the sheriff unable to see five paces. There were men and women and children screaming and wailing everywhere.

A bear flew in through one of the windows, snarling and snapping, drool and rotting flesh spraying from its mouth. Someone fired at it, the shot going through the creature and hitting Goody Dibble in the chest. And it was only then that Sheriff Pitkin understood that these things had no substance, that they were but apparitions.

Goody sat down hard, staring at the large hole in her ribs as blood bubbled from her lips.

The sheriff heard a thud on the roof, went to reload, and realized he was out of shot, that most of the others were as well.

"Fire!" someone called, and the sheriff saw that the dense clouds were more than musket smoke, that there was a red glow of flames blooming on the west side of the meetinghouse. And that was when the screaming began in earnest. People began to panic, rushing toward the front doors, only to find their way blocked by the barricade, and yet still they pressed on, massing together, piling atop one another, becoming hopelessly entangled. And to make it worse, flames began to sprout from the back of the meetinghouse, black smoke filling the room, blinding and choking people, leaving only the two windows on the sheriff's side open for escape.

"Here!" the sheriff cried. "Over here. Now!" He smashed out the remaining glass from the window with the butt of his musket and saw the Devil plucking up torches—the very torches he had ordered set—and tossing them on the roof. And with the horror of that revelation he understood the ruse: that while they were shooting at ghosts, the beast was setting the meetinghouse ablaze.

Smoke continued to fill the room, making it impossible to see and harder and harder to breathe. The ghostly creatures continued to fly about, howling and adding to the chaos.

Dorthy Dodd, covered in soot, her eyes blind with smoke and tears, scrambled for the window. The sheriff tried to help her out, but before he could, Reverend Smith, his coat on fire, dove for the window, knocking into Dorthy, the both of them tumbling out. The window was set high off the ground, and the impact of their fall left them dazed. Before either could make it to their feet, the Devil was upon them, smacking them soundly on the head with his dreadful tomahawk, splitting their skulls wide open.

"No, you damnable bastard!" the sheriff cried; he tossed aside his useless musket and grabbed an ax. He climbed into the window case, readied to jump, when someone crashed into him from behind, causing him to fall and land hard. A sharp pain shot up Sheriff Pitkin's leg and he let out a cry, clutching his ankle. He wiped furiously at his eyes, trying to clear his vision. The Devil towered before him, but the demon wasn't looking at him—its eyes were fixed on the person who'd come out of the window with him.

"Well, well," the creature said. "You are Ansel, are you not?"

Ansel was doubled over, coughing and choking, streams of black drool hanging from his mouth, but despite all that, when he heard his name, he looked up in terror.

There came a terrific crash—the roof of the meetinghouse collapsing, falling in on itself. An explosion of sparks and flame erupted, and the sheriff knew then that no one else would be leaving that doomed building.

The Devil watched the ghostly beasts flying around the flames. "It is so wonderful that the old ones have decided to join us. Take it in. It is a rare and special spectacle."

Sheriff Pitkin pushed himself to his feet, fighting to stay steady on his injured ankle. He hefted his ax and waited.

The horned demon looked at him. But it wasn't malice, or hatred, or evil that the sheriff saw in this creature's eyes, but sadness, an utter and profound sadness.

"The blood, it never ends," the Devil said ruefully, and slammed the tomahawk against the side of the sheriff's head.

Samson grabbed Ansel by the back of the neck and yanked him to his feet. Ansel screeched, flailing his arms as Samson dragged him away from the flames, over to the twin oaks, and shoved him to the ground. They both watched the meetinghouse burn, Samson on the lookout for any other survivors. There were none.

A few of the great old ones lingered about here and there, their ghostly forms drifting, growing dimmer and dimmer, their song fading.

Wolves appeared, skulking out of the shadows, sniffing, catching the scent of fresh blood. Several trotted to one of the bodies and began to feed.

Ansel started to crawl away and was met with a deep growl. The she-wolf strolled up, blocking his way, her cold eyes locked on him. Ansel froze.

"We are not done yet, Ansel," Samson said, and walked away, over to where Abitha lay on the ground.

She'd not moved, and Samson sensed nothing from her, no life, no magic. The man she called "Reverend" lay curled in a ball by her side, quivering, his eyes clenched, his hands pressed tightly over his ears. Samson nudged him and he looked up, staring horrified at Samson, then beyond Samson at the ghostly shapes and burning meetinghouse.

"Your great god could not save her then?" Samson asked.

The reverend just stared at him, and Samson saw madness taking its hold. The man's eyes went to the bloody tomahawk, grew wide and fearful.

Samson tossed the weapon away. "Death is not for you, reverend man. I have need of you. A small task."

"A task from you," the reverend said, and tittered. "Is it the Devil I now serve? Have I fallen that far?"

"I do not want your service or your soul, reverend man. I just want you to tell them, your breed of people, tell them what happened here. Tell them that the Devil, Slewfoot himself, burned down this church, killed them all . . . the men, the women, and the children. That he is wicked and cruel and shows no mercy. That he conjured demons and that they danced for him. Tell them to fear this forest, that Slewfoot waits for them there . . . awaits his chance to kill their families and eat their bones."

The reverend stood up on shaky legs, his eyes distant, disturbed. "I need to go and find my Sarah," he said, and wandered off, walking right past the wolves as though not even seeing them. The wolves glanced up from their feast, began to growl, but Samson shook his head and they let the minister pass.

Samson knelt and gently gathered Abitha's small body, cradling her against his chest; she weighed nothing to him. He stood, looked up at the orange autumn moon, nodded. "What must be done, will be done." He set golden eyes on Ansel. "You will come with me." Samson headed away, toward the gate.

Ansel shook his head. "No," he wheezed. "I will not. Cannot!"

The big wolf growled, baring her teeth, taking a few menacing steps forward.

Ansel climbed quickly to his feet and stumbled after Samson.

Samson left the village, entered the woods, following the familiar road that led back to Abitha's farm. Behind him, Ansel, his hands clutched to his chest in prayer, mumbled through trembling lips, as the she-wolf and her pack trailed along.

Sky and Creek caught up with them and zipped ahead.

As Samson walked, not a sound came from Abitha, not any sign of life. Slowly, the air around them began to change, a chilling wind blowing down from the north, pushing out the last pockets of humid air, knocking the remaining autumn leaves from their branches. The moon was now high in the sky, all the jagged fingers of the bare tree limbs clawing for its rutty glow.

They reached Abitha's farm, Samson walking past the cabin and the burned husk of the barn without so much as a glance. He marched through the dried cornstalks to the edge of the forest. There he hesitated, steadying himself. "I am ready," he whispered, and entered the dark wood.

"No," Ansel whimpered, falling back a step. "Please, I do not want to go in there." The wolves moved up, surrounding him, their blood-matted fur bristling.

Ansel followed Samson into the trees.

Samson crunched through the layers of dry leaves as he skirted the bog. When he reached the crumbling black rocks of the ancient Pawpaw, he stopped, looked up at the sapling, and let out a gasp.

All its crimson leaves were gone, the branches bare, the limbs withered, dry, and emaciated like some starving creature. He thought if it were possible for a tree to look mournful, this one did.

Samson wanted to look away, but didn't. "I have failed you. I am sorry."

A faint woeful sound drifted out of the cave, coming from the very bottom of the pit.

Ansel glanced from the cave to the twelve standing stones that circled the black rocks. "This is a cursed place," he cried. "God! Oh . . . Jesus! Jesus, help me! Save my soul! Why will you not save me!"

Samson turned on him. "You will be silent. . . . If you are not, I will tear your tongue from your mouth."

Ansel clamped his own hands to his mouth; tears began rolling down his cheeks as he fought not to scream.

Cradling Abitha tightly against his chest, Samson deftly climbed the black cluster of rocks. He laid her down at the base of the sapling, amongst the dry leaves and bones—small bones, like those of the wildfolk.

"It is time to set things to right. To make amends." Samson sucked in a deep breath and a mournful sound came up from his throat, a low keening that slowly turned into a howl, louder, then louder, the howls drifting through the trees, into the crevasse, the earth itself, all the dark places where the dead liked to hide. He called to them, trying to awaken them.

Sky and Creek flittered about, swimming, flying round and round Samson, their tiny eyes aglow.

Voices began to answer, drifting up from the pit. Those of ancient beasts and wildfolk. But they were not who Samson was seeking.

He knelt and gently slipped the chain of braided hair from around Abitha's neck. Held it out to the moon. "I know you are near," he called, and howled again, this time the wolves joining in, the sound echoing for miles in all directions. He felt them then and fell quiet, letting the echoes die away. He looked to the standing stones, waited.

A ghostly shadow appeared in front of one of the stones. The shape of a woman with long hair hanging down her face. Another appeared in front of the next stone in the circle, and one by one, after that, until twelve mothers stood in front of twelve stones.

"Three for each season, one for each cycle of the moon. The circle is complete." Samson smiled and set the braid atop Abitha's lifeless hand. "All is ready." His golden eyes drifted down to Ansel, and the wolves pressed in, giving Ansel nowhere to go.

Ansel fell to his knees, blubbering incoherently.

Samson hopped down, grabbed the man by the arm, and dragged him back up to the sapling. He forced the trembling man to kneel before the small tree. Ansel's bulging eyes darted everywhere, drool spilling from his mouth.

Samson set one long sharp claw against the man's throat. "I am the shepherd and I am the slayer. I am life and I am . . . *death!*" With that he dug his claw into the soft flesh beneath Ansel's jaw, ripping it across, opening the man's throat.

Samson held Ansel as blood pumped from his neck, dousing the trunk of the sapling, spattering onto Abitha's upturned cheek, and soaking into the ground, into the little bones all around the base of the small tree.

"Serpent!" Samson cried. "First Mother . . . Mother of all Mothers. I bring you blood. I bring you tribute!"

Samson set his golden eyes on the mothers. "Call her," he cried, demanded. "Call her now!"

One mother stepped forward, began to chant, and the others joined her, their voices rising, filling the night.

Samson thrust back his head and howled, the wolves joining him.

The wind stirred, sending the leaves swirling up all around them. Samson's fur bristled. Something was coming; he felt it slithering deep down below, circling them, moving closer and closer.

A hiss full of fury erupted, making the very ground rumble.

"Mother Earth," Samson shouted. "It is me. I have returned!"

The mothers' chanting built.

A great spectral shape rose from the ground, a serpent made of smoke and shadow, its coils wrapping around the ancient stones as it rose above Samson, poised, ready to strike, its narrow red eyes cutting into his core.

Samson gave the serpent a fierce grin, dabbed his hands into Ansel's blood, soaking his palms. "I am the shepherd and I am the slayer," he cried, and his golden eyes flashed, burned with an inner fire. "I am death and I am . . . *LIFE!*" He placed his hands on the sapling, clutching tightly around its trunk.

The great serpent struck, driving into Samson, pouring into him, a roaring blast of heated air, and for a moment he felt he would be crushed beneath her power as it burned through him.

Then she was gone, leaving Samson's heart drumming, his entire being throbbing.

Samson felt the stones tremble beneath him, felt the pulse of the earth, noticed something pushing its way up through the autumn debris. In all the places Ansel's blood touched, mushrooms and then wildflowers, dozens of them, sprouting leaves, buds, then flowers of all colors. Vines crawled all over Abitha, weaving along her arms and legs, intertwining with her long auburn hair, caressing her face.

A host of wails came from the pit below, and a menagerie of ghosts poured out from the cave—beasts and wildfolk of every description. And then the bones, the tiny bones around the sapling, began to glow, to come together, forming little skeletons, those of the wildfolk, and the skeletons, they began to dance, to jig about the tree.

Samson laughed, a loud bellow that could be heard above the entire cacophony.

Then one other ghost appeared, that of Abitha's husband, Edward. He stood just outside the circle of stones. Samson saw that his spirit was again whole, his eyes no longer hollow but bright and staring sadly at Abitha. Edward started toward Abitha, drifting heavenward with each step until he swirled away and was gone like mist in the wind.

The pulse moved up through the ground, through Samson, through his heart, into his hands, then into the sapling, pumping like blood, connecting them all. His eyes flashed and the sapling's branches regained their rigidity, reaching for the moon, then crimson leaves began to sprout along every branch. And there, a bud sprouted upon one of the limbs. Samson gasped as two more buds appeared. All three blooming, almost blazing into radiant red flowers. The three flowers opened, petals breaking loose, floating away as though weightless, and in their place, a tiny, egg-shaped fruit appeared, quickly swelling, ripening to brilliant crimson.

The mothers stepped forward, pulling their hair back to better see, their faces in awe. Sky and Creek squealed and raced around with the ghosts. The wolves howled, falling back, their eyes full of wonder.

Samson reached out, touched one of the fruits, felt its heat, grasped it in both hands, and gently twisted it from the branch. "Thank you."

He knelt next to Abitha, and there, while the ghosts circled and the little skeletons danced, he held the fruit over Abitha's mouth and squeezed, crushing the fruit. Bloodred pulp and juice dripped through Samson's fingers, dripping onto Abitha's forehead and face, slithering into her eyes, her nose, her mouth.

"I am death and I am life, and the circle . . . it will go on."

Abitha gasped.

EPILOGUE

1972, somewhere in the hills of
Monongahela National Forest, West Virginia

Mike Branson knelt down and examined the tracks. "It's a big one, for sure," he surmised. "Has to be—look at the size of those hoof-prints."

"I thought we were squirrel hunting," his longtime buddy, Tim Johnson, put in. "Bucks aren't in season."

"I don't see any game wardens about. Do you?"

"'Course not. Not out here. We're about as far away from shit as you can get."

"Then I guess it's deer season," Mike said.

Tim chuckled, tapped the shotgun his wife gave him last Christmas. "I guess it's pretty much whatever-the-fuck-we-find season then."

"Amen to that," Mike said, and pulled out his flask. The two men shared a swig of whiskey and then continued on.

The tracks led them to a small stream and then up into a narrow ravine, the surrounding cliffs growing steeper as they went.

"Oh, hell!" Tim said in a hushed voice. "Mike, look over there." He pointed up into a nearby tree.

"What?"

"There!"

Mike saw a pair of eyes staring down at them. "Is that a coon?"

"One way to find out," Tim said. He raised his shotgun and fired. The blast completely missed the animal, hitting the branch instead, splintering it and sending the raccoon tumbling to the ground.

Tim chambered another round, but the animal dashed away before he could get a bead on it. He fired anyway, kicking up the dirt and leaves as the raccoon disappeared over the rise.

Mike let out a hoot. "Now, that was some impressive shooting!" He snorted. "Being able to miss like that, at such close range, *immm-pressive*. Don't let anyone be telling you otherwise."

"Shut up," Tim said, snatching the flask away and taking a long draw.

The men continued on, following the large hoofprints. The tracks led them farther up the ravine.

"Mike, y'know, this is kinda weird, but . . . I've been all up in this valley at least a dozen times, and I don't ever recall coming across this canyon before."

"Aww, you're just drunk."

"I don't know. I am pretty damn sure I'd remember this one. I mean, look along the ridge there, at all those little caves. And some of these trees and bushes and birds and shit, they're . . . well . . . kinda strange."

"Shh, you hear that?"

"What?"

"Listen."

"Sounds like someone singing . . . a woman, I think."

"Yeah, I hear it. What's a woman doing way out here?"

"What is anyone doing way out here?"

"Probably some goddamn hippies."

"Well, if it is, we'll have to encourage them"—he tapped his shotgun—"to camp elsewheres."

They pressed onward, following the light song, sure whoever it was singing was just around the next bend. But each bend revealed another, and another, and they soon lost track of how far they'd come.

"Mike, we're going to have to turn back soon, 'less you want to spend the night out here."

"She's close. I can tell."

"You been saying that for miles. Something ain't right. It's gonna be dark soon, and I'm getting a little creeped out."

"There." Mike pointed. "Look . . . smoke."

A thin trail of smoke drifted up from just the other side of a large crop of

303

boulders. The two men hiked around and found a large tree with brilliant crimson leaves—dozens of egg-shaped fruits dangling from its branches.

"You ever seen a tree like that one before, Tim?"

Tim didn't answer; he was staring at the stick hut built into the wall of the canyon. The door and windows were draped in colorful curtains and beads, and dozens of small totems of bone and feathers were strung along the eaves. The song was coming from inside the hut.

"See there, told you it was hippies."

The smoke rose from a firepit in front of the hut. A large iron pot hung from a spit. Something was stewing inside, and whatever it was smelled divine.

The song stopped and the curtain covering the door ruffled; both men raised their rifles.

A woman peered out; she had long flowing red hair and mesmerizing green eyes and wore a necklace of braids. "Hello, gentlemen," she said in a low, soothing tone. "I am very glad to see you. I do not get much company out here."

Mike and Tim exchanged a glance.

"You out here by yourself?" Mike asked.

She laughed. "Nay, of course not. I have the birds and flowers, the trees and snakes, the fairies and the frogs, and all of Mother Earth's impish wonders. So many friends."

The smoke shifted then, even though there was no wind; its ghostly tendrils drifted and coiled around them. Mike inhaled deeply, savoring the sweet scent, and when he did, he felt a calmness, a passivity steal over him.

"I was about to start dinner. Would you two like to join me?"

Both men nodded. Mike smiled, thinking how with this woman being all alone and so far away from everything, well . . . who knew where things might go.

And as though reading his thoughts, the woman gave him an alluring smile. "You gentlemen appear tired from your long hike. Why don't you set down your rifles and take a little nap before dinner?"

Upon hearing that, Mike suddenly felt his eyelids drooping. "That sounds good," he said. "Real good." His rifle slipped from his hand and he lay down in the sand, and so did Tim—right in front of the fire.

The woman stepped out from behind the curtain, and it was then that Mike saw her legs were those of a goat. Thought *What a shame,* because he didn't much want to screw a woman with goat legs. He also noticed that she had small horns growing out from her forehead. But none of it mattered much to him now, as what he most wanted in the world was just to sleep.

Then Mike noticed something else: a fish. It came swimming out of the hut.

That ain't right, he thought.

Then he saw that it had a face, like a small child, that it was grinning at him with needlelike teeth.

"That certainly ain't right."

A raven alighted on the woman's shoulder, and sure enough, it had one of them little-kid heads too. But there were more of them, so many more, and they were suddenly everywhere—crawling, swimming, floating, scampering out of the bushes, the rocks, every little crack and crevice, all colors, shapes, and sizes. Some looked like several animals twisted together, others like tiny little naked people with insect wings and sparkling skin.

"What . . . in . . . the . . . *hell?*"

The woman walked up to the men, peered down at them. "Oh, and I forgot to mention. Samson will be joining us soon."

"Samson?" Mike muttered, his words slurred. "Who's Samson?"

"The Devil."

305

ACKNOWLEDGMENTS

First and foremost, a huge thank-you to my editors, Diana Gill and Kelly Lonesome. Some books come easy; others are much more work. This book started off as a struggle, but thanks to the expertise and guidance of these two phenomenal editors, I found the story I truly wanted to tell.

To Bethany Reis for her editorial expertise, her diligence, and for catching so many of my blunders.

To Savannah Tenderfoot at Salt & Sage Books for lending her expertise and perspective on the Pequot people.

To Evan Pritchard for his historical expertise.

An additional round of appreciation goes to my beta readers, K. M. Alexander and Redd Walitzki.

And always, a big thank-you to Julie Kane-Ritsch, for her friendship and guidance.